TREASON TRAP

Max Sargent Corporate Espionage Mystery Thriller 3

BEN COLT

Max Sargent Corporate Espionage Mystery Thrillers

available in the series by the author BEN COLT

can be read in any order

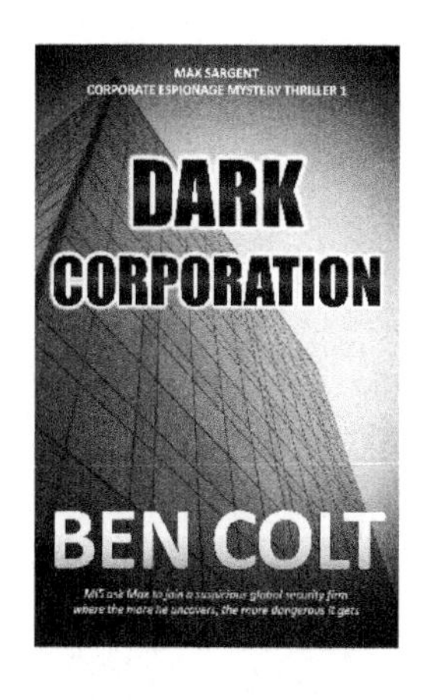

1

A small amber light started flashing on one of the screens amid the twenty other monitors filling the wall. It was three AM in the Richmond Bank's control room in central London. Carly Carter was the IT Security Manager on duty and casually glanced over to the operative who should have started to query the warning light.

"Simon, can you check that out, please? Now. Tell me what it says?"

He'd been in a semi-doze and abruptly sat up, stirring himself into action and moved closer to the screen in question. His stomach then churned with a wave of anxiety.

"Er boss, you'd better come over here," he said nervously. "I've not seen this one before."

Carly rose and strolled over to him. "Well, what does it say then," she repeated tiresomely.

Simon purposefully read out loud the message on the screen. "ALERT. DATA TRANSFER IN PROGRESS."

Underneath the warning message, a thin countdown bar appeared as they both looked on, like a fuse, denoting that some kind of download was steadily progressing.

"What on earth is this!" exclaimed Carly, staring at the screen. "We don't have data transfer programs running at this time of the night."

"What do we do boss?" asked Simon, turning to look at her.

They were both worried. There shouldn't be any type of data transfer going on, those were usually done by the IT department during office hours. They both had a nasty feeling.

"I don't understand why it's telling us there's a data transfer running?" pondered Carly again as if questioning its validity would make it go away.

She leant across Simon and typing into the keyboard, brought up an 'options' menu which would allow her to interrogate or stop the activity. To her horror, most of the menu choices were greyed out showing they weren't accessible at this time. She still clicked on them angrily trying to get a response.

"Try 'PURPOSE'?" suggested Simon pointing to the box.

Carly clicked on the selection which opened a new window. Both of them simultaneously missed a heartbeat as they quickly scanned the new piece of information.

'TRANSFERRING CUSTOMER DATA'.

"Oh shit!" cried Carly.

"Oh my God, we're screwed!" joined in Simon.

"Can you stop it?" shouted Carly urgently.

"No. The 'halt program' option isn't responding right now," said Simon, frantically clicking on the unresponsive box.

"Go into the override programming and see if you can stop it," she ordered.

Simon pressed a few keys and opened another window allowing programming code to be input. He started typing furiously, trying various interrogations of the system and attempts to cut off the program. He shook his head.

Carly looked around at the other six staff in the room, who were all looking over to her with some consternation. They'd heard something was going on and it wasn't sounding good.

She decided none of them had the expertise to tackle this better than Simon, so left him to keep trying. She scuttled back to her desk and pulled out a small booklet from the top drawer entitled, 'Richmond Bank IT Security Protocols Manual'.

She flicked straight to the back pages and found the list of emergency contacts. Running her finger down the list of senior directors with their home addresses and private contact numbers alongside, she hovered over the Group IT Director's name. For something like this she surely needed to go to her boss's boss?

Carly glanced over to Simon's screen and could see the progress bar was about a quarter of the way and relentlessly creeping along.

Returning to her Director's list she moved her finger back up to the top name, John Stevens, the Group Chief Executive. She dialled the number and gathered herself, moving back over to Simon to see if he'd had any success.

John Stevens had only been appointed CEO for Richmond Bank several months ago and had been making a great impression on the board, staff and performance. Most importantly he'd impressed the directors of the larger banking group who owned Richmond Bank, who thought he was a good choice to take the bank forward.

The Technology guys had issued some of the key directors with mobile phones which had several numbers. The first was his normal day-to-day number, which he could program to switch over to the second lesser-known emergency number, either manually or at a certain time each night.

He was fast asleep as the 'emergency' ring tone started to sound, with a battle-stations siren noise. He woke abruptly and grabbed the phone as his wife turned over and pulled the duvet over her head.

"Yes? Stevens here."

The female voice on the other end sounded nervous.

"Mr Stevens, I'm so sorry to bother you at this time. Carly Carter here. I'm the duty manager in the IT Security control room for the bank."

John Stevens immediately sat up in bed and turned on his sidelight.

"What on earth is it?"

Carly cut straight to the point. "We've got some kind of computer breach going on here, right now. It seems as though someone is hacking into our customer records!"

John Stevens gasped. "How can that be? Good God, we've spent millions before I arrived on upgrading IT security and online banking. How do you know we're being hacked?"

"I'm looking at a data transfer progress bar and it's moving as we speak. It's not our program sir. Someone outside is stealing our customer's data!"

Stevens pressed for more information. "You say data, so there's no money leaving our system?"

Carly checked with Simon, who brought up a summary of the bank's real-time transactions. At three AM only a handful of nocturnal UK customers were making minor transactions, moving money, paying bills or withdrawing small sums from cash machines. He shook his head and gave Carly a thumb's up. "I'd get an alert if any large sums were moving around at this time of the night," whispered Simon.

"No sir. We can't see any untoward cash transfers or money leakages anywhere."

Stevens' tensed shoulders relaxed, a little. "Okay, so we're not being robbed. That's good, thank the Lord. So what exactly is this 'customer data' that's being transferred somewhere?"

Carly wasn't entirely sure so winged it. "It's probably only customers' names, addresses, personal info, maybe even bank accounts and recent statements. Only information access, not the ability to withdraw money from their accounts. Our recent upgrades wouldn't allow that, at least I don't think so." Carly tried to make light of the situation but realized as she spoke that it was far more serious than she'd made it sound.

"Personal information about some of our customers," cried Stevens. "Bloody hell, this could ruin the bank!"

Carly interrupted, "I don't think it's just *some* of our customer's sir!"

"What, *all* of them?" said Stevens pathetically, "all two million of them!" Carly didn't answer. He continued, "Well, shut it down then. Stop it!" he demanded.

Carly looked over to Simon and gave him the instruction to do whatever it took to stop the transfer. The progress bar was over halfway now and as is often the case, seemed to be progressing along its ominous bar faster than before.

Simon had a problem though. "I can't just pull the plug on the system. To shut this down, I mean really stop it, we'd need to power off the entire banking operation."

Stevens could hear what Simon was saying, and shouted to Carly down the phone, "Everything's backed up, isn't it? If there's no other risk, just turn it all off!"

Simon reminded Carly, speaking even more softly this time, "We can only do that with the IT Director's security code. You'll have to call him?"

"I still heard that," cut in Stevens. "Keep me on this line and use another phone to call Bob Simmons, quickly. We need to shut it all down."

"If we shut it off, anyone in the middle of a transaction will have it voided," prompted Carly.

"That's the least of our problems. We can deal with those."

Carly threw the manual to Simon and told him to call the IT head and get his code to turn everything off. The transfer bar was two-thirds done by now. The rest of the team in the control room had gathered around Carly and Simon, but had wisely chosen to remain silent. Any unhelpful suggestions wouldn't be a good career move at this tense moment.

"What's that?" asked Carly as a new window popped up on Simon's screen.

All eight staff strained to read the message in the box. Simon read it out loud. 'SIGNIFICANT MONETARY TRANSFER BEING REQUESTED'.

"Oh my God, what the hell's that then?" asked Carly crossly.

Stevens shouted down the phone, "What's going on there Carly?"

"We've just had another alert pop up, but this one isn't an information transfer. Someone is in the process of requesting a large money transfer! We get this alert with anything over a hundred thousand."

Carly opened up the options menu and whilst most boxes

were again greyed out, she clicked on the 'DETAILS' box which was still operational.

Simon was now waiting for the IT Director to answer his phone.

Carly broke the bad news to Stevens, of what was now staring back at them from the screen.

"Sir, not good I'm afraid. There's another transfer just starting. This one's for cash."

"From who's account?" asked Stevens, "give me the details for heaven's sake!"

Carly gulped. "It's coming out of our account. The bank's account."

"You mean our own reserves, which account?"

Carly hesitated. "Our bitcoin funds account!" As she spoke a new progress bar appeared in the window and started rapidly moving across the screen. It raced towards its completion much faster than the previous bar. "It's transferring out the bank's bitcoin funds in front of my eyes sir!"

"Bitcoin!" repeated Stevens. "We've only recently started dealing in Bitcoin cryptocurrency. There can't be that much in our funds?"

"I'm getting the codes from the IT Director to shut it all down," cried out Simon, who was noting down the final instructions from a perplexed and concerned Bob Simmons on the other line.

Carly updated the Chief Exec. "Sir. The customer data transfer is almost complete. And so is the bitcoin transfer!"

Simon started to quickly type, bringing up a new screen with overall operational menus controlling the whole of the Richmond Banking system. "Almost there," he said, then shouting at Carly's phone to Stevens, "you definitely want me to shut it down sir?"

The Chief Exec paused for a second, unsure what the repercussions of this would be. "Check with Bob, I'll go with his call on it?"

Simon asked the IT Director who quickly said, "Do it!"

Simon hit the ‘Enter’ button terminating every process, transaction, transfer, cash withdrawal, bill payment and monetary handling in progress across the entire Richmond banking company.

Bob the IT Director, who had never experienced shutting down the system, was eagerly asking, “What’s happened there?”

Stevens chimed in as well. “Have the transfers been stopped?”

Carly, Simon and the other six staff stared at the screen as Simon opened the two alert boxes.

Carly relayed the messages to Stevens. “I’m sorry sir, we just missed catching the two transfers. They appear to have both gone through.”

“What does it say then?”

Carly read them out. “2,108,774 customer data records successfully transferred!”

“And the bitcoins, please give me some good news?”

“93,560 bitcoins successfully transferred.” Carly was as white as a sheet and felt like she was about to faint.

Stevens’ immediate reaction was premature, “Oh, well that’s not too….” He stopped short as his tired brain caught up and worked out the approximate value of ninety-three thousand bitcoins. “Oh my! That’s well over two billion pounds worth!”

Simon gazed into the screen, “But where’s it all gone?”

One of the IT guys watching finally chipped in. “Surely we can trace it all?”

Everyone looked at one another until Bob the IT Director replied over the phone now on speaker. “Simon, you’re gonna have to tell Stevens that tracing the transfers might be difficult, given we’ve shut the whole system down immediately after they went through!”

Simon gulped and turned to Carly, but there was no need to relay the bad news.

“I heard!” said the Chief Exec, who paused as if deciding

what to say next, but then rang off. He had some urgent calls to make, the long day ahead of him started now.

The news that Richmond Bank, part-owned by the British Government, had had all of its customer details hacked and been robbed of its own and client's entire bitcoin funds of two billion, wasn't going to go down well at all.

Much later on that same day, at sundown, an unmarked police van slowly pulled up on the side of the road down a quiet country lane. The nearby village of Harpsden just outside Henley-on-Thames was quietening after another idyllic day in the British countryside. A handful of wealthy commuters made their way home from their busy days, mostly in the city.

Inside the blacked-out van sat Max Sargent. With him were five armed police officers from the Specialist Firearms Command unit, part of London's Metropolitan Police force.

Max was the only person unarmed and was representing British Intelligence Services MI5 for this operation. The other men were all in dark blue fatigues, helmets, body armour and held their Heckler and Koch MP5 sub-machine guns. Two of them had the standard-issue Glock 17 semi-automatic handguns. The other three had Sig Sauer P228's, prompted by the team's lead and best marksman Sergeant Merrick, who favoured the German-made gun over the Glock.

The SCO19 armed response unit was formed when Central Operations merged with the Specialist Crime Directorate in 2012. Recently they were moved under the Met Ops and had been called upon by the MI5 Cyber team to facilitate a raid.

For some months MI5 Cyber unit, the team run by Max's boss Si Lawson, had been trying to track down an infamous hacker known only as Renegade. The cybercriminal and his gang had been linked to a spate of computer intrusions, blackmailing hospitals across the National Health Service of the UK.

The administrative offices controlling each targeted

regional Trust's IT systems would find an ominous message on their computer screens one day. The alert would explain that access to their NHS servers, data and files had been blocked and only a somewhat reasonable payment of between £25,000 and £100,000 would unlock their system again. Details of an offshore account were given, sometimes accompanied by a deadline by which payment had to be made.

Some of the health service offices had, after much deliberation, actually paid the money and to their relief saw their computers being unlocked and restored to normal use. Once word of this got out, other regions adopted the same view, being that their data and operational access was far too critical to be stopped by what seemed to be a small price to pay.

As the NHS was government-funded, the blackmailing scam was immediately referred to MI5's Cyber team where Max Sargent had recently started working.

Max Sargent had made the transition from a normal, everyday corporate executive of some twenty years, into operating as an undercover industrial agent for MI5. This wasn't initially a conscious choice, but after a business indiscretion of his own, MI5 gave him the chance of a clean record if he helped them with one 'observe and report' job inside a suspicious global security firm.

This then led to a second assignment at a British Arms firm where designs were being stolen. Max again found himself being the only person able to follow the trail back to the broker and buyer.

On both of his first two operations, the fine line separating normal office life from extreme danger and criminality was crossed. Greed, power and wealth, attract fraud, corruption and murder. Corporate businessmen and criminals were involved, but with such a toxic mixture of deceit and opportunity, there were also foreign intelligence services pulling strings and wanting to benefit as well.

Max had been working on this NHS Renegade case and

with his brief experience in the Royal Marine Commandos, albeit twenty years ago before his corporate career, was a good choice to accompany the armed team to this location.

"Okay lads," announced Sergeant Merrick looking around the men, "I know this has been a rather rushed call out but that's what we're here for. You've had the briefing back at base but I wanna summarise before we leave the van."

Looking to Max, Merrick continued. "The guys at Box 500 think they've finally tracked down a prolific hacker and their associates to this house. They're blackmailing hospitals. That's just not on guys. I know Max here only joined us at the HQ briefing, but he's representing their Cyber unit and has equal lead and authority alongside me."

One of the police officers screwed up his face, "Really Sarg?"

Merrick was quick to shut down the break of respect. "Let's cut the bullshit. Max here might have been sitting at a desk for a few years, but before you were even pounding the beat sunshine, Max was doing a warzone tour in the Marines and came out with the Military Cross. So don't give him any bullshit, you've not earned that right by a long way!"

The chastised officer looked remorseful. "Sorry Sarg." Then to Max, "Sorry Sir. Just a bit of bravado before we go through the door. Won't happen again."

"No problem officer," said Max calmly and unconcerned, impressed the Sarg had come down on any dissent so fast. Discipline was critical to such operations.

The Sergeant carried on. "Intel collected online implied this Renegade person has a small team with him, likely armed, hence we're going in orgy style."

Max looked at him quizzically. "Orgy style?"

Merrick elaborated, "We're going into every entry and exit point, top to bottom. We've seen the house plans and between the five of us that are armed, we'll each take our designated entry points. The front door, back door, patio doors, into the first-floor window and lastly we're covering entry into the top floor loft rooms," nodding at two of the officers with lightweight wire ladders.

"Don't worry about me guys," added Max. "I'll stay out of the way and be with Sarg here going in the front door. Remember, the reason we're going in heavy," he looked at Sarg, "orgy style as you say, is because we must secure every piece of computer equipment, laptops, desktops, iPads, server boxes, connections. That's where the evidence is."

Merrick endorsed him, "Next to your own safety and apprehending these people, secure the techie kit, guys!"

He looked around the team as if judging their readiness. Years of raids had given him the ability to check the measure of his squad just before the 'off'. He wanted passion and determination, readiness and confidence, but not too hyper, no anxiety nor hesitation. It was a tough thing to do when going through the door. One never quite knew what would be waiting to greet you on the other side.

"Right," said Merrick, "we know the house is registered to a family of five, but that can easily be a cover for the gang's base. All radios on, channel one, spread out to the nearest point opposite your entry points. We'll let the two wall-climbers get ahead then on my command, we go in!"

They all quietly poured out of the van and made their way towards the large Edwardian country house. The surrounding grounds were large and well secluded, so the neighbouring properties were all out of sight. The sun had just dipped behind the horizon, dimming the light across the property and conveniently shading the six men moving stealthily to the house.

They spread out as several moved around the perimeter to cover the rear and patio doors, another two to the end of the house to gain access up the chimney wall which had no windows, before entering the top floor windows.

Merrick and Max waited in the bushes in front of the main entrance door. The house had a few lights on behind either blind slats or half-closed curtains, and with four cars parked around the large driveway, it was clear people were inside.

The radio crackled lightly and one of the officers spoke with some urgency, "Sarg, I can see a young male adult just passing the first floor rear window, he appeared to be holding a small machine gun of some kind!"

Everyone's anxiety rose a notch. Merrick was quick to respond. "Copy. We knew there was a likelihood they'd be armed from the Dark Web intel Renegade had posted. I want everyone to hold their positions to observe and report. Let's try to establish how many are in the house with their positions?"

"Loft room light is on," reported one of the men.

"Suspected armed man still in first-floor room."

"Sarg, I just saw a male adult moving from the kitchen area to the lounge, unarmed," reported the officer trying to see through a partially blocked-out back door. "It looks like there's an adult female in the kitchen as well."

Merrick waited for anything else to be passed on, but the radio was silent for thirty seconds. It felt like a lot longer though, time was starting to speed up as they all approached the order to enter.

"Climbers start off," instructed Merrick, "when I can see you're almost ready to enter the first and loft floor windows, on my call, we'll all go in together!"

Each officer instinctively checked their MP5's safety catch was off and felt for their handgun reassuringly resting in its side holster.

Having studied available design drawings and a few old internet estate agency photos of the house, the two climbers knew there was a brick ledge alongside and above the chimney stack. As they'd been able to recce the house first-hand now, they'd decided to only use one of the ultra-light wire ladders for both of them. One of the officers threw up the end of the wire ladders and on his first attempt managed to get the small but efficient grapple hooks lodged behind the brickwork.

Testing the strain, he started to swiftly climb up the short distance to the ledging, which would give them both access to the first floor and loft windows. The moment he was up he quickly checked both windows for any movement, then signalled for the other to start climbing.

Merrick turned to Max, "We're about to go in, stay behind me, about two or three yards okay!"

He pressed his radio button, "Okay lads, take up your positions and I want you entering the premises five seconds from my mark. Any problems speak now?"

The other four officers were by now chomping at the bit and more than ready to go in.

Merrick rose and emerged from the bushes followed by Max and started quietly walking towards the front door. The other two men in the garden also started to move towards their designated back door and patio doors.

The team had studied the plans of the house and again whilst approaching the building and had opted not to use any door rams or small explosive charges. These were large men well-practised at breaking down standard household doors and windows, which in reality offered little resistance.

As Merrick judged his arrival at the front door to be in a few moments he gave the order. "Enter in five, enter in five!"

Each of the officers timed their entry to perfection and in unison, smashed into their respective house entry points at the same time.

The crashing of glass and splintering of window and door frames was truly terrifying for anyone inside. To have the sanctity, the security of their home, breached and broken into across multiple entry points was a horrific experience for anyone, armed or not.

One officer smashed the weak back door almost off its hinges and strode into the kitchen, to be greeted by the woman screaming at the top of her voice, dropping the cutlery she was gathering.

The double-glazed but flimsy locked patio doors simply

burst apart as the officer threw himself at them expecting more resistance. He almost tumbled into the man pouring himself a drink in the large lounge, who froze and looked quite horrified to see a gun-wielding policeman flying towards him.

The officer on the first floor had enough room on the ledge to put his whole weight into a shoulder barge, smashing the slightly rotting, single glazed windows inwards. Knowing the young man inside was armed it was his voice everyone heard first. He yelled out in a threatening, urgent shout, "Armed police, freeze, don't move!" to the gaping lad sitting on the bed with what appeared to be the gun.

As the officer finished his instruction to him, he'd already realized that the 'weapon' the young lad held and was loading, was a plastic replica toy gun. The darts he was pushing into the bright orange coloured magazine were made of polystyrene!

Police downstairs were now also shouting out their warnings.

The officer going through the loft windows didn't have any room for a run-up at the window frame and took several attempts to break through. As he climbed into the room, he could see a young, startled boy sitting in a bean bag on the floor, in front of a large array of computers, screens and server boxes.

The poor lad was playing his favourite war game simulator and having been interrupted, had just been taken down by another player. Both he and the officer glanced at the largest screen to see a CGI black-fatigued soldier firing at him with an MP5. The message on the TV then read, 'YOU'RE DEAD! TRY AGAIN?'. The youngster was in a trance as he looked back at the real man now in his bedroom standing over him, pointing a real MP5 into his face!

Sergeant Merrick had kicked the front door in and closely followed by Max, could see into both the kitchen and lounge. Both the man and the woman were offering no resistance and the officers around the house were starting to now call out,

"Clear!".

Max noticed someone at the top of the first flight of stairs and touched Merrick's shoulder to alert him. The Sergeant swung his MP5 round and followed the legs coming into view through the bannister rails as they descended the stairs.

"Armed police! Freeze!"

The person kept on coming down the stairs.

"Put that gun down officer!" The man in the lounge had gathered himself and was urgently pleading with the Sergeant. The figure coming down the stairs continued and came into view.

"He's just a boy! What the hell are you all doing here, this is crazy!" insisted the man now coming out to greet his ten-year-old.

The boy carried on down the stairs, in complete shock, seemingly oblivious to all the commotion. In his hand was a brightly coloured toy gun, loaded with plastic darts ready for the game he and his eighteen-year-old brother upstairs were about to play.

As Merrick instructed his team on his radio, "On me in the hall lads," the mother ran into the hall and gathered up her child. Having recovered from the shock of the devastating intrusion, she was now really scared, but the anger broke through.

"Put down those bloody guns and someone better tell me exactly what's going on here, right now?" she yelled and then started sobbing. The husband came over to her, looking at the Sergeant equally as angrily.

The two officers on the floors above were by now accompanying the young lads down the stairs as the five officers, all five family members and Max congregated in the hall. Merrick lowered his gun as did the other officers.

Max spoke in an attempt to deflect some of their anger away from the Sarg. "I'm Max Sargent with MI5 and these officers are with the Met Police." The audience was simply gobsmacked. "We've been tracking a dangerous cybercriminal, a hacker and their gang. Currently extorting money from various government establishments. The NHS to be precise."

The father cut in. "MI5? Met Police! Cyber hacking, what's any of this got to do with my family?"

Merrick replied, thankful that Max had at least shared the explanation with him. "We have it on good authority that these blackmailing crimes are being originated from this property."

The officer from the loft room added, "Sarg, this lad had a lot of computer gear in his attic room?"

The mother and father looked at one another, then at their fifteen-year-old son. "Rupert? Is this about you? You're kidding right!"

Rupert started to cry, but before completely breaking down, managed to utter through his tears, "I didn't mean it to get this far. It all got out of hand, I'm sorry, I'm sorry!"

"What have you gone and done Rupert!"

2

The Director General of MI5 was rarely kept waiting on the telephone by anyone, including the UK's top parliamentarian. However, he would allow today's exception, given the Prime Minister's unscheduled call with the President of the Government of Spain, had apparently overrun. In the circumstances this was understandable. A few incidents regarding the British territory of Gibraltar had rekindled Spain's attempts to claim the iconic headland on Spain's south coast. Relations were souring.

The DG had been asked to call in at precisely eight PM about the 'Richmond debacle'. He'd already been fully briefed with updates three times that day on what had happened in the early hours of the morning. Usually, his calls and meetings with the PM were run by him, giving the head of government the necessary briefings, updates, advice and plans. The PM listened and agreed. Today he knew the PM would be in a fluster and would want to get things off their chest first, before hearing any suggestions or actions already being taken.

The 10 Downing Street receptionist came back on the line, apologized again and finally put him through.

"Prime Minister."

"Ah yes, Director General. I assume you've had the briefings about this awful mess at Richmond Bank?"

'No apology for keeping me waiting', thought the DG who was a stickler for courtesy. "Yes, I have…" but the PM was on a roll and not listening.

"Well, I'm not happy about it. How the hell can a huge bank have all its customer's data stolen in this day and age. Didn't they have adequate security in place?"

The DG paused to check if there would be a space to answer and could hear the PM drawing for breath and about to continue on, so waited.

"The Government bailed this damn bank out during the last financial crisis, and we own forty-five per cent of them for crying out loud. And never mind the customer records, these hackers also got off with two billion pounds of bitcoin funds! For Pete's sake, this is making a fool of the bank, and the Government," the DG knew what was coming next, "and frankly me!"

The gap appeared so the DG interjected calmly, as always. "Prime Minister. I share your concerns and have been kept up to date throughout the day. Security at the bank was I gather state of the art, that's what stopped the customer's accounts from being broken into. That's good news for you to pass onto the press." The DG knew exactly what buttons to press with the PM. "However, they'd yet to apply the same security to their new bitcoin funds account, setup after the security upgrades."

"You're kidding, what idiots!"

"Indeed, Prime Minister. I have just passed this case onto the Deputy Director General's Cyber unit in MI5 and they will have full access to the PricewaterhouseCoopers fraud team and police investigations."

"Oh yes, your Cyber team, they're the bunch who recently sorted that weapons design theft case aren't they?" acknowledged the PM.

"They are, Prime Minister, the same team that have just, we believe, caught the blackmailing hacker of our NHS data and computers access."

"Really? Are you saying that's all sorted now?"

"We only raided the premises about an hour ago Prime Minister, I would normally have waited until our briefing tomorrow to give you all the facts, but I thought you'd probably like some good news this evening." The DG was a master at wrapping these politicians around his little finger.

"Can I speak about this to the press tonight Director General, who was it?"

"Yes, I'm confident enough for you to say we've ended the problem. The hacker is cooperating fully and will help cancel all current and outstanding system lockouts and hacks."

"And the money they've extorted?" asked the PM eagerly.

We're working on that, may take a couple of days to fully trace it and see what's remaining, I'll keep you posted on that of course."

"Oh, alright," said the PM like a moody child, happy one moment, sulky the next. "So, who was it?" he repeated.

The DG anticipated another flare-up but just came straight out with it. "A fifteen-year-old boy in Henley! But you can't say that to the press."

"What!" exploded the PM again.

"As you said Prime Minister, such things are possible in this day and age I'm afraid," couched the Director General. "I gather he's a computer genius, combine that knowledge and flair with some easily obtainable computer and server equipment, and you're ready to start trying to hack other systems."

"Quite unbelievable!" said the PM more calmly again. "What a superb coup for your Cyber team. Do pass on my thanks, won't you? I will perhaps just hint tonight that we're looking to tie up the NHS blackmailing issue, until we cover it on our call tomorrow, just to be sure eh?" The politician in him had returned.

"As you wish Prime Minister."

Once they'd both put the phone down the PM thought to himself, 'Good ol' MI5, they always seem to come through!'.

The Director General had a slightly different thought, 'Bloody politicians!'.

He then dialled his Deputy Director General to whom Si Lawson's Cyber unit reported. He needed the Richmond robbery sorted out quickly. It was indeed an embarrassment to the government and the country. He had no idea though the case would be so much more than a one-off bank hack.

After the raid on the Buchannon's family home near Henley, Max had spent the following day dipping in and out of the interview rooms of the family members, mainly that of the hacker Rupert.

MI5 could hand the matter over to the police, but wanted to be sure that the case was in the bag by the time they withdrew.

As a fifteen-year-old Rupert was still regarded in the eyes of the law as a child, thankfully for him he was treated completely differently than if he had been an adult. Permissions had to be granted, parents' consent sought and them being present at interviews, along with lawyers and independent advocates and witnesses. This would normally be a nightmare for the police, but fortunately, as Rupert and his parents wanted to cooperate fully, the details and admissions flowed freely.

Rupert had got himself onto the Dark Web and into the hacker's community. On the chat rooms, he'd admired stories of infamous hackers bragging about what virus they'd launched, or which company's back-office servers they'd gotten into. One thing led to another and in no time Rupert had managed to hack into his school's server. To start with he couldn't alter anything, but he had full visibility of all the pupils' reports, personal details, staff emails and even salaries.

Then after several more small-time hacks, he worked out an add-on program that did give him editing access to some lesser-protected areas of some small business systems.

At this time, his elder brother had a suspected fracture in his foot from skiing and had gone for an x-ray. The weeks passed and despite their parents chasing up the surgery to get the x-ray results, they heard nothing.

Sharing the family's frustration on the tardiness of the NHS, Rupert started probing all possible entry points to get into the National Health Service systems. He only wanted to see if he could find his brother's x-ray results.

After a sustained onslaught of attempts and advice from the Dark Web hacker community, he finally stumbled into the family's local NHS Trust's system. He was in!

Rupert found the letter sitting on the system that had been dictated by the family doctor, typed in, but not yet posted. It said that only hairline fractures had been found, which had for the most part already started to re-bind and heal. No further remedy was required. He moved the letter into the General Practitioner's 'Priority' file which was then seen by one of the administrative staff at the surgery, who duly printed and posted it to his brother.

Pleased with his success and still with access to the local NHS system, Rupert then realized he could manipulate who was given access to patients' data. More importantly, he could determine who accessed the Trust's intranet and operating servers.

He then Googled how to set up an offshore anonymous bank account and began to block use and access to the system, with an on-screen warning demanding payment to remove the lock.

Rupert was so wrapped up in his success at hacking, he had no idea of the immorality and chaos it was causing until his antics appeared on the news. By then though, he had already extorted six other Trust's and had a balance of over four-hundred-thousand pounds in his offshore account!

MI5's Cyber team had by now got to grips with the young lad's mode of operation. They placed tracer updates into all NHS systems, acting as a sticky digital tripwire. When Rupert accessed a local system and the first tracer tag attached itself to his access gateway, the game was up. He was up against the big boys of the cyber world in MI5 and immediately lost.

As soon as Rupert's location had been determined, the armed police team were pushed in. Max joined them from the Cyber team to represent MI5 on the raid. Unfortunately,

Rupert had joined in with the fake bragging on the Dark Web. He'd boasted of his armed gang, which had turned the likely mundane plain-clothed police knocking on their door, into a full-scale armed response team storming the family home. The sight of Rupert's younger and older brothers preparing their guns for a play fight hadn't helped either.

Rupert ended up returning all the money he had miraculously extorted. He would later be charged with a lifetime suspended sentence and would be put on a watch list of known cyber threat personnel. He would have to report to the police annually and declare all cyber activities and allow access into his home at any time by an investigative cyber fraud team whenever they desired to check what he was doing. Juvenile detention centres were not necessary, Rupert had learnt his lesson and was contrite. Penalties for his caper would follow him for the rest of his life.

Max Sargent was back at Thames House, MI5's headquarters overlooking Lambeth Bridge on the Thames. Amidst the congratulatory clapping from the Cyber team, he'd also endured the ribbing with comments like, "Are you sure you didn't need more armed police, to protect you from the toy guns!" and "Next time Max trying simply knocking on the door, rather than demolishing the house to get in eh!".

"Yes, yes," cut in the boss Si Lawson, "seriously though guys, great job tracing the NHS hacker. A good lesson for all of us, even an innocent-looking fifteen-year-old can give the country the run-around for a while, with a couple of good computers!"

He gestured to Vince his deputy and Max to follow him back to his office. They all sat at his meeting table. Si got straight to it.

"Celebrations over I'm afraid. Our next assignment dropped into my lap yesterday. It's a big one, direct from the PM to the DG and then the Deputy Director General onto me.

The story will break today in the news."

Vince nodded. "I think we can guess boss, is it the bank theft?"

Si chuckled, "I thought you might have already got a whiff on the grapevine here at Thames House."

Max couldn't help add, "We're not the Intelligence Service for nothing! What's the gig then?"

Si Lawson now betrayed a slight frown. "In the early hours of yesterday morning, Richmond Bank was hacked. They copied all two million customer details, but with a new security upgrade installed, weren't able to get into their accounts. That would have been disastrous, probably the end of the bank." Max and Vince were now looking concerned and concentrating on every word. This was a big deal.

Max asked, "Aren't they part government-owned?"

"They are, forty-five per cent and that's why the PM and ministers are all in a tiz," said Si. "But the account they were able to transfer everything out of, was the bank's bitcoin fund. That hadn't had the latest security put over it."

"This doesn't sound good boos, how much?" said Vince. "Bitcoin's gone through the roof over the years hasn't it?"

"Correct Vince. Ninety-three odd thousand bitcoins doesn't sound much. But at around twenty-five thousand pounds each, it was over two billion!"

"Good grief," gasped Max. "I remember when those bitcoins were just a few quid."

"Less than that," said Si. "The bitcoin cryptocurrency was launched in 2009 and were pennies to start with. The following year a bitcoin miner made the first real-world transaction when buying a Papa John's pizza in Florida for about ten thousand bitcoins! They're based on a blockchain with a ledger of all bitcoin transactions and then eventually become digital encrypted cash."

Vince had quickly looked up the prices on his mobile. "Blimey, as you say they started off at a few pence then after four years went into the hundreds. The second half of 2017 was when you wanted to have these, they went from a few thousand up to seventeen thousand that year. For the last three or four years, they've steadily climbed up to over twenty-five grand a pop!"

Si shook his head in shared disbelief. "Someone's laughing and has made a lot of money. Right, we'll have a number of the team assigned across the police and interview investigations. I think our own techie guy Alan deserves a crack at being let loose on this as well, especially when talking to the bank's IT staff."

"Let me take Alan," asked Max. "How do you want me to help?"

"I suggest you stick with the PricewaterhouseCoopers fraud guys. I've already set it up, you can join them at Richmond Bank as soon as you're ready today. Ask for an Andy Archer, he's their lead. Good guy, a bit status-driven though. They're employed by the bank and we're employed by the government, who own almost half the bank. No need to throw your weight around, let them get on with their job, but if push comes to shove, you outrank him okay!"

"And the police lead, boss?" asked Vince.

Si frowned. "Yes, this one's a bit more tricky. William Lucas. Chief Superintendent no less. I know him from old."

"Unusual for a Chief Super to lead a case like this, that would normally be down to a Chief Inspector wouldn't it," said Vince.

"Oh no, not for William. And by the way don't call him Bill or Will whatever you do," Si warned. "He's totally loyal to the Met and views all other services including us at MI5, as inferior pen-pushers. A high profile case like this will get him out from behind his desk. He'll want to ensure the Met solve it quickly and get the glory, so he'll personally oversee this one. Please tread carefully with him, any issues tell me so I can give you any cover. I still have some sway with him from when we served together, even if he does think I betrayed the cause when I left the Met."

"So we'd better make sure we say hi to him first when we get to the bank," added Max.

Si nodded. "They'll generally let you tag along in the background and do what you want, as long as it doesn't compromise their operation and investigative plans. If you're onto something tell me, then we can decide whether we hand it over to them."

Max and Vince smiled at one another knowingly.

As they left Si's office, Alan was already waiting outside. He was a younger lad whose life revolved around computers, technology, gadgets and programming. He worked with the Cyber team on several different assignments, from the safety of his desk and had access to the full expanse of facilities and labs across MI5.

He'd previously helped Max with some interesting and life-saving mobile phone app upgrades. He also had a go at tracking a Dark Web user brokering arms, designed a virus kill program and a micro-tracker for his two previous operations. He and Max had a good relationship, Alan as the inventor maker, Max as the user in the field.

Alan was excited, he was leaving the confines of Thames House and getting out into the field of operations, albeit accompanying Max with some office investigations. He'd even put on a suit.

"Alan," greeted Max, "barely recognized you in that suit, first time?"

"Pretty much," he laughed. "Can't wait to understand more about this bank's IT security. Quite impressive though, that they got hacked. Two billion in bitcoins eh, not bad for a desktop computer nerd somewhere!"

Max and Alan made their way to Richmond Bank's main offices which were halfway along Fenchurch Street near the main London station. The new glass-fronted building sat comfortably amongst the other impressive mix of new and old structures of the City's financial district. The dominating taller buildings towered above the Richmond Bank offices, including the Walkie Talkie also in Fenchurch Street, the Gherkin at St Mary Axe and the Leadenhall Cheesegrater tower.

They arrived at the plush, bright reception and Max asked for Chief Superintendent Lucas. The heavily made-up girl seemed indifferent to them until Max said they were from MI5. Then she was far more efficient, smiling at Alan, much to his delight. They were given ID passes which already included their photos, taken surreptitiously from behind the reception desk.

She pointed to the row of elevators across the atrium. "Take the lift to the sixth floor, turn right and you'll find them in conference room one."

As they exited the quiet, serene lift, Max and Alan walked into a world of commotion. Staff bustling along the corridor following instructions to gather up more information or documents. Others having been summoned to answer questions and many talking with hushed voices trying to find out what was happening and who's been asked what.

The loudest noise emanated from conference room one at the end of the hallway. The huge room, the size of a tennis court, had been given over to the investigative teams. A mishmash of desks, partitions, open areas and meeting rooms to the side, filled the large space.

Someone had placed typed signs on plain A4 paper in the areas and Max could see them denoting team areas for Richmond IT, Police, PWC and a smaller group by the MI5 sign.

The chaos seemed to be organized, as everyone knew what they were doing and everything disseminated from a tall policeman in the centre.

Max suggested Alan joined the other few MI5 staff, then approached the officer in the centre issuing instructions and monitoring proceedings.

"Chief Superintendent Lucas?" offered Max.

The wary senior Met officer looked him up and down.

"That is me, and you are?"

"Max Sargent, MI5 Cyber, Corporate," said Max. "Si Lawson asked me to attend."

The Chief Super sighed. "More from MI5? You've already got a handful of your people over there, why do you lot…" He paused and relooked at Max. "Oh yes, you're the fellow I've heard about. Executive recently turned MI5 and already got a few impressive cases under your belt."

"Beginner's luck," said Max trying to show humility.

"Nonsense. You should have joined the Met, not Si Lawson's bunch. You'd have a lot more action with us."

Max laughed politely. "I seem to be getting more than my fair share of action with Si. Anyway, where can I be of most use, William?" Max emphasised the 'William', careful to avoid 'Will' or 'Bill'! He felt there had been enough of a connection to risk calling the senior Met officer by his first name and waited to see if he'd got away with it.

Lucas paused, thinking Max was a bit cheeky, but he let it go, so suggested, "Probably best if you join the PWC bunch for now, they have less policy and forms than my Met guys. That's their lead man," he said pointing to a short, over-weight chap. "Oh, Max. If you do come up with anything, be sure to come to me first," said Lucas.

Max was reminded of what Si had told him about Lucas being desperate to solve this before MI5 got anywhere. He'd worry about that if he turned anything up. He thanked the officer and strode over to the PricewaterhouseCoopers man.

"Andy Archer is it? Max Sargent, MI5 Cyber Corporate."

The PWC partner swung round and cautiously eyed Max. "Ah yes, the ex Chief Procurement Officer. Now with MI5. What on earth brought about that career change?"

Max detected this was going to be a 'who can piss the furthest contest' and tried to resist.

"Well I thought it was a short leap from Procurement into corporate crime," trying to make light of it, "you know with all that governance, policy and security us Buyers have to be responsible for."

Andy wasn't impressed. "A big leap I'd say. Just because you've been a top procurement man doesn't really give you the right to think you're now a top corporate fraud man. I've been doing this for fifteen years, what I don't know isn't worth knowing. You have to build your skill set over the years."

"Well, I do have other skills than just procurement." Max was referring to his stint in the Commandos and regretted the inference, hoping Andy wouldn't go down that route. He didn't. "So, what's the status Andy?" said Max moving it on.

The PWC man felt there was something about Max that was more than just a procurement executive but satisfied himself by saying, "Well, I guess if you're good enough for Si Lawson's team, then you're alright Max."

He led Max over to a large notice board with lots of documents, organization charts and scribbles across everything.

Andy explained. "Whilst we work on our stuff, we coordinate everything with the Chief Super, he's the centre of the wheel so to say. The other teams do the same, the Met, your MI5 bunch and Richmond Bank's own IT Security team. We each have a progress board," pointing around the room at the other sections, "we put everything we have on the board and any team can wander round and learn from what each of us is progressing. Every few hours the Chief Super gets the leads together and we go through it all, then plan the next few hours of work, interviews and info gathering. Kind of a concentrated project management operation."

"Sounds super-efficient," agreed Max.

"Keep your eye on the bank's IT lot, they're embarrassed about this whole thing on their watch and super keen to be the ones to solve their own mess."

Max could see healthy competition in evidence, as both the Met and PWC also wanted to be the heroes.

"I'm about to interview the top execs of the bank," said Andy. "I think it's right that as the PWC lead I get my hands dirty and show the troops how to do it, don't you think?"

"Absolutely," agreed Max, wanting to add sarcasm to his voice. "Can I tag along?"

While Alan hung around with the other MI5 staff, Max accompanied Andy and his sizeable PWC fraud team to various interviews for the remainder of the day.

The Chief Exec John Stevens was doing the rounds amongst the investigative teams and had started to take the tack that his predecessor was responsible for the security upgrade, which was clearly inadequate. It was Andy who bluntly pointed out that he was responsible for ensuring it had been rolled out across all platforms, including the ill-fated bitcoin fund.

Bob Simmons the bank's IT Director took the whole thing very personally, as if someone had robbed *him*. He was more upset about the morals of the raid, than coming up with sensible suggestions as to how it could occur.

They saw directors for Operations, Finance, Human Resources and Sales, none of whom showed any hint of interest or knowledge in IT security or what could have happened.

All of the investigative teams had pooled their top technology programmers, to see if any kind of digital footprint had been left, enough to perhaps run a trace back to the hackers. They were getting nowhere fast and all agreed that the system being turned off moments after the transfers had completed, destroyed any chance they had of tracing the criminal's intrusion.

Max and Alan regrouped at the end of the day, both disheartened by sitting in the back of interviews and meetings, watching little or no progress being made.

"It feels like they're all missing something," said Max.

"Yeah," agreed Alan, "like they're looking in the wrong place. You were a top executive Max, did you know everything going on in your team?"

Max thought back to his many leadership roles. "You

know it's funny because I always thought I had a handle on everything, knew what was going on across my team, all the personalities. I really tried to be in touch with everyone no matter how senior or junior."

"So, did you know everything?" challenged Alan politely.

Max chuckled to himself. "No. It's simply not possible for the boss to know everything and everyone in their department, especially when you have hundreds of staff."

"When did you realise other things were going on under your nose, but couldn't see it?"

"Usually when it was too late. One of my directors would come to me and say we've got a bullying problem, been going on for some time. I'd never have thought the person doing the bullying was capable of it and of course, never saw anything myself. Or the sexual harassment, that was only apparent when my report showed me a printout of the texts a staff member had been sending using a company mobile. Or that I discovered key supplier contract files had been downloaded by a leaver and taken to their new job at a competitor. Or the jilted husband shouting in reception because he'd just found out his wife, in my department, was having an affair with someone else in my team!"

"Quite a lot going on then," said Alan carefully. "Max, I've got an idea..."

"I think I've got the same thought, Alan," interrupted Max. "We need to get into the roots of Richmond Bank. People like the PWC lead and the Met want to tackle the top guys, the joust, the bravado and shame. Frankly, none of them are likely to have a clue about the hack."

"Maybe the IT chap?" suggested Alan.

"Agreed, he could know more than he's letting on. But we need to spend tomorrow talking to the troops, the more junior staff. That's where we might get some interesting views about what happened. I'll tell Si and clear it with the Chief Super," said Max. "He'll probably be glad to have us out of the way!"

The following day Max and Alan walked around the

conference room looking at each of the team's boards. In particular, they wanted organization charts so they could identify the junior staff across finance, operations and IT.

The Chief Super had welcomed them trawling through the lesser important bank staff and Andy at PWC turned his nose up at the notion inexperienced, low-level staff would have any idea about the hack. Si Lawson was curious about the tactic, but trusted Max so went along with it. The other MI5 team members at the bank stayed with the activities up in the conference room. Max and Alan were free to meet with whoever they wished below mid-management level.

Rather than set themselves up in an office or interview room like the others were doing, Max wanted to go and see each staff member they put onto their random list, covering the three key departments. He knew that inviting them into an intimidating, formal interview across a desk, was not conducive to the open and casual chats he had in mind. That's when people were more likely to speak freely.

Max decided to take the operations and finance staff, while Alan was best suited to speaking with his fellow technology geeks. No scary emails were sent to the targeted staff explaining they were required to meet them, let alone any mention of MI5. Max and Alan would simply circulate around the offices asking for people by name and then either finding a quiet space or grabbing an empty room. Their style was calm and collaborative, chatty, not interrogatory.

Max worked his way through the junior staff in the Operations department and quickly found out they were mainly responsible for the retail branches, cash machines and most of the activities outside of the head office. They had little to do with the computer systems or IT.

He then met with several staff in their Finance function. Because this team would see and usually approve all spends and projects across the bank, as the money counters, they had a good insight into the work carried out by other departments.

Max homed in specifically on their views of the IT security

upgrades which were carried out months ago, just before the new Chief Exec started. One of the lower-level finance managers, Kate Martins, echoed a view that some of the IT guys working on the project lost confidence in the consulting firms brought in to support the upgrades.

"Whenever we had project status updates to track the costs of the work alongside the budgets, it was clear our IT people weren't entirely happy with what was happening," she told Max. "I know that in itself doesn't mean anything untoward was happening, I just got the feeling things weren't exactly collaborative."

Max pressed for more details. "Do you have a list of the Richmond bank IT staff on the upgrade project? Also, the outside companies involved, with all their names as well?"

"Yeah sure," said Kate shrugging her shoulders. "I've got copies of the IT security upgrade project plan, costings, consulting firms being used, it's all there."

"And everyone's names?"

"Yup, I can give you the minutes for a couple of the project meetings, they'll have the names of everyone involved, whether they attended the meeting or were logged as absent and to be copied."

Max was sure that the teams working up in the conference room must have also asked for the names of everyone involved in the IT security upgrade, but wanted to see what Alan had turned up with his chats throughout the IT team. They met in the canteen for lunch. Alan looked unsure about something.

"What's eating you then?" asked Max.

Alan looked troubled. "I don't know, nothing outstanding but I kinda feel there's something not quite right somewhere."

"Oh come on Alan, you can't just say that, break it down, tell me what the IT guys were saying to you?" challenged Max, hopeful something might turn up. He produced the lists of staff involved with the project.

Alan fought to make sense of his suspicions. "Well, a few

of them said they and their bosses had reservations about the way the project was handled. Some of the consultants were a bit ahead of themselves, telling the Richmond managers what to do, how to do it, getting overly involved in some of the final implementation stages."

"Did you get any names mentioned?"

Alan looked apologetic. "Names? Oh, no, I didn't really ask. Sorry."

Max explained. "Look, I've got all the names of everyone involved with the security upgrade. We need people to point out anyone on the lists they weren't happy with, or felt were too involved, or suspect in any way. Rather than me come marching back in with you, take these lists and go back and see just your most cooperative few staff who you felt had something to tell us. Ask for names. Let them freely accuse anyone. Tell them they'll be kept anonymous okay?"

Alan looked invigorated and grabbed the list, left his half-eaten lunch and went straight back to the IT offices.

As Max finished his meal, waiting for Alan to return, the Richmond Bank IT Director Bob Simmons strolled over.

"One of the investigators aren't you? I saw you in the conference room earlier. In the MI5 area?" said Bob tentatively, edging nearer to sit down. "I'm Bob Simmons the IT Director."

Max gestured to one of the empty seats. "Yes, Sargent. Do join me."

"So how are you MI5 guys getting on, come up with anything yet? I trust you're getting all the cooperation you need?"

"I think we are," replied Max, "time will tell."

"I noticed you've ducked out of all the top exec interviews with the other teams up there. Why's that?"

"As I mentioned to your deputy, I'm not here to sit in the back of a room and watch, there are enough people doing that already. I want to help you find out what happened here," replied Max. "That's why I'm covering the lower-ranking staff. You'd be surprised what you can find out talking to the frontline troops!"

Simmons looked surprised. "Crikey, I wouldn't have thought you guys would waste your time with junior staff who likely weren't closely involved, nor would know all the details. If you think you're onto something, come and see me. Be good for MI5 and my team here to get to the bottom of this horrible incident."

Max thought to himself, 'now we have another party desperately wanting to be the hero and beat the other teams to the prize'.

"What do you think happened then?" Max asked.

Bob shrugged. "As I've repeatedly told everyone, hackers are highly effective these days at breaking down all types of security, old and new. Today's latest unbreakable security software is tomorrow's hacker's conquest. I feel personally responsible though, after all, I'm head of the bank's IT."

He looked round as if about to impart some secret. "To be honest Max, I'm surprised John Stevens hasn't fired me yet. It happened on my watch and just maybe if we hadn't shut everything down at the time of the hack, we could have traced them!"

Max got the impression this poor IT Director would be the scapegoat and he knew it. The Chief Exec and board would be looking for someone to take the hit, once they'd found out what happened.

Alan returned looking a little more enthusiastic this time and seeing Bob sat with Max, waited for a nod to join them.

"Alan's with me," explained Max, and felt comfortable hearing what he had to say with Bob there.

Alan placed the sheets on the table. "The staff have pointed out a few names of people on the project they either didn't like, or trust, or heard their managers unhappy with."

"What's all this?" asked Bob somewhat perturbed.

Max nodded for Alan to read out the names and as he did so, Bob interjected quickly with his view of them, at the same time huffing in protest at the unorthodox method the two MI5 guys had taken.

"No, he's in the clear, wouldn't dare do anything wrong." Then, "She's totally reliable, just rubs everyone up the wrong way. Bit of an arsehole, but not a criminal!"

There were five names Alan read out, prompted by nothing more than a mention from one of the IT juniors.

"The last one was a Freddy McIntosh," said Alan, sitting back frowning, satisfied the IT Director was vouching for each of them.

Bob quickly gave his view again. "Ah yes, Freddy, good guy, used him before, an independent consultant, always helps to have a few top IT people onboard who aren't serving under a big brand name. They're free to say it as they see it. No issues with him."

Max and Alan looked slightly despondent. "That's it," said Alan.

"Well keep me posted won't you," said Bob as he got up from the table, looking a lot happier than the two of them still seated.

Alan waited until Bob had gone, he then leant across the table to Max pointing at one of the names on the list.

"Max, what I didn't say in front of him was that last name, Freddy McIntosh, came up a few times from staff questioning his authority."

"How do you mean, he was just an external consultant," said Max, "he shouldn't really have any authority, he consults and advises?"

"No, that's not what the IT chaps said. Asking lots of questions about anything he didn't already cover, including some of the final firewall protocols. They thought he had some kind of free pass to get way more involved in things than he needed to."

"Free pass from who?" asked Max, already suspecting the answer as he asked it.

"From that Bob Simmons!"

The following day Max and Alan retreated back to MI5's Thames House. Max drew up a grid on a whiteboard wall with the names of the IT, Finance and Operations Director of the bank. Also the Chief Exec and the five names of those mentioned by staff, involved with the security upgrade.

"Right Alan, we go along the list and I'll read out everything I can find and Google about each one. Previous roles, firms, press quotes, references, LinkedIn profile and network. You write it up on the board as I shout it out. Then at the end, we see if anyone knows anyone else that could be interesting!"

Max had picked up quite a talent from his previous procurement information-gathering exercises, for finding out about firms, products and markets. This also covered knowing about supplier's managers, directors, competitors and personnel. If you knew where to look and what search sites and terms to use, the data one could find on someone was astonishing.

They went through each person for the entire morning. Max called out snippets of information about each of them, with Alan furiously jotting it onto the board trying to keep up with Max's tirade of details.

Si Lawson strolled in just as they finished. "How's it going then?"

"Just finished the info gathering," said Alan proudly, happy to be showing he could do more than just gadgets and apps.

Max was already conscious from reading out the huge amount of information throughout the day, that there were a few repeated firms and crossovers between some of the names.

The three of them studied the board and Alan eagerly drew the first line between two mentions of Cambridge University. Probably nothing as it was shared by the Chief Exec and a low-level operations chap.

They called out more overlaps, eager to spot the next match. After just five minutes they were struggling to see any more.

"Let's see what we've got here," said Si moving closer to the board.

"We've got a few LinkedIn network shares," said Max, "quite usual for people who've worked together. Some people collect contacts to impress everyone else on how well connected they are, or think they are!"

"A couple of same schools," said Alan, "reciprocal social media posts on one another's Instagram pages."

"You've underlined that name for good reason by the looks of it," commented Si, pointing at 'Freddy McIntosh' on the board.

Max nodded, "That was the one the IT Director said he'd worked with before. Seems they've shared three previous companies, each one with McIntosh consulting for Simmons. Must have gotten to know one another well by now?"

Si Lawson called out to his deputy Vince, who popped his head around the door.

"Yes, boss?"

"Vince, do a quick check on two names across our criminal network and Executives Pending archives. See if we've got anything at all looking dubious or similar? They're Bob Simmons and Freddy McIntosh."

Vince disappeared.

Si added, "You don't think Max that the IT boss has anything to do with it do you?"

Max pondered. "I can't believe he would. He'd be the most obvious suspect. He has the most to lose, he mentioned to me he's waiting to get the sack about this."

"He also authorized the shut-down with the Chief Exec when they tried to stop the hack," said Alan. "It can't be him surely?"

"Yes, how convenient that because of that shut-down, no-one seems able to trace the hackers now," mused Max.

Vince came back in with a couple of printouts. "Your two names, no criminal records of any kind, but seems about ten years ago they were both suspended by a company pending dismissal allegations."

"What for?" asked Si.

"Data protection abuse. But nothing could be proven so they both got payoffs and non-disclosure deals."

Max scanned the board. "So, the three companies their paths have crossed before Richmond Bank, are a large soft drinks brand, a global hotel chain…"

"And the Jurado Data firm!" Vince read the third from the board.

Max looked through the notes. "But that was twelve years ago."

"Doesn't matter how long ago," said Si, "the connection could have been made then and nothing happened until an opportunity presented itself. Like at Richmond." Si nodded. "We've not solved anything yet, but some dots are certainly getting joined up here for further investigation. Let's not go blundering in anywhere, nor tell the others back at Richmond. Not yet anyway. Well get cracking then?"

"On what," said Alan.

"We find out more about this Jurado Data firm," answered Max. "A lot more!"

3

Over the last two decades, data had become a highly valuable commodity. With the explosion in the use of the internet, mobile communications, apps, social media and customer targeting, everyone wanted more data about people. Information was power.

Big corporations wanted to know everything about their market, trends and customer profiles, to better utilize their precious marketing spends. They wanted to target existing customers with tailored promotions to spend more. They also wanted to target new customers with personalized and audience-specific offers to draw them into their brand's clutches.

One of the many leading lights in the customer data revolution was the Jurado Data Group. Originally from Madrid and now based in prestigious offices at One The Strand, overlooking Trafalgar Square. The company was headed up by the voracious Sonia Jurado.

Not yet forty, she had conquered the European world of data, statistics and customer information and insights. A determined, unwavering force, with gravitas and drive matched by her beauty. A curvaceous five-foot-nine lady with long, sweeping black hair and dark brown eyes, olive skin and a fiery Spanish temperament simmering beneath the surface. A businesswoman not to be trifled with.

Sonia was raised in a modest family home in the town of Boadilla Del Monte, just West of Madrid. Her parents Ana and Miguel Jurado had wanted a large family, but complications with Sonia's birth made more children impossible, so they doted on their one child.

Sonia's grandparents on her mother's side had come to

Spain from Mexico for a quieter, safer life. Ana worked in a local school as an English teacher, enabling her daughter to grow up also speaking fluent English. Miguel worked in the Madrid Fire Department for many years as a fireman, being promoted to Captain.

Early on in his career, he'd once had an awful experience when attending a multi-car pile-up. One of the cars he came across, had trapped inside the parents in the front and their eight-year-old girl in the back. The same age as Sonia.

Another vehicle had ended up on top of this car crushing down the roof and buckling the side jamming the doors shut. Miguel had managed to prize apart enough of a gap in the bodywork with his crowbar, for each of the adults to get out. A fire had then started at the rear of the car when the battery had shorted out against the body. The fuel tank was just below.

Miguel only needed to break through the central door pillar of the car to have enough room to drag out the semi-conscious girl from the rear seat. The fire behind grew, adding more urgency to his fight against the thin but enduring steel strut. Another firefighter joined him. They levered the pillar. They pried and bent it, then even tried whacking it with their bars. Miguel could see the steel bending but continuing to withstand their battering. It was so frustrating for him as he knew with simple cutting equipment, they could slice through the panel in seconds and free the girl.

The fire took hold and encircled the fuel tank. His colleague finally dragged him away as they and the parents watched on. The terrified girl inside momentarily regained consciousness and cried out, "Mama!" in terror, just before the tank exploded engulfing the rear of the car with an inferno of heat and flames.

Poor Miguel never got over that day, the sight of the little girl in the back of the burning car. The sound of her calling out. That stayed with him forever, waking him in the night and driving him on a mission to improve the equipment fire fighters were issued with.

He began a crusade, reviewing, testing and recommending to his superiors what kit was sub-standard, where modifications were required, what worked well and should be more widely distributed across the Fire Services.

At the time of the horrible incident, basic air-compression metal cutters were in existence, but simply not available to the team that attended the car pile-up that day. Miguel naturally became the go-to person within Madrid's Fire Department for all topics of equipment and safety. He would act as procurement officer for their purchases, diligently ensuring the best equipment was balanced with value for money and the quantity needed by the fire-fighting teams.

During his latter career, he left the service and set up his own wholesale firm, Jurado Fire Equipment. With this, he could continue to act as advisor and buyer for the Fire Services and also have an influence on the manufacturer's designs and innovation.

Miguel improved the quality and effectiveness of many of the key rescue apparatus including fire fighters breathing gear, increased heat temperature resistance clothing and axe-bar tools. His specialities though, prompted by his awful incident with the little girl, were the improvements made to cutting equipment. These included disc cutters, jaw clamps and gap openers, mechanical scissors and latterly plasma and water-jet cutting equipment.

Sonia attended local schools and quickly found out she excelled in two things. She was a gifted mathematician and loved all things numbers and data related. She was also well known for taking on a challenge. If it was reasonably possible and someone dared her to do something, Sonia would stop at nothing to complete the task and 'win'.

As expected, not all the dares she was given were entirely legitimate and much chastisement and parent-teacher meetings followed some of the more unacceptable antics. She persuaded some classmates to steal the head teacher's armchair with her and place it at the end of the swimming pool's highest diving board. As staff struggled to retrieve it, the head's favourite chair disappeared into the deep end.

Sonia also took on the challenge of crashing the school's website to prove to the arrogant technology team it wasn't infallible. With one of the computer nerds, they devised a way of bombarding the site's server with multiple form submissions with large picture and 'execute' files attached.

Then her world crashed in on her. Ana her mother found out that her father Miguel had been having a secret affair with one of the staff at his fire equipment company. An English woman. She and Sonia were devastated.

Miguel pleaded with Ana to give him another chance, but her mother's principles reached beyond second chances for an adulterous husband, and she threw him out of the family home. Miguel retreated into the arms of his English lover where their relationship continued for many years.

Sonia loved her father and couldn't hold him responsible. She blamed the breakup of her parents entirely on the other woman and by association, she blamed the British. Coming over to her country and ruining marriages, scarring children for life. It was a hatred that never left her and continued to smoulder away from that point onwards.

At seventeen Sonia was one of a rare bunch of students each year to take on the Bachillerato course in the subject of Statistics, later called Data Science. She was starting to fully appreciate the power of information and the use and manipulation of numbers and mass data scenarios.

She excelled and was awarded a top Titulo de Bachiller of Statistics. Before she could fill out her University application forms, Sonia was approached by one of the leading data, search and algorithm firms. In 2000 at just eighteen, she started working for Yahoo!, a leading search engine company, at their Madrid offices.

During the five years Sonia worked at Yahoo!, her fascination and love of all things data were cemented. Her gift of being a statistics genius got her noticed and heard, then followed. She was promoted every year and in reflection of her employer's happiness at the contributions she made, her salary rose from €25,000 to an impressive €275,000 in five years.

However, the world of search engines was on the march and Sonia could see that the once darling of internet search, was being stalked by the many-faceted competitor Google. As Google branched out into new areas, Yahoo! bought more search engine firms. As Google expanded its advertising, Yahoo focused on the free email provision sector. It seemed much of what they did to capitalize on their past success, was perhaps misplaced or mistimed.

Her advice and finally cries of frustration were ignored by the European and Californian senior managers. Sonia knew everything was changing and decided to move on for herself. Within two years the indomitable march of Google had overtaken all other search engine firms and would continue its meteoric rise thereafter.

Sonia could see that the emergence of the internet, online shopping, mobile apps and social media, would provide new business sectors, hungry to utilize more and more information about consumers.

She moved from Madrid to one of the centre's of the business world, London, and in 2008 set up her new company Jurado Data.

The market was dominated by two main drivers; getting people's data, and then knowing how to use it.

Firms would collect basic contact information such as email lists from websites, shopping channels and large databases like business registries, clubs or subscriptions. These would then be compiled into mailing lists and sold to companies wanting to blast out email offers and promotions, much of which ended up causing the 'spam' revolution. The name comes from a Monty Python comedy sketch where everything on the café's menu includes spam. It was unavoidable, repetitive and never-ending.

Sonia had her own email crawler program which could inspect a web page's html source code and extract a copy of every email on the site, found by among other things, searching for the '@' sign. It could be directed at a business institute and trawl thousands of members pages gathering their emails within an hour, providing a valuable, sellable email list.

But this was far too basic for Sonia, who realized that there were bigger data mines to be found in large organizations, hidden just behind their off-the-shelf server firewalls and security.

As her team grew, so did the number of 'specialist programmers' she took on. This was really her job title for her 'hackers'. Sonia felt that because all they were copying was information about consumers who had freely given their details to some online shopping site or insurance company, it was fair game. It was all data that was out in the public domain, somewhere. She simply knew how to find it without asking.

Jurado Data amassed huge personal information tranches across many marketplaces, countries and population profiles. Then repeatedly sold on the lists for promotions, marketing and targeted solicitation. Insurance companies, online retailers and supermarkets all beat a path to her door, hungry to capitalize on the data revolution and land grab of new customers.

During the next ten years, her company grew its annual revenue to over five hundred million and as the sole owner, Sonia was a multi-millionaire many times over.

She had a large apartment at the end of Edgware Road overlooking Marble Arch, and villas in Madrid and Cancun, Mexico.

In 2017 one of Sonia's friends, another big name in the computer industry, suggested she bought bitcoins as an investment. Since its launch seven years prior, bitcoin prices had been flat at under a couple of hundred dollars. But there'd been a huge email campaign urging everyone to buy bitcoin. Whilst this tarnished bitcoin as another scam of some kind, the power of mass mailing did the job and prices looked as though they must surely rise. During the second quarter of that year, bitcoin started to rise.

Sonia could afford to take a punt on her friend's suggestion and bought five hundred bitcoins at eight hundred dollars each. By the time she sold them at the end of the same year, the price had rocketed to seventeen thousand dollars a bitcoin. Her original four-hundred-thousand-dollar investment was now worth eight and a half million!

Sonia never married, she simply wasn't the type to contemplate being at home looking after a husband and children. She was having too much fun running her own company and sleeping with her pick of the male staff. They were conquests, rarely relationships and the men seemed to accept this. They were flattered that their attractive strong-willed boss wanted to bed them, even if it was for just a few tantalizing nights. Like an alpha animal, she was marking her territory, gaining allegiance and loyalty.

She did well to cover her tracks, just in case a disgruntled employee thought they could leave and tell all. In addition to harshly binding contracts, non-disclosure agreements, salaries much higher than the market rates, she also had her Special Operations team. Her trusted security men, trouble-shooters, literally.

Nick Hawkins was a soldier through and through. Not an officer type, a soldier. He liked being with the lads, he liked the action and the power he had over his troops. He was never destined for the higher ranks and wouldn't have been happy behind a desk. 'A diamond in the rough that probably can't be polished', said one of his annual reports.

His six-foot-tall sturdy, fit frame was formed with decades

of military training, conflict postings, hiking and swimming. A rugged, naturally tough-looking face with a strong jawline, was hardened by stints in both hot and cold weathers, driving rain and the odd punch-up. Dark, strong wavy hair, too long really for the military, had been allowed by his Commander as a long-service concession, framed his brown discerning eyes. He sported several Green Beret and Marines related tattoos.

He spent a happy seventeen years in the British Royal Marines and within his first five years had already jumped three ranks to Colour Sergeant. There he stayed for another five years before finally being promoted to Warrant Officer Class 2, one of the most senior ranks still with direct influence over the 'troops'. Both Nick and his senior officers knew he was best placed where the action was.

Deservedly so. He was a good soldier, loyal, hard-working, tough and savvy. During his service, he saw conflict eight times, including in Afghanistan, Iraq and on a Navy Frigate called upon to raid a Somali pirate base. Whilst briefly serving in Sierra Leone he was captured by rebels and in line to be killed, when he was saved by another Commando from certain death.

Then after a decade and a half of exemplary service, that edge all good soldiers require, that steely determination, got the better of him.

His Commando Brigade's new commanding officer Lieutenant Colonel Jim Barr, came in as many new leaders do, determined to set high standards and better his predecessors. He was destined for greater things and would have a few years in charge of the Brigade to show he could up their game.

Historic loyalties and oversights went out the window with the new Commander. Slates were wiped clean, and everyone had to start from scratch building up tenure and credit with the new boss.

Within the first few days, Jim Barr as expected, gathered

the senior officers together to impress on them that standards must be raised.

"I'm aware that you're already one of the leading Commando Brigade's, but I want to be clear, we must be seen as *the* leading Brigade and I intend to make sure that happens as soon as possible." He met the gaze of everyone in the room. "Being the best starts with myself and all of you, setting a perfect, non-compromising example at all times."

When his briefing had finished and the officers started to make their way to the exit, Jim Barr was drawn to one particular Warrant Officer's hair length. It wasn't untidy, but amidst a sea of other short, tight, regulation haircuts around the room, it did stand out. He pointed to Nick Hawkins.

"You there!"

Of course, all of the remaining six officers still in the room turned round to see who was being referred to. Nick could see his Commander gesticulating at him. "Sir?"

"You can start by getting your bloody hair cut!" As the words left his mouth the Lieutenant Colonel regretted it. He instantly knew singling out a senior, long-serving veteran in front of his peers wasn't the right thing to do. But he couldn't be seen to back down now or apologise. He had to own it.

Nick was horrified. Fifteen years of duty, battle-scars, promotions, looking after numerous changes of troops and making them the best. After giving up his life for the Commandos and now ready and willing to serve this new Commander, to be told to 'get a haircut' pushed the wrong button at the wrong time. His blood boiled. He stood there, defiant, rage swelling inside him.

One of his colleagues could see his anger was about to explode and quickly tried to pull him out of the room, calling him by his nickname. "Come on Fifty me old mate, yes Sir we'll get that sorted!"

Nick spoke through gritted teeth, staring at the Commander. "Is that really the mark of your leadership and judgement?" Jim Barr was now shocked. "That you speak to me like I'm some pissing grunt on his first day. And all you have to say is get my hair cut, in front of my fellow officers!" Now Nick was also committed.

With a pounding heart, Jim Barr had to press his authority in this ridiculous stand-off he'd gotten himself into.

"Stand down Warrant Officer!" A quick apology would have sufficed, but in the heat of the moment, Jim Barr felt he had to stay firm. "It's just a bloody haircut. Leave the room and get it done and we'll say no more about it."

Something in Nick broke his restraint and without thinking, he launched himself at the Lieutenant Colonel. He closed the gap between them, but his half-heartedness knowing it was wrong, allowed his colleagues to catch him and prevent contact with the senior officer.

The dye was cast. Despite tempers calming, even apologies from both men, it was just too much of an affray to come back from, especially with witnesses. Another Commanding Officer was sent in to adjudicate over a 'formal review meeting' between the two men. Because of Nick's outstanding service, mention of a possible Court Martial was quickly dismissed by the man in charge. Loyalty and looking after your own did count for something, but after discussions and referral to a review board, the recommendation was inevitable.

Nick Hawkins was asked to resign and granted immediate discharge from the military. His pension would be kept intact and superb references provided. Contrary to the usual protocol, there would be no mention of the incident on his nor Jim Barr's records. The witnessing officers were all asked to sign NDA's and never spoke of it again.

Nick Hawkins found himself out on an unfamiliar 'civi street' and stayed with family wondering what on earth had happened to him. He was still angry though. He simply couldn't reconcile that after his dedicated service in one of the elite forces of the world, one silly incident could lead to this.

His fall from Commando Warrant Officer to ill-equipped

job hunter hit him hard. As is often the case, ex-military people naturally migrate to either the civilian services like fight-fighters or police, or end up as security guards.

After a year of trying various jobs, the easy money of security pushed itself onto Nick and he joined an independent firm grateful to have someone with such a notable service record. Cognizant of his skills, they gave him the more challenging jobs like personal protection for VIP's, thinking the excitement would match his hunger for action. But Nick was just as bored babysitting people who thought they were important and needed protecting, as he would have been doing night duty in a deserted office.

Then he was assigned for a week to an up-and-coming data firm's Spanish boss, one Sonia Jurado. He was captivated by this mesmerising woman, intelligent, determined and clearly going places.

Mid that week whilst he and Sonia had been leaving the Jurado Data offices late one evening, they were confronted by two thugs. One of Sonia's small-time Eastend data conquests her team had hacked, had somehow found out who was responsible. They wanted to teach the young Spanish upstart a lesson she wouldn't forget and had sent round a couple of his men to warn, threaten and if necessary, slap her around a bit.

They hadn't reckoned on her having a bodyguard and certainly not a Commando vet such as Nick Hawkins.

"Piss off mate, this has got nothing to do with you," they sneered. "We just wanna make sure the lady doesn't mess with our boss again and pays him for the data she stole."

Nick hadn't fully appreciated what his temporary hirer did, but came alive once more with the thrill of conflict and action.

"Sorry fellas, not today," he warned. "In fact not ever. Do yourselves a favour and run along before you get hurt."

The two men turned their attention to Nick and approached him. No one spoke to them like that and he was now also up for a beating, along with the woman.

As the first came within range, the inside of Nick's palm chopped into the man's throat with debilitating force, rendering him incapacitated and choking for breath. A swipe kick to the side of his knee sent him crashing to the ground.

The second man's concentration and forward momentum was interrupted by the sight of his friend going down so fast. He never saw the back of Nick's fist come flying into his lower jaw and cheekbone, fracturing both. Crying in agony he also fell, nursing the side of his face.

"Time to go," said Nick to Sonia, offering out his hand to guide her past the two fallen men in case they regrouped.

Sonia was impressed. By the end of the week that he'd been with her for, he'd fallen in love, saved her from a beating and she'd let him into her bed twice.

Sonia made it clear their time was a fling and she wasn't wanting any relationships. Sad to part company with this amazing woman, he returned to the security firm briefly heartbroken.

Then after a couple of days Sonia called him and offered him a permanent job as her head of security, with the promise that when the firm got bigger, his role would too. Maybe something in Operations, 'Special' Operations.

Nick was overjoyed to be reunited with her, on any terms. He just liked being around Sonia Jurado and would do anything for her. Anything.

4

The Spanish Intelligence Community was overhauled and reaffirmed in 2002, beholden to the Spanish Prime Minister and the Government.

Their three over-arching divisions cover Military Intelligence run by the Armed Forces Intelligence Centre, represented by each branch of the armed forces. Then Domestic intelligence, including the Intelligence Centre for Counter-Terrorism and Organised Crime. Finally, there is the Foreign Intelligence group overseen by the National Intelligence Centre, otherwise known as Centro Superior de Informacion de la Defensa, or CNI.

This division is led by the Director with a deputy, the Secretary General, and has three Directorate units. These cover resources, intelligence affairs and support to intelligence, each run by a Director General.

The Director of the CNI was returning to his offices having just met with Spain's Prime Minister. He fully expected one of his senior reports Eduardo Garcia, would be waiting for him impatiently in his office.

He readied himself as he approached. Eduardo was his Director General of the Support to Intelligence division, and despite being the Director's subordinate, he knew Eduardo wasn't going to be happy.

The secretary sitting outside nodded her head towards the office and whispered, "He's in there."

"Eduardo, good to see you, everything alright?" offered the CNI Director.

Eduardo rose from his seat respectfully, but his words already had a tinge of frustration in them. "That depends on how you got on with the Prime Minister. Sir?"

"You're not still angry about this Gibraltar thing, are you? I thought we'd talked about that?" replied the senior man.

"You're damn right I'm still annoyed about it." Eduardo's temper was rising already in anticipation of bad news. "How can it be right those damn British keep hold of a territory that's rightfully ours. What did the PM say then?"

The Director sat in his chair behind his desk, happy to put the large table between the two of them. He gestured for Eduardo to also sit, and waited until he did, in an attempt to calm the discussion.

"I did raise it again with the PM, who has himself spoken once more to the British Prime Minister, mainly now out of respect of yourself Eduardo. So, take that as a compliment and a favour to you."

"And?"

"He did raise it again," pausing with a sigh. "He and to be honest I as well, feel we have other more pressing agendas that need our attention right now. Gibraltar is wrapped up in so much historic and binding paperwork and agreements, it's not something the British would consider just giving up. Why would they?"

Eduardo bristled. "We had an opportunity with Brexit to make a case for Gibraltar returning to us. It's a tiny plot of land surrounded and dwarfed by Spain, it's rightfully ours!"

The Director continued calmly, masking his growing agitation. "Well, it's not ours. It belongs to Britain and has done for over three hundred years. British sovereignty was declared in 1713 in perpetuity within the Treaty of Utrecht and as you know became their colony in 1830."

"I know all the history thank you, Sir."

"Then you should also know it's not up for grabs, nor discussion anymore. The PM was embarrassed to bring it up again, just leave it now." The Director hoped his reminder of the facts would help make the point, but pressed on.

"It's not like we're going to get into any sea battles ever again. We don't need its previous strategic naval choke hold anymore. It's nothing. It's just a bloody rock! You could almost fit Gibraltar's entire population into the Las Ventas bullring stadium here in Madrid. Its whole area is only two-and-a-half square miles for Christ's sake! Who cares!"

"I do." Eduardo detected that he was quickly using up his boss's patience and took in a calming breath. "Is there nothing we can do?"

"Every time the Gibraltarians have had a vote to determine if they want to be part of Spain or Britain, they've always overwhelmingly voted to stay British."

Eduardo was out of ideas. "Maybe some improved trade deal for the Brits, or even a payment of sorts? We must have some leverage for just letting them keep hold of Gibraltar?"

"We need Britain more than they need us, Eduardo. The post-Brexit agreement stands. Spain has agreed with them that Gibraltar will participate with the Schengen European countries for freedom of movement to avoid a hard border. We co-exist happily, who governs as you say, this tiny plot of land, is frankly irrelevant."

Eduardo knew his argument was based on passion and conceding for now, rose to leave. "It's just the principle of it. They should pay, somehow!"

"Wouldn't that be great," added the Director trying to placate him, then regretting the comment, hoping it wouldn't be construed as condoning anything untoward.

Eduardo left the room, raising his eyebrows to the secretary and cursing, "Maldita Britanica eh!" She mustered an empathetic frown.

He got back to his office and strode over to the window, needing to calm himself before his next meeting with his seven Heads of teams. Looking out into the surrounding trees always seemed to help him separate himself momentarily, from the huge onerous job he had within the Spanish Intelligence Services.

The cluster of office blocks around him, circled the main 'U' shaped large smart building they were in, of red brick and cream sandstone. Unlike the CIA or MI5 HQ's, the complex just North-West of Madrid had little in the way of high walls, copious CCTV or small armies of armed security.

The Spanish Intelligence Services are situated on the Avienda Padre Huidobro, next to the motorway intersections of the A-6 and M-30, which thankfully couldn't be seen due to the lush, dense trees around the buildings. On the other side of them sat an open area with both a golf course and the National Forest Genetic Resources Centre. Secret Service, seedlings and golf, a bizarre, eclectic mix of occupants in the same area.

Eduardo Garcia was an unnaturally tall, thin Spaniard at six foot five, in his fifties with thinning hair over a narrow, aggressive face. He'd served with the Intelligence Services all his working life and rose through the ranks through sheer determination to succeed and deliver what he felt was best for his beloved Spain.

Eduardo had just as much passion, but for an entirely opposite characteristic. He hated the British.

Over the decades he'd sat across the table and squirmed at their pompous, Imperialistic attitude, their fancy use of the English language, the way they seemed to talk down to the Spanish. He felt they regarded his country as merely a convenient holiday destination, or somewhere for their gangs and villains to retreat to when the going got tough back home. He would then have to deal with their scum. But there was another reason his resentment ran deep.

His beautiful Spanish mother grew up in the hills just North of Marbella in a town called Montua. During the summer she and her friends would often hang out along the coastline with its stunning beaches and marinas in Marbella, flirting and enjoying themselves with the visiting tourists.

In the early seventies when life was much more carefree, she got involved with not one, but two British lads who were holidaying together, for fun, drink and girls. She fell for both of them and they, in turn, treated her like a queen at the start of their week-long holiday.

They played on the beach, partied, went fishing, ate together and laughed together. She knew that a decision was going to have to be made as to which of them she would sleep with. As a Catholic, it had to be one of them, or none. A three-way was out of the question for her.

The flirting got more serious, and she introduced into the conversations that she would have to pick one of them, but didn't want anyone to be upset when jilted. The inevitable night of decision arrived. But the two boys had also been talking and didn't want either to miss out. They just wanted to have fun, so they slipped crushed up sleeping tablets into her drink.

She became drowsy and they took her back to their small hotel room, by which time she was mumbling for them to send her home in a taxi. It was too late though. The last thing she remembered was the first boy starting to have his way with her, as she lay there, before passing out. Then the other lad did whatever he wanted to as well, after which they each took another turn.

When it was over, the two boys realized the enormity of what they'd done and couldn't risk her reporting them to the police for rape. So before she could wake, they both packed and were on a plane home early the next morning.

At the end of that year, Eduardo was born. She moved away from where the terrible nightmare had occurred and settled in Coslada near Madrid to bring up her baby alone.

When Eduardo was thirteen he finally persuaded his mother to tell him everything she knew about his father. She did. He was utterly devastated to hear the pitiful story of what had happened to his mother, his beautiful mother. He felt his identity had been denigrated, not even knowing which of the two lads was indeed his natural father.

Years later when Eduardo started in the Spanish Intelligence Services, one of the first things he set about was finding at least one of those men who had raped his mother.

She could only remember one of their full names so that's all he had to go after.

When he was just twenty-five, he tracked down the man, now almost fifty, to a terraced house in Croydon, South London. He engineered a visit to the Spanish Embassy there and made time one night to confront this void left inside of him.

Filled with hatred, curiosity and hope in equal measures, he knocked on the door. The man answered and Eduardo could see the goings-on behind him of a busy family home, with wife in the kitchen and several teenagers going about their evening.

Their eyes met and before a word was said, the man knew what this stranger at his door was there about.

Eduardo broke the silence. "I think you, or maybe your friend, are my father!" Silence. "1972, Marbella!"

The man instantly stepped outside and closed the front door behind him so his family couldn't see or hear anything. He was speechless for a moment, memories flooding back. Shame, confusion, shock and bewilderment all taking hold.

Then to Eduardo's horror and surprise, the man leant forward, his face defiantly up against Eduardo's and with gritted teeth said, "Listen to me you shitty little Dago, piss off outta here. I don't know what you're talking about and want nothing to do with you okay! Go!" shoving the young Spaniard away.

Eduardo was shocked to the core and left, totally dejected. He got to the end of the road with his tail between his legs, until rage overflowed. It was a stupid, small gesture, but he felt better for it. He returned to the man's house and threw a large stone through each of the front downstairs and first-floor windows, and ran.

Since that day Eduardo no longer cared about crossing that line of integrity so carefully protected within the Secret Services. If something a little dubious was required to get the job done, he wouldn't hesitate in pushing the boundaries.

Over the months and years, his hatred of the British swelled up in him and he exercised any opportunity to deny them a deal or withhold some piece of vital intelligence they needed. Whatever he could do within his growing power remit, to thwart the Brits, he did.

Gibraltar had become a festering annoyance of his for some twenty years. He really thought that the whole Brexit debacle would present an opportunity somehow, for his government and Prime Minister to introduce the topic into the confused EU negotiations. It was clear from his Director today, that the last chance for any movement on the topic had fallen flat.

Eduardo didn't know how, but if the opportunity arose, he would try again to take back Gibraltar. If not, then he would at least exact some form of 'correction' for this gross belittlement of his country. He wanted revenge.

5

Within a day the MI5 Cyber team that Si Lawson led, had gathered a comprehensive information file on the Jurado data firm. They had access to a huge array of intelligence networks and databases, as well as enhanced search facilities online, using the popular interrogation tools and site and social media and communication channels.

Josh compiled everything into a neat information summary on twenty PowerPoint slides and went into the large meeting room. Around the table sat the boss Si Lawson with his deputy Vince, Alan the techie and Max Sargent, who set the scene.

"So after Alan and I took the low road at Richmond Bank, interviewing the junior staff across Ops, Finance and IT, we started to get a few names rising to the surface."

Josh began projecting his slides to compliment what Max was talking about.

Max continued. "The bank's IT Director Bob Simmons came up, in prime position to potentially help with the hack and bitcoin theft, shut the system down after the raid and prevent tracing the hackers."

"Did he seem dodgy when you met him?" asked Vince.

"No, he appeared to take the whole thing personally as it was on his watch and was expecting to be made the scapegoat and fired anytime soon," replied Max, looking at Alan for his agreement to his summation of the key man. Alan shrugged and nodded.

"Definitely a suspect," added Si. "Carry on Max."

Josh showed them their pictures.

"Then we have this Freddy McIntosh IT consultant, who's worked for Simmons four times including at Richmond Bank. The bank staff felt he had, shall we say, favoured access all areas and was part of the digital security upgrade the bank underwent a few months ago. Asked a lot of questions. Could be thorough and just wanting to learn. Could be more than that, potentially finding out about weaknesses or details on the security access protocols?"

Vince chipped in. "When me and Max went through their crossovers, the interesting one was this Jurado Data company. That leads us nicely into what we have on them."

"Okay, let's see what you've got Josh on this Jurado lot?" led in Si.

Josh took over. "Meteoric rise in the information market," he began. Josh took them through the history of the firm, IT operations, clients, types of specialism across the data, statistics and customer profiling fields.

"Interestingly," Josh continued with a nugget of information he knew would raise eyebrows, "Jurado did a piece of work for our Richmond Bank over a year ago. Not really IT security-related as such. It was consulting to help the bank improve the way it manipulated its customer details and better promote new services in a more targeted manner."

Alan the techie jumped in. "Yeah, but that could possibly give them a whiff of that huge amount of personal data just sitting there for the copying."

"All two million customers, that would be worth a lot to a data firm like Jurado," added Max.

"Sounds intriguing, added to which there was the two billion in bitcoins," said Si, "but without being able to trace back what happened that night, how can we prove it was them? We'd have to raid them and get through every piece of data, equipment, activity history, God knows what, to find any possible hack history?"

"Nightmare, not going to happen," agreed Alan. "You'd need to get someone to talk from inside their team."

Max pondered. "Or get someone into their team?"

Si looked at Max and gave him a knowing nod. "But how? They'd need to be highly technical I'd imagine."

Their gazes settled upon the youngster Alan, who quickly affirmed, “Don’t look at me!” He was right, that would be too much to ask of him.

Josh went on. “So now I’ll walk you through the people, in particular the owner, Sonia Jurado.”

He went through her family, her father’s fire equipment company still operating under his oversight as Chairman, and her properties in Spain, London and Mexico. Josh has all her financial details, at least those that were declared, the offshore anonymous accounts would always be undisclosed and hidden. On paper, she was worth about six hundred million, but they all suspected her obvious skills with computers and data were put to good use hiding more assets away from prying eyes.

“She seems to have a small but loyal, long-serving team, not much in the way of staff turnover,” said Josh. “Feels like once you’re in, they pay or entice you enough not to want to leave. Her top people get extremely well paid, all millionaires themselves.”

“Golden handcuffs! A good way to prevent anyone leaving and dirty laundry being aired in public?” wondered Si out loud.

“Apart from the usual Directors for Sales, Finance and HR, we have a couple of others including this guy,” Josh brought up the profile picture taken from a retailer’s case studies website, “Peter Whistler, her Chief Technology Officer.”

He went through an impressive sounding IT, programming and data science background, adding, “Certainly a likely candidate to be an influential technology whizz, or maybe even hacker?”

He flicked onto another profile picture. “And finally Jurado’s Operations Director, a Nick Hawkins. Or maybe it’s Special Operations, as he’s referred to in different publications and websites.

Max sat up. “No, it can’t be, bloody hell,” he exclaimed. “It’s Fifty!”

Everyone in the room looked at him in puzzlement.

"What are you talking about Max," said Si, "you're not making any sense?"

Max repeated, "Fifty!" pointing at the screen. "My old Colour Sergeant in the Marines. Twenty years ago. Good God, what's he doing working for Jurado?"

"You served with this guy, Max?" asked Vince.

Max was shocked to see the picture but excited to find his old comrade alive and well in civi street.

"This guy was my Colour Sergeant for my brief spell in the Commandos," explained Max with pride. "Crikey we were both posted to Sierra Leone," Max's mood dropped as memories flooded back. "We fought the advancing rebels' side by side, and were captured by them." Max quietened and suddenly became contemplative.

Si cut in. "It's okay Max, you don't need to go through the details."

Josh interjected clumsily. "Is that the incident when you got the Military Cross, Max?"

Max straightened himself up and snapped out of the fog, looking around at all of them waiting on his next words.

"Fifty. That was Nick Hawkins' handle. He could always throw a dart into the fifty-point bullseye on a dart board. Uncanny really." Max nodded with pride. "Good bloke, taught me a lot. I think he did a fifteen-year stint in the Marines, long before and long after I was there. No idea what he did afterwards, I guess now I know."

Max seemed more relaxed talking about him, so Alan couldn't help but venture for more details. "What did happen with the two of you, if you're okay to tell us, might be relevant?" Si shot him a look.

"That's okay," said Max. "Our patrol got into a firefight with rebels, men were shot on both sides until three of us were surrounded, then captured." The room was silent, no one now wanting to interrupt as they could see Max envisaging events once more in his mind.

"They took us to a ruined building and were going to kill all of us. Fifty got beaten up, but my best friend was first, to be murdered, in front of our eyes. It was awful."

Max stopped as if assuming everyone could then fill in the blank as to what happened next. He realized that talking about it after all those years was liberating him, from holding it deep inside himself. He concluded the story.

"Just as the thugs were finishing off my mate, I managed to grab the gun from the guy guarding me and Fifty." Max could see Alan drop his head slightly as if to say 'and then what?'. "Well let's put it this way," pointing at Nick's picture and himself, "me and Fifty are still around. The rest of them aren't!"

The room stayed silent again, each imagining what Max had gone through and shuddering, grateful they would never have to endure anything similar. Their respect for Max went up a few more points.

Max broke the steely thoughts and smiled at each of them, lingering on the boss. "Si?"

Si Lawson leant forward onto the table, thought carefully, then addressed Max calmly and objectively. "So Max, it looks like we may have found a way to get you into Jurado Data? That's the only way we can be certain if they're behind the Richmond job. What do you think?"

Max had already wrestled with the inevitable opportunity to get an in-road and maybe even crack this assignment. He remembered Fifty had an edge to him, but that was twenty years ago. He wouldn't get involved in hacking and bank robbery, would he? He must be innocent, so Jurado must be innocent. He would take it on, not to prove they'd done it, but he hoped to prove they hadn't.

He frowned looking down at the table-top, then nodding, pronounced, "I'm up for it! It's the only way."

Max sat down with Josh and Vince to once again go through

everything they had on Jurado and Nick Hawkins. It seemed from bank accounts, property and cars, his old Colour Sergeant had done very well for himself. All thanks to his time with Jurado.

"Wow, he lives in a large house on Cheyne Walk on the Chelsea Embankment overlooking the Thames," observed Max.

Josh looked up the address on Google street view. "There it is, big, five stories with a garage." He quickly logged into the Land Registry to look up what the property was bought for. "Last sold in 2015 to a Mr Nicholas Hawkins for over eight million! Your old Commando mate *is* doing well!"

"He's just on the other side of the river to me in Clapham," said Max. "So close by all these years and I never knew it. Let's go through his standing orders and frequent purchases and try to establish somewhere I can engineer bumping into him," suggested Max.

Josh brought up Nick Hawkins' various bank statements and they quickly established which one was being used for normal living expenses. They each scanned down the last few months spend lines.

"Looks like he picks up a Starbucks every morning before going to work."

"Regular monthly transfers to some Spanish sounding lady, three grand each?" said Vince.

"Probably just a housekeeper or cleaner," said Max. "This one looks more interesting. I know that gym."

Josh read it out. "Battersea Fitness, just off Battersea Park. Looks like he has a standing order monthly membership payment going out to them."

Vince added, "It's situated about halfway between you in Clapham, Max, and him in Chelsea."

Max wondered. "Maybe that's where I make contact again, with my old Colour Sergeant. Looks like I'm off to the gym!"

Max went online and bought a trial membership and on the assumption Nick Hawkins would use the gym either early before work, or at the end of the day, started visiting the gym randomly at those times.

Battersea Fitness was a plush warehouse-style fitness centre, with large open spaces filled with all the latest training equipment, lined up in rows in front of long, mirrored walls.

Max had spent some time going through his background story with Vince, to keep it as close to the truth as possible. He wanted to avoid any slipups in case Hawkins was suspicious of his intended chance encounter.

After just four days Max was in the gym one evening, dripping with sweat on one of the cross-trainers, when his concentration on the TV ahead of him was broken by a familiar voice.

"No way! Max? You old sod, what the hell are you doing here?" Nick Hawkins had spotted him across the floor-space having just entered the gym. He'd immediately recognized one of his old Commando Brigade soldiers. Of the hundreds of men that passed through his charge, Max would always be someone indelibly stamped into his memory forever.

Max knew the unmistakable voice and feigned his utter surprise as he turned to face him, halting the cross-trainer program. He looked at Nick for a few seconds as if searching his memory to identify him.

"Fifty?"

"Yes, it's me, Nick Hawkins ya silly git. My God Max, how are you?"

Max jumped off the trainer and gave Nick a huge hug which was eagerly reciprocated.

"I'm good thanks," said Max cheerfully. "Been polishing an office seat with my arse for the last twenty years, but otherwise, all good. You look great."

Nick had managed to maintain his strong, wavy dark hair and like Max, a fit, muscly body. Fitness training was such a huge part of any soldier's regime and discipline, it often stayed with them for life.

Nick replied, "Well you know, once a soldier, always a

soldier, at least when it comes to regular exercise. Fancy bumping into you here?" He looked intrigued to hear from Max how they'd crossed paths after all those years.

Max explained. "After I recently got booted out of my last company, I was doing well in procurement and supply chain, I wanted to take time out, you know, perhaps a change in direction. I only live down the road in Clapham, so have a bit more time now to put in some training."

Nick seemed happy with the explanation. "So that's what you did when you left us?"

"Yup, joined civi street working for companies, buying this and that. Did well mind you, got to the top of the game," said Max proudly, knowing he could be looked up online.

"So what happened?" asked Nick.

"Bit stupid really, wanted to help an old boss, you know how important loyalty is to us guys. Got caught sending him some files I thought he'd find useful." Max wanted to show Nick that he wasn't beyond crossing the line if it was for a friend. He wanted Nick to realise he could be trusted and had done something that was strictly speaking, illegal.

"Interesting," said Nick. "You're right, loyalty is everything. So what are you doing now, what's the plan?"

"Don't know to be honest. I fancy a change from sitting behind a desk, could do with a bit more excitement. Ever since leaving the Marines, I've always had that gap in my life, the action I would have had if I'd stayed on like you did, after *that* day."

Nick frowned and nodded. "Yeah, I've never forgotten that day, think of it most days of the week. Poor Pete who copped it. But I've also never forgotten you, Max. You saved my bloody life mate. If it weren't for you I wouldn't be standing here. They were gonna kill us both for sure that day!"

Max nodded in agreement. The chat was going as planned.

"So what are you doing then Fifty?"

Nick chuckled. "I've not really heard that name since leaving the Marines. I did another ten years after you, made it to Warrant Officer which was high enough for me."

"You were great with the men, but I couldn't ever see you behind a desk," said Max.

"For sure. I kinda knew my time was almost up and all it took at the end was a new Commander to arrive at the Brigade who was an arsehole and that was me done."

"Well looks like you're doing pretty well now," said Max, suddenly realizing he was referring to when he'd seen Nick's property value and bank balances.

Nick looked at Max. "What do you mean Max? How would you know how I was doing?"

Max thought he'd blown it and quickly searched for a get-out. Thankfully, he spotted Nick's watch. He nodded at it.

"Come on Nick, even I know those Rolex Daytona Ceramic's are about twenty-five grand. You must be doing okay?"

Nick looked down at his rare, expensive watch. "Ah, yes, okay, you've got me there. Yes, life's been pretty good to me."

Max had got away with it, for now, but knew he would have to have his wits about him to get through much more of this chit chat. The Colour Sergeant was still as sharp as a knife. "What you been up to then?" Max asked.

"I bummed around for a bit then hooked up with my boss as security for her. Kinda been doing it ever since, Special Operations, at her firm, Jurado Data." Max was pleased Nick was being open, he didn't seem to be wanting to hide anything.

"What do they do then," asked Max, knowing full well all about the firm.

Nick chuckled coyly. "You know, a bit of this and a bit of that." Max looked puzzled, thinking that was a strange way to describe a data company. Nick picked up on it. "It's really all about customer's data, personal info and all that stuff. Kinda beyond me. I can barely remember all the bloody passwords I have around the place."

Max played along. "Sounds a bit dull for someone with your specialist skills mate."

Nick seemed desperate to tell Max more. "Ah, well we do sometimes do exciting stuff, that's why my title's Special Operations Director. I head-up security, physical security that is, not the IT things. I'm a fixer, like a trouble-shooter."

Nick now watched Max closely for his reaction, to see if there was a glimmer of interest in hearing more of what could start to drift into a darker conversation. Max again continued his pretence.

"You've got me curious Nick?"

"You should be careful Max, we know what curiosity did to the cat!" Another test.

"But cats have nine lives, I can afford to lose a couple," said Max, "tell me more?"

"I guess we damn near lost one of those lives in Sierra Leone didn't we Max?" Nick patted him on the shoulder. "We often have work on for someone like you Max, assuming you've not lost your flare for action and surprises. The money's damn good, more than you could imagine in fact. I'm sure it would make your procurement pay look like pocket money." He paused. "We may have something coming up soon, might you be interested?"

Max shrugged his shoulders, "Sounds great!"

Nick looked right into Max's eyes. "To be clear Max, you do understand what I'm saying? It might not always be, well you know, legit work."

Max suddenly rethought his innocent view of Nick, but was fast to reply with confidence. "As long as we're all looking out for one another like the old days, I'm interested."

"Well you sure as hell looked out for me Max, so I owe you. Give me your mobile and I'll check with the boss and if she agrees, I'll text you a meetup and we can chat some more okay?"

Max agreed and they swapped numbers before he retired to the changing room to shower, leaving Nick to get on with his workout.

Max tingled in the shower with nervous energy, wondering what was really happening at the Jurado firm. 'Might not always be legit work' he wondered to himself. The meeting with Fifty had gone well. He'd managed to leverage his own corporate misdemeanour, explain his availability and bring up the old times in the Commandos, where loyalty was everything. Not to mention of course, he'd saved Nick's life.

Later that evening he called Si Lawson and gave him a full account of the meeting.

"Just be careful Max, sounds like he dropped a few hints that things aren't what they seem at Jurado, so we might be onto something. But you could be entering the viper's nest?" warned Si.

"I think given I saved the guy's life, he'll look after me. I'll be fine."

"Now that you might be getting into the Jurado firm, I need to tie up a loose end at Richmond Bank for you," said Si.

"What loose end?"

"If Jurado is behind the hack and if they were assisted by the two people you found the cross-overs for, then…"

Max was ahead of him. "Bob Simmons the IT Director. Damn it, he's met me!"

"Precisely. I don't think we need to worry about the consultant bloke Freddy McIntosh yet. He's not even been pulled in. But if Simmons knows you're involved with Jurado Data or your mate Nick Hawkins, he could identify you as MI5!"

"Jesus," fretted Max. "I might have saved Fifty's life, but I dread to think what he'd do if he thought I'd double-crossed him in any way. What are you going to do?"

"I'm going to have to brief William the Chief Super, I'll say we're following up a hunch and hoping you'll get to go undercover, but that they should carry on with their 'proper' investigations back at Richmond with the executives there."

"Shouldn't they bring in McIntosh then," suggested Max.

Si thought for a moment. "I think it's time we probably got William to take in both Simmons and McIntosh for some proper interrogation, maybe one of them will crack and you can then abort your thing with Jurado."

"Better still if you can keep the two of them off the street for a while, even better," said Max. It's not worth the risk of allowing anything to tie me back to meeting Simmons, let alone him telling Jurado or Nick who I really am."

"Agreed, I'll sort that," assured Si.

Max just had to wait now and hope he got called in by Nick so he could find out more. He was fascinated to see where this might lead, but still couldn't believe this company had anything to do with the Richmond Bank raid.

Max felt certain Nick would want to see him again and sure enough the following day his mobile rang, it was Nick.

"Hi Max. I've spoken to the boss, her name is Sonia Jurado. She'd like to meet you before we do any work together. Can you come right into our offices, One The Strand, by Trafalgar Square. See you soon okay."

Max checked in with Si as he walked to Clapham Common underground, from where he took the tube seven stops to Charing Cross. It was a sunny day and he walked along The Strand the couple of hundred yards to Trafalgar Square, passing office workers and tourists going about their day in the centre of London's historic setting.

As he approached the large number One building, Nelson's column came into view. Standing resplendent in the middle of the square, it was guarded by the four large lions facing outwards. Max remembered visiting the square as a boy and being bought seeds to feed the pigeons. It seemed fun at the time, to have about twenty of the dirty birds scrambling all over him, jostling to get the food. No such scenes now as health and safety knowledge and awareness have taught visitors not to encourage or touch the pigeons.

Max entered the luxurious building and asked reception for Jurado Data. They called through. He took the lift up to the designated floor and exited into an even more modern, impressive reception.

Nick Hawkins came striding over to greet him enthusiastically.

"Let me show you around quickly. There's not a lot to see, most of what we do is inside all these computers, selling customer data and all that stuff," he gestured at the large office expanse of staff sitting at their computers.

The mostly open-plan offices were bright, cool and modern. Along the inner wall stretched a long, glass partitioned room holding rows of servers and IT equipment. Max could see it all looked state-of-the-art, with various cooling fans and vents maintaining precisely the right operating temperature for their optimum performance.

There were several meeting rooms, all filled with staff presenting to and coaching existing and potential customers, to allow Jurado more access to their data and sell them even more data. Then they'd give the hapless clients a helping hand to target audience profiles and customize promotions. It was a well-oiled machine of data bamboozlement, manipulation and impressive results delivery. Done well, a license to print money, as businesses scrambled for the attention of potential new customers.

Towards the end of the office, Max could see a larger boardroom which separated a big corner office with prime views of Trafalgar Square. An attractive, tanned, dark-haired woman sat behind a desk talking on the phone, looking straight back at him as she spoke. Max smiled. She didn't react and kept talking.

Nick continued. "Max, meet Peter, Peter Whistler, he's our technology genius." The geeky, spectacled man broke away from his PC and welcomed Max heartily. Then just as quickly, sat back down and continued his concentration on his work.

Max couldn't help but wonder if this simple looking man was the architect of the bank hack. His eyes were then drawn to a couple of the staff sat near the boardroom. What drew

Max to them was simply that they didn't look like your usual office staff. They seemed out of place, sat there at their computer screens, looking alert and moody.

Nick noticed. "Ah you've spotted the 'boys'," he leant into Max and whispered, "grumpy couple of lads, but they're okay." He took Max over to them and returned to speaking normally out loud. "These are my two Special Ops guys. Afrim and Saban. They're brothers, originally from Albania of all places."

The two men begrudgingly stood up and offered Max an awkward but very firm handshake. They sat back down in unison and returned to their keyboards, deliberately not wanting to engage in conversation.

Max could see their likeness. Both had almost shaven heads with dirty-looking stubbled faces and dark violent looking eyes. Like a pair of tigers, caged and waiting to explode with fury. Max looked at Nick questioningly.

Nick got the message, offering some explanation. "They're not customer-facing, as you can probably see, but they're a couple of whizz-kids on data profiling, PowerPoint presentations and data manipulation."

Afrim's eyes glanced up at Max and looked him up and down, then returned to his screen.

Nick whispered again. "They're part of my 'Special' Ops team if you know what I mean. Sonia and I rescued them from the East End gangland. They'd do anything for us, including any special front-line jobs. You get me." He nudged Max in the arm.

The message was clear. These two dubious looking characters were obviously Nick's strong-arm help. Max was already wondering why a straightforward so-called reputable data firm would need so much muscle on the payroll. This was all pointing in one direction, crime. And not just data crime.

"Come on, let's meet the boss," said Nick, who pulled Max aside from the two smouldering lads and started towards the office through the boardroom.

"Hang on a mo guys," said Peter Whistler as he pushed past, eager to get to Sonia ahead of them. Max and Nick stood aside and held back while Peter went into the office ahead, looking excited.

The door wasn't quite shut so Max could just hear what was said.

"Good news Sonia," said Peter. She looked up attentively to her technology guru. "That dead Christ thing you asked us to monitor, we've picked up an opportunity from the emails and..."

Sonia stopped him with a raised finger. "Tell me later Peter." She then looked at Max and Nick to show she had other people waiting. Peter looked round and nodded, then smiling, walked back past them and out.

Max was still trying to make sense of the 'dead Christ' comment he'd overheard, as he entered the minimalistic, light office and was met by Sonia Jurado.

"So you're the infamous Max Sargent," she opened with, holding out her hand.

"Not sure I'm infamous, but yes, I'm Max," taking her hand.

"Oh come now, you're being too modest," she beamed cautiously at him, inspecting every part of his face. "I rate Nick here more than any other man I've met, yet *you* saved his life. Quite something, what you did back in the Commandos, and I'm grateful you did, he's literally my right-hand man."

Max could see the strong relationship between them, but it was beyond sexual attraction, those days had long passed. It was more like a family love for one another.

"I just did what the circumstances required and got lucky. What a great office you have here, the outlook is priceless," said Max changing the subject.

Sonia looked behind her out of the windows. "Yes, it's quite something. Clients love it. It's impressive and helps with the whole status thing sadly so necessary in business." She looked at Nelson's column and huffed. "Ironic that I've worked so hard to have a daily reminder of your Brits defeating us Spanish and French at Trafalgar two hundred years ago!" She turned back to Max for a reaction.

He detected a tinge of resentment towards his nation but shrugged. "As you say that was a long time ago, who cares now eh."

"Do you remember the signal Nelson sent to his fleet before battle?"

Max dug deep back to his history lessons at school. "I think so. Wasn't it 'England expects every man will do his duty'?"

Sonia nodded. "Yes. That's a little bit how we run things here, eh Nick?"

Nick joined in with the nods. "Like the Marines Max, we value loyalty here. If you join us, even if it's shall we say, part-time for special jobs, then once you're in, you're in!"

Max took care as to how to respond this time. "Well I need a change from office work, so if you've got anything a little more exciting and challenging, then in principle I'm up for it. Depends on what you have in mind of course."

"You're giving me all the right vibes Max," the sexual innuendo wasn't lost on either Max or Nick, "so I'll leave it to Nick's judgement as to whether to involve you in something we may have coming up soon."

Her phone rang and she returned to her desk to answer it. "Lovely to meet you, Max."

"Come on mate," said Nick, "I can get back to you soon once we have more detail," ushering him out.

Max couldn't help but be drawn in by her welcoming, slightly flirty, over-confident approach to him. Her allure ran deeper than mere attractive looks. Max knew full well, Sonia Jurado had a lot more to her than met the eye and suspected he'd be finding out for himself, very soon.

6

Several years ago, Jurado Data did some work for Sonia's famous local museum in Madrid, the Prado. The data firm sold them some potential customer lists to build on the small visitor and subscribers database already established. Jurado then did a piece of work to help them target museum-goers across the country, enticing them to visit, with promotions and discount schemes.

The Museo del Prado was established two hundred years ago and features many artists and collections of Spanish monarchies over the years. Whilst also holding sculptures, it is now known as the museum of painters, with its impressive breadth and diversity of artwork. The masterpieces are all displayed at its resplendent, long building on Calle de Ruiz de Alarcon in the centre of Madrid.

In her efforts to make her child more rounded and cultured, Sonia's mother would take her to the Prado to see the beautiful paintings. As they came upon a stunning picture, she would read about it out loud with such vigour and enthusiasm, Sonia's appreciation of beautiful art was born.

The young Sonia had her favourite pieces, among which one particular painting struck her to the core and mesmerized her every time she stood in front of it. The Dead Christ Supported by an Angel, by Antonello da Messina, was painted on a panel in 1475.

The painting depicts the dead Christ being supported by a grief-stricken, crying angel, holding him up, yet out of respect, not touching his skin but his grey shawl. The brutal, bleeding wounds from his crucifixion show clearly on his side and hand. Droplets of blood can be seen around his neck and chest from the removed crown of thorns. They are located in a cemetery and the crucifixion crosses at Calvary can be made out in the background, along with the artist's birthplace town of Messina showing in the distance.

Many artists painted their renditions of Christ being held by one or more angels. The Prado has others including two by Alonso Cano painted on canvas almost two hundred years after Sonia's favourite.

But it was the enchanting painting by Antonello that captured the imagination and dreams of the young Sonia, who in later years adopted a mild obsession with the piece.

After the work her firm did with that same museum she used to visit, with *her* Dead Christ painting inside, she'd asked her IT man Whistler to access the museum's email server. He did so easily.

In an attempt to look after it and ensure the special painting was never sold or moved, they installed a simple search tag alert so that any emails mentioning the artwork name or artist could be monitored by Peter Whistler.

From time to time, emails came through of no consequence, maybe talking about moving it to another part of the museum or scheduling temporary removal for cleaning and maintenance.

But that day when Peter had rushed into Sonia's office, the email was of a graver subject matter. Peter looked on as Sonia had read out the printout. The email was from the museum Director to their Head of Communications;

'As part of our fundraising drive where identified artworks are being sold, I have agreed with the Royal Board to include Antonello's Dead Christ panel painting in the lots to be handled by Sotheby's Madrid in a few weeks.

We have had several enquiries about this piece, so it is right we submit it for auction, as opposed to agreeing to any direct sale with just one buyer.

It will be a sad loss to the Prado, but the additional funds it generates will fill a gap we have in the budget this year.

Please liaise with me tomorrow regarding collection by Sotheby's and a press release to go out next week.'

"No! They can't sell my beloved painting. No, I won't allow it!" said Sonia crossly, thrusting the piece of paper back at Peter.

"What are you going to do Sonia?" asked Peter looking highly concerned.

"I'm not sure right now, just get Nick in here at once! We'll figure out something!"

Max didn't have to wait long to hear from Nick, who called him the day after his visit to the Jurado office, inviting him to spend a long weekend with them at Sonia's Spanish villa.

Max flew into Madrid-Barajas airport where Nick was waiting to collect him in a grey Spania GTA, Spain's only real supercar. Ninety-nine cars were planned, though only fifteen had been made and sold, at prices creeping up to several million each due to the lack of supply versus demand for the ultra-rare car. The eight-litre V10 engine matches the incredible one thousand BHP of a Bugatti Veyron.

"Rare. A Spanish supercar!" admired Max.

"When in Spain!" shouted Nick across to Max above the engine howl, as they roared away from the airport.

Max enjoyed the ride for a while before asking Nick, "So is this really just a pool-villa break, or did I detect there may be something else going on during this trip?"

Nick took in a breath, this was a crossroads moment for him, and for Max. "I'm gonna be straight with you Max. If you're not up for this then just say, no issues, and I'll drop you back at the airport and we'll say no more about it."

Max tried to stay relaxed, but this sounded serious. He had to stay in with this Jurado crowd to find out if they were involved in the Richmond Bank hack, which meant he, therefore, needed Nick on his side. But he was anxious about what he was about to be told or asked to do.

Nick headed south skirting round the east side of Madrid. "You know I said we might have one of those special jobs coming up? Well, one has. We're reviewing it this weekend."

"O-k-a-y," Max said the word slowly, "and what kind of *special* job are we talking about?"

Nick led with the carrot. "Like the car?" and dropped a gear flooring the accelerator, pushing them both back in their seats.

"Yeah," screamed Max above the noise.

"For this little job, the car's yours!" Nick paused, then added, "plus half a million transferred into your account." Another pause. "I'd suggest you set up an offshore if you haven't already got one." He smiled nervously at Max in anticipation of the reply.

Max was stunned and thinking 'what the hell would he be asked to do for all that?'! He played along. "I'm interested, but cut the shit and tell me what for?"

"It's a simple little art theft. Nothing risky, nothing dangerous, we've got all the intel we need, in and out in five I reckon!" Nick slowed the powerful car down so he could study Max's reaction better. He'd put his trust in his old Commando mate and was willing him to agree, not wanting to worry about how things might have to go if he refused.

There was only one answer Max could give, even though it was against his better judgement. "Count me in Fifty! But I tell you what, it better be a bloody good plan?"

"Don't you worry Max," said Nick settling back into his seat and accelerating again, relieved at Max's answer. "Just like the old days, good intel, military precision planning, in and out, bosh, job done!"

Max couldn't help but think of the last op the two of them did together, when things didn't work out at all well for either of them!

They veered off the E-901 motorway onto the M-832 and after a minute turned off again into the Las Lagunas de las

Madres site, consisting of five large lakes near the town of Granja Avicola del Jarama.

"Welcome to Sonia's lakeside country villa, less than ten miles from the centre of Madrid." Said Nick as they drove along a single-track road beside the first large lake. Max could see this hidden paradise just off the motorway was likely to be an up-and-coming millionaire's hideaway, as they passed several large building sites with part mansions in the process of being erected.

"She bought the plot five years ago and had the villa built to her own designs. It's lovely Max, probably now worth fifteen million if it came on the market."

They rounded another small lake and Max could now see a huge villa at the end of the narrow track. It was like an oasis, with no other properties nearby, surrounded by trees and greenery amidst the bare, sandy surrounding areas.

There was a sturdy, high fence hidden with shrubbery surrounding the three-acre complex, that rose above the lake and scenery on a gentle slope. Various buildings were scattered about the site, with the large classic Spanish style mansion in the centre of the plot.

They approached the main gates which slowly lurched open on Nick's remote-control command. Inside there was a small gatehouse with one man who strolled out and waved to Nick. Max wondered if he was armed.

Nick drove up the driveway to the main house, where to Max's delight, Sonia came out of the large double front doors to greet them.

"Hi boys, welcome to my little hideaway Max, well, one of them anyway," she enthused, giving him an eye-twinkling smile. She glanced at Nick who gave her a thumbs up. "Come in, relax, chef's got an amazing dinner prepared, then we'll tell you all about our little jaunt!"

From behind Sonia, several more figures emerged from the house into the light. Peter Whistler came out first and greeted Max with his usual clipped enthusiasm, then strolled off to one of the smaller buildings beyond the driveway.

Two more men reluctantly edged out, they were Afrim and Saban, both looking sultry and closed. One of them gave Max a quick nod of acknowledgement. The other did nothing.

'Quite the rogue's gallery', thought Max to himself, 'the whole Jurado inner sanctum, and me!'.

Chief Superintendent William Lucas wasn't a fool. Si Lawson of MI5 had called him to advise they were following up a likely 'inconsequential lead' and for him to continue with the senior execs at Richmond Bank. He knew if it was Si Lawson, there would be nothing inconsequential about it. MI5 were already onto something.

He insisted that his Met Police took over the line of inquiry but when push came to shove, was politely outranked by Si. However, Lucas had been thrown something his team could act on. Si had told him about the connection between the IT Director Bob Simmons and the IT Consultant Freddy McIntosh.

"We think there might be something there worth pushing," said Si. "I suggest you bring them both in, give them the full tour treatment and see if anything drops out or one of them becomes a tell-tale."

The full tour treatment referred to putting on a bit of a show when pulling in suspects. The grand tour so to say. Using a big police station, putting them in a cell for a while. Telling them what they could go down for, what life in prison would be like, playing good cop, bad cop with them.

Si insisted, "But whatever you do William, don't let them go until you've updated me on any progress. I can't have them trotting about willy nilly when I have agents in the field on this case!"

The Chief Super had dutifully got his men to bring the two guys in with specific instructions.

Bob Simmons was in his office at the bank's HQ, when he

saw four men enter his department's open plan floor space. Two plain-clothed CID officers and two in uniform, all looking quite foreboding as they purposefully strode towards him.

He'd expected to be hauled into John Stevens office and suspended or even fired, but not this dramatic show of force from the Met.

His IT staff ducked out of the way behind desks and low partition screens, heads then popping up to see what all the commotion was about, with worried expressions on their faces.

Bob made the mistake of coming out of his office to intercept them, out of politeness and respect. He should have invited them in and shut the door for some privacy, for now, the discussion was on the open floor and in public. Perfect for the Met officers, the stage was set for drama, the audience of about sixty IT staff watched on.

The lead officer started speaking before they drew up to him. "Bob Simmons, we'd like you to accompany us to Lavender Hill police station to assist us with our inquiries, regarding the theft of personal data and bitcoin funds from this bank."

Bob started to protest, "But I thought…"

The officer continued. "You are not being charged at this time so your cooperation is voluntary, so, you do not have to say anything, but it may harm your defence if you do not mention when questioned something which you later rely on in court. Anything you do say may be given in evidence!"

"This is crazy. I had nothing to do with what happened here the other night!" One of the officers gently coaxed Bob to follow them out. His secretary grabbed his coat and briefcase and passed them to him as he went by her. "Thanks, Becky. Can you tell John Stevens what's happening? And ask him to get me the best lawyer the bank has. Lavender Hill police station. Quickly!"

The officers escorted him unceremoniously through the

building, down past reception and the hushed chatter at the unusual sight. Three policemen accompanied Bob in the waiting marked squad car, the fourth followed in a plain car.

The driver took a slightly longer route from the Richmond Bank's offices to the police station. It would take them past the long, frontage of Wandsworth prison in Clapham. Part of the 'tour'. The grim view of the prison, built in 1851, with its unforgiving high walls and solid towers surrounding the entrance, looked down on them menacingly.

The CID officer glanced at Simmons, who was trying not to look at the ominous landmark. Perhaps a little nudge was needed.

"Wandsworth prison eh, not somewhere you'd want to end up Mr Simmons. Quite a lot of white-collar serious criminals end up there these days. Nasty place, not for the likes of office workers and family men like you sir."

Bob gulped and glanced round for a quick view of the prison, thinking to himself, 'Oh my God, whatever happens, I can't end up somewhere like there!'.

A few minutes on they pulled up at Lavender Hill Police Station. A large, cream-coloured stone block on the corner of Lavender Hill and Latchmere Road. Two floors above ground and one below, with the tops of among other things, the cells, showing behind the pedestrian pavement.

There would be more drama to come as they would check him in at the duty Sargent's desk, pretend interview rooms were all in use and have to hold him briefly in a cell, another unpleasant experience, then start questioning him once his lawyer arrived. The CID officers were satisfied the 'show' might start to work its magic on this suspect if he had something to hide.

At this time, across town, the same was happening to Freddy McIntosh. The Met had already asked him for his movements and location in case they needed to speak with him. Freddy had been on high alert after events at the bank that night and suspected it was only a matter of time before they got round to him. He had worked with Bob Simmons several times before and had become a trusted ally and IT expert for the Technology Director to call on.

Freddy was at a potential new client's office in Wimbledon and in the middle of a presentation to the firm's board, when the police arrived and were shown up to the room.

Amidst his shock and profuse apologies to the horrified onlookers, Freddy was also cautioned and asked to accompany the officers to Lavender Hill Police Station. He too got the drive-by past Wandsworth Prison.

Bob Simmons and Freddy McIntosh would now undergo separate questioning at the same police station. They would be played off against one another and were each told the other was also being detained there. Police would start to gently tease them that the other was starting to give up information, with the caveat that whoever told the truth first would be looked upon favourably by any judge.

Even if it was answering simple questions, or lying at others, once they started speaking and engaging in conversation, the door was wedged open and could only be prized wider.

Freddy and Bob both started out saying nothing. As the tactics and manner of the questioning flexed and threats of charges being brought and mention of overnight stays in cells, they slowly started to answer some of the basic questions. If there was anything to say about the Richmond Bank digital robbery, one of them would surely start talking.

Sonia Jurado's chef had laid on a truly amazing dinner at the villa. The cocktails and wine had flowed freely, at least for Sonia, Max, Peter and Nick. Afrim and Saban had barely touched a drop Max observed and had kept themselves to themselves down the far end of the table. Clearly not unusual, as the only comment made about them over the crab and lobster starter was from Nick, saying simply, "Don't worry about the boys down the end, they're alright once you get to know them." Not something Max planned on doing though.

Throughout dinner, no one mentioned what was being planned. The conversation covered football, food and wine, a little about some of their pasts including Nick talking a lot about his time in the Commandos and some funny stories about their meetings with stranger, more demanding clients.

Max was listening out for any mention of previous 'special' jobs, such as the Richmond Bank hack, but either because they were oblivious to it, or extremely well-drilled, nothing came up.

It was late when Sonia rose to retire. "What a lovely evening with my boys. Tomorrow's a big day, we'll go through everything then." She turned to Max. "You've been very patient Max, you must be dying to know what we've got in mind. So let me assure you this isn't some violent crime we're planning. What I will say is that I simply want to prevent a painting that is dear to me, from being sold to some private collector and disappearing forever more. That's all."

Everyone looked at Max to assess any reaction to this snippet of tantalising information. Max stayed calm.

"Sounds reasonable to me. I'll look forward to hearing all about it in the morning."

"It's good to have you onboard," Sonia added, giving Max a cheeky smile, before sweeping up the long, curved staircase.

He couldn't help but notice a slight flinch of uneasiness from Nick, at her flirty smile. Max was starting to feel as though it wasn't just some art caper he would have to be careful about.

Once back in his room, Max thought carefully about what to tell Si Lawson. He had the ability on his mobile to call or text him using the 'Notes' app, leaving no obvious trace of the communications to anyone looking at his phone. A nice little upgrade Alan had installed for him some while ago back at MI5.

He started to type out a text. He felt that surely he had to report that some art theft was about to go down, but he didn't know anything else about it, what, when, where or how. His priority, for now, was to keep in with this crowd and find out if they did the Richmond Bank job. It felt likely but he hadn't a shred of evidence yet.

He was torn. After a few moments, he reconciled himself to the fact he had to let this play out for now. He simply couldn't afford to risk undoing what it had taken to get this far so quickly.

Deleting the text he'd started, he retyped a new message and sent it to Si. It said simply, 'At Jurado's villa, gaining their trust, nothing re Richmond yet, expecting to be tested soon, will revert when I have more, no backup required.'

Max put the phone down and slumped onto his bed. He was exhausted and the food and wine had taken their effect on his senses. 'Thank heavens I can get a good night's sleep' he thought.

At that moment, the handle of his door gently tilted and opened slowly. Max sat up, imagining one of the Albanian 'boys' was paying him a surprise visit to dispose of him.

A slender arm came round the door to grasp the handle, followed enticingly by a woman's body, swathed in a silk night gown. Max looked on wide-eyed, as Sonia Jurado slipped into the room and closed the door behind her.

She turned to him and put her finger up to her lips, then gave him a cheeky, playful smile accompanied by an excited, suppressed giggle. She approached the bedside in such a manner that made it clear there was no debate about what she wanted to happen next.

Max was stunned by her beauty and sheer brashness and confidence. He wasn't going to protest, this lady knew what she wanted and so did he. The light purple silk nightie slipped from her smooth, tanned shoulders and fell effortlessly down her body to the floor.

She stood there for a second allowing Max to take in the delights she was offering, then pulled back the single sheet and got into bed next to him. This would be his initiation, her seal of approval and their pact of mutual loyalty.

He could smell her intoxicating mix of natural alluring odours, expensive perfumes and delectable wines from the evening. His exhaustion evaporated, reinvigorated by this beautiful yet cheeky Spanish business titan.

The slumber he'd yearned for moments ago would have to wait, it was going to be some while before they finally got to sleep.

7

Over the last forty-eight hours, Peter Whistler had done his homework on the Prado museum. He already had access into their servers to obtain the email relating to Sonia's painting, so could also investigate everything else in their system, including, guards, rotas, CCTV, police and alarms.

In addition, a plethora of searches available over the internet, coupled with a few quick hacks into the public building's records and the security system provider, had given him all he needed.

The six of them had gradually appeared downstairs and congregated on the terrace by the large pool, looking down the garden at the lakes in the distance. A buffet was laid out for them by the over-efficient resident chef.

Nick Hawkins sat in a large comfortable armchair gazing out at the scenery, looking contemplative. Like most of them, he'd once had his time with the boss and shared her bed, but he sometimes found it hard to detach himself from her magnetism. Maybe a look she gave him or a touch, reminded him of what could have been a permanent relationship.

He knew how Sonia operated, he knew she couldn't be contained by one man, but that didn't stop him disliking it when she openly set upon another of her conquests. He was certain she'd gone to Max last night and whilst he owed each of them a great deal, the thought of them together just took the edge off his feelings for Max.

He snapped out of it as Max strolled out to join him. Sonia came down twenty minutes later, just as Peter seemed ready to brief them all. The Albanian boys lurked to one side as usual. Max wondered if they ever smiled. Probably not.

Sonia addressed them, without a hint of what had

transpired between her and Max. She'd always made it clear she was a free spirit, but she wouldn't rub anyone's faces in it, especially not Nick. She knew he really cared for her.

"Right boys, isn't this nice," she gleamed at everyone, lifting the mood immediately. "Peter, let's start by showing them what it is that's got my feathers so ruffled up eh?"

Peter brought up a picture of the artwork on his large laptop screen. They all looked at the enchanting painting. It drew them in. Max was fairly nonchalant about it to start with, but found the more he studied it, the more he understood its compelling beauty and sadness, and how someone could become attached to such an incredible piece of art.

Sonia continued. "Antonello's Dead Christ Supported by an Angel. I've spent my life staring at this, with my mother as a child, and latterly watching over it, to make sure we're never separated. Thanks to Peter, we found out the Prado intends to send it off to auction next week. It will then no doubt disappear from sight inside a huge yacht or hidden mansion. What I need us to do, is not a crime for money," Max checked for any reaction, "it's a crime of passion, for Spain. This painting deserves to be shared by everyone!"

Nick joined in, directing his comments mainly to Max and the boys. "The Prado is a little different from your elite museums, it's not seen as your usual theft target with priceless mater-pieces. The paintings and sculptures are not your thirty million Van Gogh Sunflowers. Judging by the security, they simply aren't expecting anyone to try to take anything from them."

Peter took over, pulling up various diagrams and pictures as he spoke. "They basically only have four levels of security to penetrate. The alarmed building itself, guards, CCTV and patrolling police cars."

"Walk us through each one," asked Sonia, sipping an expresso.

"From the original building design plans and a couple of subsequent alteration permission requests, there are six entry-exit points. The one I'm interested in is a fire escape door near the ticket office end of the building, almost directly beneath where the Dead Christ is displayed. During the day it can be opened by a security guards' fob and at night it's time-locked. I guess that's on the assumption they wouldn't need to do a mass evacuation after dark. I have gained access to their system so can open this door as required, deactivating its alarm as well. The museum only has alarms on its doors, no beams or motion detectors as the guard's patrol. It does mean that all the other time-locked doors will also open, but you'll be in and out in a few minutes so that shouldn't matter."

Nick nodded in approval and glanced at Sonia to receive a big smile back. Max was surprised at how easy this was all starting to sound like.

"Looking at the guard rotas it seems as though they normally have about eight covering the two main museum floors during the day, then six PM to two PM, five guards, then down to four up until seven AM. So probably one guard at each end of the two floors. So I suggest three AM tonight is our window."

'Tonight!' thought Max. He had to say something. "Are we sure about doing this so quickly?" he blurted.

Sonia reassured him. "Peter knows what he's talking about, trust him, he's not a novice at this." Max wondered if Peter had had some prior practice at Richmond Bank. "Best we get on with this before the Dead Christ gets shipped off to Sotheby's anytime next week. You'll be with Nick and the boys, no guns or anything like that and we're only taking the one painting, nothing else."

"So what if we come across any of these patrol guards?" asked Max.

Nick answered. "The four of us will have tranquillizer dart guns, just in case that happens. As long as we avoid any protective jackets they may be wearing and hit into skin, they'll be sleeping like a baby within three seconds!"

Peter went on with his roundup. "CCTV again is an easy

one, given you'll only need a few minutes inside, tops. I've got access to the Prado's system so will record a five-minute section then do the old trick of looping it back over when you enter the building. They'll pick it up later for sure, but it's a very slim chance any operator in their small third-floor control room will spot the splice at three AM."

Max cut in again. "We're talking about breaking into one of the best-known museums in Spain like it's a jaunt in the park. Sonia, are you really sure about this?"

Max was conscious Nick and the two boys were now looking at him curiously as if questioning his commitment, or maybe bravery to follow this through. He added, "Just checking, this is all new for me."

"I don't want any of us to get caught for such a paltry theft," explained Sonia. "It's not like we're robbing a bank!" The poorly chosen example wasn't lost on Max, nor Nick it seemed who shifted in his armchair. "I wouldn't risk it, or you guys, it's just a bloody picture after all and I'm simply saving it!"

Max held his hands up, "Okay, understood. I'm good."

Nick spoke. "The only uncertainty we have are the police patrols. It seems their brief is to frequently pass by the Prado, day and night, on their patrols. They park up there for a coffee and sometimes have a stroll, check with the guards there, all random though. Their presence is much greater during the day when all the visitors are milling about. At night they're either alongside, somewhere about the building, or very close by."

"That's our only inconsistency," agreed Peter. "I'll be back here with Sonia, with full computer systems access and radio contact with you all on one channel. Let's now go through some more detail including timings, equipment, location of the painting, transport, routes in and around the Prado and a load of other things."

"You okay Max?" asked Sonia.

Without hesitation, he replied, "Let's do this!" thinking to himself 'how on earth was he going to avoid the job let alone stop it, or tell Si, without breaking his cover!'.

Having all dozed or slept late afternoon into early evening, they were ready for the night's operation. They'd agreed that black fatigues would stand out even if just one person saw them entering the Prado, so opted for casual civilian clothing. They would each wear skin coloured face masks and baseball caps.

Inside one of the villa's outbuildings was all the equipment they required including a ten-year-old dark blue 4.8 litre V8 Porsche Cayenne and an old, small Renault. Fake plates had been put on the cars, which thanks to a trail of dodgy ownership and scrapping paperwork, rendered the cars no longer existing on the road, so untraceable.

They had a canvas case to put the twenty-nine-inch high, twenty-one-inch wide panel painting safely inside. As Max, Nick and the boys were relying heavily on Peter to handle everything except guards and police, the only other items they took were their upgraded semi-automatic compressed air dart guns. Small, light-weight rifles each had a magazine of just four hypodermic needled darts. These were filled with a rapid-onset barbiturate general anaesthetic dose of sodium pentothal.

Peter had been careful to research the volume of the dose for humans, who can react differently to the drug.

He'd warned them, "For God's sake don't use more than one dart per person. There's a high risk of giving them an overdose with very likely adverse side effects."

Nick had tried to reassure him, "We shouldn't need to use these at all. If you can get us in okay we'll try to avoid coming into contact with any of the guards if at all possible."

They put on rubber gloves and set off at two-thirty AM and drove up the A-3 past Villa de Vallecas. They pulled off at junction five to park up the small Renault in some trees at the end of the slip road. Then all together in the Cayenne, they proceeded past Moratalaz into Madrid.

As they approached the area of the museum at three AM, they turned off up the Calle de Alfonso XII which had the Real Jardin Botanico to their left. On their right lay the expansive El Retiro Park with its many walkways, plazas, monuments and lakes. They turned left and slowed down as they rounded the corner into Calle de Ruiz de Alarcon, running alongside the Prado museum up towards the plaza. This was where the main entrance and ticket offices were situated.

The large, long reddish two-story building looked like a fortress in the night's gloomy darkness. Its rectangular outline was punctuated in the middle by a round-arched shape and further along a third storey rose higher than the rest of the museum.

What they were unaware of was the small Citroen police car parked up on the other side of the museum building. Two officers had parked up by the Monumento a Velazquez statue for a quick coffee break. They also wanted to catch up on the Valencia versus Athletic Bilbao match rerun from the game earlier that evening.

The street to the front of the Prado was deserted and silent. To their right loomed several seven-storey apartment blocks and in the distance opposite the far end of the Prado, sat the pristine sandstone-built San Jeronimo el Real Church, atop its balustraded stone staircase.

Fortunately, because of the residences, there were a number of cars parked up on the right-hand side of the street. Saban pointed at an empty space and Nick quietly parked the Porsche up in the free slot.

"In position," reported Nick on the two-way radio they each had.

"Understood," said Peter, "we can see you on the map a third of the way along the East side of the Prado. Tell me when you're going towards the designated doorway and I'll engage the CCTV loop I've recorded, disable the alarms and open the time-locked exit doors including your one." Sonia nodded complimenting Peter's preparation and control.

All four men in the car strained round in all directions to check all was clear.

"Police!" whispered Max urgently. A 'POLICIA' marked white and blue car pulled round the end corner into their road.

"Get down below the window line!" growled Nick. It seemed ridiculous at the time but that was the only thing to do. The sight of four men sitting in an illegal car opposite the Prado museum, would be like waving a red rag to a bull for the police. The men pressed themselves sideways and down into their respective spaces front and rear of the medium-sized Cayenne, momentarily jostling for the lowest position achievable.

The police car slowed down as it approached them. Then it stopped. None of the four men could see as they each had their heads buried into their seats or front centre consul. They dare not look up, but they heard the police car slow and stop. Hearts were pounding. They could only wait for a tap on the window, shouting and a drawn gun pointing at them.

The two policemen were at the end of their shift and as they always did, put in one last pass of their beloved museum before going back to the station and then on home to bed.

Reluctantly they had slowed having seen something they didn't like the look of. A white windowless van was parked two cars before the Porsche and had drawn the attention of the two officers. The driver gesticulated to the other who begrudgingly got out and strolled wearily over to the van, pointing his small torch through the front driver's window. He was given a clear view of the rear, which was filled with dust sheets, pots of paint and various decorator's tools.

"Nada," he said softly to his colleague in the squad car and walked back to re-join him.

The men in the Cayenne heard their car pull away again and relaxed for a second, then froze once more. It sounded as though it had stopped again, just level with them!

The passenger policeman raised his cheap torch once more

to give a cursory look into the Porsche. It wasn't that they suspected it, but their casual attention was sparked purely because it was a nice-looking car with smoked glass windows.

The four men could see the torch light shine into their car, which was dulled by the heavily tinted windows. The Cayenne sat on the road much higher than the small, low police car and so the combination of darkened glass and the policeman looking up to see inside, gave him a murky view of an empty car.

After what seemed like an eternity, the policeman pointed forwards and the driver pulled away from them. The guys in the Porsche waited until they could hear the police car disappear into the distance and then waited another few minutes, before Nick very slowly raised his head to peer out through the windscreen. All was clear.

"Jesus, I thought I was going to have a heart attack," said Nick holding his chest. Even the two Albanian boys looked a little disturbed at the intensity of the moment. "Okay lads, masks and caps on, grab your dart guns and let's do this quickly. The only thing we're interested in is Sonia's Dead Christ, nothing else alright." Saban also had a crowbar.

Nick waited to get a nod from Max, Afrim and Saban before then radioing Peter back at the villa. "We're leaving the car now, tell me when you've deactivated the alarms, CCTV and door?"

Peter brought up various screens he'd left open, ready to activate the cut-off commands and start the CCTV loop, anxiously watched by Sonia. After a few moments, he rechecked each window, quietly praising himself each time he was happy his actions had been activated and confirmed back to him.

He clicked his radio transmit, "CCTV loop now running for the next five minutes before it loops again. The four time-locked exit doors have been released, but you'll have to pry your entry door open as it'll likely only have the push bar on the inside. Target middle or top and bottom of the door, that's where the bar bolts will be."

"And the alarm?" asked Nick impatiently, ready to get out of the car.

Peter double-checked. "Hang on a sec. It looks like I've managed to temporarily stop the alarm being transmitted to the alarm company and police station, but not the alarm going off at the Prado."

"What the hell does all that mean?"

Peter quickly assessed the predicament. "It looks like any alarms, beams, motion sensors that I'm not aware of inside the museum can still go off on-site."

"I thought you said there were no beams and sensors inside as the guards are patrolling?"

Peter looked round at Sonia, "What do you think, should we abort?"

Sonia came on the radio. "Nick, we're just not quite sure if there are any alarm triggers inside, do you want to abort?"

Nick and the others were mentally committed and ready to go. He looked at the faces of Max, Afrim and Saban, which were determined, pumped and chomping at the bit.

"Hell no, we're right here and ready, let's just get on with it. We're setting off now!"

Nick waved the others out and they all smoothly slid out of the Porsche, dart guns held close to their sides and crossed the street. Then they disappeared down some steps hidden by the low shrubbery beds set in large concrete containers.

Opposite and above them an elderly Spanish lady finding it hard to sleep, was at her sink making a tea, when she looked out of her window down onto the Prado museum. She did a double-take, as she thought she saw a couple of figures descending down the steps to the lower level, then they were gone. It was just after three AM and she was tired, but it seemed odd. Her brain briefly wrestled with whether to call the police, or go back to bed with her drink. Maybe she had imagined it, just shadows and after all, her eyesight wasn't what it used to be. She shuffled off back to bed.

The men reached the allotted fire escape door. Its flat surface flush with its surrounding frame, looked back at them mockingly, with no handle to lever or lock to pick. Saban moved forward and quietly jammed the end of the crowbar into the tiny gap between the door and frame. He was strong and levered and pushed in a rocking motion. Slowly but surely the metal wedge end started to gain vital millimetres into the widening gap being created.

He leant back and carefully, rhythmically pulled on the bar with all his might, to break the retaining bar on the other side of the door, free from its holding slot. Afrim took out the canvas bag and held it around the bar and surrounding door, ready to muffle the sound of any break or splintering.

Crack!

The door gave way and opened. The four men froze in anticipation of alarms going off all around them. The night air remained silent. They listened through the opening for any sounds from inside the museum, a guard shouting, or running towards the dulled sound of the door breaking. Nothing.

Saban quietly put down the crowbar and they all held up their dart guns and went inside, twitching from side to side as they went, constantly checking for beams, detectors or guards.

Above them, a CCTV camera observed them uselessly. Its red light was still on, but it wasn't sending any pictures back to the control room where the single observer sat. All they were seeing was the previous five minutes being replayed and fortunately, they weren't paying any attention to it anyway.

They kept clustered together and silently edged their way across the marble floor towards the staircase. The Dead Christ painting was on the floor above them in room twenty-four. They approached the edge of the large, long open space which gave you a view both ways down much of the length of the museum.

Nick waved them to keep pressed into the side, knowing they would be exposed to view from a large part of the ground floor. They skirted round a wall between them and the stairs.

He peered round and his cautious gaze was instantly met with the sight of a security guard slowly walking towards him.

Without hesitation, Nick moved into the open space to get a clear view of the stunned young man. The guard had frozen at the sight of a masked intruder in front of him on this hallowed ground. That gave Nick the time he needed to fire off a single tranquiliser dart at the guard's thigh, his largest unprotected front-facing target.

The dart shot off with a quiet thump and hiss of compressed gas and hit its mark. Before the guard could think about running or screaming, its potion, injected by the impact, started to relax him into drowsiness. He looked down at the needle and fluffy tail tuft protruding from his leg in disbelief. Then as he raised his head back up to Nick, he started to slump down to the floor. Within six seconds he was asleep.

Nick checked down both sides of the open space that all was clear, then urged the others past him and up the stairs. Max, Afrim and Saban all paused to look at the young guard lying on the hard floor. He was breathing a little heavily, but he was young and fit. He'd come round after twenty minutes with a bad headache and feeling groggy for a few hours after.

They climbed the stairs swiftly, alert to everything around them. At the top Max was first and peered around a pillar to check the main open corridor was clear. He just caught sight of another guard at the far end rounding the wall leading to one of the many satellite showrooms. A moment later he'd gone. Max waved them on and Nick overtook him and led on another fifteen yards to their destination.

The old lady in the apartment alongside, who'd seen what looked like several dark figures descending the steps at the Prado's side, had been restless in bed. 'But what if they were intruders or robbers', she kept thinking. 'Better safe than sorry,' so she reached for the phone and dialled the police.

As they all came into the room, they were greeted by their prize, hanging humbly on the wall. No cordons, no case frame, no fuss. Max and Nick stared at the mesmerizing artwork, looking into the closed eyes of the Christ and then the sobbing eyes of the Angel behind. They could see why Sonia was so captivated by this painting.

Nick radioed back to Peter and Sonia. "Just about to collect the prize!"

Peter replied, "Once you remove it, get out fast okay!" He had a feeling there may be a sensor behind the more valuable pieces that could set off the museum's alarms.

Afrim and Saban readied themselves on either side of the painted panel and looked at Nick for the nod.

"When it comes off the wall, we go, quickly!" whispered Nick, then looked at the boys.

They pulled at the panel expecting it to resist or be fixed firmly to the wall, but it came away from its resting place with ease. At the same instant, all hell broke loose as siren alarms started sounding throughout the whole museum. Not a good design, as only the man in the monitoring room upstairs, was able to see where the alarm had been set off. The guards in the building had to wait to be told by radio.

The boys thrust the panel painting into their canvas cover and Afrim let his dart gun swing to his side as he took charge of the artwork. The four of them started to make their way at pace to the stairs, when the older guard assigned to that section of the museum, came rushing out of the public toilets. Disorientated by the high-pitched alarm, he found himself facing four masked men carrying a highly suspect canvas case and holding up guns.

Nick spotted him first and held his hand up behind him to signal to the others that he would take the shot. He fired, but watched not one but two tranquillizer darts embed themselves into each of the elderly guard's thighs. He turned to see that Saban had also squeezed his trigger, too fast with all the confusion.

The guard, in his sixties with grey hair and glasses, slumped to the floor almost immediately. They all froze for a moment as Nick approached him to check he was breathing alright. He was.

Nick turned and they all ran as fast as they could, down the stairs and out of their broken, opened fire exit doorway.

The two policemen in their car on the other side of the museum heard the alarm and accelerated round to the end of the building where the entrance plaza was. The guard inside the main doors immediately let them in, grateful for backup, even though he still had no idea what had set off the alarm.

At the same time the nearby District Police Station just several hundred metres away had got the call from the elderly resident. They immediately radioed all police cars in the vicinity to respond to a possible robbery at the Prado. Five cars confirmed they were within a minute's ETA.

As the alarm started to sound, the man in the control room on the third floor had realized that something wasn't right with all the CCTV monitors. They were showing everything was quiet and normal. He'd radioed all the guards, albeit two of them were out cold, saying he had no visibility of what had happened and that they should be on high alert.

He then saw that the alarm had failed to trigger the direct signalling to the police, so-called them himself to alert them of the likely intrusion. They told him they'd already responded to a local call and police would be there during the next minute.

Nick, Max, Afrim carrying the painting and Saban all sprinted to the Porsche. Max ended up nearest the driver's door and Nick shouted for him to just get straight in and drive! They threw themselves into the car, Nick up front and the two boys dived into the rear with the painting on their laps.

"What's happening?" said Peter over the radio.

"Not now mate," snapped Nick, "we've got it, I'll revert when able!"

Max gunned the accelerator just as two police cars rounded the end of the road behind them. As he pulled away another was heading towards them along the Calle de Alberto Bosch side street to their right. Max looked at his rear-view mirror and watched it drift into line directly behind him, the driver seemed to know what he was doing.

Rather than take the remaining street to the right, Max climbed the low curb and passed between the small bollards, continuing alongside the museum on the pedestrianised area.

He passed the church steps and drew level to the Prado entrance to their left, where they saw the parked police car. He remembered from Peter's map briefing the road after the church was a one-way, so slammed on the brakes to reduce his speed back down to fifty. He turned sharp right and headed down the Calle de la Adademia in the wrong direction. The smaller police cars behind were keeping up with him.

Halfway down, another police car passed the far end of the road then either from seeing them or being told by his colleagues, skidded to a halt and started reversing back to try to block them.

Nick pointed diagonally left to the ornamental Puerta da Felipe IV ornamental archway. "Over there, go through the park gateway, too many police cars out here on the road!"

Max swung out of the one-way road just before the reversing police car got there and crossed the two separated lanes of the main road. With a couple of small adjustments, the Porsche squeezed through the tight arched entrance to the Parque de El Retiro and rumbled its way up the stone steps of the Jardin del Paterre. He drove along the walkway to the right of the grass dividing two pathways, through the ornamental gardens and past its two ponds.

The expert police driver and one other car continued to follow. The other police were all shouting at one another over their radios, thrown by the Cayenne's off-road choice, trying to agree where to now go to block off exits to the large park grounds.

"Go up the ramp and into the main park, then hopefully you can lose them there," shouted Nick, pointing to the side of the fast-approaching Jacinto Benavente statue, lit up by their headlights.

Max swerved onto the curved ramp and flicked the car out the other end. They were now into the myriad of criss-cross, tree-shrouded walkways around the huge three hundred acre park.

Saban tapped Max's shoulder to alert him to the one police car still chasing them. "Wow, this guy keeps on coming at us," said Max despairingly.

"You're gonna have to put in some nifty turns Max to lose him, I'll tell you the rough direction we need to exit the park and make for the motorway," said Nick, now looking down at the Satnav map on the dash.

The other four police cars outside of the park had organized themselves to take a section length of the park's outer edges, in the hope of maybe blocking or at least seeing the blue Porsche come out.

Max now set about accelerating hard down a pathway, then heavily braking and drifting sharply into a new avenue, hoping to put enough distance between them and the police car behind, to eventually lose them.

He executed turn after turn, keeping their general direction towards the south end of the park. The policeman in the car behind was one of Madrid's Policia best drivers. With the nippy little Renault at his command, he was starting to catchup up with the larger Porsche.

Nick leaned over and killed the Cayenne's lights.

"What the hell!" shouted Max.

"There's enough moonlight for you to see," said Nick, "the trees and hedges are dense, but he's always got your tail lights to follow. Now lose him for God's sake or we're all for it!"

The sudden disappearance of the Porsche's lights ahead of him threw the police driver for a moment and slowing, he lost thirty yards distance between them, before regaining composure. The Porsche in front started putting in an abrupt turn followed by a hard acceleration the full length of a long walkway. With its superior power on the straights, it pulled further away from the smaller car.

After a couple more similar moves, Max suddenly did a series of right, then left, then right turns. Afrim and Saban both peered out the rear and motioned Max had been successful and to continue unfollowed.

"You've lost the bastard Max, nice one!" congratulated Nick. "Now follow my direction out of here," holding up his hand as he checked the Satnav map.

Max skirted round the larger stone bollard in the centre of the pathway exit and came out onto the southerly end of the park and Avenue de Menendez Pelayo. They all looked around and amazingly there was no sign of any of the police cars.

Max drove down to the Mariano de Cavia roundabout with its fountain in the middle, turned left and a kilometre later pulled onto the A-3 motorway.

Inside the Porsche, everyone was genuinely relieved after the tense last ten minutes. "Right, let's transfer into the other car at junction six, dump this one and get back to the villa," ordered Nick checking that they each still had their rubber gloves on so no prints could have been left.

"Jesus Nick, next time you throw one of these parties, maybe keep me out of it eh!" joked Max.

They swapped into the Renault still parked under its tree covering. Saban drove.

"Had a spot of bother, alarm got triggered, lots of police," reported Nick over the radio. "Max got us out of trouble. We have the prize. Coming home!"

Sonia and Peter celebrated. Having been told not to communicate for the last fifteen minutes, they were beside themselves with anxiety and tension, imagining the worst.

Nick could now sit back and enjoy the adrenalin rush the night had given him. It had been a bit scary but very exhilarating and his old Commando friend had been impressive, corroborating his choice and trust in involving him.

Max sat there wondering what on earth he was doing.

Going undercover to find out if this lot, including his old Colour Sergeant, had anything to do with the Richmond Bank data and bitcoin theft was one thing. Which incidentally he thought to himself, had got him nowhere so far. But now robbing nationally treasured artworks from one of Spain's top museums, well that was something else!

Yet above the worry of the night's robbery, his thoughts turned to something else. 'How on earth was he going to explain all this to his boss Si Lawson, back at MI5!'

8

Chief Superintendent William Lucas had played all his cards in detaining Bob Simmons and Freddy McIntosh at the Lavender Hill police station, as requested by Si Lawson. Holding warrants, legal process and time had finally given way to the highly paid lawyers provided by the bank. In the absence of either man giving the police anything concrete to suggest they were involved, they had to be released.

As the two executives left the station together, it was the first time they'd seen one another for some days. They gave each other an assuring nod to confirm that they were each fine and had said nothing to incriminate anyone.

John Stevens, the bank's Chief Exec had told Bob Simmons that under the circumstances, he should go on garden leave with full pay until this whole sorry mess sorted itself out. Bob was glad to go home, after experiencing the delights of a police cell. Freddy McIntosh also went home, where after a long call trying to explain everything to the clients he'd been presenting to, was told they would not be using his services.

Lucas put a call into Si Lawson and apologetically explained that nothing had come out of holding the two bank staff and they'd been released. He did add that his officers all had the feeling that they definitely had something to hide.

Si had gotten straight onto the phone to Max, who'd earlier texted to say he'd be home shortly from Spain and needed to speak about something urgently.

"Are you okay Max, how did it go in Madrid? I need to update you on those two Richmond chaps we took in." Si rushed.

"What about the two bank staff?" asked Max.

"As we agreed the police held them while you had your Spanish trip with the Jurado bunch, but found nothing that would allow us to charge them. They had to be released this morning."

"I won't be able to come into the bank again anyway, so that should be fine," contemplated Max. "We just need to make sure Simmons doesn't go to the Jurado offices when I'm around, he could identify me to the others!"

"I don't think he'd go anywhere near them having had a taste of police hospitality for a couple of days. So, what did you find out in Madrid?"

Max took in a deep breath. He'd been thinking about how to tell Si on the brief flight home. "Well firstly like you, I didn't come up with anything, not even a hint, that they were involved in the bank hack. But if I'm honest, I think they had something to do with it, certainly got that feeling anyway."

"Same as the police that detained Simmons and McIntosh," agreed Si.

Max couldn't put his story off any longer. "Just let me explain okay Si, I may have taken the undercover thing too far." Si obediently remained silent. Max went on. "Sonia Jurado has this thing about one of the paintings in Madrid's Prado museum. A childhood connection. They found out from the museum's emails that they were going to auction off this painting. It's called the Dead Christ Supported by an Angel, by Antonello."

Si cut in with a prolonged, "Y-e-s," in grave anticipation.

"Before I knew what was happening, my loyalty and allegiance to them were being tested. I had to join in, otherwise my cover would have been blown." Max paused. "They stole it! We stole it! I helped them!"

"What!" exploded Si. "Tell me you're kidding Max. What happened?"

"They'd started planning it before I got out there and Nick Hawkins my Colour Sergeant must have thought I was up for this kind of thing, and maybe happy with the money. They offered me half a million and a Spania GTA!"

"What on earth's that?"

"Spain's only supercar. It's worth over a million," said Max. "Anyway, they had totally sussed out the museum, security, alarms, guards, everything, went through it all on the Saturday, then very late that night, we were off to the bloody Prado to get Sonia's painting!"

"Jesus Max. Not armed I hope? No one got hurt, did they? Anyone get caught?" Si wanted to know everything so couldn't help bombard Max with questions. He was starting to think about how he was going to deal with this mess.

"No guns, actually we just had tranquillizer dart guns. No one hurt, just a couple of guards knocked out with the darts. And no one was caught. We actually got away with it!"

"I think you'll find a dart gun is probably classed as a weapon out there! What a disaster!"

"I'm sorry Si. It was just too risky to contact you, the main thing is I'm still in with them and I'm sure they could have done the Richmond job. They certainly have all the know-how."

"Run me through their team?"

"Sonia Jurado is very much the boss. Fifty, Nick Hawkins is her right-hand man, then Peter Whistler is definitely the master technology hacker. Then you've got an odd pair of Albanian blokes Afrim and Saban, never mentioned their full names. Supposedly IT whizz kids, ex-gangland, London, couple of miserable sods, never say a word. Thugs."

"Where's this painting?" asked Si.

"No idea, I assume she'll keep it at the Madrid villa or maybe ship it out to her mansion in Cancun Mexico? What are we going to do Si?"

Si gave a long huff. "Firstly, having gone to so much trouble to stay undercover, you keep going with this bunch, for now. But we need to get something on the Richmond job quickly now, or we abort."

"And the Prado mess?" asked Max.

"I'm going to have to speak with the Deputy Director General on that one. If we know about a serious crime committed in another country, we're obliged to tell them and help however we can."

"But..."

Si continued. "I'll let the DDG decide, given the highly delicate situation we now have. At least it wasn't some full-blown armed bank heist. But I have a feeling he ain't going to be happy, one little bit. He'll probably go ape when I tell him!"

Si was sitting in front of his boss, the Deputy Director General MI5, having just spent the last six minutes explaining the whole sorry affair. The bank, Simmons and McIntosh, the Jurado connection, Max going in undercover, then getting roped into the art theft from the Prado. Si felt he couldn't have made it up, it was all so crazy and waited for the number two of the secret service to explode.

The DDG sat quietly, listening carefully to every word, giving his highly thought of Head of Cyber the time he needed to tell all. He gave the odd frown and sigh, among thoughtful and serious expressions.

But Si had not given enough credit to this wise, older, ex-politician, ex-military, well educated, diplomatic leader. He'd dealt with much worse than a mere undercover op leaving behind a bit of a mess to sort out. He didn't explode. He simply got straight down to business and his calmness was even more impressive to Si, than if he had yelled and sworn at him.

"We will have to give something to the Spanish authorities about the Prado art theft. I'll need to take a view on how much and in what form we do that, making sure we don't drop your lad right in it" said the DDG purposefully. "We've got a few things going on with them involving the Prime Minister, so I'll have to run this by the Director General and possibly the

PM before we do anything. Leave it with me for an hour."

One of his personal assistants knocked on the door to remind the DDG he had a call waiting for him from the Director General of their sister service, MI6.

Si took his leave.

Half an hour later the DDG had five minutes between more calls and meetings. He strolled out of his soundproofed office and made his way over to the holding area of his own boss, the Director General of the MI5. His team of four assistants sat at their desks, each high-ranking staff in their own right. Busy with their workload of making life easier for the top man, they briefly and politely acknowledged the DDG's presence, then got back down to work.

The quantity of information, approvals, reports, briefings, meetings, calls and decisions, would force any normal person to quit after a day. But the DG took it all in his stride. An old hand at this game and adept at balancing on the daily tightrope of getting things done, whilst keeping the politicians happy and thinking they were also involved.

He looked up at his number two who went straight in.

"Literally got two minutes I'm afraid," the DG had to be precise with his time management, otherwise the diary of the day would run away with itself. "Got more time later if you need it though?"

"Two minutes is good thanks," said the DDG, who just wanted a quick guide on being allowed to play the Jurado thing as he wanted. "Richmond Bank. One of Cyber's agents has infiltrated the Jurado Data firm, our suspects for the hack. No evidence yet but we feel we'll get it soon."

"I hope so," cut in the boss. "Likelihood they did it?"

The exchange was minimalistic, efficient. Years of being able to summarize information, enabled faster decisions and less time wasted.

"Eighty per cent. The issue is that to maintain Jurado's trust in him, our agent had to take part in a single item art theft from the Prado museum! One of vanity for Sonia Jurado. No-one hurt, they got away with it seems."

The Director General gave a wry smile. "Just when I think I've heard it all, you tell me one of your agents has helped rob the Prado!"

"I can pull him out and try another avenue of inquiry, but shouldn't we give something to the Spanish?"

The DG thought for a few moments. "No don't pull him out. Normally I'd say get him away from the inevitable trouble he's heading for, being so close to Jurado. More so now we know what they're capable of. Do you rate him?"

"Si Lawson certainly does, and I do as well. Max Sargent, he's new to us, but has already shown himself to be well equipped for all this. He sorted the Dark Corporation and weapons espionage operations."

"Well, the PM's in a real flap about the Richmond Bank job and wants us to find out who did it. He'll also support anything that helps the Spanish. We've had to knock them back again regarding their silly notion that Gibraltar belongs to them, so anything to soften that will help. Plus we don't want to waste the effort it's taken to get your man Sargent into Jurado Data. Especially if he might actually turn something up on Richmond. Needs to be soon though."

"And how much do we give the Spanish?"

"The bare minimum so we've done our bit and nothing comes back to bite us when it all comes out, as it always does. Goes without saying though, you can't give anything up that exposes your undercover agent."

"Understood Director General. We'll let this play out a little longer."

Max and Si Lawson's team were given the remainder of the day to come up with what to tell the Spanish Intelligence Service, without dropping Max in it with either the Spanish or Jurado. They had to give them something, but they also had to ensure Max got a little more time with Jurado to unearth anything on the Richmond job.

The team dialled Max into a brainstorming session and went through all sorts of ideas and options.

Everything they thought of might somehow lead back to Max and jeopardise his relationship with Nick and Sonia. In the end, they all agreed that it would have to be an anonymous tipoff that had come to light in an unrelated operation.

Regardless of Peter Whistler's careful preparation and hack into the museum, there would surely be some trace left behind, either digitally or from the equipment they used, the cars, something. They didn't need to answer that, just so long as there was enough of a possibility that someone in addition to Max being suspected, had slipped up somewhere along the line.

Max was concerned. "At some point, they're all going to look at the new boy in their little close-knit team. Me!"

"You'll just have to ride that out Max," said Si. "Play dumb, play innocent. Why would you tip off the police about a crime you helped commit? They don't know you're working with us, we've done everything required to cover that as we do for all agents going undercover."

"It feels a little complex," observed Max. "A lot of moving parts in play here!"

"It's always complex," agreed Si. "At least this way we can bargain with the Spanish that the intel is only being passed on, under the strict understanding that the Spanish authorities do not bring Jurado in until cleared by us."

"And you're right Max," said Vince, "there's a lot of gaps in the idea, and we're placing huge trust in the Spanish that they won't jump the gun and drag Jurado in, along with you as well!"

"I do believe that they'll be pretty bloody appreciative of us giving them the Prado culprits," said Si. "They might actually go for the forced delay. I think I also need to put some distance between us here at MI5 and the tipoff."

"What are you thinking boss?" asked Vince.

"I'm going to have to go cap in hand to someone in particular, in the Met," said Si. "Someone who will be only to pleased to help out MI5."

"Chief Super Lucas?" guessed Max.

Bob Simmons had hit the blossoming era of technology innovation at just the right time. In 1980 he had taken a leap of faith and embarked on a computer programming course for his degree at Brighton Polytechnic in Sussex. His timing and choice put him into one of the fastest-growing, highest demand marketplaces for the rest of his career.

Now sixty, the well-positioned start to his life seemed to have always just passed him by. He'd done okay but felt he should have done so much better. Almost securing senior roles in up-and-coming media and technology firms such as Google, eBay and the big one, Apple. But 'almost' he now knew only too well, was a polite way of dressing up 'didn't'. Those top jobs with huge salaries and the all-important share options would have made him a multi-millionaire many times over. Likely living in California and having contributed to worldwide household branded products, had been just beyond his reach.

Bob had had a good, steady career in the corporate sector, climbing up the Information Technology ladder rung by rung. Straight out of Brighton he'd joined a talented, young small firm churning out basic but popular video games. The company was destined for big things. Until the two lads that owned it went for the first cash offer from a bigger firm, swallowing up every games firm they could. The young Bob wasn't a shareholder so got three months severance and watched his two young bosses disappear off into the sunset with millions.

He then joined a high street off licence chain called Victoria Wine, at their head office in Woking Surrey. They were the UK's largest with fifteen-hundred stores and before the large supermarkets had got a hold, were the biggest drinks and tobacco sellers in the country.

The new Managing Director came in and wanted to use technology to better communicate with all the branch managers. Bob again was there at the right time and played a big mid-manager role, despite his young age, in rolling out the UK's first retail chain Electronic Point of Sale computerized system. EPOS was totally new, there were lots of niggles and long nights, but Bob and the Technology team successfully got EPOS into all shops and working as it should.

Pricing could be sent to all branches from HQ, promotions advised, stock managed automatically, and the marketeers and buyers knew what sales of any product had been on a daily basis.

The Managing Director was a huge fan of Bob and had on several occasions been quite clear that he would be given a big promotion, salary rise and bonus at the July reviews. Bob was on the up.

Until that is, he came in one day in June, to find gossip and consternation rife around the office. Apparently, the Managing Director had resigned and was likely to be leaving that day. Circumstances were sketchy but the grapevine had cottoned onto the rumour that he'd had an affair with his secretary. The husband had found out the day before and was threatening to go to the press after he'd paid the guilty MD a visit in the office to sort him out!

The Managing Director found the time that day to walk around the offices to thank staff for their work, apologise for his speedy departure and say his goodbyes. When he got round to Bob he was full of praise and compliments, which gave him the confidence to ask, "About my promotion, the one you've promised me for next month, can you tell me that's still going through?"

The outgoing MD was profusely apologetic. "I'm so sorry Bob, if it were up to me you'd get what you fully deserve. But that'll now be down to the new MD I'm afraid. Good luck

Bob!" With that, he moved on to other staff eagerly waiting for their chance to say farewell to the much-liked exiting boss.

Bob was devastated. Another 'almost'. The new MD rightly told Bob he couldn't promote him based on what he hadn't seen for himself, but suggested he would look favourably on it in say six to twelve months.

Bob resigned the following day, much to his employer's shock, but they never tried to keep him with even a small salary lift. He had no job to go to, but with the experience of installing the country's first EPOS system and demand for technology staff rising by the day, he joined one of Victoria Wine's suppliers. They were one of the largest soft drinks firms in the world. He got the big hike in salary and bonus he'd wanted, plus a nice fully expensed company car and more holiday.

At the cola firm, Bob was given a new project to lead. They wanted to improve automation at their large bottling plants, combining sales, stock and just-in-time management of ordering their packaging supplies. Bob was encouraged to pull in whatever expertise was required to get the job done, as no suitable off the shelf software products were yet available.

Enter a young Freddy McIntosh straight out of college with some basic computer skills and a large dose of energy and keenness. The recruitment agency put him forward as a cheap run around technology helper, to be at the beck and call of the project team.

Freddy's passion and helpfulness soon came to Bob's attention and he started mentoring the boy and helping him better understand everything in the fast-changing sector they worked in. In turn, Freddy would do anything for Bob and so the relationship was struck, which would continue on and off for the rest of Bob's career.

Bob moved onto a global hotel chain in a more senior IT role, this time setting up an improved customer booking and management system. Once more he brought in Freddy to help with the project.

He then spent a year in a new, fast-growing customer data firm called Jurado, where he worked for the impressive Spanish female boss. Once again he found a brief consulting role for Freddy. Everything was above board at Jurado and Bob and Sonia built an excellent relationship, including the obligatory one night stand just weeks after he joined the company.

However, people information and client data analysis just wasn't his thing and didn't quite fit his expertise, nor passion. On the other hand, one of his deputies was incredibly adept at data and statistics manipulation. He was also an amazing programmer and extremely talented at computer system security programming and data extraction. Depending on how this was utilised, it might otherwise be known as 'hacking'.

So Sonia let Bob move on to bigger things as overall IT Director at Richmond Bank and happily promoted Peter Whistler into her lead technology role, on Bob's recommendation.

Then a couple of years went by and Bob got sight of the bank's marketing team tendering for a piece of work to improve their utilization of customer promotions and communications. He was about to suggest to the Director they include his old firm Jurado, but by then Sonia's company was doing so well they were already an obvious choice to include in the tender process. He sat back and let the marketing and procurement people run their tender. Knowing that as there was a significant input required by IT, he would have a seat at the stakeholder's decision table at the end.

So as not to raise any conflict-of-interest question with his previous stint at Jurado, Bob told the procurement lead and said his deputy IT Director would stand in for him for this review. His deputy had been promoted into his senior role by Bob and was forever grateful to him for that. He'd speak his mind, but if Bob wanted something just so, he would always relent and do his boss's will.

Three customer data suppliers were shortlisted from the

extensive 'request for quotation' submissions including Jurado. Procurement then ably organized each of them to come in one after the other, to pitch their proposals to the stakeholder team.

Sonia Jurado had, by all accounts Bob later heard, swept into the room with her usual engaging, twinkle-in-the-eye charisma. Peter Whistler covered the technical parts, which went over most people's heads but impressed them, and with her marketing and sales leads also as impressive, she had the audience looking on favourably. All except the gay procurement director who took an instant disliking to this flirty wench and didn't hide their unimpressed view throughout the day.

After the three pitches, the stakeholder team then talked about each supplier and took time to agree on their individual scores for each firm, across a wide selection of measurement criteria. Such as cost, experience, references, account management, ease to implement and so on.

The final scores put Jurado and one other supplier into first place and so the frustrated procurement lead suggested they went round the table and now voted for who they'd like to award the contract to.

Bob had briefed his IT deputy about his views on Jurado being a great fit for the bank and more importantly working well with the deputy. He'd also in the past shown his number two that when it comes to these close calls, get in early with your view. Often the 'undecided' stakeholders just need a compelling, passionate steer in the right direction, to help make up their minds in your favour.

The IT man jumped right in as soon as the procurement chap had opened it up for final voting.

"I might as well go first," he'd said playing it cool. "Given the basics like costs, account team, experience etcetera are very close, it clearly comes down to how well our two IT teams can work together and implement this. Who in here could possibly know what issues we'll have to deal with, but that'll be down to me and my team to sort out. I feel confident that surely we have to therefore choose Jurado Data. They're the best fit for us, so that's my vote on behalf of IT. Bob Simmons will support my choice."

The compelling technology vote mesmerized the other stakeholders, who fearful of such unknown IT issues causing any problems, followed the specialist's vote one by one. The procurement lead saw what had happened but by the time it was his vote, the decision had been made. Jurado Data were appointed.

Bob was in the clear having declared his past with the firm and stayed out of the review process, so was reunited with Sonia and her team once more. A few weeks later he hired Freddy McIntosh to come in and join the project as a consultant, now in a far more senior and influential role.

As the work progressed, Sonia could see the huge client database the bank had, at the time, almost two million customers. That kind of data was worth a lot to a company like hers. It could be chopped up, repackaged and sold many times over, as part of other sales deals they were doing every week. The bank had many levels to its security, rightly protecting the core of their business, being their client's bank accounts and personal information.

At the time Sonia coveted the wealth of data, but from a distance. There was nothing she would dare do to make a play for it whilst she was engaged in working for the bank. Too many obvious links back to Jurado. The project completed, her firm withdrew from the bank and the tantalizing sight of so much data drifted away and out of reach, but was not forgotten by her.

The outgoing Chief Executive was retiring after forty years in the banking business. He'd help find a most suitable replacement in a John Stevens, who had to sit out a twelve-month garden leave clause in his resignation contract. So the Chief Executive had time for his swan song. He would oversee a significant security upgrade to their online banking software, systems and portal. One of the key leaders for this upgrade would be his IT Director, Bob Simmons.

Bob went about the project with the utmost integrity, ensuring the matrix team including external security and consulting firms were allocated separate boxes of work. No one part of the team had too much access or sight of the whole security upgrade. Except for himself and a strongly vetted independent IT consultant. Freddy McIntosh. The double act was back together again.

The nine-month piece of work progressed slowly to start with, as everyone familiarized themselves with the current security and operating model. Then previous recommendations, ideas and budgets were refined, after which the real work of making the upgrades could begin.

Down-times were kept to a minimum, where certain services operated by the bank had to be briefly switched off to accommodate an upgrade or software change. Where necessary though, these were usually done at four AM, the optimum time when the highest proportion of the country's population is most likely to be fast asleep.

The final part of the upgrade was the critical piece, where different work-streams started to link up and the final segments of the whole system's security were inserted.

It was during this phase that Sonia Jurado had called up Bob and suggested they had dinner to 'catchup'. She'd heard some months back that Bob was overseeing the bank's security upgrade. Then Peter Whistler had flippantly said to her that he'd love to get his hands on the bank's security gates coding, her interest in all that data was rekindled.

Sonia booked them a table for dinner at the famous Roux at the Landau restaurant in The Langham, one of London's most prestigious hotels in Portland Place off Regent Street.

The heady mix of the six-course taster menu with fine wines to match each course, along with a large dose of the flirtatious Spanish senorita Sonia, worked its magic on the hapless IT Director.

She gently pried, and prodded, then joked, sussing him out and dropping in the fantasy of a huge payoff for a little information. He joked, they laughed, he flatly refused to do anything of the kind, she worked her magic charm and once more reopened the fantasy discussion.

By the end of the meal Bob was pleasantly drunk, but had got the message that Sonia was deadly serious about him providing a few key pieces of coding and security information for Peter Whistler, to gain access to the customer records. He flatly refused to assist in anything that would give access to all the bank's customer accounts and money.

Sonia's evening wasn't finished. She needed to know that Bob would fall into line once more. He was the key to this working and would likely have to sacrifice his job for it. She needed to press home her advantage. If there was any opportunity to transfer some inconspicuous funds as well, then that door had been left open before she let him go.

Sonia did what she did so well. She'd already booked a room upstairs in The Langham and it didn't take too much persuasion to lead the starry-eyed Bob Simmons to the elevator and into the hotel room.

Bob's second marriage was on the rocks anyway, so it was a short jump for him to make, into Sonia's beckoning hotel bed. He didn't even bother calling home to say work was keeping him in town for the night.

Sonia gave him a night to remember for the rest of his life and despite being somewhat intoxicated, he managed to respond surprisingly well. That was Sonia's magic at work again.

By the time they left after breakfast in bed the following morning, Bob was Sonia's puppet. He'd agreed on behalf of himself and Freddy McIntosh, who he'd speak to later, to provide whatever they could to allow Whistler to gain access to the bank's customer data. He also agreed that if any other monetary opportunities arose, other than an individual's personal money, he would pass it on. His bizarre conscience was happy to rob from the rich investors, firms and institutions, but not the general public.

Bob had several private chats with Freddy, who was shocked to begin with, but soon relented after being told about the multi-million-pound pay out waiting.

During those last six weeks on the security upgrade, Bob ensured that Freddy was given full access to all parts of the project, as his eyes and ears. It was also quite normal for someone like Freddy to be asking more detailed questions about some of the key coding and security protocols. Better him than the more visible IT Director, who should have an overarching view and not be getting involved in the detail.

As the final weeks closed in, between Freddy and Bob, they were able to obtain critical pieces of access and encryption information. They would pass it onto Whistler, who would then come back explaining he would now need to know something else, with clear details of what was required.

Finally, the expert hacker at Jurado, felt he had enough to just possibly gain entry into the bank's system. The way it was set up and the routes he would take to get in, could really only be tried once. After this, digital openings could get closed, or codes changed, passwords routinely altered at someone's whim. It would be a one-shot opportunity for Whistler.

Once he started to attempt access to the bank, he would have to follow it through to the end. Any slipups or missing intel, and it would all be for nothing. If, and it was a big if, he got in, only then might he be able to have a look around the system to see if there were any monetary funds left open or with a lower level of security applied to them.

Peter and Sonia wouldn't leave it long before trying the hack into one of the UK's largest banks, part-owned by the government. If it worked, they knew it would change everything. They just didn't realise the scale of how much their lives would change, for better or worse.

9

Bob Simmons had expected to be summoned, questioned and probably fired, by John Stevens his new Chief Executive at Richmond Bank. He did not expect to be hauled in by the Met Police, nor put under intense questioning, spending the weekend at a police station in a cell.

The threats of jail time and the drive past Wandsworth prison had indeed had a huge effect on him, even though he tried his best not to show it. After the whole ordeal he had promised himself that if things took a turn for the worse, he would do whatever it took to avoid a prison sentence. Someone like him simply wasn't cut out for prison life.

Bob rummaged through his electronics cupboard at home and picked out one of his old pay-as-you-go throw-away mobiles. It was a pre-touch screen and just had a simple LED display and keypad, but it did what he wanted. It allowed him to make untraceable calls.

He wasn't at all happy about this whole Richmond affair and after being put under so much scrutiny by the Met, was starting to think that maybe somehow, something would give and he'd end up taking the blame. He needed to sort this out, make sure he was covered and avoid anything coming back to him.

Bob Simmons had to speak with someone who should be able to help. He would call Sonia Jurado. As he started to press in the numbers, he thought about what he would say. That then led to what he would ask for. In fact, what he would demand.

He stopped midway through the numbers. He needed to shore up his position first. He cancelled the half-dialled number and punched in a new set of numbers, for Freddy McIntosh.

A cautious man answered. “Hello?”

“Freddy. It’s me, Bob. You okay to speak for a mo?”

“Bob! What the hell are you doing calling me, they could be recording it.”

“Unlikely,” assured Bob. “You’ve seen too many spy movies,” trying to make light of the situation. “We’ve not been charged with anything, we’ve just got out of the police station and I’m using a really old phone, don’t worry, it’s fine.”

“Did you say anything to the police?” Freddy had been desperate to ask Bob this to make sure he wouldn’t be taking the hit for anyone else.

“Nothing,” confirmed Bob. “Not a word. I assume that’s the same with you otherwise they would have charged us and not let us go. They’ve got nothing on us.”

Freddy let out a sigh of relief. “Nothing from me either. Do you think we’ll be okay? The bank hack and theft are a really big deal, it’s on the news and everything. The Prime Minister has vowed to catch the culprits very soon.”

“Of course it’s a big deal, the Government own part of the bank. What happened is a bit of a slap in the face for them, makes them look daft.”

“I didn’t like being taken in by the Met, Bob. If this all goes wrong somehow, I ain’t going to prison that’s for sure,” warned Freddy.

“That’s why I’m calling Freddy. As long as you and me say nothing we’ll be fine. But all this aggro is worth a lot more to us, the risks we're taking, we’re right in the firing line while those who did the hack and took the data…”

Freddy cut in, “Not to mention two billion in bitcoins!”

“Yeah, and that, we deserve more for our troubles.”

“Agreed,” chimed in Freddy. “But what are you going to do Bob?”

“Well, that's what I want to check with you first. How do you feel about living abroad, and never returning to the UK?” It was a startling question to open with.

"What?"

"I'm going to tell Jurado we want more money. A lot more. Now we know how much bitcoin value they took, what they agreed to pay us is nothing." Bob sounded determined.

"Crikey Bob, how do you think they'll take it?" asked Freddy somewhat worried now. "You know Sonia can be a bit funny about the whole loyalty thing."

"They don't have a choice, do they. Anyway, they can easily afford it. But it does mean that if I get us more, we'll have to start new lives in another country where we'll be untouchable by the Met or any other UK agency. What do you say, Freddy?"

The line went silent for much longer than Bob had hoped for. Freddy was younger than him and engaged to be married soon. His life was ahead of him, unlike Bob about to start his second divorce and a career coming to an end anyway. But Bob needed them to both be on the same page if he was going to get anywhere with Jurado.

Freddy started umming and erring down the line. "Hmm, I'm not sure Bob," he paused, "I'll tell you what, you know, I'll do it!"

"Nice one Freddy, I'll make you very, very rich," said Bob, relieved he now had both bargaining chips for his talk with Sonia. "You can always send for Helen to join you once you're settled in your beachside villa somewhere nice eh."

"Yeah, I guess so," said Freddy, still going over everything in his mind, which kept coming back to the money. "How much more will you ask for, for me that is?"

Bob quickly imagined what he could get away with. "I'll have to see how it goes, how she reacts, but it'll be significantly more than the five million they agreed previously. They got away with two billion in bitcoins for Christ's sake! Leave it with me now, stay stum with the coppers and the bank's investigative teams and I'll update you in the next few days once I know what's happening okay."

Bob rang off and sat down, grateful that Freddy had thrown

in with him. Having them both singing off the same song sheet meant he had so much more bargaining power now for his next call. He went to the kitchen and made himself a tea to settle himself and gather his thoughts about how to play it. This would be the most important call of his life. How would she react? Was he being too greedy? What could she possibly do about it anyway, to get at him?

He dialled Sonia.

"Bob! Are you out now, I heard the police had taken you in for a couple of days. What happened, you okay?" asked Sonia with much concern. Bob couldn't quite tell if she was worried about him, or herself. She added, "Safe to talk is it?"

"Old mobile so yes. I'm fine, bit tough though, got interrogated all weekend by the Met. Not nice. But thankfully the bank's lawyers were great. I didn't have to say much."

"And Freddy?"

"Same. Got the treatment, said nothing. You'll be pleased to hear we're all in the clear, for now anyway. They're clutching at straws and have nothing, so had to let us go. But we're under the spotlight for sure."

"Thank heavens Bob, if they had anything you'd still be in there. Well done, great job."

"Yeah, well that's what I wanted to talk to you about Sonia," edged Bob. It may have just been him, but he felt the mood change on the other end of the line.

"Oh yes, how do you mean?"

Bob reminded himself of the numbers he had to play with and emboldened, sat up straight. "Come on Sonia. The five mill to Freddy and fifteen to me was for the bank's client data, which you got."

"And I can transfer you both the money whenever and wherever you want Bob, no problem. Just give me the details?"

"You know that's not why I'm calling," said Bob. "What about the bitcoins you got?"

Sonia's tone became more adversarial. "Now hang on Bob,

we agreed payment for access to the customer data. It was understood that if Peter got the chance to see if there was anything else he could access, that was down to him."

Bob countered. "But he only got access at all because of what we provided. Another two billion's worth for God's sake. That's more than anyone needs Sonia!"

"What are you suggesting Bob?"

"Look, our careers, our lives are finished here, if we get away with this. Me and Freddy need to disappear off into the sunset with enough to cover us for the rest of our lives. Better for you we're out of here." Bob's brain was juggling numbers around in readiness to see what he felt he could go for. "I think it would be much fairer, given our part, to share the bitcoin fund with us." He waited for any reaction. The line stayed silent. "I want a hundred mill for Freddy and three-hundred for me!"

Bob's familiarity with Sonia told him the continued silence from her on the phone, was even worse than her ranting and raving at him.

He couldn't help but fill in the gap. "Well? That's fair isn't it?"

After a few moments which seemed like forever to Bob, she spoke, as if having just calmed herself down. "I'm not sure I like you making demands on me like this Bob. I might almost be forgiven for confusing it with a threat, or blackmail."

Bob quickly clarified, "Oh no Sonia, I'd never do that to you. But please be fair with us. Two billion, come on!"

"Alright."

Bob detected the word was forced out through Sonia's lips. The tone held resentment, probably not about the sum, but more having to acquiesce to someone else's demands. She liked to call the shots. Bob hoped he hadn't pushed too far and was also conscious Sonia hadn't tried to negotiate the numbers down. Strange.

Sonia spoke again. "Just get the offshore accounts to Nick

or one of the boys here and we'll sort the transfers. Then within the week, you and Freddy work out a way to leave the country undetected, for good. Yes?"

The relief of getting the massive sums of money agreed upon, was tainted by the reality dawning on Bob that his life in the UK, his home, was about to end. He hadn't even thought about where to go and what to do. No matter, three-hundred million makes everything easy.

"Done," agreed Bob.

He was about to thank Sonia, but heard the line go dead as Sonia rang off. He felt sad that she had ended it that way and slightly humiliated. Rejection from her was enough to demean the most confident of men.

He returned to celebrating his windfall and new life. "Three-hundred million!" he said out loud, "oh my God!" Excitement and adrenalin washed through him. He wanted to celebrate, tell people, but of course, he couldn't. Then he remembered Freddy.

Bob dialled his number. He would be over the moon to hear the news on the new deal he'd done with Sonia for him. Lucky Freddy!

Sonia sat back in her chair in her office at One The Strand. She spun round and looked out onto Nelson's Column in the centre of Trafalgar Square. The famous landmark was framed by Admiralty Arch to the left and the multi-columned frontage of the National Gallery to the right. The traffic as always in central London, included many black taxi cabs and red double-decker buses.

She knew that Bob Simmons was completely justified in asking for a reasonable share of the bitcoin fund they'd stumbled across the other night. But she'd rather have decided on what they could have before being approached by them and put on the spot.

She was still amazed that they'd got away with the unplanned two billion transfer. Peter had gained access into the bank's system and had started transferring a copy of the customer data back to Jurado's complex system of ghost and real servers. Whilst he was waiting he'd given himself the time it took for that transfer to complete, to hunt around the software probing and testing for any other lower-level security holes to penetrate.

They'd been quite shocked when the message came back from one of Peter's interrogative trojan's saying 'ACCESS FOUND TO RICHMOND BANK BITCOIN FUND'! They were even more shocked to watch the transfer bar creep across the screen taking out over two billion pounds worth of ninety-thousand bitcoins. It was the mother of all digital smash-and-grab heists.

But Bob's call had perturbed Sonia for reasons other than paying him and Freddy a fifth of the bitcoins they'd taken. Having been taken in by the Met it was clear they were onto something and it was probably only a matter of time before someone made a mistake and got charged. If that happened it wouldn't be long before everything led back to her and it would have to be snowing in hell before she'd allow herself to do jail time.

It felt like everything had changed now. The legitimate data business she'd worked so hard to build up was now top of its game. She had billions in the bank to play with so there was no need to be working hard anymore to make another few hundred million every year. Looking around the view and then her office, she felt detached from it for the first time and her thoughts drifted towards spending more time at her other home in Cancun Mexico. Things in London and Madrid were getting a bit hot, so perhaps some time away from everything would let things settle down. If it went bad, she'd be untouchable in Mexico, where the British authorities had less sway. She'd also done some work for her local government there and felt sure they would go some way to protect her if things followed her out there.

Right now she couldn't risk Bob or Freddy slipping up and had decided that she had no intention of paying them their hundreds of millions. There was an easier way, where she wouldn't have to pay anything and could rest easy that they wouldn't talk to the police and incriminate her.

"Nick!" she shouted through her office door and meeting room outside.

Nick came in attentively, "Yes boss."

"Close the door." Nick sat in one of the chairs across the desk from her. "We may have a problem." Nick frowned. "Bob and Freddy may spill the beans. I don't know when, but I feel they're the weak link and if they do, we're all for it."

Without hesitation Nick replied. "What do you want me to do then?"

"I suggest you and the boys make sure we don't have anything to worry about," said Sonia reticently. "Pay Bob and Freddy a visit in the next day or so. You know what I mean?"

Nick realized the gravity of what Sonia was asking him to do. He screwed up his face at her as if to say 'Really, you want them killed?'.

She nodded sternly. "It's the only way. It's getting too complex now. May have to think about retreating to Cancun soon."

Nick rose. "If you're sure."

Just as Nick reached the door, Sonia had another thought.

"Oh yes, maybe, if you trust him, take Max along with you eh?"

10

Si Lawson had called Chief Superintendent William Lucas and asked if he had twenty minutes to meet him for a 'chat'. He'd also said a meet would be better than over the phone. This requested chat in itself was quite unusual and had sparked the curiosity of the senior Metropolitan Police officer and guaranteed he'd agree to meet. Si had suggested they caught up halfway along Victoria Tower Gardens South, just across the road from his MI5 HQ at Millbank.

Si exited the huge Thames House of the Secret Service and took the short walk alongside the building to the roundabout on Lambeth Bridge. He crossed the road and went down the steps to the walkway alongside the River Thames.

On the opposite bank, slender apartment high-rises jostled for position along the highly prized riverside location, with a view of both the Thames and the city's skyline. Further along the other side, Si could see the tops of the turrets of the Archbishop's official residence, Lambeth Palace. In the distance, the top of the Shard rose above its surrounding buildings at well over three hundred metres tall, a similar height to the Eiffel Tower in Paris. To his left on the other side of the river sat the recognizable London Eye landmark and tourist attraction, with its thirty-two capsules representing each of the boroughs of London.

He continued along the tree-covered walkway past the elaborate Buxton Memorial Fountain where the grassy expanse of the Gardens opened out, with the Victoria Tower of the House of Lords at the far end. Si could see Lucas waiting for him on one of the benches, each raised on a plinth looking out across the river.

"William. Thanks for making the time to see me, I do

appreciate it."

"I could hardly refuse could I now, 'let's have a chat, not over the phone', most intriguing," said Lucas.

Si wanted to reassure him, as no one liked surprises. "It's about the Richmond Bank hack and theft. We think we may be onto something, but for now, I'll have to ask you to keep this to yourself, this is off the record. Don't worry William, I'll vouch for you back at MI5 and this has gone through the DG. The PM is also aware, so you're covered okay." Si knew Lucas would want reassurance that he wouldn't be left out in the cold if anything went public, or wrong.

"I assumed it was Richmond related, though I'm surprised you've got anything, those two you asked me to bring in, the IT Director and his consultant chap, said nothing at all. What else have you got?"

Si looked out over the river and briefly watched a tourist boat go by, waiting for them to pass as if somehow they might hear what he said.

"You remember meeting one of my guys at the bank, Max Sargent?"

Lucas nodded. "Indeed, your new person, the corporate executive turned MI5 agent. Got some good form I gather."

"Having found a link between the two you kindly took into Lavender Hill, Max has managed to get in with their common denominator. It's a high-tech computer and data firm called Jurado. Run by a Spanish businesswoman, Sonia Jurado."

Lucas was impressed. "That was fast work, how'd he manage that?"

"Old Commando colleague already in there has embraced him, old loyalties and so on. Anyway, Max feels the same as your CID officers who questioned the IT guys. They seem to have all the skills to have done the bank job, he's just working on getting the evidence."

Lucas waited, he could feel the punchline was approaching. Si continued.

"So, we need him to continue to be trusted and stay

undercover within Jurado, until we crack the Richmond thing. In the meantime, Sonia Jurado and her close team managed to pull off another robbery last weekend in Madrid!"

Si waited for Lucas to see if he knew about the recent heist.

"Madrid? You don't mean the break-in at the Prado museum do you?" recollected the officer. "How do you know that was Jurado?"

The punchline. "Because Max was with them when they did it!"

Like a truly seasoned officer, the shock on Lucas' face quickly changed to a look of admiration, impressed at Si's man going above and beyond to maintain his cover, to crack *their* case.

"Okay, I can see how that will cause some issues that you might need my help with. What is it you want from me?"

Si could tell the Chief Super was starting to relish the apparent power he might now have, to 'help out' MI5.

"Having checked with the Director General, we've agreed we want to keep Max inside Jurado Data. The PM wants the Richmond case solved ASAP, this is our best lead." Si waited for a nod from Lucas, but the Met man was giving nothing until he heard what the ask was.

Si continued. "We feel we have to notify the Spanish Authorities that Jurado was responsible for the Prado theft. We can't keep something like that from them. It was just one painting and no one was hurt."

Lucas was a step ahead and relished filling in the request. "And you need me to help pass this onto the Spanish so MI5 aren't involved and your chap's cover isn't blown?"

"You've got it, William," said Si, pleased that Lucas seemed willing to help.

"I'm guessing you've got an idea about how I do this Si?"

"Yes, I have. Let's keep it brief and simple. You get one of your CID teams to log an information report to Interpol. Just tell them that it has come to light during a confidential Met operation, that Jurado did the Prado theft."

"Sounds reasonable."

"But, and this is the key part, we are only passing this on under the understanding that they cannot move on Jurado yet, as this could jeopardise an ongoing investigation."

"I like it Si," nodded Lucas. "The Spanish won't want to mess up one of the Met's operations and frankly I'd have thought they'd appreciate the tipoff, assuming they've not got anywhere with the Prado job themselves."

Lucas took a moment to go through it all again in his mind as Si patiently let it all sink in. He respected Lucas and knew if he'd missed anything, Lucas would likely call it out.

"Are we good then William?"

"We are, I'll get onto this straight away."

Interpol is the International Criminal Police Organisation based in Lyon France and operates as an administrative liaison between the law enforcement agencies of its member countries. They field communications between police forces and maintain various criminal and operational databases for their community. They serve as an intelligence hub and have no agents with the power to arrest anyone.

Si waited for him to revel in being called upon. "I'll tell you what though Si, this is a big one you owe me. But you know I'm always happy when the Met can help out you boy scouts in MI5!"

Over his career's service to Spanish Intelligence, Eduardo Garcia had managed to spread his network of loyal staff throughout the Services. Some he'd promoted, others owed him favours or been helped out of some tight spot by him. There were those who were simply afraid of him and wanted to do anything to curry favour with him, and those who worked for him and been indoctrinated into the ways Garcia liked to operate. It seemed obvious to him, that even within the Secret Service, intel from 'scouts' could give you the edge.

Diego Morales had previously worked under Garcia and

wanting to broaden his experience in Spanish Intelligence, had jumped at the opportunity to be promoted ahead of his time, into the Interpol Liaison Team in Madrid. This meant more money and another string to his CV bow, which would stand him in good stead for more senior roles in the future.

After almost a year in the department that handled all communications to and from Interpol, Diego had had enough. The work was administrative at best, passing on messages, arranging meetings and calls, pulling together projects and sharing intel.

He waited for the opportunity to catch Garcia alone one evening in the car park as they both left and asked if the influential department head would consider bringing him back into the fold, for more action and a challenge.

Eduardo had told the younger man he would keep it in mind, but no sooner had the conversation finished, he'd pushed the thought aside. After all, it was Diego who wanted to advance his career by leaving him in the first place.

Eduardo was having a meeting in his office suite when he heard an excited voice outside talking anxiously with his assistant. Angry at the disturbance and rallying to the protection of his secretary, he excused himself and came out to see what the fuss was about.

"I'm sorry Mr Garcia, Diego here was insistent he got to see you. I have explained you cannot be interrupted as you're in a meeting."

"What on earth did you want Diego? You can't come bursting in here like this. Make an appointment," admonished Eduardo, apologizing to his waiting senior managers.

Diego was determined, bordering on rude. "Mr Garcia, I really must see you now. Something important has come up which I felt you should be informed of, before I pass it to anyone else."

The notion that he might get his hands on something before those who were meant to hear it, immediately struck a chord with the high ranking official.

"Well, I am busy, so this had better be important or there'll be trouble," threatened Eduardo. He motioned Diego to follow him into his office and then waved out the four men sat bewildered at the meeting table. They could see the visitor had rattled the boss, so quickly gathered their papers and scuttled out closing the door, happy to be out of the firing line.

"Now then, what's going on?" said Eduardo sitting at his desk.

Diego held a bit of paper which was clearly the vital and valuable piece of intel he was offering to impart, but wanted to milk this chance for everything he could.

"Mr Garcia, remember you said you'd keep me in mind about transferring back into your team again. Were you serious about that?" Diego said eagerly.

Eduardo could already see where this was heading and although admiring the lad's tenacity and balls for even attempting to leverage what he had, pushed back.

"I do remember, and that stands, but before I even consider a transfer you need to be straight with me, you're already trying my patience. What do you have? I won't ask again."

Diego got the message. "It's about the robbery from the Prado. I'm pretty sure the Madrid Police haven't got any leads yet and desperately want a break to solving who did it."

"Oh, the Prado?" Eduardo smelt an opportunity coming his way. Leverage over the Police Chief was always a handy thing to have. "Quite a coup for someone to get in and out, then outrun the police in a chase through the park. What about it then, come on man?"

"I've just received a message from Interpol which was passed onto them by London's Metropolitan Police Criminal Investigation Branch."

"Yes!"

"They appear to believe they found out who robbed the Prado, during one of their unrelated operation's, so wanted to be helpful and pass on the intel."

"Really? What's the source? This operation they're

conducting?"

"They cannot divulge the operation or informant as it's ongoing."

"For God's sake man, tell me who they think robbed the Prado then?"

"The owner of the Jurado Data firm sir, a Sonia Jurado!"

"A woman?"

"Well, her team."

"I know of this company, big into selling and using customer data and all that stuff. Well, they'd certainly have the computer power to hack into the museum. The police will be interested to have this information, let me see this Interpol communication," waving at the paper.

"There one more thing though sir. I'm afraid it's been officially tagged as 'No Action Until Authorised'."

"What! You're kidding?"

When passing on operationally sensitive intel between Interpol countries, the originator can request that the intel they hand over cannot be acted upon if it might jeopardise another current investigation. The unwritten rule among enforcement agencies is to respect such requests unless a life-threatening situation arises. Otherwise, they cannot act until the originator has cleared them to, after the other operation has concluded.

"Sorry sir, we can't do anything with this, but I knew I should bring it to you first," said Diego, now pushing his luck. "I thought it would help the discussion we had, about a transfer."

Now Eduardo had the leverage. "It's not worth much if I can't do anything with it!" His manipulative mind raced through permutations of how to use this tipoff to his best advantage. A few ideas came to mind. "But you did the right thing coming to me first, have you told anyone else?"

"No."

"Make sure you keep it that way, tell no one, and then maybe I will sort out your transfer back into my department, alright?"

Diego nodded profusely and as Eduardo gestured towards the door, he backed out of the office. "Thank you, sir."

Eduardo picked up the communication paper from his desk where Diego had laid it down. He read through the wording carefully, twice, to be absolutely sure about what he had and what he could do with it. And what he couldn't.

But Eduardo was well known for bending the rules if it served his beloved Spain to do so.

He pressed the speed-dial on his desk phone to one of his most trusted senior operatives. A man who was totally loyal to his boss, without question. Someone who was just as adept at trawling through intel, as they were leading a front-line operation, or dispensing justice to someone threatening Spain's cause, or that of his boss.

"Santiago, it's me. I need you to dig up everything you can on Sonia Jurado and her Jurado Data firm? Takes priority over everything else you have. Bring it to me by the end of today?"

"Yes boss."

"And get yourself up to date with where the police are with that Prado museum art robbery."

"Yes boss. Solo?"

"Yes Santiago, work on this alone. Don't involve anyone else. Not a word."

"No problem boss."

That evening Santiago Lopez visited his superior's office with printouts and laptop. He was furnished with every piece of information about Sonia Jurado, her family, career, data and fire equipment companies, key staff profiles, properties, accounts that were accessible and everything else imaginable about a person available to the Spanish Secret Services.

Santiago also had photos and police reports from the Prado museum robbery, which now included a new piece of news. The elderly guard who had accidentally been shot twice with tranquillizer darts had not come round. He'd been rushed to hospital from the museum, but the double dose of the knockout drug had been too much for his old body to assimilate and handle. He'd recently passed away from a heart attack brought on by the volume of tranquillizer inside him. The Prado heist had now become an armed robbery-murder.

The two men poured through every detail past midnight. As they did, ideas started to form in Eduardo's mind. How he could leverage this and perhaps settle other scores.

After much discussion, Santiago left. Eduardo spun around facing away from the door and looked out his window across the moonlit surrounding trees. He was contemplative, seriously considering making the most outrageous decision of his career. He'd always got away with his unorthodox choices in the past, where he'd bucked the Services policies, or gone out on a limb alone without telling his boss. For the most part, he'd been right and where he'd been foolish, the results were of little consequence.

What he was considering was audacious to the extreme. He flip-flopped from being emboldened about the idea, then checking with himself if it was indeed possible. To then dismissing it as crazy, risking his career, risking much more if it went wrong.

He and Santiago would take an Iberia flight the next day to London. Then it would be up to how the key person at the centre of his idea reacted. He held most of the cards, so would pitch his outrageous demand, to Sonia Jurado.

11

Santiago Lopez was forty-eight and had spent more than half his life in the Spanish military and Intelligence Services. His nimble, athletic five-eleven frame gave a hint of his likely martial arts prowess, with strong legs and arms able to apply speed and power in equal measures. The short-cropped military-style haircut looked severe and was always in contrast to his kind, empathetic looking eyes. Eyes that had fooled many who had wrongly chosen to confront or challenge him.

Santiago was a true foot soldier. Once he acknowledged authority, which had to be earned, he would do exactly what he was told, to what, or who, how and when.

Straight out of college he'd joined the Spanish army and steadily worked his way up through the ranks to Captain. Superiors always migrated towards those under their command who could be completely relied on to follow their orders, be they legitimate, or somewhat more questionable.

In turn, when Santiago was in command of his own soldiers, he had little time for anyone who dared to not follow his orders to the letter. The rule was clear, do as he said and he'd look after you like a brother, defend and protect you under all circumstances. Willingly disobey him and it was often one strike and you're out. Those soldiers who did, found themselves demoted, transferred to another less prestigious posting, or simply dismissed out of the service altogether.

His reliability for taking on even the tougher, less palatable jobs, drew him to the attention of Spain's Special Operations Command. The Mando de Operaciones Especiales oversaw the various Special Operations throughout the Army, based at the Alferez Rojas Navarrete barracks in Alicante.

There, he took part in a number of more clandestine assignments, culminating in a leading role assimilating intel regarding potential terrorist attacks in Spain by factions including Al-Qaeda.

This was when his path crossed Eduardo Garcia's, then a senior director within the Spanish Intelligence Services. They worked closely together, during which time Eduardo was impressed at Santiago's extreme loyalty to his superiors and ability to simply get on with what he was directed to do, without question.

The assignment they both worked on came to a climax in 2004 when a number of coordinated bomb attacks were undertaken against the Cercanias commuter train system of Madrid.

They had gathered enough intel to know something was likely to go down, but were not in a position to know who, when or where the attacks would be instigated. One hundred and ninety-two people were killed and over two thousand injured.

Special Operations and Secret Services weren't able to prevent the attacks and blame and anger ran rife, tensions were high. Once again Santiago shone through as a logical, pragmatic leader dealing with the facts and uninterested in blame or arguing. Then his ability to follow orders came to the fore, when some of the suspected terrorists were located.

Eduardo Garcia was so incensed at the atrocities they had committed, he took Santiago aside and as he set off to the location, told him that they would not want to take such murderers alive. They should receive their swift justice as soon as Santiago and his men were able to deliver it.

Santiago still checked with his own superior, who influenced now by Garcia, gave a simple nod of agreement.

Three suspected Al-Qaeda men were holed up in a suburb of Madrid, having raised suspicions with locals with their comings and goings.

Santiago and his men took over from the local police who

had surrounded the building. Negotiations were stopped as they had no hostages and smoke and gas grenades were fired into the house, with all exits covered. The soldiers went in so fast, with gas masks and infra-red goggles, the men inside didn't have a chance.

There had been gun shots as two of them fired wildly around themselves, hoping to hit anyone coming at them through the thick smoke. One was shot dead in the return fire, the other wounded, had dropped his weapon to give himself up and be taken in alive. The third was cornered in a room holding explosives and threatening to blow up himself and those nearby.

Santiago had come into the first room where the terrorist was now being held under armed guard. Without a word, he calmly raised his Sig Sauer 226 nine-millimetre handgun and shot him in the heart twice.

He then went across the landing into the other room to find the last terrorist in the far corner, shouting threats at them that he would set off the small device. Assessing that the explosive would be localized, he waved the other soldiers to exit the room and doorway. As Santiago slide through the half-open doorway to leave, he casually tossed back into the room a mini-fragmentation grenade, then closed the door behind him.

The shouting from inside became more urgent and two seconds later there was a small explosion as the grenade detonated at the terrorist's feet. This was closely followed by a slightly larger explosion which was their handheld device being set off by the grenade fragments.

When the soldiers went back in, the terrorist had disappeared into thousands of particles across the floor, walls and ceiling of the room.

Three months later Eduardo Garcia offered Santiago a more senior job with him in his Support to Intelligence division of the Spanish Secret Service. Over fifteen years their close but strictly professional relationship strengthened to one of inseparable trust and loyalty. Santiago was Eduardo's right-hand man, his confidant, bodyguard and trouble-shooter, literally.

Sonia Jurado had just finished joining a presentation in her meeting room, to a large insurance company they were pitching to. Her Sales Manager felt they were almost ready to commit to Jurado Data, to handle their customer database and new custom targeting campaigns. It just needed a little persuasion in the right direction, something they were well-rehearsed at doing, by using their 'closer'. Sonia was brought in. She flattered, sold, impressed, flirted and negotiated. After fifteen minutes the insurance firm's Operations Director was ready to talk contracts.

She returned to her adjoining office as the phone rang. An external call.

"Sonia here," she said politely.

"Sonia Jurado?" said the man at the other end.

"Yes, who is this?"

"My name is Eduardo. I'm calling from the Spanish Embassy in London. I need to see you about a most delicate matter, can you meet me now?"

Sonia was trying to take in the various shocks of what had been said, 'embassy, delicate matter, meet now!'.

"Erm, what's this about," gathering her thoughts, "I'm rather busy, can you email me and we can diarise something properly?"

"That's not going to work for me. I must insist that you meet me at once, I'm only up the road in Belgrave Square."

"You need to tell me what's going on, or I'm hanging up!"

"I work for the Spanish Government. I can assure you it's in your best interests to see me," said Eduardo more insistently. "This is a once-only lifeline!"

Sonia huffed, "Alright, where?"

"I'll wait for you in Belgrave Square gardens, they're private, right opposite our Embassy which is number twenty-four on a corner of the square. Shall we say in fifteen minutes?"

"Okay," said Sonia highly disgruntled about the whole thing.

"Oh and Ms Jurado, come alone please, it really is a delicate matter."

Sonia grabbed her bag and left the office, much to the surprise of Nick and the two Albanian boys. She always told them where she was going. Exiting onto the Strand, she caught the first taxi that approached. They always pulled over for her at once.

They rounded Trafalgar Square and passed through Admiralty Arch onto the strait of The Mall. Ahead of them was the magnificent Buckingham Palace, which sat behind the large, fountained Victoria Memorial. Turning right they went along Constitution Hill, alongside the Palace's high spiked garden wall, and over Hyde Park corner roundabout.

Within ten minutes the taxi dropped her off across the road from the elongated, cream Embassy building, with Spanish and European flags above the entrance.

Sonia was greeted by a military-looking man. It was Santiago.

"Ms Jurado? I work for Eduardo, will you come this way please." It wasn't a question.

He led her past the statue of Christopher Columbus and through one of the low-level black metal barred gates into the private gardens. The five-acre plot was dense with trees and shrubs and provided a concealed, private area for residents and the many surrounding Embassies.

He led her over to a tall distinguished-looking man who rose from a secluded bench.

"Sonia Jurado, thank you so much for agreeing to see me. I am Eduardo. Before we start, would you mind?" he gestured towards Santiago who had produced a small metal detector from his jacket and was waiting in readiness.

Taken by surprise again, she agreed and he flashed the

electronic baton around her person expertly, only detecting a bunch of keys and mobile phone in her bag. He took the mobile.

Eduardo explained, "This is off the record you understand."

They sat. "Can you please tell me what all this cloak and dagger is about now!" Sonia didn't like not being in control.

"Of course," said Eduardo, who had decided not to dance around with this confident looking businesswoman. "I know you were behind the recent Prado museum break-in and theft!"

The words hung in the air and for Sonia, time seemed to stop for a moment, as her world crashed in on her. She quickly gathered herself back up.

"I don't know what you're talking about, this is ridiculous!"

Eduardo expected this standard denial. "Come, come, Sonia, I may call you Sonia, yes? We both know you arranged to take Antonello's Dead Christ painting, which I assume you still have somewhere. That's an incredibly serious crime."

"What, an art theft?" Sonia fell right into the basic trap of addressing details of the crime rather than another denial.

Eduardo didn't bother pointing this out. "Why yes, haven't you heard? The guard your men shot twice with the tranquillizer darts, has unfortunately died!"

Sonia looked shocked and surprised yet again. Eduardo went on. "It's now being treated as armed robbery-murder."

"What part of the government did you say you work for?"

"I didn't. But I'm in the Intelligence Services."

"Why would you think a reputable businesswoman like me had anything to do with this?" she demanded.

Eduardo's patience was thinning now. "As I said when I called, I'd like to help you out of this, but I need you to be honest with me. You haven't been charged, we're not being recorded, this is off the record."

Sonia continued to frown, so he pushed on with his ace

card.

"Of course if you want to continue playing games then my friend Santiago here will escort you to the Embassy over there," he pointed to the building through the trees just thirty yards away, "where you'll be charged, detained pending extradition back to Madrid, face trial, and then spend twenty years in one of our finest penitentiaries. And trust me, there's nothing fine about them!"

Sonia felt she had no way out of this and was relieved the Richmond Bank hack hadn't been mentioned yet. 'Surely if he knew about that he'd have said something by now? No, this all seemed to be about the Prado break-in', she thought.

"Alright, let's say for the sake of argument I did the Prado job, for good reason I might add, why are you offering to help me?"

"That's better," said Eduardo sarcastically. "Why did you go to the trouble of hacking and breaking into the Prado, with millions worth of fine art all around, and have your men, who did a great job by the way, take just one painting, the Dead Christ?"

"For our country!"

"Explain?"

"My mother took me to see that painting since I was a little girl, it's beautiful…"

"Indeed it is," he agreed.

"I found out that the museum was about to auction it off to raise some funds. I simply couldn't have that piece, which our country owns, disappearing off into a foreign private collection."

"Admirable. So, a theft not for personal gain, but patriotic vanity. Are you a patriot Sonia?"

"I guess so."

"Tell me about your parents Sonia?" Eduardo and Santiago had done their research. "Your father?"

Sonia looked startled at the change of tack, then figured she knew where the question was leading. "You mean his fire equipment business or his affair?"

Eduardo shrugged, letting Sonia work out what he wanted her to say.

She continued begrudgingly. "He had an affair with some British girl which split up my parents."

"British, you say? How do you feel about that?" Eduardo wanted to know if Sonia shared the same hatred he had for them.

"I despise them frankly! She ruined my life and my parents' lives. How's that relevant though?"

"We share the same hatred, Sonia. My mother was raped by two English lads!" Sonia reeled at the shocking and personal disclosure. Eduardo had found their common enemy and pushed their combined anger. "I still don't know who my father even is! I found one of the lads and confronted him years later."

"What happened," said Sonia empathetically and hopeful.

"He told me to piss off!"

"Oh my God, I'm so sorry. That's awful."

Eduardo gazed at the sky for a moment, partly lost in the memory of his mother and partly for dramatic effect. Sonia was coming round to where he wanted her for the big ask he needed to put to her.

"Your team. The blokes you have to hack into high-security museums, rob them and evade all of Madrid's police. They seem pretty good. Ex-military I'm guessing?"

"They are good and totally loyal to me," said Sonia proudly. "Yup, some with a military background," thinking of Nick and Max, "the rest with varied past's," imagining the Albanian mobsters, Peter's IT genius and Max again in corporations.

Eduardo paused, checking with himself he was committed to putting his proposition to this determined, Spanish woman. He glanced round to make sure no one was nearby, just Santiago standing behind them, ever watchful.

"Your robbery of the Prado is commendable, but a guard

was killed. That's a really big deal, Sonia." He looked straight at her now. "So, if I'm going to make that disappear and prevent a jail sentence for you and your friends, then I have a really big ask of you in return."

Sonia's ever-present call to a challenge started to rise to the surface. "Go on."

"I want to humiliate," he corrected himself, "I want *us* to humiliate, the British!" He checked her reaction.

Her face looked puzzled, but with a tinge of interest and excitement. Just what he wanted to see in her.

"How?"

"I want you and your team, to steal one of the Crown jewels!"

Sonia felt she'd had her share of surprises in the last half an hour, but this! Her face screwed up in rejection and amusement at this preposterous suggestion.

"That's ridiculous! You're mad!"

Eduardo quickly tried to smooth over the idea and her reaction. "It's not ridiculous at all. You have the men you need, the skills, the equipment at your disposal and the hacking ability to pull it off. Plus you have my considerable resources, in confidence of course."

"But the Crown jewels! It's impossible!"

"No, it's entirely possible. Everyone just assumes it's impossible. It's a building, with alarms, CCTV, guards. It's just another Prado, but on steroids shall we say!"

Sonia looked as though she was thinking to herself whether such a heist was achievable, so Eduardo continued to coach her along.

"Santiago here is the best operative I've ever known. He will join your team." They looked round at him, he gave Sonia a reassuring nod and smile. "Of course you all need to do your own research on this before you commit, that's understandable. I just want an initial 'yes in principle' from you today and we can leave here as partners?"

Sonia's mind was exploding, wrestling with the tight

corner she was backed into, envisaging trying to break into the Tower of London of all places. Was it achievable, what would happen if they got caught, what if they succeeded? She concluded that she didn't want to be escorted over to the Spanish Embassy and arrested today, so surely there was no harm in looking into this more with the boys.

Her life in Spain and the UK was finished anyway, especially with the Richmond Bank investigation looking as though it might be closing in on them.

She took in a deep breath then let out a long sigh. Eduardo watched in eager anticipation. "Well?"

"I'll look at it, but no promises!"

"Excellent!" commended Eduardo happily. "Can you imagine the fuss it'll cause and embarrassment of the Brits if you manage to pull this off? They'll be the laughingstock of the entire world."

Sonia allowed herself a smile, thinking, 'I've already crossed the line with the bank and museum jobs, I guess, in for a penny, in for a pound!'.

The first thing we need to sort," said Eduardo getting back down to business, "is the painting."

"What about it?"

"You need to return it. As good faith. I'll make sure the museum isn't allowed to sell it on. It will stay at the Prado for evermore after this. And the great thing is that following its theft, it'll probably be the number one attraction at the Prado for years to come!"

"How do I return it?

"Entirely up to you. Post it back to the Prado, leave it at a police station, whatever you want, as long as it can't be traced back to you or your team."

"Okay," agreed Sonia, "consider it done."

"There is also I'm afraid a more vulgar point I must mention." Eduardo was momentarily serious.

"Oh, what's that?" said Sonia looking a little worried.

"Just so we're clear. This is all in complete confidence

between the two of us. I decide who I tell back at our Intelligence Services, you can share it with your team of course. I hope your trust in them isn't misplaced. If this gets out in any form, if you or anyone you involve says a word of this, or threatens to speak out… then my friend here, will kill every one of you. I guarantee it!"

Sonia looked back at Santiago. The smile had gone and he looked deadly serious this time. She believed he would indeed kill them. She tried to keep it business-like. "Understood."

"Good. Thank you," said Eduardo, hoping it didn't put too much of a downer on proceedings. "I'll be in touch soon, don't try to contact me, just get your team busy on assessing the job in hand, getting familiar with everything. Planning, options, every eventuality, getting in, getting out, overcoming the security, the casings the jewels are in. Become Crown jewel and Tower experts. I'm guessing you'll need to also think about finding someone to help you on the inside. Someone with knowledge of the security system, in the control room, staff in residence, a Beefeater, one of the soldiers there. Lots to think about, but I know you can do this Sonia."

Eduardo rose. Sonia's mind was spinning as she stood up. She felt tiny next to him. Then one thought pushed through.

"Just one final question," she said. "How on earth did you find out about our Prado venture?"

"In the spirit of partnership and trust, I don't think there's any harm in telling you," pondered Eduardo. "I got a tipoff from Interpol. Someone in their community found out during an entirely unrelated operation. No idea who though."

Sonia was intrigued. "But who, *in their community*?"

Eduardo gave a slight shrug of his shoulders as if it was of no importance.

"I think it was from the Met, here in London!"

12

It was five AM. The two Policia officers raced through the streets of Madrid, anxious and excited at the radio call they'd just received from their Sargent back at the police station. They'd been instructed to go to a certain destination immediately.

Their Sergeant had told them he'd just received an anonymous untraceable call. The caller had said that if he wanted to solve a major national crime, he should send police to this puzzling location.

The men in the car were both wondering if they were about to discover a dead body. That was often something they had to respond to, where a passing member of the public had found a corpse but didn't want to get involved or be identified.

They pulled up at one of the entrances to Madrid's La Almundena cemetery. They'd been told to go to one of the more well-known residents there. That of the statue and mausoleum of Spain's first famous female bullfighter, Juanita Cruz.

They walked quickly past the vast rows of headstones and could see in the distance the statue of the female bullfighter. She struck a magnificent pose holding her matador's hat and traje de luces tunic, espada sword and swirling muleta cape.

They approached more carefully as they closed in. Nothing seemed wrong, no dead bodies, just a number of wreaths and flowers left by tourists and locals.

One of the officers then noticed a large flower arrangement that appeared odd in shape. It was a rectangle, rather than the usual rounded form. He went over to it and as he started to raise it up for a closer inspection, some of the flowers lying over it fell away, revealing a large canvas covering. There was something solid inside.

The two policemen gathered around the strange object and one of them untied the drawstrings at the top end. The canvas covering partially fell down each side.

Their jaws dropped at the sight in front of them.

"Cristo muerto de Antonello!" exclaimed one officer quietly in disbelief.

Their eyes fell upon the tearful angel gently supporting the dead Christ. It was the recently stolen painting from the Prado museum!

Sonia had instructed one of her staff at the villa to drop off the artwork in the middle of the night. Then, later on, using a temporary burner phone with a muffled microphone, call the local police station.

"Shame after all the effort and risks we took to get that painting," said Nick, talking to Sonia in her office.

"Maybe, but we've got the result I wanted," she replied. "The Dead Christ will now stay at the Prado. It was worth it."

"Nice touch leaving it by Juanita's statue."

She chuckled. "Well on the basis one strong woman managed to take the painting, with the help of you guys, I felt it was befitting that another strong, leading woman returned it. But it seems it's come at a price!"

Sonia had come back from her meeting with Eduardo and Santiago, and immediately told Nick everything. The dead guard, the threat of twenty years in a Spanish prison and the outrageous proposal that they somehow look into the feasibility of stealing one of the Crown jewels.

They'd already worked out why Eduardo had suggested just one item. Many of the separate priceless treasures had their own security-laden, bomb-proof cabinets they each sat within. It would simply be impossible to think that anyone would have enough time to steal the whole collection. They needed to work out which jewel or crown was the easiest to take, with the most impact.

Sonia had already asked Peter to begin researching everything about the jewels and the Tower. But their attention was drawn away from starting to look into this huge challenge. They were more concerned with how this supposed tipoff had reached the Spanish Secret Services, via Interpol and the Met.

"How on earth could anyone the Met have anything to do with, possibly have known what we were planning with the Prado?" repeated Sonia.

"There's no way Peter, Afrim or Saban would have said anything, one-hundred per cent safe with them," said Nick.

Sonia looked at him sternly. "Then what about your Max friend?"

"Max? No way."

"He's the obvious newbie in the pack, you've only just got to know him again after what, twenty years?"

"Why would anyone shop themselves?" challenged Nick. "No. You don't pull off something like that, then tipoff the authorities that you were part of the crime. Can't be him."

"Undercover in some way maybe?" pushed Sonia.

"Not Max. He's been sitting in an office since he left the Marines. I looked him up, twenty years of hard labour in corporations. Impressive career, never thought he had that in him." Nick was defensive. "Anyway, if he was undercover for someone, again, you don't join in with the caper yourself and then drop us all in it afterwards. He's as guilty as we are!"

Sonia had to agree with the logic. "He did seem pretty convincing in mucking in with you guys that night. Got you out of there through the park. Is that really all because of your couple of years together in the Commandos?"

"Loyalties and trust run very deep when you serve together, especially when you fight side by side in a conflict zone like me and Max did." Nick was resolute. "He saved my bloody life for heaven's sake. Honestly, Sonia, I trust him. What about your staff at the villa?" he said trying to divert attention away from Max.

Sonia pondered for a moment. “Chef, no.” She thought more. “House staff, a possibility, maybe at a stretch? The housekeeper does sometimes use agency cleaners. But how would they possibly know what we did? No agency staff were on when we were there.”

“Rumours, gossip, seeing or hearing any of the preparations, the equipment, the cars in the outhouse?” said Nick, thinking they were onto something.

“But how would any of that get back to the Met in London, unless they were running some sort of international investigation on something in Madrid?” queried Sonia.

“You don’t think it’s got anything to do with the Richmond job, do you? The Met are all over that one,” said Nick.

“I can’t see how it could?”

“You’ve got me and the boys handling Bob and Freddy, you said you thought it was only a matter of time before one of them may say something?”

“But they couldn’t possibly know what we were up to in Madrid that weekend, they were both being questioned by the Met at the same time you’re at the Prado,” mused Sonia. “No, there’s no link between them and the museum.”

Nick thought back to the time when Bob and Freddy worked for them. Bob had been close to Sonia for about a year, that was a long time to get to know her.

The potential link hit him. “Hang on a mo, I think I’ve got it!” Sonia looked up. “Bob knew perfectly well how much you loved the Dead Christ painting at the Prado, your childhood connection with it, how protective you are of it.”

Sonia completed the thought process. “It wouldn’t be a huge assumption would it, to think that I just might have something to do with its theft, if he saw it in the news?”

They both thought it through to themselves. “Na, still doesn’t feel right to me,” said Nick. “Anyway, what’s done is done, your Spanish Intelligence Services chap knows now and we’re lumbered with having to try to pull off what’ll be the most talked-about robbery worldwide, whether we like it or not!"

"About that. I assume you trust Max enough to include him in the Tower job? Let's not give him any details yet okay. See if he's interested in a Prado mark two, but nothing giving away what, where or how yet."

Nich shrugged a shoulder, "Alright, but I'm sure he's fine, and we'll need him for something like this."

Sonia shook her head. "Bob and Freddy are too much of a liability now, for potentially talking about the Richmond hack, and now possibly Bob's the leak for the Prado job. Either way, you and your boys need to get on with paying them both a visit!"

"Shame. They're decent fellas."

Freddy McIntosh rented a studio apartment on Brixton Road in South London. His address was innocently shown in the phone book available online, so could be looked up by anyone.

His work profile on the business directory LinkedIn also gave his past and more importantly current employment details. He was providing consultancy support to a media company based in Leicester Square.

Afrim and Saban easily found the information they wanted on Bob Simmons' regular IT consulting protégé. They had passed him in the office years ago when he briefly worked at Jurado Data with Bob, but were never really introduced to him. But they had to be careful as he could recognize them.

As most consultants like to get into the office early, given they're being paid a day rate and have to work longer hours, the boys expected him to arrive in Leicester Square between seven and eight AM.

The underground tube from Brixton went four stops on the Victoria line to Green Park, then two stops on the Piccadilly line to Leicester Square. This took about fifteen minutes. They would wait for him in one of the small café's on Brixton Road, between his flat and the station, from about six-forty onwards.

The next morning the two Albanian boys took up positions with their coffees, in two different cafés along the short distance of two hundred metres. They waited, trying not to make it too obvious that they were each watching the road outside like hawks, waiting for their prey to pass by.

At seven AM Freddy kissed his fiancée goodbye and exited the flat onto Brixton Road. Afrim almost missed him as he went by the window he was sat behind. He quickly sent the pre-typed text to Saban who was further ahead, saying simply 'Now'. He then waited for Freddy to continue another twenty yards before cautiously leaving the café.

Fortunately, Brixton Road was always very busy at this time, with hundreds of commuters constantly pouring down the pavements and into the transport hub of the area, being the underground station. The multitude of workers provided good cover for them to each follow Freddy at a distance, as everyone went about their robotic daily travel with little concern or acknowledgement of anyone else.

Freddy turned into the large glass-fronted entrance of the underground and flashed his Oyster travel card over the turnstile machine. It promptly clicked open for him, as other travellers bunched up behind, huffing at the apparent slowness of the equipment. Everyone was always rushing to minimise their wasted travel time.

Afrim was about eight travellers behind him, with Saban close by using a different entry gate. They kept their distance, adjusting themselves to put others between them and Freddy whenever they thought he might look round.

The throng descended towards the Victoria line Northbound platform and just as Freddy emerged onto the concrete promenade, a tube train was about to depart.

The two boys held back for a moment, disappearing into the crowd. If Freddy got onto the train they didn't want to be seen by him as he pulled away. Nor did they want to find themselves on an almost empty platform right next to him if he missed the train.

Freddy moved towards the closing door as if to dodge inside, but a burly builder moved across the opening thinking no one else was going to come onboard. He then saw Freddy but it was too late and told him to, "Take the next one mate."

The boys held back and allowed more people to pour onto the platform to once again give them cover. The next train would be about four minutes away. It felt like a long four minutes to them.

Finally, with the platform packed with the next round of waiting commuters, they closed in. Afrim slowly and cautiously positioned himself just ten feet to Freddy's right. Saban drew in closer behind Freddy, who was now nearest to the platform edge being the first to arrive on the recently vacated platform.

The sound of the train signalled its approach, with its accompanying rush of air being pushed down the tunnel ahead of it.

Afrim's timing was perfect. He jostled carelessly into the suited gentleman next to him who immediately cried out somewhat alarmed, "What are you doing man, stop pushing, just be careful!"

The distraction was enough to draw the attention of any of the surrounding commuters who cared to look up, including Freddy.

The train exited from the dark tunnel and started to slow as it made its way along the platform. Saban was now directly behind Freddy.

Freddy looked at the businessman complaining of being jostled, then something triggered in his sight and memory. The man next to him. 'Surely it couldn't be?'.

"Afr…!"

He only managed to get out part of the name of the man he'd seen across the other travellers. Saban had disguised a gentle but firm push in the back as the natural anticipative movement of the crowd preparing to board the train.

Freddy's body connected with the live and earthed electrical rails receiving six-hundred and thirty volts of direct current through his body. Simultaneously the unforgiving underside of the train's leading lower-edge smashed into his head, then body, like a sledgehammer hitting a rag doll. He died instantly.

Moments later several commuters realized what had happened, and screamed out, though there was nothing to be seen as the train continued masking poor Freddy from view, eventually stopping.

Amid the confusion and chaos that followed, the two boys disappeared into the crowds. Saban moved to the end of the platform through the concerned people craning their heads to see what had happened. He would later catch the train to the next station once it was moved out of the way. Afrim quietly lost himself in the crowds exiting and entering the platforms and then back out onto the street above, mingled in with more commuters around the station's entrance.

Freddy McIntosh's death would be treated as an 'accident, possibly suicide' with the case file left open for three months, but nothing more would be done about it, no witnesses came forward. He became another unfortunate statistic of deaths on the railways.

The driver of the tube would from that day on, be haunted by the sight of someone disappearing under his train, every time he pulled into a new station. He resigned three months later from anxiety and stress.

Nick collected Max from his home on Clapham Common, having already called Bob Simmons. He'd arranged to drop into Bob's home and meet him alone, to get the details of his offshore account for the newly agreed Richmond Bank share.

"Nice home Max, you've done okay on civi street ol' pal," commented Nick as he leaned down to take in the large detached, gated house.

"I've done alright thanks," replied Max. "Corporates pay well when you save them hundreds of millions in better deals with suppliers."

"Ever thought what you'd do if *you* had hundreds of millions?"

Max detected the normally fun question sounded a little more serious than just a fantasy. He played along.

"Haven't we all? Lots of fast cars and lots of properties around the world," he joked.

"So you'd be happy to live abroad? Nothing keeping you here in Blighty?"

Max could feel this was leading somewhere. "No, not I guess. If I did have that much money then I suppose there are a lot warmer, exotic places I'd rather be than cold, dark, wet Britain for six months of the year."

Nick changed tack, satisfied with Max's replies. "You did well in Madrid, Max. Sonia and I appreciate you coming in with us at short notice. You were great, getting us out of there."

"I have to say it was kinda fun wasn't it," pretended Max. "Got the adrenalin pumping and reminded what I know I've missed by opting out of the Marines all those years ago. The action man's still inside me, deep down I suppose."

"It certainly is Max." Nick paused to check himself before trusting his old comrade once more. "How would you feel about helping us with another job? A bit like the Prado?"

Max didn't betray the surge of concern inside him. "What, another museum, you're kidding?"

"It'll be much more of a challenge this next one. Harder, more dangerous, higher profile, big consequences!"

"Jesus Nick, the Prado was a one-off for me. Sounds like you're planning to rob a Vegas casino!"

Nick laughed. "No nothing like that. But seriously Max, if we had something big, might you be up for it? If we were successful, you'd get your hundreds of millions and could buy that beachfront house abroad you've always wanted? Ten if you like."

Max thought to himself that getting involved with the Prado theft was going beyond the call of duty and agreeing to another crime, bigger and more dangerous, would not be supported by his MI5 employers. Yet he was still trying to stay in line to find out anything about the Richmond job, so couldn't afford to fall out with Nick.

"You're serious aren't you?" he looked to Nick who nodded. "Bloody hell Nick, you don't half drop in a bombshell, don't you! Can you let me think about it?"

Nick didn't expect Max to agree right off the cuff, so took the consolation of at least not being rejected out of hand.

"Of course. Big decision as you say, but don't take too long, we need to know if you're in or not. It's got the backing of a much higher authority."

"How do you mean?"

"Let's just say the job has the support of a foreign power, so we'll get protection if anything were to go wrong." Nick was being liberal with the truth.

"You guys done anything like this job or the Prado before?" asked Max casually.

"Kind of. Didn't involve me or the boys though."

"Oh, how do you mean?"

"Well, we weren't needed to do anything, like at the Prado. It was all sort of done remotely," said Nick coyly.

Max was right. This sounded very much like the Richmond job. But still all hearsay, no actual proof or a direct link. Max braced himself for the straight question.

"What job was that then, sounds interesting?"

Nick looked at him suspiciously for a second, then shook his head. "Na. I don't want to burden you with all that nonsense. Forget I mentioned it."

"Sure," replied Max quickly. "So what are we doing now then?" He could see they were heading towards Roehampton and Putney.

"Kinda related to what we've been talking about. Need to pay someone a visit. Might get a bit frisky. Probably have to go Commando on them." He turned to Max. "You up for that? Be just like the old days."

Max thought quickly. He didn't want to risk going down another criminal rabbit hole and have Si Lawson wondering if he'd taken leave of his senses again. He'd already used up a lot of credit with the job in Madrid.

"Hmm, I'm okay with the Prado type thing where no-one gets hurt, Nick. Don't want to be strong-arming a civi though. Can I pass on this?"

Nick chose not to mention one of the Prado guards had died and given Max had spent twenty years in an office, was prepared to let him sit it out on this one.

"Okay, if you're sure Max. Perhaps you can just wait outside the house by the car and make sure no one disturbs me when I have my little chat with the guy inside?"

"No problem," said Max.

They came upon the picturesque Putney Heath in the middle of south London. Nick drove alongside the green expanse, then turned into Telegraph Road which led them into a hidden enclave of about forty very nice homes spread over a handful of narrow cul-de-sac streets. He proceeded to the end road and the end house. It was the home of Bob Simmons!

The short driveway led up to a large family home. All was quiet though. Nick turned the car around and parked up fifteen yards away from the house, facing back out the drive. Max hoped this was for convenience and not to get away quickly.

"Be about ten minutes okay?" said Nick as he got out. Max also climbed out and sat against the warm engine bonnet, his back to the house.

From inside, Bob Simmons peered out to see Nick Hawkins his old Jurado colleague approaching the front door. He could see someone else down the driveway, waiting by a car.

"Bob, how are you?" greeted Nick coming in.

"I've been better," said the Richmond Bank IT Director. "Who's the passenger out there?"

"Oh just a pal, don't worry about him, he's not coming in." Bob looked again at the figure by the car. He couldn't see them properly, but for a moment, they seemed familiar.

Nick tried to relax him. "You old devil! Asking Sonia for more money! Three-hundred million no less. Best get lost abroad before the soon-to-be ex-wife hears about that and puts it in your divorce settlement eh!" he joked, looking round the house to make sure they were alone.

"Ha Ha," said Bob sarcastically. "This isn't funny. I'm not happy about being pulled in by the Met for two days. They know something I'm sure of it."

"If they knew anything you wouldn't be here at home with me would you?" assured Nick. "But while we're on that subject, did you or Freddy say anything to them, anything at all, that could come back to us?" Bob could see Nick's body language change, and not for the better.

"No! Absolutely nothing. But let me tell you lot at Jurado, if it does all come out, I won't take the fall and go to prison. No way!"

Nick changed tack to surprise Bob. "And what about any mention of Prado?"

"What? I' don't even know what you're talking about?"

"Oh come on, you know about the Prado job, what did you say to the Met about that?" pushed Nick.

"I've absolutely no idea who or what the Prado is," insisted Bob. He then remembered from a long past holiday in Spain. "Isn't that the name of some museum?"

Nick felt more assured that maybe Bob didn't know anything about their Prado trip, he was after all being detained at the time. He looked at him and his expression changed from interrogator, to relaxed friend once more.

"I've had enough of all these questions Nick, you know you can trust me. Let's get on with this account stuff now," he said moving towards his office which overlooked the driveway.

As Bob leant down to find the piece of paper with his offshore bank details, he looked out at the other man still standing by the car.

"What's your chap's name, I'm sure I've seen him somewhere before?"

"Unlikely," said Nick, "it's Max."

"Maybe not," said Bob.

When they'd met in the Richmond Bank canteen Max had introduced himself as just 'Sargent'.

Just as Bob grabbed the sheet of paper, he felt a tiny scratch on the side of his neck. He instinctively held his hand to it and turning abruptly cried out, "What was that! Ouch, that hurt!"

He then saw Nick standing beside him holding a small, empty syringe with a tiny hypodermic needle attached. Nick stood back.

"I'm sorry Bob"

"What the hell have you gone and done Nick!"

"We remembered you telling us once, years ago, that you have an extreme allergic reaction to wasp stings."

Bob looked at the syringe, "What was that?" He could already feel pain crawling through his body emanating from his neck. His face screwed up in horror.

"Hyaluronidase, phosphatase acid, histamine, dopamine and a whole bunch of other things I can't pronounce. I never was any good at biology or chemistry. Put simply, it's wasp sting venom!" said Nick putting away the syringe.

Bob clumsily swiped at his desktop sending a paper-weight flying towards the window, to try and alert the man outside. It smashed through the glass. Max turned round and started to come towards the house, wondering what was going on.

The pain searing through Bob's body was crippling, as his cells and organs were touched by the venom, causing a catastrophic deterioration reaction. His oesophagus and larynx started to slowly swell, restricting his breathing.

As he gazed at the man outside now running to the front door his eyes were struggling to focus properly on the man's face. He crumpled to his knees.

Max came rushing into the room. "Christ Nick, what's happened?" he shouted.

Nick merely collected up the piece of paper on the desk and Bob's laptop.

As Bob's brain struggled to assimilate the sounds, he knew deep down he'd heard that voice before. The pain collapsed him onto the floor, as cells gave way to the poisonous reaction and vital organs started to give up functioning. The pain throughout his whole body was making him unconscious.

Bob looked up with the last of his strength and recognized Max from the bank's canteen!

He tried to reach out but couldn't anymore, as he attempted to whisper out loud Max's surname. "Ss..."

The word was cut-off as his throat closed up and he suffered a heart attack. Bob Simmons slumped onto the carpet at their feet, dead.

13

Max had barely spoken to Nick during the car ride home. He felt contempt towards his old Colour Sergeant. How could he have gone so bad? Was this just misplaced loyalty to the mesmerising Sonia Jurado? Or was it what it often came down to, the money?

The instant he saw Bob Simmons writhing in agony at Nick's feet, he knew he'd been poisoned somehow. In the car, Nick had glibly said a wasp had stung him on the neck and he'd had an allergic reaction, but knew that Max didn't believe that for one second. Max had said they should call the police, but Nick said he'd do that later. With the Prado and this new job on the horizon, he didn't want to have to explain why he was there.

Max felt this was yet another clue tying Jurado to the Richmond job. They clearly used Bob Simmons and were now discarding him. But he still had no solid evidence.

Nick had asked Max in the car, "What do you think he was trying to say, at the end? It almost sounded like he recognized you and was trying to say your name, Sargent?"

"He was clearly about to say 'save me', given the state the poor chap was in," said Max thinking fast.

Nick thought for a moment and accepted that explanation, given Bob hadn't reacted to seeing him outside or being told his name was Max.

"If this is all too much for you Max, I'll understand," said Nick. "Perhaps that big job I mentioned isn't for you after all?"

"Perhaps not," agreed Max. "As I said, I'll go for adventure and money, but this kind of thing, people getting hurt, I can't sign up to that Nick."

"That wasn't your view in Sierra Leone."

Max shot him a look. "That's a low blow and you know it. A war zone. Survival. Saving you!" said Max crossly. "I mean not on civi street."

"If it makes any difference Max, you kinda have already drawn blood on civi as well."

"What do you mean?"

"That guard at the Prado we accidentally tranquillized twice."

"Yes?" said Max, worried he wasn't going to like what he was going to be told next.

"He died I'm afraid." Nick let that hang for a while, Max was silent. "You're one of us now Max. Have a think about the next job anyway okay?"

"It's not for me, but thanks."

As soon as Max got back home and Nick had gone, he got straight on the phone to Si Lawson at MI5 and got right to it.

"Si, things are going sour I'm afraid. I've just come from Bob Simmons home in the middle of Putney Heath. I didn't see it but am pretty certain Nick Hawkins just scrubbed him out. Claimed it was a wasp sting he was allergic to!"

"Oh my God Max. This is bad," said Si. "I've just caught an alert that the other chap you were onto, Freddy McIntosh…"

Max cut in, "Don't tell me he's dead as well?"

"I'm afraid so."

"How? When?"

"Early this morning, fell under a tube train at his Brixton station. They're putting it down as accident or suicide."

"Accident suicide my arse," said Max. "If it wasn't my old sergeant Nick, then I've got a good idea who it could have been. Couple of nasty Albanians Nick and Sonia have on the payroll. Afrim and Saban something or other."

"Police have already interviewed some travellers and checked CCTV. Nothing of any interest. If he was murdered, they were good. No trace at all."

Max was angry. "But surely Si, me witnessing Nick killing Simmons and both him and McIntosh mysteriously dying with Nick etcetera involved, that's enough to haul them all in isn't it?"

"So you did see Nick kill Simmons then?"

"Well no, I was outside. Really? Come on, he did something Si. Simmons recognized me from when I met him at the bank and was about to call out my name! That would have put the cat amongst the pigeons, for me!"

"Look Max, I think we can agree that the Jurado lot pulled off the Richmond job, but as you know we have to get some hard evidence." Si shared his frustration. "We think we know it all, but we've got nothing to hand over to police let alone succeed with a prosecution."

"There's something else I found out just now. Bigger!" said Max.

"What do you mean?"

"In the car Nick was asking me if I wanted to do another job with them. Bigger than Prado. Worth hundreds of millions, to me that is. Can't you just pull them all in?"

"What else did he say about this 'next job'?"

Max thought back. "He was saying it'll have consequences and that it'll be dangerous. He also said something about being backed by a foreign power!"

"What foreign power? When, where, anything else?" coaxed Si eager for more detail.

"Sorry Si, that is literally everything he said. He wouldn't tell me anymore but wants me to think about joining them."
"What did you say to that?"

"No, of course!" fumed Max. "I've already helped rob the Prado, oh and by the way, I gather one of the guards which Nick and the Albanians tranquillized, has died, and I've near as damn it been present when Simmons got it in the neck!"

"This is becoming a mess!" concluded Si.

"I can't carry on undercover. At what point am I seen to go from MI5 to Jurado criminal? The lines are getting very blurred right now Si!"

"Okay Max, don't worry, we need to get them all in and for you to have nothing more to do with them," said Si, thinking things through. "Hang tight and I'll go see the Deputy Director General now and check if we can wrap this up. Okay?"

Max huffed, still wound up. "I'm sure once they're in front of the police and they go through their computer equipment at the Strand office, something will turn up."

Si called off and immediately rang up to the DDG's team of personal assistants.

"Yes Si, Chuck here?"

"Chuck, I need ten minutes, no, five will do, with the DDG? It's urgent, so as soon as possible please?"

"Everything's always urgent," Chuck replied unhelpfully. "He's chokka today, but, let's see, I can do nine fifty-five tomorrow morning if that suits?"

"No Chuck, that doesn't suit!" replied Si crossly. Knowing he had to negotiate his way past Chuck, he quickly calmed again before saying, "the DDG won't be happy with you or me if I don't update him on a pressing operation we have running right now." Then he played his ace card. "I've already got two dead people just today!"

That did the trick. "Oh, I see. Well, I can give you your five minutes if you come up now and wait til he finishes his current meeting," agreed Chuck. "I can then hold his next appointment briefly til you're done."

Not wanting to wait for the lifts, Si strode upstairs to the MI5 senior director's floor at Thames House. He went along the corridor beside the various offices and rooms, their modern and classical styles clashing badly with each new appointment's personal tastes. He gave Chuck a nod and sat outside the DDG's large, glass, soundproofed office.

Si could see a distinguished Asian man sitting in front of the DDG. It looked as though he was being told in no uncertain terms that something was not acceptable. The DDG rarely got flustered or cross, on the surface, but it looked as though he was most unhappy with the other man, who appeared completely admonished.

Chuck leaned over to Si and whispered an explanation. "Someone from the Chinese embassy. It's still kicking off in Hong Kong!" Then mimicking Queen Victoria's prude voice, "We are not amused!"

Since handing Hong Kong back to the Chinese in 1997, they'd waited a decade before slowly starting to change things. But the world and people of Hong Kong were onto it, protesting, complaining, but to little avail. Rules were changing, freedoms reducing, leaders being swapped out and controls strengthened. It seemed the wonderful old British colony was losing its wonder and slowly becoming absorbed by the mighty new owner, China.

The Chinese man stood, gave a slight bow and exited the office, watched closely by the DDG who seemed to be in a trance. He was merely thinking through how this whole Hong Kong debacle was going to turn out and how to pitch his next report to the Director General and Prime Minister.

He looked up. "Si Lawson. Very clever."

"I'm sorry sir?"

"Managing to get to see me when you're not in my diary. Must be important?" Which really meant 'this had better be important!'.

"It is," said Si closing the door quickly and sitting.

Si then proceeded to tell him everything he knew about the Jurado undercover operation with Max, including the deaths of Simmons and McIntosh, knowing they did the Richmond job but couldn't yet prove it. Finally, Nick Hawkins' offer for Max to help them with this next, bigger job.

The DDG asked, "Does Max feel he can get proof on the bank hack? We still need to solve that for the PM."

"We all know they did it so it's only a matter of time before we get something firm on them. Max just doesn't want to continue being involved in criminal activities, he's worried it'll reflect badly on MI5, and him!"

"We'll worry about that, not him," said the DDG. "I'm more concerned about this big, dangerous next job they're planning, with so-called 'foreign backing'. That's something we must know more about?"

"I agree sir. I was inclined to bring them all in, but that'll leave us nowhere with Richmond and this other job."

"It sounds like we have our way forward then," summarized the DDG. "Keep Max in with them. He's got to find out about this other job with the foreign backer, I don't like the sound of that at all. And get proof on their involvement with Richmond Bank."

"Understood sir," said Si leaving.

"You'd better make sure you cover this off with Max, so he knows we're behind him all the way. We don't leave our frontline agents out in the cold if things go wrong, as long as all the checks and balances are in order."

"Will do, he's a good chap, if anyone can sort their way through this, Max can."

"Let's just hope this Jurado bunch don't cotton onto him before we get what we want!"

After Peter Whistler had recovered from the shock of the challenge Sonia had told him about, he'd set to work with his usual gusto. Eliciting the help of Afrim and Saban, both equally adept at researching, assessing and planning, they busily hit the internet to find out everything they could about the Crown jewels and the Tower of London.

They each took categories away, did the research, then dropped their files onto a shared drive. After a few hours work, they then swapped subject matters, then started the research all over. This was how they would get three people's takes on what they could find, gather and interpret.

At the end of the day, with a few hard-working stragglers still in the Jurado Data offices, Sonia and Nick took the three of them out to an amazing seven-course taster menu at the high-quality Square restaurant in Mayfair. Not a word was said about the Tower and their day's findings. After dinner, they returned to the now deserted offices at One The Strand and settled into the large meeting room by Sonia's office.

Sonia opened. "Before we hear all about your findings guys, let me tell you where we are with all this." The four men shuffled in their seats as if to get comfortable, always content to hear her soft voice speak to them.

"I'm convinced that Bob nor Freddy said anything to the Met police about the Richmond job and given they were freed, it would appear they've got nothing that leads them to us or incriminates us. So good job with that, though I do feel it may only be a matter of time before something comes up that connects us to the bank hack and bitcoin transfer. So, hold that thought okay," she said, raising her hand and gathering her thoughts.

None of the men interrupted her, Peter and Nick just gave a slight, dutiful nod. Sonia continued.

"Amazingly we also seem to have got away with the Prado Dead Christ thing, despite apparently the Met possibly knowing something about it and passing this onto the Spanish Secret Services. Whilst the painting's been returned and will now be safe there once more, I think it's a fair assumption that the walls will close in on us soon for this as well."

The reality of possibly being caught, started to hit Peter who gave a prolonged frown.

Sonia assured him. "Don't worry Peter, I've got it covered." He relaxed. "Having been seen by this Eduardo chap at our embassy, we find ourselves in the position of having to do this one last job. We've no choice really, so if it's at all possible, we will."

There was no argument from the men, now hanging on her next words for what they'd each figured out by themselves.

Sonia gave them a comforting smile. "But let me tell you clearly, the moment we get clear from this job, we'll all get the hell out of this country on a private jet back to my place in Mexico! We'll be safe there."

The men were relieved to hear this and Nick added, "Thank heavens that's your view, Sonia. I think we were all starting to feel the pressure is building what with everything going on. I'm definitely in, we need to leave this all behind us the second we get out of the Tower." The others nodded, Nick looked at Peter, "Assuming that's possible Peter?"

Sonia said, "Over to you guys, tell us all about the Tower of London!"

Peter took over, referring to the notes and files they accumulated, with accompanying pictures to show them on his laptop.

"Probably the most famous, historic fortress in the world. Your embassy friend couldn't have picked a more challenging task for us, at least on the face of it."

Sonia and Nick got their first hint that this crazy idea just might have legs.

"William the Conqueror came over here in 1066 and decided to build the most impressive, dominating and oppressive fortress there ever was, right in the centre of London. The White Tower in the centre of today's much larger complex, was started during the 1070s and must have been a hell of a sight to Londoners at the time. He wanted us Brits to know who was boss and somewhere to use as a home, fortress, prison, armoury and bank. Masons came over from France, the labour was provided by the English and the Tower was finished around 1090, along with another thirty-five other castles all over the place."

"Not too much of a history lesson," suggested Sonia. Peter flicked over a few pages of notes.

"We all know that throughout its ten centuries of existence, this place has been seen as a symbol of the Crown, our monarchy, but also a reminder of respect, dominance and fear. Kings, queens, rivals and enemies have all been imprisoned here, tortured here, even murdered and executed here. 1471

Henry VI was murdered in the chapel, then the two children of his rival Edward IV, the Princes in the Tower, vanished in 1483. Their skeletons were discovered in 1674."

Sonia looked tired of the comings and goings of the British monarch's in-fighting. Peter pushed on wanting to give a flavour of the incredible history they were considering trespassing on. History they'd likely be adding to whether they succeeded or failed!

"Elizabeth the first, Lady Jane Grey, Guy Fawkes and Sir Walter Raleigh were all sent to the Tower. Lady Grey was executed by Henry VIII on Tower Green in 1554, she was only seventeen. We were even shooting German spies there in the last war."

Sonia looked impatient so Peter flicked past more pages.

"More relevant to our task in hand then. Firstly the Yeoman Warders or Beefeaters, been around since Edward IV 1461 as the royal bodyguards. So-called because they were allowed to eat as much beef as they wanted from the King's table! They were Tower and Monarch guards, but as we know they now really just provide tours for the three million annual visitors. Also, do a few ceremonial duties like the daily Key Ceremony unlocking and locking the main gates and so on."

"How many of them," asked Sonia.

"Thirty-seven plus one Chief Warder," said Peter. "They're all ex-armed forces of minimum twenty-two years service and must be deemed to be exemplary with good conduct medals. They swear the oath of royal allegiance and all live at the Tower with their families."

"A nice home if you can get it," joked Nick mimicking a Beefeater being able to tell someone 'I live at the Tower of London'."

"That brings me to another big influencer to our little jaunt there," said Peter. "There's basically a whole thriving town within the walls! You've got the thirty-eight Beefeaters, plus their families, and all the rest of the live-in staff, management, doctor, chaplain, maintenance… and the garrison!"

"How many are we talking in all?" asked Nick.

"Over one hundred and fifty people permanently at the Tower!"

"What about this garrison, that doesn't sound great?" said Sonia.

"It's not," agreed Peter. "This is where information on the web starts to dry up like a puddle in Arizona. We couldn't find anything anywhere online that told us how many soldiers are based at the Tower. All we got was that the Tower is the HQ of the Royal Regiment of Fusiliers, so it sounds like there could be a lot of them. Duties include ceremonial stuff and of course, protecting the Crown jewels! They carry loaded SA80 assault weapons."

"Any guess as to how many?" asked Nick, looking concerned.

"No idea. Ten maybe permanently? More for ceremonies, bands and big events?"

"Okay move on, we'll worry about that later," suggested Sonia.

"We're going to have to talk about it sometime," insisted Nick.

"Well obviously any plans will have to include totally avoiding contact with the armed guards," said Sonia curtly, "keep going Peter."

"Now onto the site and buildings." He pulled up a map of the complex. "There are a few entrances to the Tower. The main one through the Middle and Byward Towers including drawbridge and portcullis which everyone uses to this day. Two small doors on Tower Wharf by the river."

"What about getting in through them?

"No dice. You'd have to blow open the large wooden doors and then you're at the opposite end of the site to the jewels, with the guard's barracks in between. Lastly, via the Thames, you had Traitor's Gate. But that's long since been bricked up."

"Great!"

"You have a thirty-metre-wide dry moat, then a thirty-five-foot outer rampart wall, followed by a sixty-foot inner rampart wall."

"Where exactly are the crown jewels?" asked Sonia.

"Everyone who hasn't visited there, always assume they're in the actual Tower of London, the White Tower in the middle," started Peter.

Nick interrupted. "They're actually not in the White Tower, they're kept in the old Waterloo Barracks building."

"Precisely," said Peter. "Now called the Waterloo Block at the far end to the river, with the Chapel on one side and the Fusiliers barracks and museum right next to it on the other."

They studied the plan in more detail, with Peter going through each part of the site, buildings, walkways, greens and views, using photos pulled from the internet.

"Tell us about the Crown jewels themselves?" asked Sonia. "The embassy guy said we only need to take one item, what's the choice we have?"

Peter pulled up a new file. "There are over one hundred and forty items in the collection including swords, robes, rings and trumpets. There's a few smaller consort crowns and coronets. However, the real goodies of the whole collection are better known as the coronation regalia, used for crowing sovereigns since 1641 and occasional big ceremonies and the like. The first is the most sacred crown, of the eleventh century's Edward the Confessor. Weighs well over two kilograms." He pulled up a picture of each item as he spoke about them.

"Next is the gold sovereign's orb with a cross on top, which symbolizes the Christian world. They place it on the sovereign's right hand before it's put on the altar. Then we have the sceptre with cross, and rod with dove signifying the Holy Ghost. The monarch receives these in each hand just before crowning, signifying their control of uprisings, and gathering in and controlling men who stray."

Sonia sat up staring at the picture of the sceptre with cross. "Oh my God, look at the ice on that one. It's huge. Is it real?"

"It sure is. The Cullinan I or Star of Africa diamond. The largest quality white cut diamond in the world, at over five hundred and thirty carats!"

The single teardrop-shaped diamond was exquisite, even just its picture twinkled back at them tantalisingly. At one hundred and six grams, seventy-four facets and several inches across and high, it was huge. It sat near the top of the three-foot-long golden staff in its gold wire cradle, from which it can be removed to also be hung from the Cullinan II diamond as a pendant. Over the rest of the sceptre, another three hundred and thirty-three other smaller diamonds paled into insignificance, along with emeralds, rubies, sapphires and a round amethyst.

A rough diamond of over three thousand one hundred carats was discovered in South Africa in 1905, by the Premier mining firm, whose chairman was Thomas Cullinan. Having failed to sell it in London, the Transvaal government bought it for £150,000 and in respect and good faith, presented it as a gift to the United Kingdom's sovereign King Edward VII in 1907. Parliament was undecided on whether to accept the gift, but Winston Churchill persuaded the king to oblige.

Rather than transport it to the UK on the assigned armed steamboat in a guarded safe, the real Cullinan I was posted by registered mail in a plain box. The diamond onboard the steamboat was a fake to deter would-be thieves.

From the original massive raw stone, nine Cullinan diamonds were cleaved by Joseph Asscher in Amsterdam, the largest being the Star of Africa. The Cullinan I. Its closest sibling is the Cullinan II at three hundred and seventeen carats, which is mounted in the Imperial Crown.

Peter continued to the next slide. "I've saved the best til last. The Imperial State crown. This is the one the monarch wears after their coronation and for things like the state opening of parliament. This is *the* Queen's, or King's crown!"

Sonia, Nick and even the Albanian boys were impressed. Not just at the majestic appearance of the world's most famous crown, but knowing the power it symbolizes, its history and significance.

"It has over two-thousand eight-hundred diamonds including the Cullinan II which can be removed and used for a pendant with its larger Cullinan I. Also seventeen sapphires, eleven emeralds, two-hundred and sixty-nine pearls and four rubies including the Black Prince's. It's been around since the fifteenth century in ten versions, with Oliver Cromwell breaking up most of the crown jewels after the execution of King Charles I. It's been in its current form since 1937."

"So, if we're going to take anything," said Nick, "It's surely got to be the Imperial crown?" looking at Sonia.

She didn't seem so sure. "Perhaps," she said thoughtfully. "Okay, nice roundup Peter, now what about the actual security of these Crown jewels? If we can't get past that, the whole thing's off and I've got a difficult conversation with this embassy Eduardo fella!"

Peter looked despondent. "Ah, that's where information on the web dries up again. All we found was that a huge refurbishment took place in 2012, which means a massive security upgrade. Cost supposedly three million. We also know there's a large vault for the jewels." He stopped there.

Nick and Sonia waited for him to carry on. "Yes, well, what else then?"

"No, that's it! That is everything we could find. There's nothing online, in records, mentions by Beefeater tours, about the actual security surrounding the jewels! The public gets spirited past them on a moving walkway to manage a steady, fast flow in the jewel room. The jewels are inside bomb-proof glass cabinets and I can't find any way of getting into the security system they use!"

"What, so that's the end of that, is it?" said Nick leaning back in his chair resignedly.

"Come on guys, this is pathetic," said Sonia. "Just because we can't find an ABC guide to stealing the Crown jewels on the internet! What a surprise! Of course not, they're not going to publish their security info, are they! So how do we get to find out Peter?"

He pondered. "Well, the easiest way is for someone to get me access into the Tower's system, servers, or even just their intranet."

"How?"

"It only needs a dongle to be plugged into any one of their computers that's part of the system. I can then see if I can get access and start to have a look around. That may tell us more about the security there."

Nick had a thought. "Sonia, didn't you say the embassy chap said you'd need an insider?"

"He did."

"Let's face it, he's right," said Nick. "There's no way we can possibly do any of this without someone giving us the inside track on what goes on there. Peter needs all the info on CCTV, security, alarms, beams, guards, feeds to the police. We're blind at the moment."

"What about if you knew one of the soldiers posted there?" asked Peter.

Nick thought about it but quickly dismissed the idea. "Na, no chance. They'll be a lot younger than me and there's no way you'd turn one soldier against Queen and country. Betraying what they've signed up for and betraying their mates there, let alone having anything to do with stealing the Crown jewels. What we're talking about, it's treason!"

The word hung there for a moment, making them all appreciate how serious what they were contemplating really was.

"What about the staff at the Tower, maintenance, cleaners, there must be someone who might jump ship, for a lot of money?" suggested Sonia, trying to push the 'treason' word out of her mind.

"Maybe if I get into the system I can look at the staff list, do some research on everyone," mused Peter.

"Hang on," said Nick, "what about the Beefeaters? They'll

be more my age with their minimum of twenty-odd years of service. Do we have access to a list of these thirty-eight Yeoman Warders, Peter?"

Afrim leant over and showed Peter which file he thought he remembered putting some information into. Peter found it.

"Ah yes, here we are. They put all the Beefeater names onto some board somewhere. Here's a snapshot by some tourist we found on Pinterest."

Nick shuffled his chair closer and peered at the picture listing the names of the Warders. He scanned each one, delving into his memories of service in the Marines, hoping maybe a name sounded familiar.

"Well?" asked Sonia. "Recognise anyone?"

Nick started to shake his head. "Nope," as he finished going through the columns of names.

"Look again!"

Nick huffed but obliged Sonia.

No one made a sound, to let him concentrate fully on the screen.

"No way!" exclaimed Nick. "Barney Smith! I missed it the first time. I wonder if that's the Barney Smith I think I met out in Afghanistan? It couldn't be, he was just a bloody cook! Great food though. We weren't close mates but had a few chats with him out there. Nice chap, grumpy sod though."

They all looked at Nick and Sonia gave one of her cheeky smiles. "Maybe our way in?"

Nick's mobile rang, it was Max.

"Hi mate," said Nick, "you okay, it's quite late?"

"I'm fine thanks Nick, just a quick call," said Max. "I've given a lot of thought to what you said to me, and, well, it's hard to turn down such a big payday if that's really still on offer, for this big job you mentioned."

"What are you saying then, Max?"

"Count me in!"

14

Barney Smith was a large Scotsman in his fifties with greying hair and round face, which changed from jovial to sulky as quickly as his demeanour and mood could also. Twenty-five years in the army had gone by quickly, helped by numerous postings abroad, many different jobs including a gunner, engineering, catering and training, and also three marriages and three divorces. Ex-wives all agreed he was always far too 'up and down all the time'.

In 2006 he'd been posted to Kandahar in Afghanistan with the 105 Regiment Royal Artillery, a rare foreign assignment, in support of other regiments on the front line including the Marine Commandos. At that time Barney had opted to try his hand in the regiment's catering division and was working as one of many chefs turning out great nosh for the combative and support soldiers out there. His toad in the hole, sausages in Yorkshire pudding batter, was always the talk of the camps there.

That's where he'd come across one of the more senior green beret Commandos, Colour Sergeant Nick Hawkins, or as everyone seemed to refer to him as, Fifty.

They got talking because of Fifty's over-enthusiastic requests and pleading for Barney to amend the weekly menu to include more of his special 'toad in the hole'. They found they had a couple of memorable things in common. They both wanted to find something after their duty to the Queen that would make them lots of money. And they both supported Manchester United football club.

Barney had eventually left the army and with no family or wife to return to, nor entrepreneurial idea or business to set up, he consoled himself with the security and comforts of becoming a Yeoman Warder at the Tower of London.

There was a great community within the Tower walls, a village atmosphere, free accommodation, good pay, prestige and a bit of a challenge for him to conquer. Not the challenge of being on a battlefield, or stripping down a tank, but the challenge of memorizing all the historical facts and figures of the Tower. A prerequisite to being able to handle throngs of eager, inquisitive tourists.

He'd settled into life at the Tower, got over his nerves doing up to eight tours a week for visitors, whose top questions were always, 'are the crown jewels real?' and 'where did they carry out the executions?'.

But his demons shadowed him wherever he went and over the last four years at the Tower, he'd been summoned by the Chief Warder on four occasions for unprofessional, rude behaviour. The complaints came from both members of the public and his fellow Beaffeaters, one citing 'constantly grumpy, miserable attitude towards them and the job making them feel depressed!'.

The Chief Warder had on the last visit to his office, given Barney a written warning. Which meant one more half-justified complaint and he would join a very short list of Warders who since their beginnings, had been dismissed. Their names had been removed from the honours board.

Unfortunately, this only served to fuel his high's and low's, more so the low's and Barney himself knew it was only a matter of time before the inevitable happened. Over the last few days, he had started to think about the wording of his resignation letter and what on earth he'd then do with himself when he left the Tower village.

It was then he found a message left in his apartment by reception, for him to call back a number, the note said, 'Really miss your toad in the hole, our team ManU not doing so well these days!'. He took a few moments to think about it, everyone liked his toad in the hole, then he remembered who this must be. Fifty!

Nick was just leaving the Strand office to meet with Barney. He'd offered to take him to lunch on his day off at Le Gavroche restaurant in Upper Brook Street just off Park Lane.

"You've got Peter's special mini-USB stick?"

Nick patted his pocket. "Yup."

"Offer him twenty-five million," said Sonia, "and go up to fifty if you have to. We've got all that bitcoin fund to play with. None of this works without someone like him with us, and he's the only one we've identified so far Nick."

Sonia was flush with cash in the bank with her own fortune in the UK and the several billion offshore. She could afford to throw it around to get people like Max and this Barney Smith on board.

"Will do, he's a Scotsman so I suspect if he's got nothing better going on, he'll take the twenty-five."

"Just one other thing," said Sonia before Nick left her office, "how are you feeling about bringing Max in, completely?"

Nick could tell the question was loaded. "I was happy to have him with us, we need more people than we've got so someone like him will really help us. Why?"

"If you believe Simmons was telling you the truth about not knowing we did the Prado job and let's assume Freddy didn't know either or say anything, that only leaves Max doesn't it?" Sonia gave Nick a spurious look.

"I see where you're coming from, but I still vouch for him," defended Nick. "Still doesn't make any sense he'd snitch on a job that he helped us with?"

"Just until I say, Nick, let's bring Max in but I don't want him knowing any of the details about the Tower and Crown jewels. Keep him warm, fluffy info's fine, but nothing that could incriminate us if we fell out with him for some reason?"

Nick shrugged his shoulders and gave her a puzzled frown, but agreed.

Meeting someone you served with in a conflict zone after fifteen years, was like greeting your long-lost brother. Nick and Barney embraced outside the restaurant and immediately struck up a comfortable, enthusiastic exchange of information about what they did in the services, families, jobs and passions. The grumpy old Scot was on good form and on a high, pleased to reminisce about the good old days when he was in the army, with a like-minded soul.

Nick asked the chef at the famous restaurant to come and meet Barney and insisted he shared his secret way of doing toad in the hole. They had a fabulous meal and a couple of bottles of very expensive wine.

By the end of the meal, Barney had given Nick all the background and circumstances he needed to know, to ascertain there might be a chance he would consider helping them, but he had to tread carefully. It was a big ask.

Nick settled the bill to Barney's delight, especially as it came to almost five-hundred pounds, and suggested they continued their time together on a stroll in Hyde Park. They crossed over the two lanes of Park Lane and started walking past Speakers Corner near Marble Arch.

"I'm glad you've done so well for yourself Fifty," praised Barney with genuine feeling. "We always thought we'd make it big didn't we. At least one of us has eh."

"What if I was to say you could hit the big time, within the next week or two?" Nick tensed waiting to see his reaction.

Barney thought he was joking. "What big time? Lottery win!"

"Twenty-five million cash, and then disappear abroad forevermore." Nick put on his best 'serious' tone.

"What?"

"I mean it, Barney."

"What in hell's name would I have to do to get twenty-five million? I don't like the sound of this, must be totally screwy!"

"All I need is some information, a few hours of your time, a USB stick put into a PC and then one night's work," explained Nick, simplifying it all.

"What?" Nick could see Barney's brain churning through

the last few statements trying to compute what was happening. His eyebrows then narrowed and his face took on a look of sheer horror. Turning his head slowly to Nick and looking him dead in the eyes, he said, "You're not thinking of doing anything stupid at the Tower are you?"

They sat on a bench near the Reformer's Tree memorial and Nick committed himself and the Jurado team. He told Barney what they were planning, what they were being forced to plan.

Barney listened in shock, interjecting occasionally with "Don't tell me anymore, I don't want to hear it" and "I suppose it could be possible" and then "twenty-five million doesn't sound much for what you're asking".

Nick had gambled everything on taking him into their confidence. If he'd said no then we're sunk anyway, if he shopped them they would go to prison. But after half an hour of Nick's best persuasion and the way Barney felt about his employment at the Tower, his army service and the way his life had turned out, he was starting to come closer to agreeing.

Nick played his ace card. "Barney, you deserve so much more and this will get you everything you've ever wanted. You'll be able to do anything you want, have anything you want. I know I can persuade my boss that the appropriate fee for your services, should be doubled!"

Barney froze for a moment. Then lurched at Nick, to give him a light, long hug. He sobbed once and fought back a tear. Then before releasing his embrace, whispered softly into Nick's ear, "So that's fifty million pounds, and I get paid whether you succeed or fail, yes?"

Barney was thinking to himself, 'There's no way on earth anyone's going to get into the vault, not in a million years!'.

Nick got out a digital recorder and placed it on the bench between them and they spent the next hour and a half going through everything Barney knew about the Tower and Crown jewels. He knew a lot from his privileged role as Beefeater, tour guide and Tower historian.

Barney explained the missing information about the soldiers there. He told Nick that "They rotate duty at the Tower between five Guards regiments, the Grenadiers, Coldstream, Scots, Irish and Welsh. There are precisely fifteen soldiers there, along with six NCO's and one officer." Twenty-two, more than Peter had guessed, not good.

He didn't know exactly how many CCTV cameras but there were a lot, especially in and around the jewel room, maybe up to a hundred, covering every single part of each room from many angles. He said, "The CCTV could be accessed by the on-site management team and was monitored day and night offsite somewhere by a security firm."

"Motion alarms were installed but so as to avoid false callouts from the police or guards, had been given five-minute delays so staff had plenty of time to cancel them. After all, who would be stupid enough to try to steal any of the Crown jewels!"

"Because of the presence of the soldier guards, most doorways throughout the Tower and jewel house have kept their original old thick wooden doors, hinges and bolts. They are either locked with sliding bars or old locks and keys."

Barney said "The Met police including the fast response armed squad were on twenty-four-seven alert to respond to anything at the Tower within eight minutes or less. I can't remember the last time this was ever required, given there are armed soldiers on-site, but I think the Met do a response drill every few months, just to keep everyone on their toes."

"What about this Waterloo Block and gaining entry?" asked Nick.

"The Waterloo Block was built in 1845 originally to house up to one thousand soldiers. The Crown jewels have been there since 1967 and there was a major refurb and upgrade done in 2012. The building comprises mainly museum space with offices upstairs and of course the lower level vault or crypt."

Nick held up his hand for Barney to stop for a moment,

while they waited for a couple of elderly ladies to slowly stroll past them. "Go on," he said, checking the digital recorder was still recording. "What about entry and exit points?"

"This long building has the two tall octagonal turrets on either side of the central entrance and square larger turrets on the front corners. There are four floors, the underground vaults, three normal floors and a small roof space. The ground floor windows have all been blacked out and bricked up behind the window facades. There are quite a few ground floor doorways but they're all thick wooden, bolted, heavy doors, two in the centre front being the main entrance and rear doors, a single door front left end, another rear left. Then there are two more single doors at the chapel end and another two at the barracks end where visitors are ejected after their visit."

"What about the roof," posed Nick.

"I've been up there a few times. There are two small central access doors, one to each end of the slate roof with lead flashing. There are about twelve roof vents and nine or so skylights."

"How are those two roof doors locked?"

"Just a key and sliding bolt."

Nick was thinking through how they were going to get into the building, avoiding the soldiers on the ground floor outside.

"And the jewel room, casings and vault? It's near impossible to get any information on these, especially as cameras are forbidden in there?"

Barney sighed. "Okay, assuming you can somehow get into the whole security system, this is where I'm afraid it gets hard, no, impossible."

"Just take me through it," insisted Nick.

"The underground vault was installed in 1967. The walls are lined with six-inch thick steel panels encased inside reinforced concrete, underground. So no access whatsoever to tunnel in there through that. To control the one-way flow of three million visitors every year, the monarch's Crown jewels regalia inside the main vault, have a moving walkway passing on either side of the display casings. Dark walls, velvet display stands and dim lighting all serve to enhance the focus and dazzling presentation of the jewels, as well as hide the many CCTV cameras and air circulation vents."

"How big are the vents?"

"Maybe big enough for a cat! Not people."

"And the vault access, the doors?"

Barney shook his head dismissively. "Steel doors maybe ten inches thick, weighing perhaps a ton or more each door, and with multiple two-inch diameter steel bar bolts. Two doors each end of the main vault to allow for the two lines of visitors entry and exit of the jewel room."

Nick frowned. With the best will in the world, he couldn't see how they could get through such fortifications. Barney read his mind.

"Sorry, Fifty, no-one's gonna crack into that vault. It's for the Crown jewels for God's sake! Even if you have the right equipment, you'd need a day undisturbed to make any impression on it!"

Nick was pensive. "Has anyone ever tried to steal the crown jewels before?"

"Oh yes," said Barney sarcastically cheerful.

"Really?" said Nick with interest, but misplaced.

"In 1671! Not since, and for good reason," laughed Barney. "A Colonel Blood and accomplices got the Jewel House Keeper drunk, beat him up and made off with the Imperial State Crown, Sceptre and Orb. Remember this is pre alarms, vaults, CCTV and so on."

"What happened to them?"

"The Keeper's son returned and raised the alarm, the jewels were recovered and can you believe it, Charles II pardoned Colonel Blood. Despite his treasonous theft, the King granted him five hundred pounds worth of land for his troubles!"

Nick chatted with Barney for another twenty minutes firing lots of quick answer questions at him. Many questions were about if and when such things like cleaning and maintenance were done in the jewel rooms, as clearly this couldn't be done during visiting hours. The recorder took everything in, to later be played back in its entirety to the others back at the Jurado offices.

"You mentioned something about a USB stick, Fifty?" said Barney, hoping they were almost done now and thinking of the fortune coming his way soon.

"Right. Before we give this a green light, I just need you to put this USB device into a computer at the Tower," explained Nick.

"Simple, I'll shove it into the back of mine," said Barney nonchalantly.

"Do you have full access to the management and security systems and servers?"

"No."

"Then that's no good," said Nick. Holding it up, "This has got to go into a PC that has full access all systems, who's would that be then?"

"My boss the Chief Warder would have access to everything."

"Can you get this into his PC, without being caught, and also so that he can't see it when it's in? It needs to be in there permanently," insisted Nick.

Barney visualized his boss's small office. "Should be okay, he has a desktop tower PC but it's under his desk on the floor, the back of it is covered by the desk panel."

"Great!" said Nick passing him the small stick.

"But if this is wifi I won't have his local password?"

"No need, this works independently of wifi, it has a micro sim in it so will transmit out of the Tower directly to us," smiled Nick. Barney took the stick carefully.

"Anything else Fifty?"

"I'll contact you if we have any other burning questions and we'll need you for at least one more meeting for the final plan briefing, okay?"

"No problem," said Barney, thinking this was going to be the easiest fifty million he'd ever dreamt of. "Just checking, you don't of course want me to be involved when you do this, if you do this, do you?"

Nick gave him a surprised look. "Well of course we do Barney! You don't think we're paying you all that money for that quick verbal tour of the Tower, do you? You'll be right there with us old chap. We'll need you to help get us in!"

"What!" Barney looked shocked and went slightly white.

"We'll tell you what you need to do at the briefing once we've figured it out ourselves," said Nick, "but don't worry, you'll be leaving with us when the job's done and onto a plane straight out of the country!"

Barney realized Nick was deadly serious about thinking this theft of the Crown jewels could actually be done. He must have gone completely mad!

"But what about the steel vault?"

"Well, it's not always shut, is it?"

Barney looked bemused, then the penny dropped from a conversation they'd had earlier.

"And how the hell are you going to deal with the soldiers all around outside? You can't just walk through the front door?"

Nick gave Barney a big hug and patted his back.

"You just leave that to Fifty me ol' son! We'll stay well clear of the guards."

15

The Tower's Chief Yeoman Warder was making his way back to his small office for a nice cup of tea. It had been a busy morning. He liked to run a tight ship with his thirty-seven Beefeaters. Politeness, punctuality, smart uniforms and hard work were the order of the day. Having served at the Tower himself for almost fifteen years after an exemplary military service himself, he didn't like any loose ends or worries. But right now he had exactly that on his mind. Barney Smith.

He liked Barney, he was diligent and mostly an affable chap. He just couldn't tolerate those mood swings. He was certain that Barney had some kind of mental health issue, bi-polar or something, that really needed diagnosing and seeing to.

After three verbal warnings and one written warning, he felt the writing was on the wall. Barney was going to mess it up again, somehow. Then he'd have to be dismissed.

But that would reflect badly on him, the Chief Warder and he couldn't have that. He was going to have to bite the bullet and sit Barney down one day, soon, and ever so politely and carefully suggest he considered resigning. Before the next complaint.

He didn't relish the prospect though of broaching the subject with someone as volatile as Barney. He could get angry, or start crying or storm out, much to their equal embarrassment. That would be awful and reflect badly on him again. People might think he was bullying staff. Barney could raise a constructive dismissal allegation.

The thought of it all started to stress the Chief out, so he put the matter to one side. He could deal with it later. What he needed now was that cup of tea.

He pushed the narrow wooden door aside and entered his cosy office. "What on earth…!" he exclaimed.

He was greeted with the bizarre sight of the backside of one of his Beefeaters in full uniform, grovelling on the ground on all fours! The man quickly stood up. It was Barney Smith.

"Sorry Sir!" Barney said quickly.

"What the hell are you doing down there man? In fact, why are you even in my office," asked the Chief, who now noticed Barney was clutching something in his hand.

Barney fumbled for the right words. "I'm sorry sir, you see, oh, it's a bit awkward to explain…"

"Spit it out, man!"

"Well, I wanted to have a quiet word with you, sir. It's about all these warnings you've had to give me."

The Chief's interest sparked, "Oh yes?"

"I'm worried that I might slip up again and frankly, I don't want to do anything to bring myself, or you, or the Tower into disrepute."

The Chief's stress quickly evaporated as he detected Barney might be about to suggest some kind of compromise deal to leave. "Go on."

"Well now's probably a bad time, but I just wanted to see if we could discuss the option of me resigning, so I maintain my clean sheet? I haven't decided yet mind you, it's just something I've been thinking about, just wanted to sound you out about it? Never mind, I'm sorry I barged in," said Barney as he shuffled towards the door.

"Hang on!" said the Chief. "Look, Barney. I've been thinking about it as well and frankly, I think it might be a good idea, for you to consider at least." He patted Barney's shoulder. "When you're ready to come and see me about it, I'll do everything in my power to make it all okay for you, if and when you leave."

"Thank you, sir, I appreciate that, leave it with me then?"

Barney opened the door and was almost out when the Chief called out again. "One last thing Barney!"

"Sir?"

"What's that you've got in your hand?"

Barney looked down at his clasped fingers apologetically.

"Well?" demanded the Chief.

Barney slowly opened them up. "It's just my long service medal sir, it fell off my tunic whilst I was waiting for you. I'm sorry sir, I'll get the clasp fixed immediately!"

The Chief glanced at the purple ribboned medal with the Queen's head on the coin. "That's quite alright Barney. Run along now. Can't keep the visitors waiting!" said the Chief, relieved that Barney seemed open to the suggestion of an amicable resignation discussion. One less worry.

"Of course, sir," said Barney as he exited. He shut the door behind him and had a wry smile on his face.

Hidden behind the desk panel, Nick's special dongle stick was now securely plugged into one of the free USB ports of the Chief's computer.

Peter Whistler lived in an impressive mansion on the Crown Estate in Oxshott Surrey. Neighbours included footballers, pop stars, entrepreneurs and bankers. Most of the houses sat behind large electric gates, hiding the pools, tennis courts, cherished supercars and new Range Rovers.

He and Sonia had decided to use the house as their base for the final planning and build-up to the Tower job, as Sonia and Nick's London homes were less private and weren't suitable for storing equipment.

The team had been busy working non-stop on reviewing the details that Barney had given Nick. Relooking into the layout of the site, drawing up plans, options, entry and escape, covering all eventualities of what could go wrong and dealing with guards.

A plan was starting to fall into place, which gave everyone renewed vigour in their separate activities. Peter had a direct plug into the Tower's servers and had gained access to their emails and security system. He was now monitoring communications and their diaries for any opportunities coming up where the vault would be open, out of visiting hours. He was also figuring out the best way to deal with the various elements of the security system including alarms, feeds to the police and monitoring station and the CCTV.

Sonia was making a number of calls and pulling in favours including obtaining a particular piece of kit from her father's fire equipment operation. She was also arranging for a private jet to be available on standby, at nearby north-west London Denham aerodrome.

Nick, Saban and Afrim were handling the sourcing of numerous items of equipment and ordnance. Long past and somewhat dodgy ex-military contacts were being sought, along with some even more undesirable East End mobsters. These people could get their hands on specialized kit, most weapons and military technology within days, for the right price.

They now had the basis of a detailed plan which they would run by Barney Smith, whose view and participation would be critical if they were to have any chance of success.

Sonia would also now update the Spanish embassy man Eduardo on what they were thinking. There were a couple of areas that required his help. In particular, how they would get into the Waterloo Block and then escape from it, likely amidst utter chaos.

She was conscious of his insistence that his man Santiago must also join the mission, so that had to be organized. They also wanted to bring in Max Sargent, but not too early just in case he did have something to do with leaking information out. They would include him once the job had a date and he could be watched closely by Nick, who still trusted him implicitly. They needed another pair of hands anyway, so had to take the chance with him and just manage it carefully.

Everything was coming together nicely, for the most outrageous, daring, high profile attempted break-in and theft the world had ever seen.

Then the break they'd waited for suddenly appeared one day, as Peter was looking through the emails being sent around the Tower's senior staff. He almost missed the innocuous title, but once he'd read its contents his heart missed a beat! This was it, their one opportunity. Everything they'd planned would have to hinge around this event and date, in just several days time! He got on the phone to Sonia and read it out to her.

Subject;	*Travelator repair*
From;	*Head of Maintenance*
To;	*Governor of the Tower of London, Captain of the Tower Guards, Head of Security, Chief Yeoman Warder*

Complaints are now coming in on a daily basis regarding the grinding noise of the right-hand lane moving walkway in the main crown jewels vault room.

So as not to disrupt visitors by closing the exhibit during the day, I need to urgently request an out of hours maintenance slot be diarized this Thursday, for my team and the manufacturers specialist to have access.

The travelator will have to be dismantled, the metal grind issue located, replaced, filed or adjusted, then reassembled.

I've scheduled work to commence at 9pm. They estimate the job could take six to eight hours, the cleaning team are booked for 6am in plenty of time before we open for visitors.

Please liaise with your teams to grant vault access and necessary security provision.

Sonia had replied, "Oh my God Peter! This is it. It's the only chance we'll get. Tell the others!"

Nick had called Max to tell him the job was on and that he'd pick him up from his home later that day. "Make sure you lock up, if all goes well Max, you won't be returning there again anytime soon!"

Whilst waiting for Nick, Max had rung Si Lawson at MI5 and told him *the job* looked as though it was going ahead in the next few days and he would message as soon as he knew what was happening, or got more information proving the Richmond hack was done by Jurado.

Si had jokingly said to Max, "Try not to rob any more museums or banks eh!"

"Not funny thanks Si."

Nick collected Max and drove down the A3, then off into Oxshott.

"So what's the job then?" Max asked.

But Nick was still being cautious. "Not now Max, let's just all gather together tonight, then we spend all day tomorrow going through the briefings, ready for the job tomorrow night." He checked Max, who gave no reaction. "A bit like we did for the Prado thing. That went pretty well didn't it?"

"I guess so."

They pulled into the gated entrance with a short driveway, leading up to a large, new-looking mansion. The grounds were surrounded by trees or fencing and was completely private from other nearby properties. There were already quite a few cars parked up. Max prepared himself to put on the show of his life, again.

As they got out of the car Nick came round to Max's side. "Oh just one thing Max, hope you understand old pal, but no mobiles from here in?" He held out his hand waiting for Max to hand over his phone.

Max hid his shock at the request and casually placed it into Nick's palm. "Sure. Who would I possibly want to call anyway," thinking to himself, how on earth would he get a message to Si now. He assumed they'll be watching him more closely. He felt bare without his mobile, but he'd just have to go with it and worry about communicating when the time came. For now, he had to play along.

He followed Nick inside the sumptuous house, with marble

floors, high ceilings, quality décor and finishes. From the hallway, Max could see through to the rear where there was a large patio and pool, and long well-kept lawn leading down to a tennis court at the far end. Around the hall, there was a plush office, a snooker room, a small stairway leading down to the cinema, a large open-plan kitchen, an extravagant dining room and a comfortable lounge.

Sonia came out to greet Max with a single friendly kiss on the cheek, followed by Peter Whistler, who scurried off again into the office. Saban and Afrim were playing snooker and as expected barely looked up or acknowledged Max's presence.

"And this is Santiago Lopez, Max," introduced Nick.

The trim, powerful man stepped up to Max with a smile and gave him a very firm handshake.

"Hola mi amigo."

From his stature, buzz-cut and handshake, Max was already deducing this was a tough, military man not to be trifled with.

"Max Sargent," he offered, then looking at Nick. "And Santiago is joining us…?"

"He represents, shall we say, the interested party."

Max knew the top Spanish speaking countries were Mexico, Columbia, Argentina and Spain, and had to ask him, "Where are you from Santiago?"

"Espana," he replied. Then added, "Forgive me, I do speak English, I just always start with Spanish in case people I meet speak my mother language, it's far easier for me."

"No hablo Espanol," joked Max.

"I didn't know you spoke Spanish Max?" said Nick.

"I don't," said Max. Nick and Santiago laughed politely, while Max was wondering what organization this Santiago represented. When Nick had told him 'foreign power', surely he didn't mean government authority, the Spanish Intelligence Services? Or could it be a corrupt business or even the mafia?

"And have you handed over your mobile as well?" Max

asked, expecting him to say yes.

Nick quickly chipped in. "Ar yes, Santiago, house rules from here onwards, sorry, I wasn't here when you arrived. No mobiles," holding out his hand and nodding at it.

Santiago looked shocked, but seeing there was maybe some play-acting going on, perhaps for Max's benefit, handed over his mobile, shrugging it off.

Max couldn't tell if Nick had genuinely forgotten to ask, or that the trust levels for himself were starting to crack.

"Come on Max," said Nick, "let's get a drink and sit outside while we're waiting for Peter's chef to work his magic on our dinner."

"He's got a chef as well," said Max, "do you all have chef's?"

"You'll be able to get your own chef soon eh Max," joked Nick, pouring himself a freshly squeezed orange juice with a dash of vodka.

Max got the same drink and they sat by the pool. "Fifty, if this is all going down tomorrow night, I'm here, ready to go, you know you can trust me, I think you'll understand me asking you again what it is we're going to be doing?"

"Patience Max," said Nick patting Max on the knee, "all will be revealed tomorrow I promise. We've put in a lot of work and research, including insiders, into preparing for this. You'll see that tomorrow, I think you'll be impressed, once you get over the shock of the bloody-mindedness of what we're attempting."

Max was boiling with frustration inside, desperate to find out what on earth he was now signing up to with this bunch.

"I assume from the fact Peter's running around like a madman, that there's a heavy reliance on him sorting out the technology and security elements? You mentioned a while back that you'd done other jobs that didn't involve you having to be present? Come on Nick, give me some assurances and comfort, I'm feeling pretty exposed here?" Max was desperate to find out more.

Nick sat back and gave a reconciliatory sigh. "Well, I suppose we'll all be off to Mexico tomorrow night so there's no harm telling you. Did you hear about that London bank, that recently got hacked into?"

'Bingo!' thought Max, hiding his excitement. He played along.

"I think I saw something on the news. Wasn't it Richmond bank, the one the government part-owns?"

Nick was now showing off. "Yup. We did that!"

"You're kidding," said Max, wishing he had a recording device. "Wasn't there something about bitcoins?" he said innocently.

"Sure was. It was mainly Peter who managed to get into their system, with a little help from the bank's IT Director." Nick paused, "He was the chap we visited the other day, the one with the wasp sting."

"Let me guess," said Max, "he was going to talk or something?"

"Probably. Anyway, Peter got in for the customer data, couldn't get into the private accounts, then low and behold, found out they hadn't upgraded the security of the bank's bitcoin fund, so syphoned off about two billion!"

"If I had that much I'd disappear. I wouldn't be contemplating yet another risky job, like we are now?"

"Well, we kinda owe someone," Nick pondered on his words. "That's not quite right, let's just say we found ourselves in a position of *having* to do this job tomorrow."

"Is that why Santiago is here?"

"You could look at it that way, but he'll be another useful pair of hands. Sonia says we shouldn't be fooled by the big smiles."

Max thought to himself, 'I never was!'. He was also trying to think about how he could get a message to Si Lawson.

Inside, Sonia came into the office where Peter was going through his part to play for the Tower job, checking access and programs were setup ready.

"I forgot to ask Peter, did you go through Bob Simmons' laptop, the one Nick retrieved for us?" she asked.

Peter looked up but not at Sonia, slightly irritated by the interruption. "Honestly, no, as you can see I've been a little bit busy since then, with the small job you've given me of hacking into the bloody Tower of London security system! Why is Bob's laptop such a big deal anyway?"

"Okay, okay, you're doing brilliantly as always Peter. Keep it up, priority the Tower. I just wanted you to check if there's anything on there that might tell us if he snitched to the Met or someone else, about the Richmond or Prado jobs. Someone out there can't be trusted and I don't want it messing anything up."

"I'll get round to it maybe tomorrow, I can set up an access and search program to get into it, without deleting all the files with a reset."

Sonia was satisfied with that and didn't want to put any more pressure or requests on her technology guru. "All okay for tomorrow then?"

Peter momentarily gave up concentrating on what he was doing and turned to Sonia with a sigh.

"Yes, all okay, but I'm going to have to do things differently. I've not been able to get access to the right things at both the Tower servers and simultaneously the outside security firm's system. Looping CCTV's and disarming selected beams and alarms can't be done."

"What does that mean for the boys going in?"

"I'll explain it all tomorrow, but basically I can buy them time up to the point they get to the vault room. Then all hell will break loose at the Tower, but guards and staff there won't be able to notify anyone outside, like police or extra security. I'm going to break off all the Tower's comms with the outside world, just long enough for the job I hope. Of course, people around the outside of the Tower complex will then know something's up, but we can delay them getting in."

Sonia looked dismayed. "Are we still okay to do this?"

"Oh yes, we've still got all this sorted, don't worry, I'm across everything that'll happen. The boys should have a clear path in and out, as long as they deal with everyone inside the building, and we can keep those soldiers at bay in their barracks of course!"

Sonia forced a smile. "Let's hope so! Come on, let's join the others for dinner."

The following day Peter, Sonia, Nick, Max, Afrim, Saban and Santigo all assembled in the lounge. Peter had linked his laptop to the huge television on the wall. Max settled himself down on the sofa and felt quite tense, waiting for the big reveal of what the job was. He was reminded that everyone else seemed to know what the target was but him. He was clearly on their 'suspicious list'.

Peter pressed the mouse button and the first slide came up onto the screen. It hit Max like a train! The picture was an aerial view of the Tower of London site. It showed the whole of the surrounding dry moat, the double rampart walls and other buildings, all encircling the famous square White Tower in the middle, with its distinctive corner turrets. It took Max all of a second to work out what the likely target was going to be from such a picture!

"Tell me you're kidding!" he said. The others knew it would be a shock to him and laughed at seeing Max's face drop.

Nick reassured him. "This is it, Max. The big one. I know you'll be fine, we dealt with much worse in the Marine's didn't we?"

Sonia also wanted to make him feel supported, she couldn't have anyone bailing at this time. "Max my dear, just trust us, Peter's got this whole thing covered. Let him explain everything and if you're still unsure at the end of the day, we'll talk about leaving you out."

The others looked surprised for a moment, then they and Max all figured any option to not do this would never happen. They were in it now, right up to their necks. And so was Max, who sat there dumbfounded. He just wanted to call Si on his mobile and have the cavalry sent in to bust up this whole operation, right now. Be he couldn't do that. No phone, and besides, looking round the room it was clear to him that any dissent in the ranks would have a queue of them waiting their turn to bump him off!

Max thought to himself 'get me out of here!' but added for the benefit of his audience, "Tell me all about it then?"

The whole morning was spent with Peter taking the lead as the mastermind of the operation, explaining every last detail from start to finish. How they'd get into the complex, then the Waterloo Block, past guards and down into the vault area where they'd be doing the maintenance. He went through what the security was, alarms, CCTV, locks, Beefeaters and guards. Critically Peter and Nick talked through what their insider, Barney Smith, would be doing. His role was 'key' to the success of the whole operation.

Then Sonia showed them what the prize was. They didn't need to take anything more than a single Crown jewel item. Given the critical time constraints, she explained how they would get their hands on the star prize.

Nick then covered off disabling the guards and preventing them from all rushing into the block and trapping them in the underground vault area. Also their retreat and exit from the building and the Tower site.

Listening carefully Max couldn't believe that he was actually starting to think this could work! They seemed to have got intel on every piece of the jigsaw puzzle. He'd then jolt himself back to the reality, that he was about to take part in what would be the most audacious, treasonous robbery in history. Did these people really believe they'd be safe anywhere after this? As he contemplated just hopping over the walls of the mansion and do a runner, he had to remind himself that MI5 would want to know exactly who this powerful backer was.

It sounded from Nick as though someone had something

against the Jurado team and was forcing them to do this. Surely not for money, there were easier targets than the Tower and besides, how could you ever sell any of the crown jewels, unless of course to a private collector. Or was this simply to humiliate the monarchy, or the police, or the whole of the United Kingdom?

After lunch, they all went into the large double garage which adjoined the main house, where Max could see all the equipment laid out. There seemed to be an awful lot of stuff that had to be carried in, but Max realized that spread across himself and the other four men going in, it was possible, despite the unusual means of entry they were planning.

Neatly arranged around the garage floor were their modes of transport, electronic devices, various weapons, specialist grenades, masks, radio communications, cutting equipment and other strange-looking items including small, compressed gas canisters.

Nick and Peter explained each item and asked the men to examine and check the kit assigned to them. Max looked through his pile of equipment, holding each item one by one. He couldn't help but be impressed with the thought, planning, technology and preparation these guys had done. With this kit, he found himself again thinking 'this absurd heist could work!'.

At the end, Sonia suggested, "Why don't you all relax now for a few hours. We'll go through everything once more in quick version at say six PM, then plenty of time to get your kit and be ready to leave here at midnight. Peter and I will leave earlier and set up at my Edgware Road apartment. There's a dark moon tonight with cloud cover, so there'll only be street lighting in the City with low visibility at the Tower. Good news for us!"

Nick came over to Max to check his Commando friend was still in good shape for the job. "Now you've heard everything, Max, you okay with it all?"

Max nodded. "I'd never have thought it was possible. I

have to take my hat off to your guys, you seem to have covered all the bases pretty well under the circumstances. You've taken this very seriously haven't you, especially Peter."

"This is serious stuff! Having a rather large fund does also help get things sorted fast," said Nick.

Max dived in, to see if there was any doubt in Nick's mind. "You do realize this is treason!"

Nick laughed. "Oh come on Max, that's a bit strong. Anyway, that's when you betray the sovereign."

"Or your country!" added Max.

Nick hesitated for a moment. Max thought just maybe he detected a hint of self-questioning, then he turned to Max changing the subject. "Come on Max, challenge you to a few frames of snooker," pulling him off to the games room.

As they passed the office Max looked longingly at the computers spread across the large desk. They seemed to look back at him tantalizingly, beckoning him to risk using them for just one minute to get a message out to Si at MI5. But it was clear to him, that his old Colour Sergeant was going to stick to him like glue from now until the job was done. He couldn't send for backup, nor tell Si what was happening, and if he bailed out, they'd kill him. Max was trapped. A treason trap!

Later, while they were playing snooker, Sonia got a call from Eduardo Garcia, a final check-in.

"So you're all set to go in tonight, well done Sonia," he said.

She checked with him, "You just make sure you've got your contributions all lined up, if either of them fails, the whole thing's screwed."

"Don't you worry," said Eduardo, "my men will get you full access to the building we've spoken about, just go to the delivery bay as I told you. They'll make sure your boys get to the top alright."

"And the exit?"

"Yes all arranged. My man will be on standby by one AM onwards and can be there in five minutes."

"Good," said Sonia. "we just might be able to pull off this crazy idea of yours. We'll see!"

Eduardo chuckled to himself. "This will be such an insult to the British, so embarrassing for them! For you and me Sonia, this is payback, they'll be the laughingstock of the whole world. It'll be their ultimate humiliation!"

16

The skyscraper at 122 Leadenhall is one of the tallest buildings in the City of London, at seven-hundred and thirty-eight feet high. Affectionately known as the 'Cheesegrater', due to its wedge shape resembling the kitchen utensil, it towers above most of the buildings clustered about the Bishopsgate financial district, near the River Thames.

From the top, there is a view across all of London and to its south are landmarks including The Shard, HMS Belfast on the Thames and Tower Bridge. Also, the Cheesegrater looks down onto one of the most iconic sites in the world just seven hundred meters away.... The Tower of London!

Neighbouring tall buildings also have nicknames representative of their shapes including the Gherkin at St Mary Axe, the Walkie-talkie on 20 Fenchurch, the Scalpel on Lime Street and the even taller Twentytwo Bishopsgate tower.

Through his connections, Eduardo Garcia had managed to influence the Spanish Operations Director at the security firm in charge of the Cheesegrater's nightwatchmen. They had been given strict instructions to give a stunt team confidential access to the building and roof. The team were apparently to be filmed making a night-time jump, descending across the Thames for a wealthy man's engagement party being held near the top of The Shard on the opposite bank.

At half-past midnight Nick drove the white, windowless van off Leadenhall Street and along St Mary Axe. The Cheesegrater loomed into the dark night sky above them. Just before reaching the bottom of the Gherkin, he peeled off left into Undershaft, a narrow dead-end alley that curved back around the base of the wedge-shaped building. He pulled up by the courier's entrance, which was completely concealed from the passing roads.

Nick pulled on his balaclava and fastened his helmet and got out with Max, Saban, Afrim and Santiago. They were all dressed in black fatigues and balaclavas. Each of their helmets had a neat flip-down night vision scope attached to the fronts. They had parachute packs strapped onto their backs and carried large black canvas bags stuffed full of their equipment.

The building's glass side doors immediately opened and they were greeted by a Spanish speaking uniformed guard, eager to hear all about their stunt. Santiago spoke to him in their native tongue and strung him along with the made-up story about the rich man's party and the jump they'd been permitted to do by the London Authorities. He stressed that absolute secrecy had to be maintained until the morning. Only then could he share any pictures on social media as he was likely desperate to do.

The Spaniard led them to the lifts and stopped talking once inside. Standing amidst the other five men all in black, faces concealed, clutching curious-looking bags, he felt quite intimidated and looked it as well. They travelled up past the forty-five floors inhabited mostly by financial institutions, money firms and banks, up to the top floors. The three floors above the offices were filled with plant equipment, generators and a mass of large pipework.

He led them through a corridor, up some steps and using his electronic pass key, opened the last outer door to the roof. They were forty-eight floors above street level. The cool air rushed past them as they all went out onto the glass-walled roof terrace. It was littered with vents, more pipes, two small cranes for window cleaners and a flat covered enclosure at each end.

The guard asked Santiago if he could stay and watch, but was told in no uncertain terms in Spanish, to leave them and lock the door behind him so their preparation wouldn't be disturbed.

"But what if you change your minds and want to be let

back into the building?"

"We won't change our minds. We're committed now!" said Santiago with Nick nodding in agreement.

The guard shrugged. "Okay then. Good luck. Happy landings!"

Max suddenly felt the finality of the situation he'd gotten himself into, weigh down on him like a ton of bricks. Here he was with a bunch of criminals, who after today would be infamous forever more, looking down on London, about to attempt the most brazen robbery of all time!

His mind raced for alternative options, ways to get out of this mess. Could he raise the alarm, or break off mid-air and escape? He now knew Jurado did the Richmond hack, but he still wasn't quite sure what foreign power, likely Spanish related, was behind this job. Surely MI5 could figure that out. Did he really have to go along with this tonight in order to get to the truth? But his thoughts kept coming back to one clear fact and that was if he tried anything stupid, they would kill him.

Nick snapped him away from his thoughts. "Right lads, firstly for Christ's sake just a reminder, no skydiving off the edge. You've got to inflate your ram-air wing before you leave the edge of the building. At seven hundred-odd feet up, if you jumped then pulled the rip cord, your chute will just about open as you hit the pavement below."

They moved towards the far end which overlooked the Tower of London and Tower Bridge beyond.

"You've got to throw out your air foil wing and inflate the cells between the two nylon sheets before you jump." Nick looked up at the dark sky assessing the breeze. "There a slight northerly wind coming from our left, so face into that to inflate your chute, jump off the end there, then turn as quickly as you can."

They all looked through the glass side panels, imagining performing Nick's instructions.

"But there's another building right there after we jump

off?" said Max pointing at the dark structure just lower than where they were.

"That's the Scalpel building," said Nick, "yeah don't go and land your arse on the top of that sodding thing. As we'll only have just gone airborne and the wind will try to push us towards the Thames, make sure you go to the right of it."

As they looked down they could see another lower building to the right of the Scalpel. "And we have to clear that one there," added Santiago.

"Right, but after then it's plain sailing over to the Tower. And for Christ's sake, don't bloody miss the Waterloo Block roof! Do that and you're finished. You'll probably land right on top of one of the guard's bayonets!"

Max could see his old Colour Sergeant was loving this. He was back in the Commandos, reliving the excitement of battle, leading his squad once again.

"Okay lads, attach your bags, get ready to throw out your chutes behind you, face that way and jump as soon as the wing inflates. Then I want the next one in place and doing the same within seconds!"

They each clipped their kit bags to the front of their harnesses and made their way onto the flat roof in the corner.

Max's heart was thumping out of his chest. The last time he'd parachuted was twenty years ago and even then he only did his obligatory four jumps in the Marines. Added to that this was a night jump and almost right away having to avoid a couple of other buildings! He cautiously stepped up, fourth in line with Nick after him.

He checked his harness once more, tuned into the breeze direction and concentrated on Nick's instructions, going through them in his mind.

He suddenly realized that Afrim had already opened his black chute and been pulled off the roof before actually jumping! They all watched as he struggled to gain control of the inflated wing above him. He turned to the right and was on his way, steering past the Scalpel and over the other building. He was fine.

Saban was already also in the air! 'Shit!' thought Max, 'this is all happening so fast!'. He shuffled along nearer the edge behind Santiago, who let his chute unfurl from its pack and catch the breeze. He stood there for a moment, in full control of it, before then commandingly letting it gently lift him from the platform and out into the gloom, turning simultaneously.

Max stepped to the edge. He could see the others gracefully and silently glide towards the Tower. 'This was it!'.

"You'll be fine mate," assured Nick beside him, getting ready to follow.

Max opened his chute pack just as a stronger gust of wind took hold of it, instantly wrenching him towards the edge before he was ready and had grabbed the guide pulls. He glanced at Nick just before being pulled off the ledge and out into space.

The chute hadn't fully inflated and Max immediately dropped three floors down the side of the glass, before it fully filled with air. Grasping for the black steering chords, he finally got hold of them and yanked down hard, just in time to steer around the sharp, angled edge of the Scalpel building.

Because he'd lost a little height Max was now looking as though he might not clear the next lower building. Wrestling with the chords, feeling for which tugs would slow his descent, he drifted across the roof and had to raise his legs into the air to clear the last edge of the office's roof!

At last he was in clean air. Max found himself having to constantly correct against the northerly breeze trying to veer him to his right towards the Thames. It seemed ages ago since he was dragged off the top of the Cheesegrater, but he was now gliding towards his target, which looked very small from a distance.

He looked down at Fenchurch Street station terminal as he passed over it and also picked out the offices of Richmond Bank. There was a calming silence up in the cool air above

London's dim glow from the streetlights.

Ahead, Afrim and Saban had already landed on the Waterloo Block roof and were gathering in their chutes. Max passed over the grassy knoll of Tower Hill and couldn't help thinking of all those who'd been executed there.

He was now descending towards the perimeter of the Tower site and constantly adjusted his trajectory as he steered himself to the roof, which as he neared, thankfully started to look a lot larger.

Over the dry moat, he scanned all around to see if there was anyone that would see them all flying in. Everywhere was deserted, with no tourist attractions, bars or restaurants open in the vicinity. Next to the Waterloo Block, the White Tower stood out in the dim light, looking magnificent as if coldly watching his approach. Max stole a quick thought of wondering what William the Conqueror would make of him dropping out of the sky onto this hallowed, royal site!

Max passed over Legge's Mount on the corner of the ramparts, then between the Devereux and Flint inner rampart towers. Pulling hard on the chords, he slowed himself right down to gently land on the slate roof of the Waterloo Block. The accommodating gentle slope of the roof aided his landing and he quietly walked off his momentum a few steps down its side and onto the flat, lead-covered walkway to the rear edge of the building.

At the front of the building at ground level, the two guards were both standing inside their guard huts. Whilst giving them some protection from the night's chill, the wooden boxes also served as a sound dampener. Neither of them heard the airborne intruders or their gentle roof landings three storeys above and behind them.

The maintenance men with accompanying guards down in the vault had been locked into the building since earlier that evening. They had made good progress, having dismantled the faulty walkway and located the metal-on-metal grinding point. They'd cut this away and were starting to fit a replacement part. Due to health and safety regulations, the large steel doors at both ends of the vault room had to be left open. No one could be shut inside the vault.

Seconds after Max landed, he turned to watch Nick land perfectly, gathering in his chute as he crouched down and joined him. They unbuckled their harnesses, chute packs and unclipped their kit bags. Laying them down on the lead roof covering, by one of the small roof access doors. They each started to unpack their equipment.

Max unzipped his bag and amongst the various items spread out inside ready for his use, on the top sat the one he didn't relish picking up. A silenced Glock 17 handgun.

They finished taking their equipment from the bags and fitting it to belts, backpacks, holsters and slings around their shoulders. They each looked at one another and nodded in readiness to go. Max noticed that Afrim and Saban both held Heckler and Koch MP5 submachine guns.

Just then they heard a key gently turning in the lock of one of the small black roof access doors. Instinctively they pointed their weapons at the door as it slowly opened. A face peered round.

"Barney!" whispered Nick. "Jesus, thank God."

Barney stared at all the weapons aimed at him. "Okay, okay, stop pointing those bloody guns at me, jees, gave me a heart attack."

"Well done mate, you made it. Have you done all your tasks?" asked Nick in hushed tones.

"Bloody hell, it wasn't easy I can tell you, but yes, all done," said Barney coming out onto the roof. He was dressed in casual clothes, jeans, a polo shirt and leather jacket.

"The entrances?" checked Nick.

"Yes, the key holes of the main gates at the Byward Tower and the two on Tower Wharf have all been filled with that glue gumption you gave me. No one's getting in or out of this place in a hurry. It'll take them ages to agree on how to sort those doors without destroying such prized historical artefacts!"

"Great, that stops the police all crashing our party later when they all figure out what's happening here. Now, what about the barracks?"

Barney shook his head in disbelief that he'd dared to try this more challenging task. "Just a few minutes ago I placed one of those dummy cyanide gas grenades outside each of the four exit doors around the Fusiliers HQ. God, I was terrified, Nick. I had to wait for those two guards below us to tuck themselves into their huts, before I could place the grenade on the steps outside the barracks main entrance. If they'd looked over I would have been in full view! As soon as any one of those guards tries to go in or out, they'll spot the devices. It won't hold them for long! What if they know they're fakes?"

"Any delay to those soldiers getting involved is welcome," said Nick. "They'd be fools to contemplate risking setting off a hydrogen cyanide gas grenade marked with the poison skull and the letters 'HCN' on it. With those red motion sensor beams you switched on that Peter fitted, they won't risk going anywhere near those things!"

"Fair enough," agreed Barney.

"What's security like inside here, for protecting the maintenance going on in the vault?"

"I'm not entirely sure, but my guess would be," he looked skyward imagining everyone who'd be there, "three or four maintenance, a couple of Tower staff overseeing them, two Beefeaters, armed police maybe just one or two and probably one of the armed guardsmen."

"Sounds like a lot!" whispered Santiago.

"I'd say that's pretty light," argued Barney. "They're not expecting any problems so that's just routine security for an overnight maintenance job. We are after all locked up in a fortress!"

"We need to stay alert anyway," said Nick looking at the others. "That's still a fair amount of fire power down there."

"Anyway, you'd better get on with it now!" prompted Barney who just wanted to get out of there now.

"Right Barney, you stay up here now and wait for us to get back. Here's a radio on the same wavelength as ours. Listen in only, no chatter."

Nick handed Barney an electronic device the size of a melon, showing him the switch on the end. "When we've gone, turn this on okay?"

"What is it?" asked Barney holding the metallic framed instrument.

"Just a little more confusion and delaying tactics," said Nick. "This little baby will scramble all mobile devices and Wi-Fi signals for a couple of hundred yards! No one will be able to make any calls when this is on, including us! But we've got our radio comms on a different frequency, so we can all carry on talking to one another."

Barney looked impressed, then settled himself down alongside the access door, ready to flick the switch. Nick began to lead the others past him and down a stairway into the Waterloo Block.

He got on the radio back to Peter and Sonia. "All landed, perimeter doors sealed, HCN's in place, scrambler about to be activated, we're going in now! Guard status?"

At Sonia's apartment overlooking Marble Arch, Peter acknowledged him and checked the CCTV again. "Received. Minimum ten people down there. Looks like at least four are armed," he reported, corroborating Barney's estimate. "Freezing the Waterloo Block CCTV pictures except in the vault. Disabling landline and network feeds out of the complex, right now! Good luck!"

Peter quickly set to work on his several computers, starting the activation of various blocker, virus and access programs he'd got ready to be switched on. With the exception of the vault CCTV feed going out to the external security firm, his programs blocked all communication lines in and out of the Tower site. This included the server links, alarm feeds to police and security, landline and fibre broadband. This was complimented at the same time by Barney activating the mobile's scrambler on the roof.

Next, Peter was able to freeze the CCTV pictures throughout the Waterloo Block, which went to the Tower's viewing applications and the security firm's control room. All that is, apart from those in the underground vault, where staff were moving around and still needed to be viewable by anyone monitoring them. He would freeze those shortly. Because there was likely no movement in other parts of the building, the frozen CCTV pictures gave the impression of continuous, quiet, darkened empty rooms and corridors.

Sonia and Peter were glued to their screens and the team radio. Behind them on another desk sat Bob Simmons' laptop, the one Nick had taken from his home during his fateful visit.

Earlier that evening when they arrived at the apartment and Peter was setting things up for the night ahead, Sonia had reminded him to crack Simmons' user password and see if anything in his emails and files incriminated him snitching. Peter had set his program to work on gaining access to the laptop, along with a list of search keywords to hunt for, once it was in.

The searches included words and phrases like 'met police', 'prado museum', richmond hack', 'bitcoin' and as requested by Sonia, 'max sargent'!

With their attention focused on Peter's computers supporting the team at the Tower, they hadn't noticed that the program on Simmons' laptop had gained entry and had already produced a list of files that included some of the search criteria words. One of the many 'search results' waiting on the screen was for the word, 'Sargent'!

At the Tower almost all of the one hundred and seventy staff, Beefeaters, guards and community were fast asleep. It was almost one AM. Just three people were using the internet for web browsing and two others were speaking to their family on their mobiles.

The connections went off. The web pages disappeared and the calls were ended, with 'no signal' and 'wifi not found' messages displayed.

It was late, they were all tired and occasionally the signal did tend to drop out. All five of them tutted, then switched off their devices, happy to be prompted to turn in for their well-deserved sleep. Only one of them, a soldier, thought to themselves they would report the outage all the same. But in the morning.

17

Nick led the men quickly and quietly down the central stairs of the Waterloo Block. As if checking to see if alarms started ringing, he stopped and looked up at one of the many CCTV cameras in a corner. Nothing, all remained quiet. Peter's frozen pictures must be working, for now.

Nick, Santiago and Max were in front, each holding up their tranquillizer guns, with handguns holstered at their sides. Their night vision scopes were down in front of one eye. It was a strange assimilation for Max's brain to acclimatize to the mix of normal direct sight in the dim rooms and a world cast in bright green, showing up every detail of his view.

At the rear Afrim and Saban didn't bother using their night vision, allowing their eyes to get accustomed to the dark surroundings. They provided the heavy artillery in case of any clashes with multiple armed soldiers and brazenly had their machine guns up at eye level. They were all anxiously twisting in every direction, checking there was no one about to surprise them. Tensions were high.

The upper two floors of the building with offices and museum sections were deserted. On each floor, they parted from the stairway in both directions, moving along just ten yards into each floor space and corridor to ensure no one was present. Once it was clear, they regrouped.

Having passed by the top floor, mainly office space, they started coming into display areas on the first floor. Valuable paintings, ornaments and suits of armour seemed to look upon them disapprovingly. Their eerie shadows from the lit-up green eye displays, crept along the walls as they passed by.

They froze!

A soft whistling noise started from one of the display

rooms past the area they were in. They'd all agreed earlier in the evening, that anyone they came across should be silenced, preferably with the dart guns and they would only defer to their ballistic weapons if they got into a firefight.

Afrim and Saban were ready but Max held his hand over their MP5's and pushed them down, then putting a finger to his lips signifying 'too noisy!'.

Santiago was nearest and slowly moved towards the tuneful whistling. Max followed. Dart guns raised.

In the adjoining room, one of the Beefeaters had told the others downstairs, he would do a quick wander round the floors, as he needed the loo anyway. He was glad to get out of the vault room and stretch his legs. He was frankly bored of just standing there watching the maintenance guys fuss and fiddle about with fixing the travelator. They'd already been in there for four hours straight.

He stood examining a medieval mace and chain inside its display cabinet, imagining the damage a spiked iron ball would inflict on some poor combatant's head. He heard a tiny creak of a floorboard and turned.

To his utter surprise, expecting to be quite alone, he was confronted with two completely dark figures both pointing some sort of gun right at him. The black silhouettes were punctuated by a strange green glow across half of their eyes.

Santiago squeezed his trigger, only to be greeted with a hiss as the compressed air rushed past the dart body that had failed to seat itself snugly into the chamber.

The Beefeater started to draw breath to yell out, just as Max's dart embedded itself into the man's thigh. The sharp pinprick cut off his scream, as he looked down at the dart end's tuft sticking out of his leg. He looked back at Max and Santiago, wobbled slightly, eyes rolled, and he slumped onto the wooden floor out cold.

"Christ, Santiago," fumed Nick, "sort your bloody gun out will you! Nice Max."

Afrim pushed past and pulled out a plastic zip tie cable

from a bunch in his pocket and bound the unconscious man's wrists together.

Max felt awful about darting the innocent man. It pricked his conscience about what the hell he was doing here, assisting with the robbery of the crown jewels with a bunch of criminals, tranquillizing bystanders! He had to think fast, time was running out, should he act now, could he take them on, hold them, call for security downstairs?

His thoughts were interrupted by Nick who spoke quietly but seemed agitated by the lapse of professionalism. "Right, the floor's finally clear," staring at Santiago. "The ground floor below and those exits have got to be secured, and fast. You know what to do, the doors you're each covering. Stay alert for anyone patrolling, then sort the doors quickly. Regroup in the room near the top of the stairs to the vault!"

They each rechecked the compressed gas canisters they had slung over their backs. Nick led again to the staircase and proceeded down the steps, bending down as he went to get the earliest view he could of the ground floor below. He didn't want any more surprise encounters.

As they reached the bottom, they again checked around themselves in all directions, then split up off to their designated points.

Santiago made his way to the room they would meet at, double-checking his dart gun as he went. He would wait near to the top of the stairway leading down to the underground vault and jewel room. He moved against the wall into a shadow and would ensure anyone else leaving the vaults was put to sleep as they ascended the stairs.

Afrim and Saban moved swiftly through the rooms and corridors along the length of the building, to handle the two single exit doorways at each end and the single door near the front and rear corners.

Nick walked the short distance to the main entrance and Max did the same for the large doors at the centre rear.

Max approached his thick double doors and with a final

check that all was clear, unslung the foot-long cylindrical canister. At its end was a metal nozzle. He removed the plastic trigger guard and readied himself, adjusting his distance and aim, pointing it at the top corner of the doors.

He squeezed the trigger and the compressed foam shot out at its target, instantly bonding itself to the old wooden doors and the surrounding frame. As it hit the mark Max could see it immediately starting to expand and steadily moved his aim, to shoot an even covering over the entire outer rim of the doors. He then moved down the centre opening line where the doors met and finally covered over the entire face panels of each door.

The industrial-grade closed-cell spray polyurethane foam, often used in buildings as gap fillers, mixed the isocyanate and polyol resin at the nozzle. The highly sticky substance then expands to around fifty times the volume of its liquid state within a minute. Being a high-density mix with no trapped air pockets, it forms an almost impenetrable solid mass, which with the hardener accelerator, fully sets in just five minutes.

Max finished and stood back to admire his work. The whole door opening was covered with over a foot thick yellowy blob, still expanding like some old horror movie.

No one would be opening these doors anytime soon and charging in to interrupt their visit. Though Max did now start to feel somewhat ashamed at ruining the undoubted history of these old doors. His thoughts returned to how and when he could prevent this shameful raid. He simply had to do something before it was too late.

As he came back to the middle of the floor, Nick was also just returning from spraying the main entrance doors. "Wow, that stuff's awesome! They won't be having many visitors tomorrow that's for sure!"

They slowly made their way to the meeting point where Santiago was waiting and after a minute they were re-joined by Afrim and Saban. Both of the Albanians actually looked pleased with themselves, impressed with the expanding foam guns, just as Nick and Max were.

They crept around the top of the stairs leading down to the crown jewels room in the vault and could hear voices and clanging from the maintenance work. Nick and Saban both unzipped pockets and each took out two gas grenades, looking like green cans of fizzy pop with a ring pull on the end.

Inside the cans were an aerosol mixture of carfentanil and remifentanil, fast-acting synthetic opioid anaesthetic drugs. The knock-out gas would be dispersed in the form of a fine invisible mist that would fill every corner of the room.

Nick gathered them closer. "Once we throw these down into the vault area we're going to have to wait at least thirty seconds for the gas to put them all to sleep. We can't go down before, in case any of the armed guards start wildly shooting at the entrances. Let's just hope none of them has a gas mask."

Santiago added, "And that they don't have enough time to close the vault doors. If they do, we're finished."

Nick nodded for them all to start fitting their mini gas masks and clicked his radio to update Peter and Sonia.

"Building doors sealed, freeze the vault CCTV now, ready to dispense the....hold!" He abruptly stopped whispering. Someone was coming towards the bottom of the stairs!

They all instinctively crouched down as Nick peered over the stairway railing and looked down on an armed guardsman in khaki fatigues coming onto the first steps. He hadn't yet looked up, not suspecting for a moment there would be a bunch of armed intruders waiting there!

Nick leant over the rail holding his dart gun and without hesitation fired down a tranquillizer dart into the soft trapezius shoulder muscle of the soldier. The man immediately held his free hand up to the dart and to Nick's alarm, grasped the tufted syringe and yanked it out. But the fluid had already gone into him and was making its way into his nervous system at pace.

With his last bit of normal strength, the soldier looked up and saw Nick staring down at him, dart gun still raised. Nick knew they had to act now and pushed Saban forward and started to go down the stairs to the small landing halfway. The guard was beginning to topple. Nick could see he was fighting the drug but was succumbing to the wave of sleep flowing through him.

The soldier had no doubt in his deteriorating state that the intruders were criminals, with their black suits, masks and helmets. In one last determined wrench of energy, he tried to raise up his gun. It felt like ten times the weight. He got it level and was able to pull the trigger once, firing off a single round into the wall beside him. Sandstone splintered off with shards of masonry and dust. He then collapsed onto the first few steps and was out cold.

"Go!" shouted Nick to Saban and they both ventured down the stairs past the slumped soldier. Peering round the end of the wall they could see through a holding room and into the main vault. The large steel doors were open and with the sound of the guard's gunshot, the mix of staff, travelator technicians, police and Beefeaters, were momentarily disorientated.

They quickly pulled the canister pins and threw the gas grenades hard into the area. Nick pitched his first one fast into the far end of the vault, wanting to capture anyone by the other set of vault doors. His second hit the end of the crown jewels display cases and bounced sideways inside the jewel room.

Saban's first also fell short into the vault, but having got the measure of his aim and power needed, he sent his next grenade into the far end. All four gas cans were now furiously hissing.

They both retreated back up the staircase, amidst frantic yelling and shouts from the men inside the vault, as they reacted to what they thought were explosive grenades.

"Grenade!" shouted one of the Beefeaters.

The two armed policemen both started shouting, "Gas! It's gas!"

The anaesthetic aerosol filling the air quickly took hold of the jewels vault and rooms on either end. All the occupants started inhaling the gas and quickly began feeling its effects.

One of the Tower staff began issuing instructions. "Everyone out of the vault, then close the doors." He pointed to half the people to go to the far doors and the rest to follow him to the near set of doors. But there were already five people dropping to their knees. Where the canisters had landed next to them, they were the first to inhale the sleep-inducing mist.

At the far end, one of the armed policemen and two maintenance staff had got out of the vault room and were starting to close the heavy steel doors, keen to separate themselves from the debilitating gas. The policeman urged on the other two and with gritted teeth, they managed to fully close the two thick doors. The maintenance men were now on the ground starting to drift off.

With the last of his strength, the officer pulled down hard on each door's locking wheel, spinning it round and sliding the thick bars in place. Only the keys would allow this entrance to be reopened again. The policeman collapsed to the floor, succumbing to sleep for the next half an hour as the others would.

Of the remainder, only one Beefeater, one repairer and the other policeman were exiting the remaining open entrance vault doors, nearest to the stairway.

"We can't close the vault with people inside?" gasped the officer, struggling to stand.

"We have to close the vault," insisted the Beefeater coughing, "the crown jewels must be protected!"

The uniformed policeman made it out of the vault and dropped to the floor breathing heavily, taking in more of the gas.

"Push these doors!" shouted the Warder to the other man, but he was also losing the energy to stand. He then peeled back trying to get away from the gas canister still hissing yards away on the inside. Then he fell.

The Beefeater, spurred on by sheer duty, almost managed to close one of the strong doors, before he himself dropped onto his knees, his body weight finished closing the door ready to be bolted. But the second door had to be shut as well, before they could be locked.

He held his now feeble hand out to the one remaining open door, willing it to close. He coughed, then slumped, as the anaesthetic penetrated his body and forced him past drowsiness and into a deep sleep.

The single gunshot inside the Waterloo Block had made both the soldiers outside the front of the building jump. It was the last thing they expected to hear in the middle of the night, when maintenance work was being done inside. They came out of their guard huts, one went to the nearest single doorway near the end of the block, for which he had a key.

The other ran to the main entrance. As he did so he glanced over to the Fusiliers barracks to his right, hoping to see more of his fellow guards appearing. It was then that he noticed a small object sitting in the middle of the main entrance doorstep. It appeared to have tiny light beams emitting from it spreading in all directions for about five yards.

He stopped and trotted over to the barracks to see what this strange thing was. As he got closer the painted lettering on the canister came into focus, 'HCN'. He knew the 'CN' was the abbreviation for cyanide and immediately realized it was some sort of motion-activated poison gas grenade.

The shot had also alerted most of the soldiers sleeping in their quarters and several were already making their way out of rooms towards the main door.

The duty soldier outside yelled out to them, holding up his hand.

"Stop! Stop!" he shouted urgently. "Motion grenade. Cyanide gas! Don't come out of the doorway!" They halted, peering through the doors at the sinister-looking grenade outside, blocking their exit. "Check the other exits from the building," he instructed. He needed them out into the yard and helping him investigate what caused the gunshot in the Waterloo building.

"If the other doors have gas grenades, find a way to exit the barracks through the lower floor windows. We have to find out what that gunshot was!"

The other soldiers inside quickly obeyed the duty guard's instructions, scuttling off to stop the other doors being used before they were checked. Men woke other men, some grabbed their guns, others hastily pulled on part of their uniforms, just in case it was some sort of perverse drill or test.

The first duty guard slotted his key into the Waterloo Block's single door and turned the lock to open it. He heard the bolt inside the locking mechanism slide back, but when he pushed to open the door, it was solid, it didn't budge at all. Puzzled, but desperate to get in, he stepped back and put his considerable weight and power into barging open the door. It stayed immovable. The hardened, expanded foam mass around the entire inside of the door held fast.

The moment Peter had heard from Nick they were at the top of the vault stairs, he had frozen the CCTV pictures for the jewel room. They knew this would inevitably get the alarm sounded, but wanted to buy any time they could with the possibility anyone monitoring it might think it was a feed glitch. Anything other than watching grenades flying into the vault and everyone panicking, then being rendered unconscious.

They were all unaware that it had long since been the policy of the Tower not to use loud sounding alarm bells or sirens on the site. These were deemed far too intrusive in the City. After all, this was a fortress with almost two hundred people living there, including around sixty of them being either soldiers or Beefeaters. Why on earth would they need bells going off in the middle of London, surely no-one would ever be foolhardy enough to attempt a crime inside those hallowed rampart walls!

On the other side of town, north of the City in Walthamstow, two security operatives were watching a wall of CCTV live feeds from the Tower of London. All had been still in the Waterloo Block with no movement whatsoever throughout the building, except for the maintenance going on in the underground floor.

The operatives had missed the tiny change in picture quality when Peter had frozen the building's CCTV pictures. But now, staring straight at the people working in the vault room all frozen in time, they'd sat bolt upright to check and refresh the feed.

The pictures remained frozen, showing the repair men, staff, police and Beefeaters all captured mid-motion, now quite still. One of them had seen the soldier just leave before the picture froze.

He picked up the phone and called straight through to the Tower's Head of Security, but to his surprise, got no ring tone. Nothing. The line was dead. He then tried the Fusiliers barracks. No line.

Now he was panicking. He called the police!

18

The five men on the upper part of the stairway all listened out for any remaining sounds coming from the floor below. It had been a minute since Nick and Saban had thrown the gas grenades in and convinced everyone must have been knocked out, they crept down.

Each of them wondered if they would be faced with impenetrable steel doors securely shut and bolted. They'd heard the shouts to close the vault doors and thought they'd even heard a few being closed and bolted.

Max eyed each of the others, trying to assess if he could stop this by holding them all at gunpoint.

Again he was interrupted by events moving too fast to gather his thoughts. They reached the bottom of the staircase and as they rounded the wall, one by one, they gazed at the sight in front of them in amazement.

Between them and the vault, three men lay on the ground. One of the massive steel doors had been pushed closed, but to their relief, the other door was still open. They edged over to it and now got a clear view into the vault of the most iconic collection of sovereign regalia in the world… the Crown Jewels!

The five of them walked into the vault to find more men out cold on the floor spread around the room. One of the travelators was disassembled with pieces, parts and tools strewn nearby on a dust sheet.

At the far end, they could see the other pair of vault doors had been shut and locked. Given the silence, they could safely assume that anyone on the other side of the closed doors must have eventually succumbed to the knock-out gas.

They all stood there for a few moments staring through

their gas mask goggles, at the wonders in front of them in their various display cases. The room was well lit for the maintenance work and the hundreds of diamonds, jewels and gems, gold and pearls, sparkled mockingly at them from behind their bombproof casings.

Afrim and Saban set about securing the wrists of every man on the floor with their zip ties. Santiago unslung a bag from his shoulder and began taking out a new piece of equipment they would now require. This left Nick and Max continuing to be mesmerized by the monarch's crowns, sceptres and other regalia, resting on their dark velvet displays.

Max could feel the hairs on the back of his neck stand up. How far could this go before his protection by MI5 ran out and he was classed simply as one of the gang that robbed the Tower of London. He would have to do something soon.

"You okay Max?" Nick's question jolted Max out of his glazing over. "You look a little unsure about all this?" Nick could see the reality of what they were doing had hit Max hard, standing there in front of these famous, historical, royal symbols.

"Yeah, I'm good," feigned Max. "You can't but help be captivated by this lot eh?"

"Quite so," agreed Nick. "Right, Santiago, let's get cracking on this. I want us to be out of here in a minute or two, no messing about. We're just going for the one item Sonia chose!"

As soon as the police had been alerted by the security firm in Walthamstow, a priority command had been sent to the Met police special operations team. They in turn had mobilized the uniformed branch, the armed police team and the officers who had special training to respond to sites of major interest. These included museums, other vaults with high-value items, banks that held large amounts of cash, safety deposit box premises, and top of the list, the Tower of London.

Calls into staff at the Tower had all failed and with no calls having been received from the Tower, initial assumptions had been a communications failure. However, a total cut out of computer feeds, police feed, landlines and mobiles had never happened before, so there was an anxious edge in the tones of the various officers giving commands.

At least eight police patrol cars, the armed team and ten other senior or specialist officers were now well on their way to the Tower. They would begin arriving at the main entrance within minutes.

In the meantime, the soldiers trapped in their barracks had seen the cyanide gas grenades outside each of their building's exit points. They had to assume they were all real and posed a significant danger to them and the Tower community.

The soldiers had therefore gone down to the lower floor where the windows faced out into a trench walkway around the building, just below the courtyard ground level. Several of the windows furthest away from the external doors had been broken and soldiers were now starting to climb through, many with their guns to join their comrades at the doors of the Waterloo Block.

With all the commotion, many of the community there were starting to appear from their houses and apartments. Managers, Beefeaters, families, staff, cautiously approached the rear of the White Tower to see what was happening. Some looked quite alarmed at the sight of soldiers climbing out of their barracks' windows, shouting, rushing about and congregating at the doorways to the Jewel House.

But the guards were met with solid, unopenable, thick wooden barriers. Keys were fetched from security, locks tried and re-tried and strong soldiers attempting to run at the doors in the hope of being the one to gain entry first.

The officer of the soldiers was faced with the biggest decision of his army career. A gunshot had clearly been heard from inside, yet they couldn't get in. Someone or something was deliberately preventing that. They weren't able to smash ground floor windows, they were false facades with brickwork behind the black glass. His men didn't have any explosives to blow open a doorway. But the damage was what put him off. Damage to this historical building, and indeed doors, would never be forgiven if it wasn't warranted.

The only real option was to pick the single access doorway at the rear of the building and order his soldiers to blast their way through it using their guns. What a mess, and noise that would make. No, he would wait another minute or so and see if any of the doors relented to his men's attempts to get in.

Santiago had the small industrial angle grinder ready and tapped the trigger to test it. The powerful fifty-four-volt battery clipped into the end of the handle butt, spun the circular blade at well over a hundred revolutions a second. The 125mm steel disc with cutting diamonds vacuum-brazed to its edge, would cut through the sheet layers of laminated glass and plastic polycarbonate, slowly but surely.

They had considered a water jet cutter, but without a plentiful supply of water, this was discounted. Sonia's fire equipment firm was starting to provide fire services with the latest cutting discs. These could pretty much cut into anything the rescue services would ever encounter, including for example bullet proof windows of VIP armoured cars.

"Right here," said Nick pointing above the centre of a panel of the first bullet-proof glass case. "Just do three cuts to make a triangle large enough to get our hand into."

This glass case had three items of regalia inside. One of them was the prize Eduardo Garcia had suggested to Sonia, who had been drawn to it since seeing the pictures of all the jewels that Peter had shown them in the briefing.

In the middle of the glass cabinet, raised up high, was the sovereign's orb, measuring six and a half inches in diameter. Made for Charles II's coronation in 1661 it has been used at all subsequent monarch's crowning's. Consisting of gold with diamonds, emeralds, pearls and rubies, it was slightly damaged by Colonel Blood when he attempted to steal some of the crown jewels. But they weren't after the orb.

Slotted into holders on the sides of the orb's raised display mount, were the rod and sceptre. The hole Santiago was lining up to cut, was directly level with the top of the sceptre. That is where the sparkling jewel sat that they were after, in its wire cradle made of gold, near the top of the golden shaft. The largest diamond in the world.

The Star of Africa! The Cullinan I!

Santiago looked at Nick and gulped as he readied the angle grinder.

Nick nodded. "Do it!"

Santiago pressed the trigger and the steely disc instantly spun at its operating speed. He slowly moved its edge onto the toughened glass. The blade seemed reluctant to penetrate the surface of the shiny glass, but when he applied more pressure, the diamond edge started to bite into the smooth pane. Glass dust and fragments flew into the air. The men felt for the comfort of their gas masks still protecting them.

Santiago pushed and the five-inch-wide disc began cutting into the glass. It gained purchase on the material and broke through, spraying glass dust into the inside of the display. It took about fifteen seconds for him to cut the first line.

He withdrew it and went straight in for the next cut, now with confidence. Nick, Max, Afrim and Saban all watched closely, as the illusive, incredible artefact was slowly giving itself up to them.

Santiago made two more slices and the triangle of laminated glass dropped through into the cabinet. He retreated and shut off the angle grinder, looking at the hole in disbelief. No one said anything, each almost afraid to be the one to move forward and grab this piece of priceless history.

"Max? Do you want to do the honours then?" suggested Nick, much to Max's utter horror.

Max imagined quickly drawing his Glock and putting an end to this. He could see that only the Albanians had their hands constantly on their Heckler machine guns. Nick and Santiago's Glock's were safely holstered with neither of them paying the guns any attention.

"Well, get on with it!" spurred on Nick. "Remember, just the Star of Africa diamond. Pull it out of its holding cradle, the whole staff won't fit through! Then carefully bring it out the hole, don't drop it whatever you do or we'll have to cut another hole. We really need to get out of here, God only knows what's going on outside!"

Nick pressed his radio to update Sonia and Peter. "Hole cut. Going for the Star now. Get our bloody exit transport here asap. I suspect all hell's going to break loose!"

Max rolled up the sleeve of his fatigues and carefully started to insert his hand and arm into the triangular hole in the casing glass. The room was silent, the tension was deafening!

Samuel Morales started up the machine he was sitting in. The two Pratt and Whitney engines prompted the rotor blades above him to start turning. Pumps, turbines, electrics and motors all chimed and wurred into action. He needed to be quick as alarms would be raised. Helicopters didn't usually have take-off rights after sunset at RAF Northolt in northwest London.

Eduardo Garcia had again used his considerable influence to find a particular pilot in the Spanish Air Force. He needed someone who would follow orders without question, even for a job that was clearly criminal. But loyalty to their country had to come above integrity in such circumstances.

A senior officer within Eduardo's extended network had recommended Captain Morales, who was stationed at Los Llanos airbase just south of Albecete in Spain. The pilot was one of their best helicopter officers, having flown the two

Eurocopters, AS532 Cougars and AS332 Super Pumas, and the NH90's. He could fly any helicopter.

Eduardo had then got one of his team to assist Samuel in getting a tour of RAF Northolt on one of their regular exchange visits. In particular, to include a comprehensive tour of London's Air Ambulance setup there, where they operated two red McDonnell Douglas MD902 Explorers.

They took Samuel through their minimal security, key storage and office layout. Even a quick five-minute flight up and around the aerodrome! The helicopters were always left fully fuelled and ready to respond to emergency calls at a moment's notice.

At midnight he'd easily jumped over the insignificant five-foot-high metal railing barrier alongside West End Road, at the end of the main runway. He'd then trotted four hundred metres in the dark across the grassy outfield to the Air Ambulance helicopters, one in the hangar, one outside.

A quietly broken glass door window and a picked lock and he had the keys he required.

He now had his feet on the antitorque tail control pedals. One hand was on the collective pitch control with throttle and the other, the cyclic pitch control lever. He commandingly and smoothly lifted the red helicopter up into the air.

Peter looked round at Sonia. "Blimey! I think we're going to do it!" He then noticed the open laptop of Bob Simmons still sitting on the desk behind them and could see his program had broken in and had a number of search results waiting to be interrogated on the screen.

Nodding over to the laptop he mentioned to Sonia, "Just so you know, the searches are waiting from Bob's laptop over there!"

Despite the criticality of the situation reported to them back at the Tower, Sonia had patiently waited to see if Bob's PC might give her any clues as to him or anyone else telling the Met about their Prado theft.

She went over and began looking down the list of results. Immediately, one particular line shouted out of the screen at her.

The search had found something hidden within Bob's system files with the keyword 'Sargent'!

"What the....!" She clicked on the line to open the file or document the keyword had been found in. A private diary opened up in a Word document. She quickly read through some of the entries and could see that Bob had been keeping daily records of the aftermath following the bank hack.

In particular, Bob had noted down each of his meetings or conversations with the investigative team and other directors of the bank.

The entry highlighted by the work search read;

'Met with a Max Sargent of MI5 in the canteen, they had no leads but were questioning junior IT staff'!

Sonia was in shock, then exploded with rage effing and blinding at the laptop, making Peter jump.

He turned round. "What's the matter?"

"I knew it, I knew there was something about Max," raged Sonia. "Nick and his bloody trust and army loyalty!"

"For God's sake, what's the problem with Max?"

"He's MI5! Part of the investigative team looking into the bank raid. Bob met him!"

"Oh my," said Peter. "We're screwed!"

"No, we're not," hissed Sonia. "Give me that radio mike!"

Just to the rear of the Waterloo Block, round from the two visitors exit doors at one end, about six guardsmen had just been ordered to breach the single access door using force if necessary. "And that means your bloody weapons!" the officer had yelled at them.

They all tried to push the door in, hoping to break the lock through the wooden frame, but with no success. They were now looking at one another, none of them wanting to be the first to start shooting at a historic doorway at the Tower of London, causing damage and waking half the City. But orders were orders. If this all went wrong, the officer would take the can for it.

One of the soldiers raised his SA80 assault gun, made by Heckler and Koch, paused, and then fired several rounds into the door lock area. Splinters of hard wood flew in all directions. Pieces hit some of the soldiers who were only seven feet away, with their backs up against one of the inner rampart walls below the Brick Tower.

A few chipped indentations were starting to appear in the thick wooden door. The wood had taken the bullets pretty well, aided by the thick, hard foam behind, absorbing their impact. But the soldiers could see with sustained firing around the door's perimeter, they could likely gain entry. They started to take it in turns to unload their magazines into the steadfast door.

At the main entrance to the Tower of London, most of the police cars, vans, armed response team and officers had arrived. Already many of them had congregated right outside the entrance. They'd accessed the first outer door under the Middle Tower which Barney hadn't tampered with, and were now shouting to a couple of Beefeaters on the inside of the main wooden doors under the Byward Tower.

With the police demanding to be let in, the hapless Warders simply couldn't insert the old keys into their locks to open the doors. There was some kind of hardened glue in the key holes blocking them. With urgent frustration on both sides, it would be a while before those main doors would be opened!

Max had the Star of Africa diamond in his grasp and was manipulating it with his fingers, to get it out of the wire cradle holding it to the sceptre. It wasn't easy, with his arm extended through the angular hole Santiago had cut, he was juggling the gem from its mount, making sure not to drop it. The others watched closely, willing him on.

His concentration and the night's silence was suddenly broken by the sound of gun fire above them, down the other end of the building. A lot of gun fire. It was the soldiers shooting their way through the rear access door. This added considerable urgency and anxiety to the task. They had to get out now before it was too late. They risked all being trapped in the vault!

And then, the stone freed itself from the last corner of wire capturing it. Max had managed to get the huge diamond out of its cradle! He held the magnificent Cullinan I in his hand, on the other side of the glass.

At the same time, their team radio crackled in each of their earpieces, signifying Peter and Sonia were about to speak.

It was Sonia's voice that came over the airwaves, sounding angry, urgent. All five of them in the vault heard what she had to say.

"Nick! Max is with MI5! He's played you, us, for fools!"

The shocking announcement gave Max a split second to grab his Glock from its holster with his free hand. He raised it up at Nick and twitched its aim from him to the others and back.

Nick and Santiago were still in shock trying to comprehend the astonishing revelation from Sonia. Of the two Albanians, Afrim had raised his Heckler and Koch machine gun up at Max, but with him still holding their prize in his hand, inside the casing, stopped himself from firing. His breathing was heavy though, from pure rage.

Nick held his hands up. "Okay, calm down everyone! Max, you're pointing your gun at me for God's sake, tell me there's been a mistake here?"

"What's happening Nick?" asked Sonia over the radio.

Nick slowly raised his hand to his radio button, checking Max could see what he was doing. "Max has the Star, but still inside the casing, and is now pointing his gun at us!" He paused to think. "Can you repeat and clarify what you said?"

Sonia came straight back. "Max is MI5! Do you want me to draw you a picture! Peter found Bob's diary in his laptop. Bob met Max at Richmond Bank. He was part of the MI5 investigating team for God's sake!"

Max tightened his grip on the gun. Nick looked up at him disbelievingly. Despite Sonia's claims, the evidence, he still wanted to believe there'd been some mistake. He wanted Max to explain it away. His comrade, whom he'd trusted, with his life.

"Tell me it's not true Max, please?"

Max frowned. He ignored the question and nodded to Afrim. "Make him drop the gun!"

"I can't do that Max. We need to get out of here. Give me the diamond and we'll leave you here, alive and say no more about it?"

"I can't do that Nick. We stay here, calmly, until the soldiers break in and get down here. That way no one dies!"

Nick slowly moved his hand down towards his holstered gun. He knew he had to break this deadlock and if they were caught, his life was over anyway. He had nothing to lose.

"No Nick!" shouted Max. "Don't do it, I'll shoot!"

"No you won't Max. You've saved my life before, you won't shoot me in cold blood now. And besides, if you pull that trigger, Afrim will unload his magazine into you in an instant." He curled his fingers around the Glock and slowly pulled it from its holster.

At that moment Max knew he was beaten. He wouldn't kill this man, his Commando Colour Sergeant. Seeing Max's reticence to pull his trigger, Saban and Santiago now both grabbed their guns as well.

Max stared down the barrels of two Glocks and two MP5's. "I'll drop it!" he threatened, waving the Star of Africa around inside the glass case.

Nick shook his head. "No you won't Max, it's not worth

dying for. I would never shoot you. But these guys will!"

Max sighed. "What now?"

"Give us the diamond and then we kill you!" sneered Santiago.

Nick cut in angrily. "No! No! Max, you once saved my life and I've been grateful ever since. Not a day's gone by when I haven't been thankful to you for letting me live my life. Now it's my turn to save your life! I give you my word, my word as a Marine comrade. When you hand over the diamond, we'll leave you here, alive! I promise!"

Santiago spoke again staring at Max down his gun sights.

"Make your mind up quickly, we must leave, right now. What's it to be, live, or die?"

He raised his aim from Max's chest to his head. Afrim and Saban were also itching to waste him.

The shooting upstairs was now being interjected with shouting and splintering, as the soldiers were kicking in a hole in the foam-covered door, big enough for them to climb through. Max felt his job was done, he'd delayed them long enough, they'd never get out with the Star, not past the guards.

"Okay Nick. I'll take you at your word!"

Max slowly lowered his Glock and dropped it onto the floor. Looking straight into the eyes of each of the four men surrounding him. He carefully retrieved his arm back through the hole in the glass. The large diamond came out of its tomb, sparkling even more under the vault room's direct lighting. Max offered it out.

Nick took it from him, stared into it for a moment, then it was gone, into one of his zipper pockets, like a piece of common jewellery.

"Now we kill him and go!" said Santiago again.

"Don't you bloody even think about it," snarled Nick.

"But he can just follow us?"

Nick turned to Max and thought quickly for a few seconds, noticing again the triangular hole in the display case behind Max.

"Sorry mate, I need you to put your arm through the hole again?"

"What?"

"Just do it, Max, it'll be alright I promise."

Max obliged with some puzzlement, then realized what Nick intended, as he saw him unsling the canister from around his back.

Before Max could object and withdraw his arm, Nick had levelled the nozzle of the cylinder and briefly squirted liquid foam around the hole and over Max's arm. The tacky substance immediately started expanding as Santiago held Max's shoulder preventing him from pulling away. Within moments it had formed a hard seal with enough hold that he could no longer move his arm out. It continued to foam and set around the hole, locking him there.

Max was horrified. "Really? You're leaving me here like this, with my arm inside one of the crown jewels cases?"

Nick lowered the canister and smiled. "You once told me what the crime was that we're committing here tonight."

"Yeah, it's treason!" said Max crossly.

"Then call this, your treason trap!"

Nick gestured for the others to get moving back out of the single open vault door.

"Fifty?" called out Max.

"Don't call me that again," replied Nick. "We're even now!." He then disappeared out of the vault.

Max was thankful they hadn't shot him. He stood there in the crown jewels vault in black fatigues, wearing a gas mask, surrounded by unconscious officials. His hand was glued inside a bomb-proof display unit and the Star of Africa priceless diamond missing. 'Oh my God! I've got some explaining to do!' he thought to himself.

Afrim and Saban led Santiago and Nick back up the staircase, machine guns at the ready. They could hear soldiers yelling and starting to enter the building through the dismembered doorway at the far end.

Nick quickly radioed Sonia. "Got the Star, on our way to the roof. See you soon!"

Sonia and Peter looked at one another, then quickly gathered what they needed and left the apartment. They'd drive the short distance to Denham Airport up the A40 in just over twenty minutes.

The four men ran through the display rooms, past paintings and artefacts, towards the central stairway. Afrim reached the bottom of the steps and stood guard there, watching down the corridor as the others rushed by and up the stairs.

At that moment the first soldier through the broken door ran out into the corridor, not expecting to come across anyone until the vault area. He was met with a burst of bullets from Afrim's MP5. Four rounds hit the brave soldier across his midriff. He slumped down dead, sliding a few feet with his forward momentum. His gun clattered ahead across the floor.

Two more soldiers arrived at the wall behind their fallen comrade and one quickly darted from behind the brickwork and fired a burst down the corridor towards the stairs.

Nick shouted to Afrim, "Come on, let's go!"

But Afrim wanted one more go at the approaching men, to slow them down and hold them back from chasing. He tapped the trigger and sent another seven rounds into the edge of the wall where the soldiers were, as more arrived there.

One of them dived across the floor low down, firing as he went, into the general direction of where Afrim stood. Several bullets whizzed past Afrim, but one caught him. The round passed straight through the side of his neck ripping through his jugular vein. Blood started spurting out instantly.

He fell down onto the bottom two steps, clutching his neck, trying to stop the bleeding. But it was hopeless and as Nick watched him, he knew that Afrim would be dead within thirty seconds. He left him and followed the others up the stairs.

Saban looked round at Nick for reassurance his brother would be okay. But Nick looked back up at him, then shook his head. Saban gritted his teeth for a moment, then turned and proceeded up the stairs, distraught and fuming.

Guards had now roped off the area around each of the assumed cyanide gas grenades. The police were still outside the main entrance and the congregation of Beefeaters, staff, families and soldiers outside the Waterloo Block, all looked up, as the unmistakable red Air Ambulance helicopter approached the Tower.

Given the multiple gun shots everyone had heard coming from inside the building, it seemed reasonable that the helicopter ambulance would have been called in to attend.

The front of the helicopter rose slightly as Samuel Morales began slowing its speed. He flew over the dry moat and started to come to a controlled hover over the roof of the Waterloo Block. Looking down he could see all the people in the courtyard behind the White Tower. He could also see one figure on the roof, Barney Smith, crouching down as the rotor blades buffeted him.

One of the guards that had come into the building had turned round and climbed back out again. He ran round to the front and hurriedly reported to his officer.

"Sir! Exchanging fire with several intruders inside, one man down I'm afraid. They appear to have come from the vault area. They're now making their way up the stairs." He looked at the red helicopter hovering above them and the Waterloo Block. "That must be their escape! Sir!"

Nick, Saban and Santiago made their way up the stairs and could now hear the footsteps of the pursuing soldiers two floors below them.

"Move it!" shouted Nick.

They reached the roof access door and burst through and out onto the lead-covered walkway. The red helicopter was hovering loudly just in front of them, above the roof apex. The force of the air from the rotor blades pushed down on them with immense pressure. Its side doors were slid back to the open position, awaiting its hastily departing passengers to board.

Two soldiers had run up the Bowyer Tower, which had the nearest turret behind the centre of the Waterloo Block roof, just sixty feet away.

"Barney, lock the door! Saban, Santiago, get up in there!" screamed Nick over the noise, pointing at the waiting helicopter.

The two men fought against the rushing air, up the slate roof slope. Samuel adjusted his position to get the helicopter as near to the top of the roof as possible. He constantly watched where his rotor blades were, mindful of avoiding the nearby round central and square corner turrets at the front of the building.

The guard in the courtyard asked the officer, "Shall I give the order to shoot on the helicopter, Sir?"

The officer looked up and was drawn to the prominent lettering on the red helicopter's side, saying 'London Air Ambulance'. What if they were wrong? Could he fire upon an emergency services aircraft here in the middle of the City, the Tower? The risks were greater than the benefits.

"No, not yet, stand down!"

Saban flung himself up into the helicopter and shuffled to the far side, closing the other unwanted sliding door. As he turned, Santiago was already clambering up inside as well. Nick saw that Barney was still fumbling to lock the roof access door. He could hear the soldiers approaching on the other side. The lock slid across inside its mechanism just as the first guard grabbed the door handle.

Nick climbed up into the helicopter and turned to give Barney a hand, as the minute adjustments the pilot was making to steady them, caused a slight wobbling of the craft in the air.

He then noticed two soldiers appear on top of the turret opposite them. They had a clear view of the Waterloo Block roof and the helicopter. The soldiers hadn't got the order to hold fire, from their officer down in the courtyard.

They both raised their weapons and shouted in unison,

"Halt! Halt! Land on the roof! Now! Or we'll open fire!"

Saban leant past Nick and Santiago and fired a burst at them, splintering stonework off the historical turret. The soldiers ducked down behind the masonry.

Barney struggled up the slope of the roof towards them. The helicopter rose in the air, just as he lunged for the floor inside. But with the sudden movement, he missed getting a firm hold and slipped down onto one of the landing skid rails. He frantically grabbed it crying out, "Help me!"

Nick bent down and started to wrestle Barney up into the cabin, shouting to the pilot, "Go! Jesus, just go!"

Samuel manoeuvred his control stick and started to pull upwards into the air.

The two soldiers reappeared on the turret and choosing not to fire upon the helicopter for fear of it crash landing on the Tower, one of them fired a single shot. The round hit where the soldier had aimed for. The thigh of the man hanging onto the skid. Barney yelled out!

The helicopter rose more, making it even harder for Barney to pull himself up as it pulled away from him. Nick was struggling to heave him up inside. The craft cleared the turrets and Samuel leant the helicopter down and powered forward heading briefly towards the main entrance.

The thrust of its movement and the buffeting air was too much for Barney and Nick to battle with. Barney was losing his grip and Nick couldn't do anything to regain his hold on the Beefeater.

As the helicopter began to veer to the right, that created the final pull to dislodge Barney's hold on the rail. Nick watched from the cabin, as Barney looked up at him and lost his hold. He fell, descending down into space. The turn then made Nick lose sight of Barney, but he heard the sickening thud, as Barney's body hit the grass-covered solid ground below.

There were screams underneath them from staff. Beefeaters encircled the body of one of their own Warders, lying motionless, in the middle of Tower Green.

The helicopter passed over the throng of helpless police still outside the surrounding moat and walls and rose above Tower Hill gathering speed as it went.

The police helicopter would arrive at the Tower in less than a minute. Too late though to follow the fleeing red Air Ambulance, now on its way to Denham aerodrome.

Inside the cabin Nick, Saban and Santiago allowed themselves congratulatory pats on the back, including Samuel Morales up front.

Nick slid shut the side door and unzipped his pocket to take out the diamond. He held it up. One of the most coveted items of the crown jewels. The Star of Africa. From the royal sceptre itself. The diamond continued to sparkle at them even in the darkened cabin, oblivious to the trials of the team who had now stolen it, from the Tower of London.

Nick radioed through to Sonia in the car with Peter. "We have it! Tell your government man, we have it!"

19

Max Sargent sat outside the MI5 Deputy Director General's office with Si Lawson. The meeting they were waiting to have would likely decide their fate. The DDG was currently in with the head of MI5, the Director General. It was almost nine AM.

A lot had happened since one thirty AM earlier that same morning. Max was discovered by the soldiers, trapped inside the crown jewels vault, having apparently been left behind by his fellow thieves!

The first soldiers on the scene instinctively knew not to announce outside the building that the precious Cullinan I diamond was missing from the royal sceptre. No one wanted to be the bearer of such bad news.

Whilst they didn't initially believe Max's rushed story to them, they soon acknowledged that he might indeed be with MI5 as he claimed. He certainly seemed to know the names of the right people. They agreed that only the Governor of the Tower should be told what had happened to the Star of Africa. They knew that officers, police and the government ministers well above their pay grade would decide how that particular piece of news would be handled!

The soldiers tended to the ten or so staff who had been rendered unconscious by the gas. With the help of arriving paramedics, those who were suffering badly from the drug inhalation were given naloxone and opioid antagonists, to help overcome the side effects.

Within an hour entry into the Tower premises had been gained, once the glue in the main entrance and Wharf doors had been drilled out and the locks dismantled. The swell of police and officials surging through the Tower site quickly organized itself, only allowing a select few to understand what had really happened. The rest handled the messaging to the large community of people that worked and lived within the Tower walls. Given the majority of the site's community and staff were complaining that this 'test drill' had been taken too far in its realism, the top brass went with that as the story. 'It was all a drill'! The Beefeater falling from the Air Ambulance was a terrible accident!

Later that morning everyone there would be reminded about their obligations to the Official Secrets Act they had each contracted to. No speaking to anyone about 'the drill', or grand theories about what might have taken place were forbidden to be communicated in any way whatsoever. Outside of the top team, no one even knew the Star of Africa had been taken.

During the next hour, the scrambler on the roof interrupting the Wi-Fi and airwaves was found, and disabled. Communications, feeds, telephone lines and CCTV were restored, once Peter Whistler's blockers had been detected and cancelled. The bodies of the fallen soldier, Barney Smith and Afrim were secretly taken into the chapel next door, to await private transport out of the site.

The bomb disposal squad had discovered the hydrogen cyanide gas canisters were fake, after trying to disable one of them with their explosive ordnance disposal robot. Work would start soon on removing the hardened foam from the inside of all the doors to the Waterloo Block. A new larger maintenance team would finish the jewel room travelator repair and replace the damaged display unit.

Max had been cut away from his foam vice trap and whisked out of the rear broken door exit and into the now safe barracks next door. He was then given army fatigues and taken by armed police to New Scotland Yard's Curtis Green building at Victoria Embankment. There he was allowed to make a call, which he put into his MI5 boss Si Lawson. He then started to set things up for his release back into MI5's custody.

Max hadn't yet been questioned at New Scotland Yard, who were quite dismayed when the order from up high, instructed them to deliver him to the MI5 headquarters at Thames House Millbank. Once there, still under armed police guard as a courtesy to the Met, Max spent the next few hours with various expert interrogators, MI5 officials and his boss Si Lawson.

Max told them everything he could about the Richmond bank hack, the whole Jurado team and their Prado robbery. He explained the predicament he found himself in and that if he hadn't gone along with it, having only found out about the Tower heist yesterday, they would have killed him. Max then described in detail the build-up and events of the whole Tower plan and execution.

After several hours of his clear, measured and honest account of everything he knew, officials could see he was telling the truth. Their natural default of suspicion gradually got replaced with their gratefulness of having a man on the inside of such a mind-blowingly brilliant criminal job. After all, with Max's help they already now knew who did it, an idea of why, reference potentially a Spanish 'power' and how the job was done.

Max started to feel his colleagues' trust and respect slowly return. Many shared their admiration for what he'd had to go through. The cases of both the Richmond Bank and Tower of London thefts were effectively both solved, but not concluded. That would only happen once the perpetrators were brought to justice.

During the last few hours, all the information Max provided had been assimilated, checked and summarized in a large dossier. This was then discussed by various heads of department including from the Tower, the police, the military, MI5, MI6, the Mayor of London and the Palace.

A further refined dossier now with options and recommendations, was next given to the Prime Minister, the Home Secretary, the Foreign Secretary, the Defence Secretary and MI5's Director General. Having just returned from 10 Downing Street, the DG was now speaking with his Deputy in his office just along the corridor.

"You okay Max?" asked Si Lawson, as they shared a couch outside the DDG's office.

Max puffed out a breath of air. "It's been a busy twenty-four hours, but yes, I am. I'm just glad everyone's come round to the predicament I was in and you guys are supporting me."

"I think we're all clear about the mess *we* got you into. You've always got cover when such operations have involvement and sanction from the top, as this did."

"I couldn't help thinking I would be locked up forever for treason, when I was stuck there in that damn vault room!" Max mused pensively.

"Well, strictly speaking, you did commit treason! Betrayal of the monarch and country! Look on the bright side though, you'll probably be the first person in history that then won't be charged for it!"

"Only *probably*? Second anyway, apparently, Colonel Blood got let off by King Charles II!"

"Look out, here he comes now," whispered Si as he noticed the DDG returning from his meeting with the top MI5 man.

He walked past them and sounded serious, "In you come you two!" Si thought he detected a slight creasing to the corner of his mouth. A frown, or admiring smirk?

They followed him into the sound-proofed glass office overlooking Lambeth Bridge on the Thames, closed the door and sat. Si and Max both felt like they were seeing the headmaster and about to get six of the cane.

The DDG slumped into his large leather chair, throwing the dossier onto the desk. "What a God-awful mess!"

The pair of them each thought 'this wasn't going to be good!'. Both frowned and knew not to speak until they were given their cue to.

"But...."

Maybe there was hope?

"And it's a big but," said the DDG, "thanks to you Max, the PM is on your side! You've solved the Richmond puzzle and we know everything about the Tower job from earlier this morning. Might even be able to go after his bitcoins and even get the Cullinan back?"

Max thought it felt like a lot longer ago since he was robbing the Tower of London than *this morning*. But it seemed he wasn't about to be locked up inside it after all!

The DDG continued. "We're now playing a game with the clock ticking. The top priority is to retrieve the Cullinan I diamond. We need it back in that bloody sceptre in the next forty-eight hours, tops!"

There was a pause, so Si spoke. "Are we okay with Max, boss?" He wanted to make sure, for Max's benefit, that he wasn't going to have to endure any repercussions, disciplinaries or even charges for what had happened.

The DDG looked at Max. "Thanks to your full account of everything and frankly your bravery, your two previous assignments with us here in MI5, and the full backing of your boss here," looking at Si, "and myself and the Director General, you're in the clear!"

"Thank God!" said Max.

"Outside of the top echelons, no one will ever know you were there. So don't go off bragging you helped steal one of the crown jewels will you!"

"About that sir," asked Max, "will everyone really accept the 'drill' story?"

"They haven't any other choice. Unless someone in the know blurts it out, at pain of death though," he smiled, "then I'd say we have a brief window to get that Star back where it belongs."

"But what about the Tower, visitors, the doors, even the bullet holes inside sir?"

The DDG patted the dossier. "Everyone involved has agreed that the Tower will be closed for today, following the security drill 'accident'. As a mark of respect to the Beefeater who died. Barney Smith." Max pulled a face. "Yes, despite him being one of the Jurado gang and helping them."

"We can't run with that, everything has to support the theft never happening! Anyway, they all reckon that by visitors opening time tomorrow morning, they will have everything back to normal. The doors will be cleaned, repaired or replaced if needs be with exact, aged replicas. Bullet holes filled and blended back into the stonework and the vault room including display case, fully restored, as if nothing happened there earlier!"

"You're not suggesting you believe we can get the Cullinan diamond back within twenty-four hours, are you?" ventured Max. Si gave him a look, hoping his question wouldn't be taken as impertinent. Max continued, "As I've told everyone, many times, they'll be well on their way, in fact almost there now, to Cancun."

The DDG let Max's tone pass this time. Max had been through a great deal and must be tired. "Air traffic control noted a small Gulfstream jet leaving Denham at one-fifty AM heading in the direction of Florida, Cuba, or as you suggest, Mexico. So no, I'm not suggesting we get the diamond back in a day. A *couple* of days though, yes, I am!"

"So how can you reopen the Tower tomorrow with no diamond in the sceptre?"

"There will be, at least it will look as though it's there. It'll simply be a replica! Amazing how realistic they are these days, tinted cubic zirconia or whatever the hell it's called."

Si spoke. "Sir, you implied we could get the diamond back in a couple of days?"

Max added, "We know where Sonia Jurado's villa is, just south of Cancun International airport, on the beach. Why can't you just get the Mexican Intelligence Services or army to storm the place, arrest them all and get our diamond back?" Max was tired and his tone showed signs of frustration.

"In normal circumstances we'd do just that, mount a joint

operation, go in and sort it," explained the DDG. "But Mexico isn't normal, at all!"

"How do you mean sir?"

"Firstly, relations with their various Services aren't entirely open or two-way. They still have a lot of corruption to deal with out there, at all levels, you get what I mean? The Foreign Secretary has already asked for their cooperation, but we can't tell them exactly what it's about!" He feigned a sarcastic tone, "Excuse me, we've lost one of our crown jewels, can we get it back by force from one of your beloved citizens!"

Si was taken aback at the DDG's momentary lapse of extreme professionalism, but agreed nonetheless. "Understood sir."

The DDG continued. "No, we have to sort this mess out ourselves, and besides, Jurado has done some work for the Mexican authorities. Some legitimate, some not it seems, so if they get wind of any moves against her, we suspect they'll rally round and defend her. No, they can't know what our problem is, nor be involved with what we're going to do about it."

"What is the plan sir?" asked Si, knowing that if the dossier on the desk in front of them had been to the top and back, there would be a plan.

The DDG rested a hand protectively on top of the dossier. "In confidence gentlemen. Assuming Jurado has the Star of Africa with her, which she must do, we'll send our guys into her Cancun villa and take it back, at any cost!"

"Can I ask how sir?" said Si. "You can't just drive up to her villa without raising suspicion from the local authorities?"

"Quite so. Instead, we'll have a handful of operatives," looking at Max, "indeed Commandos you'll be pleased to hear Max, who will approach the villa by the sea, infiltrate the premises and take the diamond back by whatever means necessary!"

Max was bursting with questions. "How do you get

Commandos out to Cancun, then back here with the Star in two days, assuming they manage to grab it in the first place, sir?"

The DDG allowed himself a wry smile. "Our Flagship of the fleet is on an ambassadorial and manoeuvres trip with the US Navy in Miami. We've already agreed on a slight change in the exercises it'll be doing, so it's now on its way to a point north of Havana in the Gulf of Mexico. That will place it in striking range of the Merlin helicopters, who will deliver the Commandos just off the shores of Cancun!"

"Blimey!" gasped Max. "We don't mess about here do we!"

"Not when someone tries to humiliate the United Kingdom by stealing a crown jewel!" The DDG sounded determined. "We're already talking to the Spanish authorities about suspects who might have planned backing an international scandal theft, but again, it's slow without them knowing exactly what the issue is."

"Forgive me, the Navy's Flagship is…?" asked Max.

"HMS Queen Elizabeth. Our newest, most advanced aircraft carrier! The Commandos are assigned to her and on board anyway."

"When's this happening sir?" asked Si.

"Tonight, Mexico time, so with the six-hour time difference, in about twenty hours."

"May I ask which Commando unit is on the carrier?"

The DDG paused, deciding whether to disclose this piece of information. He knew it might stir a reaction from the ex-Commando sat in front of him. "It's Four-Two Commando unit, Max. Your old team!"

Max somehow thought it might be, he didn't know how, he just had a feeling that fate was either mocking him, or drawing him in. Flashbacks of his training, of Fifty and the incident in Sierra Leone all came rushing back to him in a jumble of pride, determination and anxiety.

The other two men in the room waited quietly for Max to

speak next, wanting to gauge his reaction, make sure he was okay with his old unit being involved in what could be viewed as mopping up Max's mission.

Max's demons were thrust aside by his anger at what Jurado had done, to him and the UK. He wanted payback, and he wanted to right the wrongs of being involved with the Tower caper and not being able to stop it earlier. He simply had to ask, no, demand.

"Sir. Given everything that's happened, with my involvement, solving the Richmond hack and the information I've provided about the Tower and Jurado… I must ask, insist, that I am allowed to join the Commando team that goes into Cancun?"

There, he'd said it. Max waited for the put-down, the excuses, the reasons why it wouldn't be appropriate after twenty years on civi street, not to mention the dangers. He looked up at the DDG, then to Si.

The DDG watched Max closely, then spoke. "We thought you just might ask that Max. Having someone in the team who knows the Jurado bunch, their personalities, would certainly help. You are ex-military, albeit a while back, but your Military Cross counts for a lot around here. You've already proved yourself to us with several assignments. So in answer to your question, I will support it as long as the person who knows you best does, your boss! Si?"

Si Lawson quickly went through in his mind everything he knew about Max and all they'd been through in such a short time together. Max had impressed him and MI5, with front-line operations, more than most hardened agents. The answer was easy.

"Absolutely sir. If Max is up for it, then I know he'll do what he has to, to get that Cullinan diamond back for us." Si then pondered. "But Max is sitting with us here in London, Cancun's a long way away?"

The DDG had it covered. "We've already got your tickets, Max, just in case. You'll leave for a Heathrow to Miami flight in ninety minutes. One of the Merlin's from the carrier will collect you at Miami International and take you to the Flagship in the Gulf. One of my chaps will fill you and Si in with all the details on the way to the airport via your home. Good luck Max, we need that crown jewel back with us here!"

"Thank you, sir, I won't let you down!" said Max.

"I hope so, I'm staking my, and the country's reputation on it!" Max and Si stood and left for the door. "And Max, you'd better get as much sleep as you can on the flight over there. You've got another busy forty-eight-hour stint ahead of you, again!"

Eduardo Garcia had received the call from Sonia Jurado when she was on her way to Denham aerodrome, telling him the mission had been a success. She had the Star of Africa diamond with her and was retreating back to her Cancun villa. The Mexican authorities would never entertain any question of deporting her back to the UK for trial.

He couldn't help but laugh with Sonia over the phone. They had pulled off the ultimate insult against the British. Their revenge was sweet, for their families' personal oppression and dealings with Englishmen, and for their refusal to hand back Gibraltar to Spain. Eduardo was elated.

He told Sonia to keep the diamond for now as it may be useful in the future. Santiago would stay with her and the Star of Africa as additional security until he could arrange for his safe passage back to Spain, where he would also then be untouchable by the British.

What he didn't tell her though, was the backup idea he'd formulated in his devious mind. He wanted Santiago there, with the Cullinan I, to keep an eye on it. To make sure Sonia didn't think about selling it to the highest bidder. Some Chinese or Russian oligarch would pay many, many billions to add the Star of Africa crown jewel to their private collection.

His plan was to now humiliate the British, twice. The first had been achieved with the embarrassing theft of the diamond from the Tower of London. And then he would humiliate them again, by stealing the march on any of the British Intelligence Services trying to retrieve it. He would have his own Spanish Intelligence Services miraculously recapture the jewel. He could then triumphantly return the UK's precious royal diamond himself. Surely it could be used as leverage in the future to reopen negotiations about Gibraltar. But that was for another time. One theft, two insults. Eduardo knew how to ring the most out of any advantage.

He'd barely slept since speaking with Sonia and had got into his office early to start trawling through the British news outlets. He looked up the main newspapers online, the Times, FT, Daily Mail, Telegraph, eager to get a first glimpse of the headlines he'd fantasized about. He was expecting to see 'Outrageous theft of crown jewels!' or 'Shame on us, Star of Africa stolen!' even "Sovereign and nation insulted by Cullinan theft!'.

To his utter disbelief though, no such headlines appeared. He frantically searched through the web pages, assuming that it was possibly too early for the first editions to have captured the crown jewels theft in time before going to print.

Then, on the third page of the Times, he saw something that made his heart miss a beat. The article title was simply 'Accidental Death at Tower of London'.

"No, no, that can't be all there is! What about the diamond theft?" he said out loud to himself, fury mounting.

He read the article, the first paragraph of which said, 'Last night during a routine security drill, a Tower of London Warder Beefeater was accidentally killed when he fell from an Air Ambulance rescue helicopter. The Tower will be closed to the public today as a mark of respect.'. He read on, but there was no mention of the diamond theft from the vault, nor the fire-fight with soldiers, nor the gas or sealed doors!

He convinced himself this was a one-off error of

misunderstanding. As was often the case when news first comes out, it can take a little time for the facts to become clear. Eduardo now turned on his television and tuned into the BBC and Sky News channels. He flicked between the two for twenty minutes, waiting to catch the correct headlines about the crown jewels robbery.

But there was no mention whatsoever on the TV. Not even the Beefeater death made their news! He couldn't believe it. He wanted to pick up the phone and put in an anonymous call himself to one of the stations. But call tracing technology was commonplace now.

He consoled himself with the inevitable likelihood that something so huge would require more time to agree a proper press release. He was sure that was the explanation. The British authorities were working out how on earth they could best pitch this awful news, this insult to the UK, in the most favourable light possible.

'That'll be interesting. It'll get out, it has to', he thought. 'There's no way the Brits can sweep this under their damn red carpet much longer!'.

No. He had to do something about this. He wasn't going to let them get away with it, he wanted the world to know they'd let their crown jewels vault be robbed.

Eduardo noticed his personal assistant had just arrived and called out to her.

"Morning. Am I right in thinking we have the Princess visiting London tomorrow, one of the museum's or something?"

"Yes, that's right. She's having a tour of the Imperial War Museum. Keeping up relations and all that."

Eduardo came out of his office to see her. "Really? Get my palace contact on the phone, I'd like to add a little something onto her itinerary for tomorrow."

"Of course, Eduardo, what did you have in mind?"

"I'd like them to arrange a personal viewing for her.... Of their famous crown jewels!"

"Of course."

"And also get me the jeweller to our Royal family. I think it would be good for them to accompany the Princess on that visit. For inspiration you understand."

Eduardo retreated back into his office to take the two calls. This would prevent the British from trying to cover it all up any longer. They'd have to accept his visiting Royalty's request to view the collection, it would look odd if they didn't.

He knew the real Star of Africa was now in Mexico, not the Tower of London. With the Spanish Princess and their family's jewel expert there, nothing could stop the public humiliation when it became clear the real Cullinan I was missing!

Eduardo began to wonder if he should move things along sooner than he'd planned out in Cancun. He needed surety. He needed to be back in control and now felt vulnerable having the Star being held by Sonia Jurado.

He sent a brief text with instructions. To Santiago!

20

The Gulfstream jet landed at Cancun airport and taxied to a VIP station off the runway, where one of Sonia's villa staff was waiting to meet them.

Sonia Jurado was well known in the area, not by the public, but well known to those that mattered, the officials. The mayor, the police, the military, the airport security and customs control. Over the years of numerous events and parties at her villa, consulting work for various authorities, favours, financial help and back-handed contributions, she had built up a protective network around her private villa, that any billionaire drug baron would envy.

It was the start of a beautiful new day in Cancun, with the sun already making its appearance for another hot one. Their black stretch Lincoln limousine headed south from the airport down the Mexico 307, past the Cancun Country Club, for another eight miles. They then turned off left passing through the yellow stone entrance pillars to the Bahia Petempich area.

The police station right next to the only way into the resort area had already been fully briefed by their Chief. Sonia had called him and asked for them to be extra vigilant with any suspicious foreign or military type visitors, following a particularly 'sensitive' business deal she'd recently closed. The Chief was only too pleased to be of service to Sonia.

For years they'd joked with one another at parties that he should have a beautiful swimming pool added to his villa. He'd argued that he simply couldn't justify the cost of having it built retrospectively at his beloved property. Though he'd fantasized with Sonia about what magnificent designs he'd have for his pool, if he ever won the Mexican Loteria.

Then one day he and his family returned home from a

three-week European vacation, to find their dream pool complex had been built. Sonia had paid for the pool, with workmen toiling day and night to have it ready for the Chief's return. She greeted her old friend on their arrival, holding a bottle of champagne. The wife was overcome with gratitude, the kids all jumped straight into their new pool, and the Chief would do anything for Sonia forevermore. For Sonia, it was a mere sixty thousand dollars, but money well spent.

They drove another three miles through the dense trees which provided a natural barrier for the Caracol shoreline. Turning left they drove another two miles just parallel to the beach, behind the various hidden villas, resorts and hotel complexes. This road didn't lead anywhere, it was a dead end. Sonia's villa was the very last property on the road, half a mile from her nearest neighbour. The electric iron gates opened to reveal a staff member with a holstered gun, waiting to greet them into her private, secure, luxurious home and grounds.

Sonia, Peter, Nick, Saban and Santiago all climbed out of the limo, tired but happy to be safe. They were physically and emotionally drained after the last day's activities including the long flight over. They'd had little sleep, too pumped up after events at the Tower and enough adrenalin spikes to last a lifetime.

"Welcome to my lovely home," enthused Sonia, spreading her arms out to show off the amazing beachfront property, which Santiago and Saban had never seen before.

Behind and beyond the villa and gardens lay miles of thick, impassable trees and foliage. The only access was via the protected road they'd just come down. There was a tennis court to the side and a bungalow villa tucked to the back on the site for a couple of resident staff. The large, cream painted villa sat in the centre of the compound and looked out across an amazing pool area onto the long, sandy beach. A wooden jetty protruded out over the clear, turquoise waters and had a couple of boats resting alongside it on the still sea.

"Staff will show you to your rooms," said Sonia. "We'll

lie low here for a while. We're safe here. The Brits will have been told everything by your friend Max and likely know we're here!" she shook her head at Nick in jest, but then shrugged. "But that's fine, they can't touch us here. The authorities will protect us. The English will just have to stew in their own juice. We're safe now!"

Sonia dug into her Gucci handbag and casually pulled out the largest diamond in the world, the Cullinan I from the crown jewels! It seemed completely out of place here. She held it up and it came to life in the direct Mexican sunshine.

Incredible displays of light shot out, flickering, twinkling and bedazzling as she turned it around. The four men marvelled at it, at their accomplishment. But looking upon this symbol of the British monarchy, this historical jewel, they were each reminded of the gravity of what they'd done. They knew this wasn't over quite yet!

Sonia detected the contemplative mood so felt more reassurance was needed. "And this little beauty is also quite safe here with us. Nothing can touch us now!"

As they went into the villa, despite the protective ring around her complex, Sonia felt a hint of concern creep into her mind. Perhaps the sleeping giant they had now awakened, would not share her confidence in their safety!

Max slept for most of the nine-and-a-half-hour flight to Miami from Heathrow. MI5 knew he needed to be rested and the DDG had insisted he got a flatbed in first class.

The British Airways A380 double-deck Airbus touched down early afternoon local time and taxied to the terminal. As Max came out of the plane, he immediately saw a man standing inside the walkway tunnel holding up a small card with 'MAX S' written on it. Max went over to him.

"Max Sargent sir?" checked the man. Max nodded. "Only hand luggage I gather?" he said.

"Yup."

"Great. I'm your Miami Airport VIP Liaison Manager, welcome to Miami Mr Sargent. Please come this way." He opened the small door of the covered walkway near the plane's door, as disembarking passengers looked on with curiosity. He led Max down the metal steps onto the concrete. The huge plane towered above them.

"This way sir," he said, pointing to a luxurious version of a golf buggy. "You've already been cleared through arrivals, customs and border control, no need to go through the terminal for all that nonsense."

"I wish it was this easy when I go on holidays," joked Max.

The VIP man forced a laugh. "I don't often get told someone has the full aircraft to aircraft transfer clearance. Your government must have swung things with ours, you must be important and in a hurry sir?"

"Indeed I am."

They drove out onto one of the many marked routes along the side of the runways and taxiing lanes. Then round the terminal buildings towards a corner of the concrete expanse, where Max could see a large, grey helicopter waiting, rotor blades turning. It was one of the Merlin's from the Queen Elizabeth aircraft carrier.

One of the crew greeted Max, took his hand luggage and invited him up into the helicopter cabin. Max tried to make himself comfortable, in the uncomfortable seat. The headphones went some way to dampening the deafening noise and allowed the Merlin HC4 pilot to greet Max and explain that they had already refuelled. They would be flying over three hundred miles to join the carrier in the Gulf, their flight time would be just over two hours. That would give Max plenty of time to rest up, join the other Commandos, briefing, preparation and be taken to Cancun that night!

The flight didn't seem long. Max was left to his thoughts amidst the noise of the helicopter. He found himself going over the build-up to their visit to the Tower. He then went through every detail of the night, from jumping off the

Cheesegrater, right through to getting himself stuck in the vault room. Could he have stopped it sooner? What would they have done if he'd tried? Nick's words to him returned, when he told Max that *he* wouldn't shoot him, but the others would!

Tonight would give him the chance to fully redeem himself to his superiors and more importantly to himself. His thoughts then went through all the scenarios of what awaited him later. After all, they weren't going to invite them in for dinner and hand over the diamond on a dessert dish! It was inevitably going to be messy and that held big concerns for him, again.

The Merlin pilots started to communicate with the carrier as they approached. The Queen Elizabeth was moving across the calm sea at twenty-five knots. They slowed down and started to hover over the allotted space on the flight deck.

An officer came out to greet Max, who thanked the crew.

"Come with me sir, the 'Commy' wants to meet you and your boss is waiting to call through as well."

He led Max into the bottom of the control tower, then down a couple of floors and along a narrow corridor. Passing seamen saluted the officer with Max and gave him a curious look, surprised to see a civilian being taken on board. They had no idea what for.

They went into the officer's quarters and down to the boardroom at the end.

"Commodore Clarkson, this is Max Sargent. Just arrived on board from Miami," introduced the officer, who then left, closing the door.

Max instinctively saluted the senior Navy man in charge of the Flagship of the Fleet, "Sir!", surprised that the habit and mark of respect had stayed with him twenty years after leaving the Marines.

"At ease Max," said the Commodore holding out his hand. "No need to salute me, you're a civilian after all, but the gesture is appreciated. Have a seat and welcome aboard."

"Thank you sir," said Max, "what an impressive carrier

you have here."

"It should be for the billions we spent on it. Sixty-five-thousand-ton displacement, nine levels below the flight deck, sixty aircraft, almost a thousand feet long and a crew of seven hundred. We've got enough firepower on this to obliterate a small country!"

"Very impressive! Apologies for having this slight detour forced on you, hopefully, everything's been explained?"

"After being briefed by the PM, my First Sea Lord has given me all the details. Just a few of my senior officers know what's happening, along with the Merlin crews, the three Commandos and their officer."

"Three, sir, only three?" checked Max who was expecting a larger team to be going in with him.

"Why yes, three of our best will be more than adequate, plus you Max. That's all the space we'll have on the Merlin taking you, plus room for the compressed raiding craft. Your team will fill you in with all the details."

"Right sir," agreed Max, with thoughts of a large team surrounding the villa evaporating.

Clarkson leant over to his speakerphone. "I've been asked to get your boss at MI5 on the blower, let's call him now." He eyed Max curiously as the secure line went through to Si Lawson in London.

"Thank you, Commodore," said Si over the speaker. "Max, just wanted to touch base before you go in tonight. You don't need me to tell you how critical this is, not just for MI5 and the government, but everyone here, and the country. We simply cannot allow anyone to make a mockery of us. The Commodore's been given a message from the PM, for you and the chaps going. The Four-Two officer will give it to you and your guys when you're briefed."

"Okay Si, thanks."

"One other thing, our hunch about the robbery's backer, this Spanish power, it's all starting to look like it's not a criminal organization, but someone within their government or Intelligence Services."

"What makes you think that?" asked Max.

"From the info you gave us, we found your Santiago Lopez buried within their Agency, works for one of their top diplomats, an Eduardo Garcia. Santiago might be working alone, but now something else's come up which doesn't feel right as well."

"What's that?"

"The King of Spain's daughter is here tomorrow on a diplomatic trip visiting the War Museum. Her team have now requested she has a private viewing of the regalia crown jewels. With their Royal family's jeweller in toe. We've put them off until tomorrow evening after the Tower closes to the public and she's finished at the museum."

"What! But what about the refurbishment, the replica?" Then thinking about it Max added, "Sounds suspicious?"

"Very. Like someone wants it known the real Star of Africa isn't there, I agree," said Si. "The refurb part is fine. While you've been sleeping during your first-class flight over there, it's been frantic at the Tower. Can you believe though, most things have been replaced or repaired during today, it's evening here now, and by the time the Tower opens in the morning, it'll all be done. No one will ever know or see what happened the other night!"

"And the replica Cullinan?"

"That's the point I wanted to make Max. The replica will do its job for tomorrow's public, but..."

Max was ahead of him and interjected, "We need to have the real one back in its place before the Princess and her jeweller view it? Damn, is that even possible with the timings, flight time back to you is about ten hours and that's assuming we get it back from the villa and then the carrier?"

"Don't worry Max, it's all been thrashed out by people better at this than you and me. Yes, it can be done, your Four-Two officer will explain it and thanks to the Commodore's help, I know we *can* do this Max!"

They ended the call with Si. The Commodore asked the same officer from earlier to take Max to the Royal Marine's Lieutenant Colonel who was overseeing the raid.

They went down more stairs and along corridors in the rabbit warren of a city on the sea and finally went into another much smaller meeting room. The senior officer greeted Max, as three other Marines stood to attention. They'd been specially picked for their outstanding records, achievements and skills. Each of them introduced themselves to Max, they were Blake, Hall and the marksman sniper, Marsh.

Their initial scepticism about a civilian even being considered to accompany them on a dangerous raid, was soon replaced with respect. Si Lawson had submitted his summary of Max with this discerning audience in mind. They were given top-level impressive details of Max's previous two operations with MI5. Along with information about his brief time as a Commando twenty years ago, with their same unit Four-Two. The shared links were beginning to form before they'd even met him. And of course, there was also what had taken place out in Sierra Leone, leading to Max's honorary discharge, but with the Military Cross pinned to his uniform.

Despite these men having served for much longer than Max's two years in the Commandos, they had each felt this man deserved their respect and support. They wanted him to be good, after all, they might have to rely on him for their own safety on the mission. A mission that had been clearly outlined to them. To retrieve the Star of Africa for the United Kingdom.

Max was given time to tell them all the pertinent details he could about what had happened and with the accompanying files already compiled and sent over, he went through each member of the Jurado team. The three Commandos listened intently, knowing information was power and advantage, to be ignored at one's peril.

Next, the Lieutenant Colonel took them through the mission plan including maps and aerial pictures of the villa complex. There were even photographs over the years of parts of the grounds and inside the villa, gained from local paper cuttings and social media covered events held there.

"We've got two Merlin HC4's onboard, each with a range of about five hundred miles," said the officer. "By the time we need to go later tonight, the carrier will still be around two hundred and fifty miles from Cancun. Less than two hours flying time in the Merlin. Once it's dropped you guys off it'll need to high-tail it back here pronto before it takes a swim."

He could see his Marine's looking slightly perturbed at the thought of being left at the villa and asked to make their own way back.

"Don't worry lads, that's where the second Merlin comes in. That will leave the carrier precisely forty minutes after the first, to come and collect you from either the beach of the villa or out at sea. We reckon if you haven't got the whole thing sorted within half an hour, you're probably all dead anyway!"

The men laughed it off.

"Only joking of course," the Lieutenant Colonel patted Marsh on the shoulder. "It'll be dark when you approach Cancun, but not dark enough to get you in too close. From the villa's first floor balcony their line of sight to the horizon, with binoculars, is over three miles. So the Merlin will drop you into the water three and a half miles out with the compressed inflatable and silenced outboard. It should only take you about ten minutes to get ashore from there, landing a little way up the beach from the villa."

He then went through the options of approach for the four men, how they should spread out, provide cover and infiltrate the villa, depending on where the Jurado men were. More details, plans and discussion about engagement with the 'enemy'.

"Ah yes, that leads me on nicely to a message we've been sent, by the Prime Minister." The officer took out the thin slip of typed paper and placed it on the table in front of them. "I'll let you read it."

TOP SECRET, FOR YOUR EYES ONLY
TO BE DESTROYED ONCE READ

I wanted to wish you luck on behalf of HM Government and the many Services involved with the predicament we find ourselves in ref the Cullinan I crown jewel.

You must obtain possession of this most treasured piece of our nation's history, regalia and pride. We cannot and will not be intimidated by anyone threatening our position on the world's stage, by such a heinous crime.

Thank you for doing your duty tonight. The perpetrators, each and everyone, should not be allowed to speak of this.

The PM.

The last line held in the air as they each read the note. They re-read it to be sure they understood. It was subtle but clear. No survivors!

Max looked at the other three as they nodded to one another to reaffirm their understanding of how important this was, and their pact.

The Lieutenant Colonel picked up the piece of paper, grabbed a lighter and touched its flame to the corner. They all watched it burn up into black ash within moments.

"Me and the Commodore will be on your radios and with your body cameras, we'll be able to see what's going on. We'll let you guys get on with the job, but we're there if you need any direction and fine-tuning of the pickup when it's over."

"Sir?" said Max. "One thing's bothering me. The timings. If…" he corrected himself, "*when* we get the Star back, we wait for the second Merlin, then two hours back to the Queen Elizabeth, two hours to Miami, then ten plus back to London. I can't see how it'll work, won't it be too tight?"

The others hadn't done the maths but now nodded in unison.

The officer smiled. "Absolutely right Max. Plus we've got

the loss of the six hours time difference! We need to shave off quite a few hours to all that if we're going to get the stone back in its place, for the Princess of Spain to gaze upon tomorrow evening."

They were curious, but could see the officer had it under control, somehow.

"Let me take you through what we've got planned!"

21

Max, Blake, Hall and Marsh had taken time after their briefing, to eat and chill briefly before getting ready for the off. One of the chef's had prepared them a simple fillet steak, pasta and side salad, with freshly squeezed orange juice. Perfect. They watched a couple of the old original 'Tom and Jerry' cartoons, with the cat and mouse chasing around the house beating the hell out of one another.

Then it was off to select and prepare their equipment. This included silenced MP5 machine guns, grenades, flash stuns and Glock 17 handguns. Marsh had his sniper rifle with an infra-red scope option and would provide longer range cover if able to.

Max, however, upon seeing the Glock laid out for him, screwed up his face a little.

"What's the matter, Max?" Hall asked him.

"I know the 17 is the standard issue but is there a choice at all?"

"Crikey Max, are you kidding, we've got whatever you could imagine somewhere here, just name it? Rocket launchers, Gatlings, anything!"

"Someone I worked with recently, highly recommended the Sig 228. I don't suppose you've got one of them have you?" asked Max.

"Ah, old school eh!" Blake had been listening and delved into one of the ordnance drawers, pulling out the handgun in question. "The Sig Sauer P228! You and your friend know your stuff. This is probably one of the best there is for weight, size, power, accuracy and reliability. Personally, I'll stick with my Glock, that's what I've been brought up with, but I like your choice." He handed it over with some boxes of rounds and spare clips. "Here's the silencer for it."

All geared up and in black fatigues, which Max was becoming very familiar with by now, they came onto the flight deck. Once again, the Merlin was waiting, rotor blades spinning relentlessly.

The large helicopter rose up from the runway into the late evening dull sky and veered off over the sea, buffeting the flight deck crew kneeling against the torrents of air.

During the flight, the four men went through a final equipment check. The radio and bodycams were tested to ensure their Lieutenant Colonel and Commodore with support technicians were receiving them.

They also each checked they had a particular item tucked away in their zipped pockets. This would form part of the plan to start shaving time off the unforgiving schedule they faced.

"Five minutes out lads," reported one of the two pilots. After the two-hour trip, it was ten PM.

On the cabin floor between them, sat a huge bundle of tightly folded PVC with a small but powerful outboard motor on top. It was attached to the rear panel of the inflatable raiding craft, its shiny propellor glinting in the darkness.

Blake held out his hand in the middle of them, the others put a hand on top. "This is it boys, failure not an option, we must get that diamond back. Once we go ashore and along the beach, you Max and Marsh go centre, me and Hall to the sides. I'll cover the entrance far side in case anyone tries to get away, or if we get any unwanted locals trying to help out. Stay online. Let's do this!"

The Merlin passed the mark four miles out from the shoreline and started to slow right down from its cruising speed of one hundred and sixty miles an hour. As it tilted back raising the nose, the craft started to reduce height and within moments, came to a flat hover above the sea below. The pilot kept lowering until the huge helicopter was just ten feet above the calm, clear water.

Blake grabbed the red pull handle of the bulky package and

as they shoved it out the door, tugged the cord, activating the compressed air canister fixed inside the rolls of PVC material. The folded lump immediately inflated, growing in size and taking the shape of a small four-man landing craft.

The outboard motor flipped into place as the last of the air forced the PVC into its final, taught shape of a small, low, black speed boat. Hall threw down a full plastic fuel can into the waiting craft, which just needed plugging into the waiting fuel line of the motor.

They each positioned themselves on the edge of the cabin sliding doorway and jumped down. Max and Blake managed to land directly into the inflatable, the other two jumped into the water, grabbing the sides of the boat and adeptly swinging themselves inside.

The Merlin throttled up and rose above them like a giant hornet. It then turned and started back to the carrier with just over half its fuel left. Another twenty miles and it would have been too far for the return trip.

They checked their bearings and set off, skimming effortlessly across the near-flat sea. The small but powerful motor did its job admirably, speeding them along at around twenty-five miles an hour. Its adapted exhaust silencer almost completely dampened its output to a soft burbling buzz.

After several minutes they could see a couple of lights ahead and to their left.

"That's the villa chaps," pointed Blake and aimed the boat slightly further to the right, ensuring their landing point was far enough away from the target.

At the villa, the team had enjoyed a marvellous dinner cooked by Sonia's chef, sitting out by the pool under a large gazebo. The drinks had flowed and they were all tired after the Tower job and long flight back. None of them thought for one moment that anyone could possibly be onto them, at least not for another day or so. They would look to increase security tomorrow both at the villa and the resort entrance with more police. Tensions had gone, the mood was triumphant and relaxed.

Sonia had gone to bed, Nick Hawkins and Peter Whistler were relaxing in the lounge where the ex-Commando was showing the IT guru the latest Beretta handgun. Santiago was in the kitchen at the rear, snooping around for more delectable snacks and Saban had gone to his room to change into his swimming trunks to go for a dip in the pool.

Max and the three Commandos quietly beached their craft, cutting the motor. They pulled the inflatable into the shrubbery lining the shore beyond the sand and quietly made their way down the beach hugging the foliage. They could see a jetty with the two boats ahead and several of the villa's exterior lights on a balcony and around the pool.

As they reached the corner of the grounds they squatted down low in a final gathering before splitting up. Nothing was said, this was merely the opportunity for anyone to raise any suggested changes to the plan, now they were on-site rather than looking at aerial photos and maps. All seemed quiet.

Blake continued on down the beach to cut in near the driveway entrance gate. Hall broke away and headed straight inland along the side perimeter of the property. He passed behind a triple garage. A long, black limousine was parked up in front on the tarmac and a couple of colourful beach buggies sat neatly lined up to the side.

Max and Marsh now crawled up the sandy, sloped clearing that had been made through the foliage, for the villa residents to access the beach and jetty. Marsh unslung his L115A3 long-range sniper rifle and started to search around the site through the twenty-five times magnification telescopic sights.

The weapon was favoured by the British military for snipers and with an accurate range of just over a kilometre, he would have no trouble pinpointing anything around the villa right in front of him. He needed a better vantage point and had already earmarked the roof of the pool gazebo, which could easily be climbed onto via one of the large barbeque stoves.

Blake held up his silenced MP5 as he approached the gates

from the inside of the perimeter. With no-one there, he continued alongside the short driveway using a few solitary trees as cover, to get closer to the villa. Hall had proceeded along his side of the site and was now starting to crawl across the thick grassy lawn towards the rear kitchen doors.

At that moment all four of them froze. Someone slid back one of the patio doors from the lounge to the pool area and came out. It was Saban. With only his trunks on and clutching a towel, they could all see he was unarmed.

Blake came on the radio in a hushed voice. “Hold! Hold everyone. Single target by the pool. Marsh ready?”

They watched him as he slid the door closed behind him and strolled across the large patio expanse to the pool.

“Saban. Albanian,” whispered Max in confirmation.

Marsh watched him now through his sights. With the magnification and their closeness, Saban’s head and shoulders filled his round telescopic view-piece. The sniper followed him with the precise crosshairs.

Saban threw his towel down near the edge of the pool and approached the diving board. From inside the lounge, Peter glanced over Nick as they were chatting and watched the young Albanian step up onto the diving board. He then continued listening to Nick.

“Take the shot Marsh!” instructed Blake quietly.

Saban stood up straight on the fibreglass board and gazed up at the stars above him. It was a clear, cool night. Despite his life-long bond with his brother Afrim, he was pragmatic and found he’d quickly resigned himself to his death back at the Tower. With time to think about it during the long flight back to Cancun, he’d surprised himself further by managing to let go of the rage and need for revenge. He felt at peace with everything, safe, here with Sonia in this hidden away oasis.

He breathed in and walked along the diving board. Then with a small half jump, he bounced on the end and did a high, lingering jack-knife dive up into the air, then started to straighten out as he entered the pool, outstretched hands first.

Peter looked up from admiring Nick's new gun and noticed Saban's perfect dive from inside the lounge, then he disappeared from view below the level of the couch opposite him and into the pool.

As Saban's fingers touched the water, Marsh's bullet hit into his back and passed through his heart. It killed him instantly before he even heard the faint 'phut' noise coming from the sniper's silencer muzzle.

The round exited out of his chest and fell into the pool under the diving board. Marsh had meticulously followed every movement of the dive and had waited until Saban was about to enter the water. He didn't want him to have the time to make any sound and couldn't risk the bullet hitting the villa having passed through him.

Saban went into the water and a red stain of blood emanated from both sides of his torso, as he slowly sank into the deep end.

The four men around the villa quickly scanned the building for any signs of hurried movement or noise. All still quiet, no one had seen what had happened outside.

"Report?" said Blake, "all clear here at the front."

"Saban dead in the pool," said Marsh, "two men in the lounge, seated, talking."

"One man in the rear kitchen," added Hall.

"Sonia, any staff?" asked Max.

"Not visible at the moment." Blake moved closer to the villa. "Marsh take up covering position, Max and Hall, get ready to go in! Don't kill the woman Sonia or the ex-Commando Nick yet, we need to know where the diamond is, they'll know."

Max crawled up the sand to the end of the pool area, keeping low once he was able to see Peter and Nick more clearly through the patio doors across the pool. Marsh skirted round the bushes and quickly climbed the barbeque and up onto the flat, solid gazebo roof. He lay down and had a view of three sides of the villa and the staff bungalow at the rear.

The approaching men each took one of their stun grenades and got ready for Blake's count.

"We go in on zero. Three, two, one…"

Simultaneously Blake ran up to the front entrance and leading with his heavy metal MP5 gun, crashed through one of the full-length glass panels next to the front door. He then threw his stun grenade into the lounge.

Max drew his arm back and threw his grenade at the pool patio doors, smashing through them and falling into the lounge as well. He started running towards the patio doors using the smoke inside as cover.

Hall rose to his feet, ran towards the kitchen and just as Santiago spotted him, hurled his flash grenade through a window.

Each of the three grenades exploded with an almighty one hundred and seventy decibel bang and accompanying blinding light flash, momentarily disorientating anyone nearby.

As Hall started firing into the kitchen where his target had been standing, Santiago had dived behind the central worktop and was scuttling from the room towards the stairs. His gun was in his bedroom and he needed to put some distance between himself and everything happening downstairs.

Marsh had just lined up Peter in his sights when the two flash bombs went off in the lounge, instantly distracting his aim by enough for him to miss his target by inches. Nick had rolled off the sofa away from Peter, who still held his new gun. The old Marine was disorientated but instincts kicked in, and he was already making for a Glock in the table drawer nearby.

Peter was stunned and dazed by the two loud bangs near him and briefly blinded by the flashes. He curled up where he sat on the couch in reaction to the loud explosions, confused and frightened. Marsh outside on the gazebo couldn't yet see him again for the smoke in the room.

Peter quickly gathered his thoughts, though he was still temporarily deafened and finding it hard to focus properly. He realized he was still holding Nick's brand-new loaded Beretta APX. He raised it up and started firing wildly into the smoke and what looked like an intruder coming through the patio doors.

Max saw Peter raise the gun in disbelief, not what he'd expected to be greeted with! As the flashes from the Beretta started and bullets began flying in his direction, Max used all his power to launch himself sideways. He felt something bite him in the leg, left calf muscle. As he flew through the air, he twisted his body round and just as he started to land on a small side table, he fired off a single round from his silenced Sig.

The bullet hit Peter in the chest, passing through a lung, the edge of his heart and smashing through his spine, before emerging into the back of the thick couch he was on.

Max crashed through the table, collapsing it to the floor with him uncomfortably on top. The Beretta ceased firing and fell to the floor, as Peter slumped back, then slid a few inches down the smooth leather. He died two seconds later.

Sonia was brought out of her light sleep by the three loud bangs, then shooting, coming from downstairs. The grenades seemed to shake the whole house and sounded like they were set off in her room they were so loud. Though shocked to the core, she got up and rushed to her dressing room. She'd hidden an old mini-Uzi machine gun there years ago as a backup for who knows what. She'd never used it before, but mow grabbed it from the back of the drawer it lay in.

Marsh was waiting for the smoke to clear in the lounge, then noticed movement in the bungalow doorway. The sole armed staff member was coming out, holding up his handgun, looking startled but determined. Marsh swung his long, silenced barrel across and within a second had the man in his crosshairs.

'Bap!' The decisive headshot felled him immediately.

Time to join the others. Marsh climbed down from the gazebo and made his way around the pool to the villa's patio doors.

Nick was opening the drawer and grabbing the Glock inside, just as Blake came into the lounge from the entrance hall. Max knelt up from the floor and could now see Nick as the smoke disseminated. Nick raised the gun.

"Freeze!" shouted Blake.

"Don't move!" yelled Max.

They were on either side of Nick pointing their guns right at him. Nick would be dead before he turned to face either one of them, let alone fire his gun off. He held his gun hand up slightly, in submission.

"Okay, okay!" Nick looked over at Peter's body on the couch. These guys were serious.

Only now did Nick look upon his intruders. He did a double-take at Max. His mind couldn't believe what his eyes saw in front of him.

"Max? It's you? How the hell did you get out here, and so fast?" Nick's face was screwed up in utter confusion and disbelief.

Hall had come into the empty kitchen and then skirted around the central workstation. With Blake and Max confronting someone in the lounge, he knew that his man, Santiago, must have gone upstairs.

Santiago was now in his bedroom. Sonia had come out of her room and was nervously waiting on the first-floor landing.

Hall approached the bottom of the stairs and as he swung round to look up to see if anyone was there, Sonia held her mini-Uzi over the balustrade and fired in his general direction.

The weapon sprayed the bottom of the staircase with the magazine's full twenty rounds in less than two seconds. Walls, floor, stairs and ornaments were peppered with 9mm bullets. Despite trying to avoid the hailstorm of lead, Hall wasn't fast enough. Three rounds struck into the Commando at the bottom of the stairs, dropping him to the ground hard. Lifeless.

The gunfire from the stairs barely made the men in the lounge flinch, each staring at one another, Nick surrounded.

He could see another man approaching the doors. He was outnumbered.

"Drop the gun Nick!" demanded Max with gritted teeth.

"Max, I trusted you?"

"And I trusted you Fifty, I had no idea what you were going to get me involved with. I was only following up on the Richmond case!"

Nick recognized some of the gear the men had. "Commandos? Max, you came here with Commandos. Which unit you guys from?" he asked looking at Blake.

Max cut in, "Same as ours Fifty, Four-Two!"

"You're kidding! There's irony for you eh? Our old unit here to kill me and get the Star!"

"You've gone bad Fifty!"

"MI5?" questioned Nick. "You? What the hell happened to you. To us? We were supposed to be on the good side?"

"I am on the good side!" asserted Max. "Please Nick, drop the gun?"

"You won't shoot me, Max, you saved my life once, and I saved yours back at the Tower," whispered Nick, his grip on the Glock tightening as if he was about to try something.

"As you once said to me, Nick. I won't shoot you, but *they* will!"

Marsh slowly entered the room, sniper rifle held up.

Nick didn't really know what compelled him to give it a go. Honour maybe. Not wanting to be caught alive and spend life in prison. Going out in a blaze of glory. He didn't know. He just had to do something.

The moment Nick started to raise his gun to Blake, his chest seemed to explode. Marsh, Blake… and Max all fired several shots at Nick. The spattering effect around the upper part of his chest, twisted and turned his body with the harsh velocity impact of the slugs. He fell to the ground.

Upstairs, Santiago had got what he wanted from his bedroom and was starting to climb down from his balcony outside.

Sonia could see she had emptied the Uzi magazine and had no defence left. On hearing the continued shooting coming from downstairs in the lounge, she called out, throwing the Uzi down the stairs.

"I give up! Don't shoot! Please don't shoot?" She started slowly coming down, step by step, hands held high.

Blake then Max slowly came out of the lounge into the hall, followed by Marsh. They saw their fallen comrade at the bottom of the stairs. His murderer descending towards him. All three turned their guns onto Sonia.

"Please! I'm so sorry. I didn't even know he was there, I panicked!" she protested feebly.

"Hall's down, she bloody shot him!" sneered Marsh.

"Come down Sonia, keep your hands raised," said Max.

"Max?" She looked shocked, then horrified, then outraged. "How did you get here?" Sonia then noticed Nick's bloodied body behind them in the lounge. "How could you? He was your old Sergeant. One of you!"

"Not any more Sonia. You saw to that didn't you," said Max.

Marsh and Blake knew how to threaten someone to quickly give up information in such stressful circumstances.

"I say we waste her now," said Marsh.

"You have shot our friend here," agreed Blake nodding to Hall's body.

Sonia was desperate. Hands raised even higher in submission. "Please! I'll do anything! We did your stupid Richmond Bank, and yes, the Tower of London job. But you know that, Max was there with us!"

The bodycams were recording everything as the Lieutenant Colonel and Commodore watched back in the depths of the aircraft carrier.

Max was quick to ask the key question. "Who put you up to the Tower job? Helped you sort things? This Spanish power? Who?"

Sonia shook her head. "Someone from the embassy,

worked with Santiago, maybe his boss."

"A name?" asked Max again.

"I didn't get his full name," pleaded Sonia, "Eduardo, no surname. Intelligence Services or something."

"Why?"

"Revenge. He hates you Brits. He wanted to humiliate the UK!"

"Did you really think we'd let you get away with one of the crown jewels," said Blake.

Sonia realized what else she could impress them with, maybe in trade for her life. "You want the diamond back, don't you? I'll give you the Cullinan for my freedom, yes?"

She moved down the stairs cautiously, checking they would let her pass and led them into the office. She went around the large desk and bent down.

"Careful lady," said Marsh, "anything stupid and it's the last thing you do!"

"Okay, I'm getting you your bloody diamond! He forced us to do the job! Blackmailed me after finding out we did a job in Madrid." She slowly pulled out the lowest drawer down the side of the desk and pulled out the paperwork inside, throwing it on the floor. The drawer now looked empty.

She hooked her nail under a tiny tab on the edge of the drawer base and slowly lifted up the false panel. They all looked inside, expecting to see the Star of Africa.

It was empty!

"Yes?" inquired Blake impatiently.

They all heard the sound of the noisy Volkswagen Beetle engine turning over outside, then after a few splutters, firing up and revving.

Sonia looked up in horror. "The buggies? Santiago!"

"What?"

"He must have seen me put it here!" pleaded Sonia.

"Guy's, hold this one, be useful to take her back to give us all the info and confess," said Max, starting back towards the hall, "I'll go after this one!"

Blake replied as Max left, "We already have all the info, sorry Max, orders!"

He calmly and efficiently levelled his gun at Sonia's head. She looked into the dark end of the barrel. He fired. Max turned his head back quickly.

"Marsh and I will sort things out here Max, just get it back for us!"

Max felt for Sonia as he ran through the lounge towards the sound of the beach buggy outside. The slight limp he had from the bullet graze on his calf, mostly ran itself off as he came out onto the pool area. He could see Santiago pulling away from the driveway and heading off for the sandy shoreline.

'No you don't!' he thought.

22

Santiago had earlier received the text from his boss Eduardo Garcia saying, 'Take diamond by whatever means and go to the Cancun safehouse. I will arrange transportation to Cuba by boat'. The tip of Cuba was only one-hundred and thirty miles away, an easy trip for a powerful motor launch.

Santiago had planned to hold them all at gunpoint after dinner, find out where the diamond was, tie them up, shoot anyone that gave him any trouble. Then flee to the Spanish Intelligence Services' secret apartment in Cancun.

But during the long boozy dinner, the atmosphere was relaxed and people were coming and going during the many courses. Santiago was paying a visit to the bathroom when he caught a glimpse of Sonia placing something into the lower desk drawer in the office. The group had then moved out to the pool area for desserts and more drinks and that was when he took a chance and came back inside.

Checking they were all still outside, laughing and joking and that the staff had retreated to their bungalow, he quickly crept into the study. Frantically searching the lower drawers all he could find was dull paperwork. Then he noticed the base inside the drawer was slightly raised at a higher level than the underneath of the wooden pull-out. He realized it had a false bottom and quickly opened it up.

The Star of Africa sat there innocently, loose, in the drawer. He quickly pocketed it, put everything back as it was and managed to go up to his room and hide it. He'd been in the office no more than twenty seconds. He intended to leave for the safehouse later in the night when everyone was asleep. But when the villa was stormed, he had to take advantage of the confusion and leave, there and then.

After climbing down his balcony, he'd run down the side of the gardens to the garages. The driveway swept around the villa and would afford the intruders time to intercept him before the exit gates. So he took one of the beach buggies. He could go north along the shoreline and later cut up through one of the hotel complexes, back to Cancun.

Both had their keys in the ignition, so he grabbed the first buggy's key and only threw it into the foliage once he'd successfully started the other one.

Max sprinted to the remaining buggy and jumped in, placing the Sig on the passenger seat. No Keys! When Max was nineteen he'd built his own beach buggy from the ground up, using a VW Beetle floor pan and 1300cc engine. The fibreglass body fixed on top, then wiring, seats and lights completed the kit car. He forced out the ignition key-holder from the dash and touched the permanent red live wire to the starter power feed. The engine cranked over, then fired into life with a noisy rumble produced by the two trombone tailpipes.

He gunned the accelerator and wheel-spun off the driveway, across the lawn and onto the top of the sandy beach. The wide rear tyres dug into the soft surface searching for more grip, assisted by the lightness of the vehicle. Max flew onto the beach, swerving left to follow the other buggy ahead.

Neither of them turned their lights on, but it was then that Santiago realized the other buggy was chasing after him. With no rear-view mirrors, he turned round to see what he'd already heard. A narrow strip of sand pushed his buggy into the shallow water for a moment, spray shooting in all directions as he ploughed through then back onto the sand. Re-energised to escape his pursuer, he floored the pedal.

Max watched Santiago briefly slowed by the water and drew closer, collecting up his Sig from the seat beside him. It would be easier for him to shoot forwards, than for Santiago to aim behind. He fired a shot in the direction of the fleeing VW, more to see if Santiago would give himself up. The buggy ahead continued at pace.

Max dropped down a gear and the wide tyres now floated over the soft sand at speed. The loose surface offered the effect of drifting on a wet or slightly icy covering, the slightest twitch on the wheel, started the buggy drifting. Max instantly counteracted any understeer and kept the buggy pretty straight. He was gaining on Santiago, who was struggling with the odd swerve on the difficult sandy surface.

As Max got closer, Santiago turned and fired two wild shots back at Max. One went through his windscreen on the passenger side, sending a large crack across the glass. Max returned fire with three rounds. One pierced Santiago's front screen, one splintered through the fibreglass bodywork. But the third nicked the inlet manifold at the base of the exposed carburettor at the rear of the buggy.

Santiago immediately felt the slight loss in power, as air diluted the fuel mix going into the flat-four cylinders.

Up ahead Max could see a sand-covered mound about seven feet high, across half of the beach strip. He looked at Santiago's speed dropping off slightly and could smell a whiff of fuel in the air. He guessed he would avoid the mound and take the direct, flat route past it. Max was closing the gap between them. He surveyed the sight ahead, the buggies speeds, the mound, the distance. As soon as the vision hit him, he accelerated hard.

Santiago was wrestling with his vehicle trying to coach more speed out of it and didn't see Max close in towards him. The leading buggy aimed at the flat beach, as Max continued to power towards the mound on Santiago's right. By the moment Max had almost caught up and Santiago turned his head to see him, Max was already driving up the mound just trailing behind.

He glanced across at Santiago who looked back over at him puzzled, thinking Max was trying to overtake him. Max's momentum carried his buggy up the mound. As he continued to power on, he started to turn in towards the other buggy alongside and now below him.

The instant Santiago realized what was happening, it was too late. Max adjusted his aim at the last moment, before launching his speeding buggy off the top of the mound and into the air.

Santiago looked up at the underneath of Max's vehicle as it careered towards him from above and to the side. Max braced himself, clutching his steering wheel.

Santiago opened his mouth to cry out, just as the front axle torsion bars of Max's buggy slammed into his cockpit, with the VW's full weight and momentum.

The unyielding metal crushed Santiago, as Max heard the sickening crunch of bones and came to a rest on top of the other beach buggy.

Max gathered himself up from the jarring impact, listening out for any signs of movement underneath him. The night air was cool and only the calming, constant sound of the water rippling onto the beach could be heard.

He climbed out of his seat, holding his Sig and slowly peered round into the other buggy. It was a mess! The front of his own VW had squashed Santiago into the steering column without mercy. His torso seemed to be entirely flattened into and around the steering wheel. Blood was dripping from his red-stained shirt, his arms limp, drooped into the footwell.

Max's first instinct was to tell the others. "Max here. I caught up with Santiago!"

"Do you have him secured?" asked Marsh back at the villa.

"No. He's dead now."

"What about the diamond?" said Blake.

With all of his concentration on the buggy chase and conclusion, Max needed the prompt to remind him what he was after. He picked his way around Santiago's body and pockets, those he could reach that weren't pinned down by the chassis on top. His fingers came across something hard. He slid it out and wiped the blood from it.

"I have it!" he announced to the others. Relief all round.

The Lieutenant Colonel and Commodore back in the carrier control room shook hands.

The LC came over the radio. “Well done lads! Max, do you have your pickup receptacle intact?”

Max fumbled into one of his zipped-up pockets and pulled out a folded jumble.

“I’ve got it, yes.”

“Great, we need to get that thing back to us pronto,” said the LC eagerly. “The Reaper’s in your area, activate the homer and tell us when you let it fly!”

“Will do.” Max sat down on the sand and briefly held the deep graze on his lower leg. The bleeding had stopped.

Soon after the men had left the carrier in the Merlin earlier on, the control team had launched another aircraft from the flight deck. The General Atomics MQ9 Reaper drone would follow them and keep an eye on progress from above, during the entire villa raid. The LC and Commodore had watched the small ghostly white figures move around the complex from their eye in the sky.

The remote-controlled drone was a sizable aircraft in itself, at over ten metres long with a wingspan of twice that. It was capable of almost three hundred miles an hour and had a range of well over a thousand miles. This was more than enough to have it follow and view the operation undetected high above. It could also stay in the airspace above the villa for more than enough time, waiting to be called upon.

Now the Reaper drone, controlled by its two ‘pilots’ in the carrier’s operations room, had a new task. It had been specially fitted with several add-on pieces of equipment.

Max unravelled the rolled-up eight-metre luminous wire cord, carefully arranging it on the sand and checking it was fully untangled. Next, he laid out the small, strong bag, about four inches square. The canvas had been impregnated with flexible liquid polystyrene. In the event it accidentally fell into the sea, it would float, with its beacon continuing to operate for recovery. He pulled at it, testing the strength of the stitching and metal loopholes.

He then flicked the small switch on the waterproof homing device at the bottom of the bag. A red light started flashing. He now carefully placed the Cullinan I diamond into the sturdy canvas bag and threaded the strong metal carabiner hook through the bag closing loops. He screwed the lock over the carabiner sprung clip to double fasten it and rechecked it was attached to the brightly coloured wireline.

Finally, he picked up the deflated balloon on the other end of the wire and opened the tiny, compressed helium canister. The balloon, also a bright luminous colour, inflated in seconds to about a metre in diameter and fought against Max's hold, wanting to start rising into the sky.

"Max here. Beacon activated. Package ready. Waiting to release?"

The LC looked over to the two drone controllers who nodded. They had positioned the drone, so it was now several miles away and ready to return to where Max was.

"Okay Max, the Reaper's a few miles out and incoming. We have the beacon on the radar to guide the drone right onto it. Release now!"

Max let the balloon go and it swirled upwards taking the line, which scampered briefly across the sand and then it was gone.

"Released!"

Max fixed his gaze on the small bag as it left him and rose up. He watched the bright balloon and line until his neck was sore from tilting it back. He then heard the distant, faint noise high up above him. It was getting closer, but barely distinguishable above the lapping water on the beach.

The Reaper had been fitted with a V-shaped yoke comprising of two outstretched six-foot-long metal receptacle arms, attached to its nose. The skyhook, or surface-to-air recovery system, was invented by Robert Fulton in the nineteen-fifties for the CIA, originally to pick up people needing a hasty extraction.

At the front of the drone, a locking clamp would engage as soon as the wireline hit the back of the yoke. This would hold the package firm until the drone's return to the aircraft carrier.

Lastly, a plastic sealed buoyancy tank had been installed into the drone. This was just in case of any failure causing it to fall into the sea with its priceless package, keeping it afloat so it could be recovered. Everything had been thought of to guarantee the safe return of the diamond.

The controller steering the drone held a large joystick and could now see the bright balloon and line ahead of the Reaper on one of his screens. The homing device in the drone was drawing it precisely onto the beacon inside the bag. Just as he was a hundred yards out, he pressed a 'MERGE CONTROL' button on his consul. This allowed him to manually lift the drone up slightly, so the yoke caught the middle of the cable.

The metal wire hit one of the capture arms and snapped into the clamp which locked it in place. The precious bag on the end of the short line trailed underneath the Reaper with little buffeting and was now held there tightly. The balloon trailed along the top of the drone and burst within a minute, with the constant air pressure compressing it.

The Reaper circled around and headed back to the Queen Elizabeth carrier, with its most prized package, worth hundreds of times the value of the high-tech military drone.

Max walked back along the beach and by the time he got back to the clearing in front of the villa, Blake and Marsh were waiting for him. They had carried out Hall's body. No one would ever be left behind. The three men embraced, weary from the emotions of the last twenty-five minutes and thankful they had made it and accomplished the mission.

Marsh had done a quick sweep of the villa and gathered up a bagful of mobile phones and computers. These would no doubt provide yet more evidence of Jurado's crimes and communications. Maybe even help recover the bank's stolen bitcoin funds.

Fifteen minutes later they spotted the second Merlin

helicopter coming towards them. With no signs of any local police, Blake asked the pilots to land on the beach to pick them up.

They shielded their eyes from the sandstorm created by the helicopter and after carefully lifting their dead comrade on board, they climbed on themselves.

"What a way to visit such a beautiful place," said Marsh, "in the dark and amidst flash-bangs and bullets!"

"Yeah, some visit eh!" agreed Blake.

Max shook his head. "Let's get the hell out of here and go home! Nice work lads!"

The F-35A fighter jet pulled away from the aircraft carrier and powered up into the night sky over the Gulf of Mexico.

The Reaper drone had got back in just over an hour. The crown jewel had been safely retrieved from the protective bag on the clamped wire underneath. Live images from a special camera were transmitted to an expert located in London, who verified the authenticity of the diamond. It was placed in a sealed box and given to the F35 pilot. He would return it to London, direct from the carrier.

Powered by a single Pratt and Whitney with an afterburner, the F-35A aircraft was capable of supersonic speeds of 1.5 Mach. It could fly at heights up to fifty thousand feet, far above commercial aeroplanes which flew at between thirty and forty thousand. At 1100 miles per hour, well beyond the speed of sound, it was the fastest way of returning the Star of Africa the four and a half thousand miles home. But its flight range over the Atlantic Ocean was only fifteen hundred miles.

The close relationship between the United Kingdom and the United States of America had made overcoming this problem an easy task. Especially as the Queen Elizabeth was taking part in manoeuvres with the US Navy. The Commodore hadn't needed to involve the British Government with the request, nor did he have to explain why he required the assistance of the United States Air Force. His US Navy counterparts had happily sorted that out for him.

The huge USAF Boeing KC class tanker was already in the right zone for the first of two mid-air refuels the jet would require. They rendezvoused about five hundred miles southeast of New York.

The fighter jet was fitted with a retractable refuelling receiver probe. Once the two planes' flight speeds were aligned, the probe was inserted into the tanker trailing drogue, a conical basket with the flexible fuel line attached. The fuel valve then opened allowing the tanker operators to dispense the fuel to the accompanying jet fighter.

Fifteen hundred miles on towards London and the F35 was next met by a Royal Air Force Voyager KC Mk 2. The same refuelling procedure then allowed the pilot to complete the four and a half thousand-mile non-stop trip.

The usual travel time from carrier to Miami, then commercial flight onto Heathrow, would have taken about fourteen hours. The fighter jet pilot landed at RAF Northolt less than five hours after taking off from the carrier.

With the time difference, it was almost midday. The same day that the Spanish Princess was due to visit the Tower of London at six PM!

23

The Princess of Spain and her entourage had spent the afternoon being given a personal tour of the Imperial War Museum. Seeing so many artefacts of historical battles, artwork and documents had been fascinating, but the Princess was particularly looking forward to the visit that had been added to her day's agenda at the last minute. She had been granted a private viewing of the crown jewels!

Her entourage consisted of Spanish government officials, their Foreign Ambassador, bodyguards both Spanish and Metropolitan police protection officers and staff from the Spanish Royal household.

As the throng of dignitaries moved around the museum, there was one particular man that stood out above all the rest. Eduardo Garcia was in attendance, accompanying his country's Princess. At six foot five inches tall he towered above everyone else.

He'd flown over early that morning. Over the last twenty-four hours, Eduardo had been in despair at the lack of coverage or announcement of the crown jewels being robbed. The British news channels and papers had continued with minimal mention of the Beefeater's accidental death during a security drill the other night.

He'd been so incensed at being cheated his moment of glory, his humiliation of the United Kingdom, that he'd arranged to be included on the Princess' tour. He just couldn't help himself. He wanted to be there in person to watch, as the Spanish Royal jeweller announced to all those important British onlookers, that the diamond was a fake and the real Cullinan I was missing!

With the Tower reopening after just one day, he'd figured

they had put a replica stone in the royal sceptre for the benefit of keeping up appearances for visitors.

He'd received a text from his man Santiago in Cancun, telling him that he had the diamond and would make his way to the safehouse. Though he did wonder why he hadn't heard from Santiago since then, at least he knew the real Star of Africa had to still be in Mexico.

The tour around the museum had felt like an eternity to him. He couldn't wait to go to the Tower of London and witness the big reveal, that the British were using fakes in their Crown jewels on public display. News of this would then have to be made public.

Tonight's dinner at the Spanish Embassy in London would be one he could truly enjoy, at the expense of the embarrassed British VIP's who would be in attendance.

At around four-thirty PM, they were bidding their farewells to the museum directors, experts and tour guides, and set off in the motorcade of black Range Rovers. Unfortunately, Eduardo had to endure one last stop, before they went to the Tower.

The Princess had especially asked if she could experience one of those English traditions the tourists often tagged into their visits, at some expense. Tea at The Ritz!

'Bloody British with their stupid tea-time!' thought Eduardo. 'How annoying!'.

The Palm Court of the famous hotel had been fully blocked out for the Spanish visitors. They sat surrounded by the golden chandeliers, marble columns and mirrored walls. Even Eduardo begrudgingly admitted the selection of pastries, teacakes, scones and finely cut sandwiches were delicious. But glancing at his watch, he just wanted to be on their way to the Tower.

Finally, at a quarter to six, the courtier announced they would be leaving for their final engagement before returning to the embassy.

The procession of cars made their way past Buckingham

Palace and the Houses of Parliament and Big Ben, then over Waterloo Bridge. Along the A3200 up to London Bridge and under the Shard to Tower Bridge Road.

As they crossed over the most famous bridge in the world, Eduardo could see the fortress to their left, that was the Tower of London. He gazed at it, imagining what had taken place there just several nights ago. Then looking at the other people in his car, he couldn't help but think to himself, 'if only you knew what I know, that so-called impregnable castle was robbed of their precious crown jewels, and *I* arranged it!'.

They skirted around the site's perimeter then turned left past Tower Hill, before coming to park up right by the entrance to the famous landmark. The four corner towers of the White Tower in the centre, three square and one round, rose above the other turrets and buildings around it.

Eduardo noticed the additional armed soldiers and Met police in the area and wondered if they were for the benefit of the Princess, or a hangover from events the other night.

A small gathering of officials waited to greet them at the entrance including the Tower's Constable, the most senior person there and Britain's own Crown Jeweller. Traditionally the only person allowed to handle the precious regalia.

As they were led across the raised walkway over the dry moat and through the Tower's entrance, Eduardo was pleased to see a select press corps accompanying them in.

"Will the photographers be coming into the jewel room with the Princess?" he innocently asked one of the officials.

"Oh no sir, any such visits from foreign royalty are considered a private affair. The media will only come as far as the courtyard outside the Waterloo Block."

Eduardo allowed himself a huge grin. 'That's near enough' he thought to himself, imagining addressing them after the big reveal, saying how horrified they were to discover the British trying to pass off a fake Cullinan to Spain's Princess!

Forgoing the offer of a longer tour due to time constraints, the Spanish contingency was taken along Water Lane within the battlements and past the Bloody Tower, where the two young Princes were believed to have been murdered. They then passed Tower Green on their left and walked up the wide steps with the ominous White Tower looming over them on the right.

They approached the Waterloo Block and all filed in through the main visitor's entrance, above which the lettering stated proudly 'The Crown Jewels'. As they went through a couple of display rooms, Eduardo scanned for any signs of damage from the other night's raid. To his dismay, everything looked perfect, timeless and undisturbed.

'How the hell have they managed to cover everything up!' he wondered.

They descended down the stairs and approached the large, open steel vault room doors. Armed security now appeared overwhelming in the lessening space. Eduardo jostled amongst the other enthusiastic people to get his first glimpse of the crown jewels inside. Aided with his considerable height advantage, he saw into the jewel room for the first time.

To his amazement, the row of regalia on display had no protective glass cabinets on top. Visiting royalty were traditionally allowed to look upon the crown jewels with their own eyes, not through bombproof strengthened glass. These had been removed earlier right after the Tower was closed to the public at five-thirty.

The collection of crowns and rods looked truly mesmerizing, sparkling and enchanting. Unique.

Everyone filed into the jewel room and adjusted themselves across the floor space. The moving walkways had been turned off so as to afford the Princess a longer, closer look. Armed police stood in front of the jewels, reminding people not to get too close or try to reach out and touch anything.

Eduardo fixed his stare onto the one jewel he was here for. He stared intently at the large diamond, the replica, in the royal sceptre. It twinkled back at him. But he was no expert.

He had made sure someone else could properly inspect the stone and reveal its true makeup.

The Constable of the Tower said a few words of welcome to the Princess and briefly explained each of the regalia on display. The Princess was dumb-struck and could barely speak, when she was invited to step forward and have an up-close look at the collection.

The Spanish Royal jeweller was also having the treat of his life being invited to inspect the Crown jewels. He had already asked if he could take a closer look without touching. The Crown Jeweller nodded to signal now was the time and invited him forward. He humbly and cautiously stepped up to the nearest display to him. The orb with rod and sceptre.

Again, first checking for permission, he raised his single eyepiece magnification loupe and went in closer to the nearest large item in front of him. The Star of Africa at the top of the royal sceptre!

Eduardo thought his heartbeat could be heard by everyone in the vault room it was beating so hard and fast! No one in the vault said a word, as the jeweller and the Princess studied the displays.

The jeweller examined the large diamond, looking for its unique characteristics, its colour, brilliance, clarity and like a one-of-a-kind birthmark, a known minuscule inclusion the Royal diamond was known to have.

He made a few 'Ooh's' and 'Arr's' as he looked through his loupe, taking care not to touch anything. Then, whilst continuing to inspect the diamond, his lips parted ready to speak. Eduardo felt like he was about to faint with the anxiety and stress of it all!

"Well gentlemen, I confess I have to tell you…" he paused as if choosing his next words carefully, "and with all my experience, I have to say…"

'Now the truth!' thought Eduardo.

"…This is, truly, *the* most magnificent diamond I've ever seen in the whole world!"

Time felt like it froze, to Eduardo!

"I am honoured that you have granted us the pleasure of viewing the famous Cullinan I in person!"

"It's beautiful," added the Princess, "and so big!"

Years of resentment, wanting revenge, his determination to embarrass the British, his desire to get Gibraltar back, to even scores, humiliate this proud, no arrogant nation, all boiled up inside Eduardo, and exploded. He yelled out before even having an instant to check himself.

"What! No! Look again, man? It's obviously not the real Star of Africa!"

The armed police braced themselves and immediately asked the Princess and jeweller to move away from the displays. Soldiers outside the vault moved in on the disturbance. Some of the onlookers were startled by Eduardo's outburst and the police's abrupt, but understandable reaction.

"It's a replica for God's sake. I don't believe it, what did you lot do, how have you done this? Princess, this is a joke!"

More armed police moved in, jostling unforgivingly past the dignitaries in the room, towards Eduardo Garcia!

The following day Max was back at MI5 HQ at Thames House, with Si Lawson.

"Max you did brilliantly out in Cancun, we're so proud of you and the other guys. I'm so sorry about Hall."

"They were good men. It was a privilege to serve with them. Kind of made me think about what I gave up, leaving the Commandos so young," said Max.

"The PM's happy. Looks like we'll get his bank's bitcoin funds back from Jurado's offshore accounts. They're being accessed today using the computers taken from the villa. Not to mention everyone involved are all so happy to have the Cullinan I back!"

"Thank God we got the diamond, and getting it back in

time was a miracle?"

Si explained. "Well you know that the F35 brought it back to Northolt in a third of the normal time it would have taken. The Star was then driven back to the Tower by a sizable armed motorcade with police motorbikes escort stopping traffic at junctions ahead. They were going to stop visitors from entering the Waterloo Block for twenty minutes later that afternoon. But given the Princess wasn't due until six, they had a full half-hour after closing the Tower to the public, to replace the replica with the real Cullinan I diamond."

"What about this Eduardo chap? You obviously knew he was behind the Tower plan, at least put Sonia up to it."

"With the evidence you and the team had gathered, we knew yesterday Eduardo Garcia, the CNI's Director General of the Support to Intelligence division, was our man. Sonia named him and his number came up on her phone. There aren't many Eduardo's high up in Spain's Centro Superior de Informacion de la Defensa, and he was Santiago's boss. Also, we caught up with the Air Ambulance pilot and the director of the Cheesegrater's security firm. Both gave us names leading back to Garcia. I spoke to the CNI Director who said Garcia always had a thing about the British. His mother was apparently raped by two English lads, he never knew his father and ever since has likely harboured a desire for revenge and humiliation."

"So if you knew he was behind the robbery, how come you let this Eduardo chap inside the vault room last night?" asked Max.

"The Princess' tour day had already started and Eduardo had gotten himself included on the invite list. The plan was to intercept him on their way back to the Spanish Embassy after they visited the Tower, or if necessary when he left the embassy today."

"Why wait?"

"Red tape," sighed Si. "He has diplomatic immunity and we only got the all-clear from Spain as the Princess's party, with Eduardo in tow, arrived at the Tower. Our PM had to get authorization from Spain's Prime Minister to revoke Garcia's immunity, so we could then arrest him. They basically offered him up to us, ashamed and embarrassed about the whole thing. They won't breathe a word of all this to anyone, and I'm not sure the whole crazy story would be believed anyway!"

Si shrugged. "We didn't know he'd have a tantrum and drop himself in it even more in the jewel room, once he saw we'd got the real diamond back in its place. Spain's Royal family aren't too happy with him either, putting the Princess in such an awkward position like that. It was a right old kerfuffle dragging him out of the vault and taking him away after the press outside had left!"

"So what will happen to him now?"

"My guess is he'll have a closed court trial, maybe at the Old Bailey, no-one will know about it though. Then he'll do time in one of our nicer prisons, after which he'll be deported back to Spain, where they'll try him themselves and put him inside one of their jails! Silly sod. At least we and the Spanish will give him the opportunity of reducing his sentence by agreeing to a strict non-disclosure contract, never to speak of anything related to this debacle. If he does, he stays inside! Even when he eventually gets out, just one word about it and he'll be dragged back again. We've heard the last of Garcia for sure!"

Max shook his head in disbelief. "I can't get over how my simple investigation of the bank hack, escalated into such an outrageous set of events. Crimes, subterfuge, robberies, murders and then stealing one of our nation's crown jewels!"

Si took out an envelope from his desk and placed it in front of Max. "Well after one last pat on the back, you'll have to forget about the whole affair, never to speak of it again. It didn't happen!" He nodded at the envelope. "For you!"

Max tore it open and pulled out a compliment slip. On the top was printed, '10 Downing Street, Office of the Prime Minister'.

Underneath was a short, hand-written note. It said simply;

Nice job Max, with thanks from me and your country.
Though try to avoid all treason traps in the future!
The PM.

Max was stunned and immensely proud of what they'd achieved. And to get the nod from the top parliamentarian was a bonus!

He was just about to read it for a second time, savouring the words, when Si took the piece of paper out of his hand and lit it with a match over his waste bin.

Max looked surprised, "Wait!," but then he nodded at his boss and feigned a frown. They watched the white paper turn to black crispy ash and drop into the bin.

"You know how it is, Max! This is MI5!"

THE END

Max Sargent Corporate Espionage Mystery Thrillers

available in the series by the author BEN COLT

can be read in any order

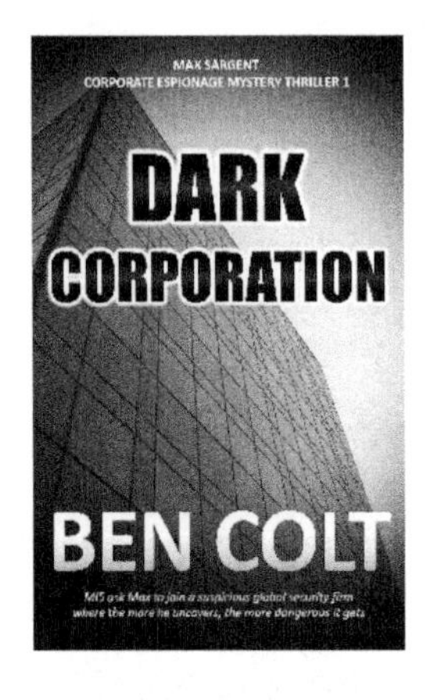

ABOUT THE AUTHOR

BEN COLT

He grew up in the house previously owned by notorious British-Soviet double-agent Kim Philby.
A senior executive of three decades in the corporate world, having been a management consultant and Chief Procurement Officer for many big brand companies in various industries.
Most of his roles had a global remit, which took him around the world on business to many different countries and cities.
His procurement teams had a privileged role in firms, with unquestioned business-wide access and control of large spends, suppliers and intellectual property.
His extensive procurement and management experience gives him first-hand insight of the potential for corporate corruption and espionage, to quickly become dangerous.

www.BenColt.com